Passage of the Acolyte

PART ONE

JAMES M. VARGO

Copyright © 2011 James M. Vargo
All rights reserved.

ISBN-13: 978-1456511791
ISBN-10: 1456511793

For all who listened

A special thanks to:
http://karenswhimsy.com/public-domain-images/ for their wonderful cover art. (Edmund Dulac, Ulalume, 1921)

CONTENTS

BOOK ONE   *page*

1	Emissary	8
2	The King's Festival	27
3	The Tournament	50
4	Alliance	67
5	The Vinery of Ristle	88
6	A House in the Green	98
7	The Arrither Road	124
8	The Haunt of Dagoraust	146
9	Three's a Charm	175
10	Ainiald	194
11	A Thief in the Night	219
12	Fire in the Night	252
13	Revelation	270
14	Northern Fire	283

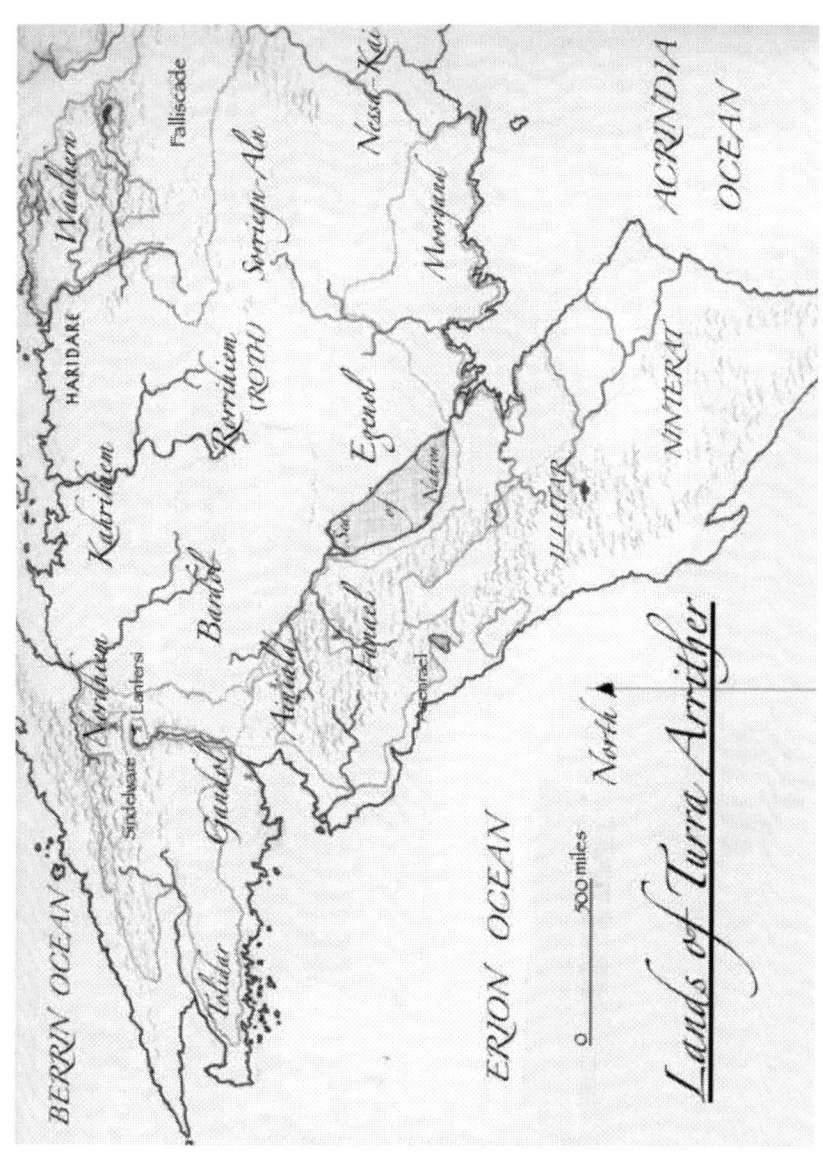

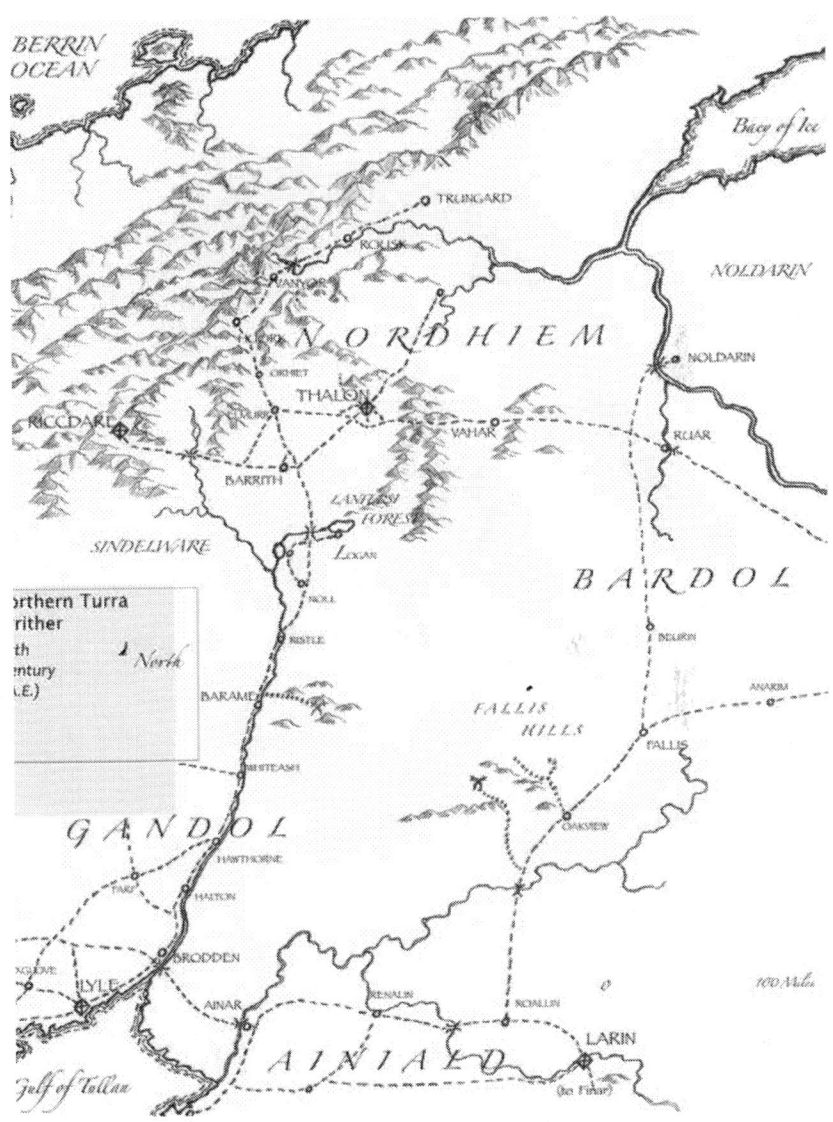

Chapter One – Emissary

When the doorbell rang at the manor Greynol Arowen called home, however rare, the visit could be lumped into three categories: the happenstance passerby curious about the plaque outside the door that read, Idarill House; or a merchant peddling spoons or some other ware the old man did not want or need; or perhaps a formal letter from Lord Vesgar or a noble in the city, inviting him to a proper function in Vanyor beneath the foothills where he lived. He never went. But it was a particular visit three years earlier, a messenger bearing an official letter that subtly snuffed out the last vestiges of his life's work – the announcement of his retirement.

"On the occasion of your seventy-seventh birthday, your service to Fawarra and the Holy-Exarch will have ended. The time you have offered in service to the faith by your consecration is most appreciated. May Fasduen bless your final days."

"Please find Idarill House a welcome retreat to live out your remaining years until a new master is selected, and our reaffirmation and commitment to Vanyor and northern Nordhiem will continue…"

And so it went.

Greynol learned to discover solace in the simpler things in life. He felt at once abandoned and free. In the shadows of a great hall that formed the heart of the manor, he studied; the meager glow of the hearth and a candle lamp that fluttered from an unchecked draft his only light. With bent fingers, he traced the words of a dusty library of books – the scrutiny of his gaze etched lines upon his face; but otherwise, his look was vibrant and beneath his years.

His mind was sharp, and here in the quietness of his retirement, time drifted from memory. But for Greynol, it felt as if something in time had waited, like a storm poised upon the horizon – something a holy man could recognize.

A noise disturbed the silence of his study as the front door flew open. Greynol made no motion as sunlight poured into the parlor – a boy stepped through.

"Good morning, Greynol. Are you home?" he called. Entering the main hall, he noticed the elder seated in his usual place within the embrace of a cushy armchair.

"I said, 'good morning'."

"Yes, Rhen, and a pleasant morning to you," replied Greynol, blue eyes never straying from the Tuirowan script.

The boy glanced about, perplexed on seeing the darkness. "Sir, it is a beautiful day outside, yet you enclose yourself in shadow."

The old man lifted his gaze. "I am well aware of the day, Rhen. I rise each day before the dawn breaks. Besides, I have seen enough fair summer days to last two lifetimes."

Rhen paid little attention to the boast and began to clear off a cluttered table in the center of the room. "Plates, cups, silverware galore...have you been too busy to bother with simple chores, like cleaning up after yourself?" he asked, in his arms a hefty pile.

"I was reading and must have lost track of the time," replied Greynol, putting on a less sour expression. "Anyway, it's *your* job."

Rhen stepped closer for a look.

"Which book today?"

"The Third Volume of Tuirowe," answered Greynol with pride.

"Oh, that," quipped Rhen, starting at once towards the eastern corridor and kitchen.

"'Oh, that,' indeed," muttered Greynol, "ignorance is the plague of Nordhiem."

His words fell on deaf ears.

Soon the hallway began to glow with light as the boy pulled back curtains and opened blinds along the way. He returned to the room with a clean cloth, bowl, and pitcher of water, and set them upon the table.

"I cannot imagine why you would want to sit in solitude for so long – it reminds me of wintertime," said Rhen, wiping the surface clean.

"But I am at peace with my surroundings, not in a dark dungeon. And I had company: the cats played beneath my chair; doves nested in the rafters; and spiders wove webs in the corner above the mantle. I was hardly alone."

"You call that company?"

Once finished, Rhen started for the stairs leading to the balcony that circled the main hall. "I'm going up top to get some air in here," he said with a foot upon the step.

Greynol nodded and relinquished his study to start the day. He stood and stretched, setting the book on a stand beside his chair. Soon sunlight began to enter the hall as one by one shutters were thrown open to expose a bright azure sky. The air stirred, warmed by the sun, and the chamber transformed from its previous gloom into a cheery summerhouse. The doves tested their wings, circling the rafters twice before flying out an open window to greet the morning. Rhen continued his work sweeping the loft and wiping the railings, and shelves, where books stood in uneven rows, he straightened and dusted. Once everything was set in order, Greynol invited him to the kitchen.

This was Monday, the fourth of Orist, and the boy's third visit to Idarill since late spring. The cold winds and snow had long ended and normalcy of life returned to Vanyor. Rhen welcomed another summer of assisting the old man, climbing the foothills early in the week. The pay was fair and it felt a joy to get out his cramped family home in the city. As for his earnings, Greynol never missed a payout.

During a lunch of eggs, salted bacon, and oatcakes, a polite conversation struck up: Rhen spoke of happenings in Vanyor, the usual fill of family events and local gossip, little that concerned the old man, but he listened with regard. And Greynol, for his part, told stories of adventure and battle that he seemed to recall very well. Rhen sat wide-eyed and fully attentive of such talk, as a boy would. He often wondered if the elder, at his age, learned of these things or lived them, for he knew so many fantastic tales. But they were timeworn stories, and whether his own or no, Greynol had given up on such silly things as adventure – at least the boy thought it so.

To Rhen, Greynol was the *Sage of Idarill*, a title given by some of the old-timers in the city; or *Greyhood*, a term used for the dress of an acolyte, which he claimed to be. Rhen understood little about these things to question him, observing what he took in during chores, or heard through their polite discussions. There appeared only an ordinary way of life: he tended his horse, milked the cow, and planted a garden – he seemed just like anybody else. But once below the surface there appeared more than the ordinary. The old man possessed odd, if not marvelous artifacts of science and nature; he prayed an awful lot, "for no good reason"; and there seemed an uncommon sense about him, at times wizened and fatherly, other times youthful and exuberant. And to his wonderment, Rhen found no explanation for the traveling clothes that sat ready beside his bed.

"Eighty must be too old for riding," he thought many times over. Greynol dismissed any occasion the subject came up.

Later in the day Rhen completed his chores: he dusted the remaining rooms, tended the stable, and at last, wiped clean the old carven sign above the front door.

"He would be proud to see you so diligent," said Greynol, watching from the foyer.

"Who would?"

"Idarill, of course. This is his house."

"Why would he care, he's long dead. And if it weren't for those gravestones out back, I'd never give it another thought. No one in Vanyor has graves in his yard like you do, and I'm glad for that."

"He still approves," replied Greynol with a wry grin.

Rhen gave a shudder and a look that said, "Please change the subject."

Picking up his stepstool, he shut the door behind them. He and Greynol took their seats beside the fire as a breeze swept into the room and shadows lengthened across the rafters. Greynol felt expectation in the wind.

"Well, is there anything else you need before I leave?" asked the boy. He leaned comfortably upon a soft cushioned chair, looking about the room like a young master inspecting his estate. "Seems every time I return some new problem arises. This house is older than you and I put together."

Greynol did not respond. He suddenly grew disconnected, as one listening to a far off conversation. His expression turned dour. Once proud eyes softened and Rhen recognized the change.

"Sir, is something wrong? You seem different now."

Greynol turned his attention to the boy. He opened his mouth to speak, but found the words difficult to form. "Something comes, Rhen – an answer to a long awaited question. Now that it is here I fear to learn it," he uttered at last.

Rhen slunk down in his seat. "This kind of talk is strange – you are acting strange. You appeared fine only moments ago. Maybe something you have eaten, something spoiled. A bad egg, perhaps...although I feel fine."

"I have no intention of frightening you," he replied, trying to muster a smile. "What I sense the end of a long drawn out chapter."

"The end you should expect is of the day. You do frighten me with such talk. You sound as if you expect to..."

The boy hesitated with the last – he had not the courage to speak a foreboding word and make it come true, as his kith and kin were apt to believe. Although Nordic and a Turrar on his father's side, Greynol held no such folklore to heart.

"Die, Rhen. Is that what you were trying to say? Death is not the enemy at the gate, and it speaks sweeter words than these," he replied coldly.

The boy, now agitated to the point of tears, pouted in the face of the unknown; he had rarely seen this side of the old man before, the mysterious Acolyte he knew nothing about. Rhen enjoyed his time with Greynol, the wise and wonderful elder with a sharp tongue and an eager smile. He brooded for a moment of uneasy expectation, finally daring to break his silence.

"I understand little about your other ways, sir, the acolyte or greyhood they call you down below. Some say you are a wizard. I do not listen to them."

"People speak most when they know least. Do I seem a wizard? I have seen sorcerers in my day, and their ways are altogether different than yours or mine. Believe what you may in the talk of common folk – their advice is sound in everyday affairs. I find no deceit in their assumptions."

"But what of your titles: Sage, Acolyte, and Greyhood?"

"All part of the whole, Rhen. Remember, there is more than meets the eye in most things. Your father understood as a young lad brought here by his father that the acolytes, starting with Idarill over one-hundred fifty years ago, taught more than just grammar, science, and rhetoric, but offered an altogether new teaching."

"Fawarra?"

"Yes, something more than mere sorcery. Now straighten your shirt and press down that mop of brown you call hair – we have a visitor."

The boy held his breath, fearing to make a sound. He paused, and then relented.

"Now what are you saying? What visitor? I believe your ears have flown out the window with your mind."

That moment came a low rapping sound upon the front door. Rhen's heart sank.

"What sort of trickery is this?"

"Fret not, I am the reason for these feelings. I would never put you into danger. Now please, do as I say and answer the door while I wait here."

Rhen obeyed. What else could he do? Without a word of protest, he marched into the parlor. The knock came again, louder than before. Swallowing hard the boy reached for the doorknob. His head swam with fearful thoughts as the brass turned in his hand. Peering around the corner, he prepared to face some great evil; but to his surprise, it was only a man. He felt foolish to think otherwise.

"May I help you?" asked Rhen, his senses restored, bowing to a dusty traveler.

"I have a message for Acolyte Greynol Arowen. I am told he resides here," answered the man, an emissary. He reached into a mud-splashed pouch and pulled out a scroll.

"Greynol lives here – this is his residence. And I am his retainer. You may leave the message with me and I shall take it to him."

The man lurched back, almost frightened. "No, I must see he receives this personally – those are my orders."

Rhen was taken aback.

"What keeps you boy?" called Greynol, losing patience.

Rhen returned at once. "There is a messenger and he wishes to see you. He has a scroll of some sort."

"Send him in at once."

Greynol threw a mantle over his shoulders and stood with arms folded – he appeared most imposing in this manner. Rhen led the young man into the hall where he stood waiting.

"Bring our visitor some food and wine. He must be hungry after his ride," Greynol instructed. Rhen nodded and ran back down the hallway towards the kitchen and pantry.

"Please take a seat," said the Acolyte, motioning a hand towards Rhen's empty chair. The messenger complied. Weary legs overcame any fear of *the Lord of Idarill*.

"Thank you for your hospitality. I am Caron, an emissary of Lord Durn of Barame," he said, gazing awkwardly about the large room.

"You came from Gandol? Quite a distance to travel, even for a messenger," replied Greynol as he retook his seat.

"I have ridden five days since leaving Barame. The border remains open, for now; otherwise, rarely would I venture so far north. Prelate Feron has advised my lord concerning the scroll and its accompanying message – my orders were to bring both directly to you. The messages arrived from Fanael; although time was lost during winter where the mountain passes grow inaccessible. There it seems the scroll sat for a time before making its way to Barame. I for one will be glad to be parted of it."

Caron removed a container from his pouch and handed it to Greynol who slid the scroll out and examined it. "The seal is broken," remarked the Acolyte. "Did Feron open this?"

"No, he left it alone. The seal was torn before arriving in Barame. You can see plainly it is the Red Dragon – the Seal of Illutar."

"How many know about this?"

"That is hard to say: Lord Durn, Feron, and whoever handled it earlier."

"Have you read it?"

The emissary shook his head with a sudden snap. "Indeed no, my pride goes before me. I kept its contents from my eyes and spoke to no one about it. Those were my direct orders."

"Yes, of course. Forgive my questioning – one finds trust fleeting these days."

"That is why I will gladly journey the long road home and be rid of this burden. Never before have I felt so much distress over such a thing."

"What troubles you?"

Caron shrugged his shoulders in embarrassment. "The fear of what I bore overcame me – even my dreams were haunted in its care. I did not read the message, yet I felt a dread about it."

"Then I release you of it; now the burden is mine alone," replied Greynol, the scroll held tightly in his grip. "You must be tired. Will you not remain the night for your trouble? There are many rooms in Idarill."

"No thank you. I have a place in town set aside for the evening. I hope to depart at first light."

"As you wish," replied Greynol as politely as he could muster, although his eyes shown with gravity. "You mentioned a second note?"

"Indeed, one that accompanied the scroll from Fanael. Lord

Durn was careful to scrutinize it as it concerns the scroll," replied Caron, reaching into his pocket to pull out two folded pieces of parchment. He read the message aloud:

To the Lord Acolyte of Vanyor,

The scroll presented before you now came to me out of the forests north of Rottian found upon a man slain along the Southern Road. His name was Sahr, son of Aram, and he hailed from the city of Gunkar, where I am lord. The enemy pierced his heart with a fell sword and the scroll hung upon it as a forewarning – the Raugulon have a way with subtleties.

The enemy is cunning, none should rejoice in receiving any gift they offer, unless that soul is a fool or traitor. I trust that you, Greynol Arowen, are neither, for an Acolyte lives under the cost of his discipline. Nordhiem is far from Ninterat and the abode of the Black Coven, but at the price of a man's death, I warn you not to take this message lightly.

Open war lay upon Fanael; little time can I spare upon the needs of one. My judgment is to send this scroll to you unopened and unmolested, for fell are the enchantments of the enemy. I pray it reaches you in good time. Fare well in our common struggle against the enemies of Fawarra. May many unspoiled days greet you.

Yours sincerely,
Lord Dhormal of Gunkar

"Well, safe to say neither of his hopes came true: it arrives late and opened," uttered Greynol, staring blankly at the scroll. The emissary looked on unsure. He folded the note and placed it into the old man's trembling hand. The two sat in silence for a moment, long enough to reveal a clumsy spy around the corner.

"Rhen, I hear your sniffling in the hall – come on out!"

A shuffle of timid feet carried the boy from his hiding place in the hallway. "Yes sir, here I am. Forgive me. I did not want to disturb you while you both while you were talking...I did not hear much," he answered, carrying a tray loaded with bread, cheese, and a carafe of wine.

"You heard enough. It is late and time for you to go home.

Come back in a week, just as always, then I will tell you what I can."

"But..."

"Next time, Rhen," replied Greynol, putting an end to all argument. He removed the tray from the boy's hands and led him to the door. Rhen was hastened away and soon descended the hill into the city.

Greynol brooded now. He looked on as the messenger devoured his meal, washing it down with wine until sated. "The robust vintage of the Central Valley has none to compare, but Nordic wine will have to do for now," said the Acolyte in a polite voice, breaking his silence.

"Indeed. Gandol vineyards have no equal, but never have I tasted the fruit of Nordhiem. It manages just fine," replied Caron, finishing a second glass.

The messenger gave a yawn and stretched his aching back. "I too am anxious to put this day to an end," he said finally, standing to gather his things. "Thank you for your kindness. With your leave I shall go now to my bed."

"By all means. May Fawarra bless the road before you."

"Thank you, sir. Blessings come rarely these days. Farewell."

Caron, like Rhen before him, departed Idarill upon his steed, disappearing into the growing shadows of the Vanyor Dale.

Greynol regained his familiar solitude. The scroll now rested upon his knees, heavy and reeking of darkness and curse. The torn open dragon seal looked more a glob of sanguine ichor than wax; the words inked upon the scroll's outer parchment were penned in blood. Forty years of silent waiting lay before him, but faced with the answer to the questions of his past he found fear.

"Aram, why was your son killed, and why does his blood mingle with my grief?" muttered Greynol, his voice wavering. "Had I known...had I known so many things."

He unrolled the scroll; it felt weighted in his hands. The words upon it were also scrolled in blood, those of whom he would not guess. He drew a breath and began to read:

To Greynol Arowen,

Belated greetings. My long search has borne fruit — years of toil and the labor of many servants seeking word of your whereabouts. My first name, Dariat, you knew not, but that name is now dead. I am Fauglir, leader of armies and wielder of powerful magic. I owe a great deal to you.

This message serves as an invitation of sorts. Please heed my request for your presence is greatly desired in Asengard. It is in Asengard that I shall begin my reign — my brethren to guide me. Should you choose to remain in that bitter land of your seclusion you shall be called upon again, under less cordial terms.

I bid you come also to Asenrael, land of the Farrian, soon to be my own. I desire your presence, a witness to my coming victory.

I summon you by a name out of your past, Arowen, a man of courage and valor; unlike Greynol, the Acolyte who hides in the far reaches of the North — a coward in wait. Only one can prevail. With eyes that see far and wide we await your call and anticipate our first meeting.

Lord Fauglir, son of Arowen and Aliane

The scroll fell from his hands. "My God, what has happened? What have I done?"

Despite the warmth of a highland summer, Greynol found himself immersed in bitterness and cold. His senses were muted. He reread the words of the scroll over and again. His mind drifted from consciousness as a dark spell, like a nightmare, took hold. He took no food and drank only when necessary — water or wine for strength. He battled within, tearing at his robes, calling out a dirge seldom heard in all Turra Arrither — Tuirowan lamentations to dispel the darkness. By the sixth night after receiving the scroll, he regained much of his lost strength. True sight returned and a new vigor, but the specter of dread remained.

He knelt beside his bed with hands clasped and arms

outstretched. The scroll lay upon a table in front of the bedroom window where a candle lamp offered its mild light. A smooth round stone sat beside it and appeared to brood in anger with a deep red glow of its own.

During the night, a storm swept down from the mountains. Lightening flashed in a brilliant display and thunder shook the foundation of Idarill itself. Greynol paid no heed until a gust of wind blew through the house slamming his bedroom door and causing the candle to flicker. Then came a second blast and the candle went out.

"Very well then, time for bed," he thought.

Sleep would not come so easily. Startled by a burst of lightening just outside his window, Greynol saw two dark figures upon a crested hill opposite the house. Illuminated by the storm the silhouettes watched, each one menacing against a blackened sky. One had wings and took to the air unabated by the wind, and the second loped down the hill to the western edge of the yard near the graveyard.

Greynol backed away from the window, lifted the stone and climbed into bed, looking like one whom just awoke from an unpleasant dream. Soon the glow of virescent eyes appeared at the window glaring back at him. Then came the sound of claws upon the roof and scratching above his head. The stone in his hands turned a bright blue against the verdant luminescence of the watcher outside the window.

"This is Idarill, House of Fawarra, as long as I am its keeper. Go back to your hiding!" called Greynol, but the scratching only grew louder and the walls began to pound. Dark voices bellowed outside with curses and ranting.

"This is Idarill, House of Fawarra..." he repeated, but the noise stopped and the watcher backed away.

Greynol hastened to the window. The two figures gathered again upon the hill, but the one on foot directed the other away. The winged creature obeyed, taking to the night skies – a flash of fire revealing its flight. The remaining creature watched for a moment, then let out an angry wail heard plainly throughout the house despite the wind and thunder. Its eyes flashed. Turning back, it ran into the wilderness for good.

"Well, I suppose that's over," said Greynol, climbing back into bed. For the first time in six nights, he dreamed in peace.

"Hello Greynol, are you home?" started another day at Idarill, the morning after that stormy night. Rhen slammed the door behind him and ran into the hall. The mood was quite different today.

The boy entered the room, met at once by the sweet fragrance of olibanum. Smoke rose from a bowl and drifted slowly into the rafters where Greynol searched through shelves of books.

"You are early," he said. "Ignore the mess for now, I've plenty to do."

The Acolyte, seen in the light of the upper windows, dressed plainly in a long hooded robe of dove-gray sewn of thick highland wool with a rope belt tied about his waist. Rhen thought him noble. "Not quite the furs and golden-weave of Lord Vesgar, but certainly worthy of a bow," he thought. And bow he did.

"You could stand beside the Lord of Vanyor and be proud – Vesgar might grow jealous if you did," said the boy giggling.

"Is that so?" replied Greynol, waving off the compliment. "That would be a sight indeed. I must have needed a good cleaning up."

Rhen immediately saw a new energy in the old man and lightness in his step. Greynol returned below, placing a pile of clothes and books upon his favorite chair. Out of a pocket came the smooth stone that he placed on top. The boy had seen it before.

"May I?" he asked. Greynol gave a nod.

Rhen picked up the oval-shaped stone; it felt like a giant pebble in his hands. "Tell me the story again," he said smiling. In an odd gesture, he held the stone to his ear as one listening.

"Again? Well, as you know, you hold a Timlet Stone from the Island of Tuirowe; also called 'Timlet' by common folk these days. These stones have a unique smoothness and pearl-like luster, and if you hold them to the sun, they gleam like stained glass. There lie many such gems along the shores of Tuirowe across the Straight of Farria-Sire."

"You see, long ago, before men came to Turra Arrither, save the Mihtrir whom have always been here, the Farrian lived in the Farria-Sire, which is a long way from Vanyor mind you. 'The People of the Jewels' your folk call them without affection. These Farrian were the Blessed Race and conversed openly with Fawarra, their God, but that was a long time ago and before many things happened. In those days, common men lived in Tuirowe and could hear the voice of Fawarra as it came across the water, falling like dew upon the shore – upon these very stones. They are precious to us, a witness to the gifts of Fawarra; and it is told, if one listens closely you may hear his voice."

"Like a shell from the ocean?"

"Yes Rhen, like a shell," replied Greynol with a laugh.

Rhen returned the stone to its resting place. "Greynol, are most Acolytes from Tuirowe? Have you been there?"

"Also, no. No man returns there now. Its passage is closed to mortal men. Some have been told to glimpse its tall misty peaks from the sea far away. But my lineage *is* from Tuirowe, on my mother's side.

"I would like to see it one day."

"Only say that when you are old and quite finished with this world."

"If your ancestry goes back there, why do you live in Nordhiem?"

"More questions?" asked Greynol, sorting through a rack of vials. "I am Nordic also: I began my youth here in Nordhiem, a farmer's son, not far from this very place. Now if you do not mind, chores remain to be done, starting with the pantry. Talk will come later."

Rhen obeyed and ran off to the kitchen. He lifted what he could carry at one time and placed items carefully into wooden crates. Lost in his work, helped greatly by the uplifting fragrances that drifted about the house, questions swirled in his young mind.

The matter that concerned him most regarded the scroll; a week had passed since the emissaries strange visit. He had not forgotten.

He completed his chores, clearing the pantry and loading every perishable item into a wagon that waited outside the kitchen door. Following Greynol's specific instructions he cleaned the stable and brushed Toryche, the acolyte's aging black palfrey, gathered eggs and crated the chickens, placing them also upon the buckboard. The boy's spirit soared light as a feather and he knew exactly what to do.

"No breaking plates today," he thought.

An hour past lunch, Rhen heard the clock above the fireplace strike one and awoke as from a dream. "Questions! You have avoided my questions!" he said with a start.

He found himself in the kitchen with a broom in hand, as Greynol prepared a late lunch upon the stove.

"You would have made me work all day then send me home without knowing a thing," he cried.

"No son, I intend on answering what I can. Thank you for working so hard; the air is light today and I fear you have been caught up in it."

"Indeed," he miffed.

Greynol wore a sympathetic grin. "Forgive me, Rhen. Now come and eat something – the bread is fresh and butter sweet."

They sat comfortably at table, a large oak buffet that could easily seat ten men; a remnant of busier times at Idarill. Soon the house would stand-alone. Rhen ate his fill of bread and honey, and scrambled eggs hot off the skillet. The boy had his milk and Greynol tea – the old man's thoughts swam over a steaming cup.

"Thank you for lunch, sir. Can I now ask you what I've waited so long to ask?" said the boy finally.

"As you wish."

"Well, first of all there is the matter of the scroll that arrived here on my last visit, although I have seen nothing of it today. Secondly, where in the world are you going? After all, you had me load the wagon out back as one going on a long trip."

Greynol smiled kindly. "The wagon you will be pulling home with the cow. She can mange it. And the chickens you can take to your family too. The cats will do no good here alone – they too shall go with you."

Rhen's eyes grew wide. "But where are you headed? Are you not returning?"

"I must journey south – a long road awaits me."

"But what did that message say that you should leave so suddenly?" asked the boy, his shoulders sloped under the weight of the news.

"It is an invitation to lands far away, but not so distant in my memories. It seems the terms of my former life have not ended as I once thought. Nothing more need I tell you."

"But you are too old to journey to some strange place. An elder cannot go on adventures."

Greynol smiled. "Am I so old, Rhen? It is true; I have lived a full life. But this is no foolish quest, only a path started long ago. There remain many untold things – bitter recollections I hold within, even now."

Rhen felt helpless, but offered his service as any good servant would. "Is there anything I can do to help?" he asked. "I don't understand what you are saying, but I wish to assist you. I am your retainer."

"Thank you, Rhen. Return to your family. A boy of twelve makes a good squire, but not a fighter. Go back home and remember me in your prayers," replied Greynol. Trembling, he reached into a pocket and pulled out a small purse.

"For your services – give this to your parents, they will use the money wisely. This will cover your pay for the remainder of summer. Explain to your mother and father that I am leaving and your work here has finished."

"But what of Idarill?"

Greynol leaned back and glanced around, filled with glad memories.

"The House will await its new Master; that decision remains with Prelate Wetherton and his superiors to decide. I will leave a key above Toryche's stall – come back with your father to check on things if you should journey this way. Another will take my place in good time – Vanyor will not be forsaken."

Rhen realized this would be their last conversation. He looked about trying to picture the home as it were; the dark stained floors many times passed over by his broom. "But when do you leave?" he asked.

"Soon. The festival begins next month in Thalon and there I can better plan my journey. Wetherton is an old friend who is also wise; he shall be my aide. The details of my passage must be concealed and I will say no more of it – it is for your own good. Come now, let us finish what remains and get you home," said Greynol, leading the boy outside into the bright courtyard.

Together they secured the cow to the cart. Everything was loaded save a small amount of provisions that Greynol kept for himself. The crates were leveled and at last came two unhappy felines, placed in a basket and covered until they arrived at their new destination.

"Very well, then. Everything is set."

"Greynol sir, this is a sudden goodbye. Will I ever see you again?"

" 'All comes out in the wash' I always say," replied Greynol, placing a hand upon the boy's brow. "All things will be known in time – every deed from every man. Recall all you have learned here: continue to work hard, fight less with your siblings, speak well of your parents, and be strong when trials come."

"Strong, like you right now?"

Greynol straightened up, taken aback by the comment; in a small way, the boy understood.

"Yes Rhen, like me right now."

Rhen embraced the elder who helped him to the wagon. The boy took the reins, wiping away his tears before starting away. Greynol watched as the wagon rolled down the path with its precious load, wheels creaking as it rounded the bend and out of sight for good. He turned aside hiding a tear of his own; his time at Idarill soon to end. Days later he locked the door for good, keeping a key for himself, the other he placed in the barn. He and Toryche took to the road once again, prepared for everything and nothing at once, and the scroll went with him to return to its owner.

Quiet rumor spread throughout Vanyor, to those who cared about *the Sage of Idarill* and his disappearance. Speculators surmised the old man went mad and died alone and lost in the wilderness. No one dare discover for himself out of fear or superstition regarding 'the House upon the Hill'; and so it remained in state.

Another source of conjecture came from outsiders: travelers in the city asking questions about the Acolyte and his whereabouts, but all that could be gathered were rumors. The most reliable concerned a certain Rhen in the city.

"A boy knew this Greynol first hand. I had to pry his little mind to gather that the Acolyte ventures to Thalon," spoke one in the interested company to a second hidden within his cloak.

"Then we too prepare for Thalon," he replied.

Chapter Two – The King's Festival

Andro Rhine stumbled out of a coarse cloth tilt onto the turf outside Thalon's southwest gate; the smells of a fresh blaze and dampened grass a reminder that he was far from home. A circle of tents hemmed him in, cradled between two equally important trading routes. His party was one cluster of many spread about the fields surrounding the grand capital of Nordhiem, all in anticipation of the King's Festival, for the city was full.

The shadows of night faded and a breeze breathed life into the fair mid-summer morning. Andro took it in like a fine draught. He ran his fingers evenly through locks of burnished gold, rarely out of place, and let them fall loosely across broad shoulders. Eyes of jade, keen to every undercurrent and watchful thing, real or imagined, reflected the forest of his Logan home. He flexed his sinewy frame and straightened an ivy-colored sark that hung loose across soft brown trousers. Stag-leather boots completed the look of a young, out of place, woodsman.

About a large fire in the center of camp, his kinsfolk gathered for breakfast. Andro strode forward with the swagger of a confident young man, having turned twenty just ten days earlier, and proceeded to trip over a tent stake while they all watched.

"Ah, still weak in the knees. I told you time on the saddle takes its toll," said his father, Audin. He offered a firm hand and pulled Andro to his feet. The elder Rhine stroked his beard and gave him the once over.

"I'm fine, really. A three-day ride out of Logan is hardly a bother, and certainly not my last time out and about," replied Andro, dusting off his pants.

"Join us for breakfast then."

Audin retook his seat upon a fine carven chair that looked clearly out of place at a campsite, appropriate instead in a fine dining hall. The Rhine pride and profession rest in the skill of carpentry, and Audin's craft drew notice, even in Logan. He loaded a years worth of crafts, from ladles to ladders, for the ride north to Thalon – there was no finer place to sell, and at a good price, than during the festival. Andro had no skill in the family business.

Andro shrugged his shoulders. "I'll take my breakfast later. Rogan and I have a long day ahead. I'm certain we will remain in the city until after dark."

"After dark?" questioned Audin. "You better keep an eye on your friend – this is his first festival, you know. Look ahead. Thalon's gate is only a stone's throw away, but once through it you walk in a different world, full of cautions."

Andro nodded. He heard the warning before.

A young man crawled out of a tent at Andro's back and stared up through a tuft of brown hair cut just above the brow. He shook his head and muttered, "I heard my name, then realized how late it must be."

"Half past nine, Rogan Pinehurst," replied Audin, taking a puff of his pipe.

"I must have overslept. Up late last night – too many anxious thoughts, too many cheerful sounds," he said. At eighteen and a fellow Logander and neighbor to Andro, Rogan could barely contain his excitement. He lifted a hand to shield his eyes. "The city looks even more impressive in the daylight."

"First time in Thalon," replied Audin, "you might enjoy yourself if you're not careful,"

"Oh, I'll be careful. This is a kingdom of Turrar, after all."

"Indeed."

The look Audin offered was familiar and disconcerting. Andro feigned a smile; never glad to face his father's sensibilities. He gave Rogan a tug on the sleeve. "If you are ready, we should get going. We can grab something to eat once inside the city."

Rogan answered with a nod, and they started at once for the gate.

The mid-summer festival brought the fullness of glory upon Nordhiem and its King Anor II. On the calendars of the West, this was the first of Gare, seventh month of the year 1653 AE. (The Age of the Easterling). The King's Festival began in 1513 AE by declaration of Ardule I, a leader of renown and patriarch of the current Nordic line. In those days, beastly Durag invaded Trungard and Huork from the north in great number, and with them hoards of savage Gonar – tribal men from the frozen plains. But they were routed, and Nordic armies sent the scourge back into the wilderness. King Ardule declared victory over their enemies and proclaimed a time of celebration and unification – days of merriment began.

The capital city of Thalon began its week of festivities bright and full of splendor: flags flew proud in the breeze above the battlements, and standards lined the five roads leading to the five city gates, all framed before the King's Mount whose iron gaze guarded the city from the north. Snowy white with gold trim embroidered thick about the edge and a soaring golden eagle in its center, the symbol of Hawe, the old war-god of the northern race, the standard of Nordhiem once again became a call to reunite old alliances.

Slipping through the crowds, Andro and Rogan drank in the sights of Thalon and its pageantry. The common races of the North paraded before their eyes: Turrar arrived from every reach of Nordhiem, and even Andro understood what a thick-skinned, hardheaded people were those that ruled the Vanadium Range and Arrahurm Plain. Their shirts and breeches were coarse, and stag leather patterned their vests, belts, and boots. Noblemen processed in silken doublets and capes of fur, while women arrived in rich full dresses of fine silk trimmed with mink and golden-weave.

Mihtrir numbers were no less. Farmers and landsmen, they were Thalon's western neighbors from Carrinth. Renown in the kingdoms of the West, they distinguished themselves as the first men to settle in any part of Turra Arrither, even before the Farrian. Plain folk and smallish compared to the tall Turrar, Mihtrir were courteous to most. They lived happily without king or kingdom; serving, but never ones to sway to tyrants – and the Turrar loved them as their own. Their brethren, the sturdy Kuirian, did not farm, but lived in the mountains to build, mine, and beat metal.

Loganders and others of Northern Gandol entered the city, although far less in number. They were a well-mannered people who enjoyed allegiance with Nordhiem; a sentiment unshared throughout the rest of Gandol and its King, Raeletin the Fifth. Present also were Bardol horsemen who arrived upon well-bred steeds, and several other races unknown to Andro and Rogan.

The city overflowed with the influx of visitors and outpouring of its people. Manors and inns stood bursting at their doorposts and crowds spilled onto the streets, even in the early hours. The strain of song and tankards of mead clanging out on the concourse became the norm – it was a fair time for most. Andro and Rogan slipped beneath their raised mugs, and the press of vendors who worked zealously to sell their handicrafts and delicacies.

"And to think, this is only the first morning of the first day," said Rogan, his eyes bright with expectation.

"It's not official until the Parade of Lords begins, a little past noon," replied Andro, no less enthusiastic. He took a sudden left turn onto a narrower lane, then right into a dusky alleyway still thick with people, but of a diminished appeal. They approached an inn set away from the bright and open where no longer a sign of welcome hung.

"This place has no name?" said Rogan gapingly, met at once by a row of backs and the clamor of a tavern crowd. The rank of grime and ale filled his nose

"The sign is most likely stolen. I believe they call it 'Diegal's'," answered Andro, pushing his way inside.

The pub reeked of pipe smoke and spilt beer, which suited the unsavory mob – the young Loganders found themselves suddenly out of place. Andro looked this way and that, searching for a familiar face while Rogan stood close at his back, one hand upon the money pouch tucked beneath his belt.

"Are you sure this is the right place? I mean, would Armond spend time in an establishment like this?" shouted Rogan above the din.

Andro smiled.

"Yes to both," he answered, pointing out a broad-shouldered man seated at a table along the back wall. "There he is."

"*He comes alone?*" wondered Rogan as they approached, only to discover a smaller man seated across the table, hidden behind the first man's brawn.

"Well, look who we have here!" called Andro. He slapped the back of the larger man who turned suddenly with a flash of angry blue eyes, but catching Andro's smile he gave a shout.

"Andro, you made it! It's about time, old friend. And Rogan, I wasn't sure you'd come. Fine it is to see you outside of Logan."

"It's nice to be away from Logan."

Armond jumped to his feet, nearly matching Andro's height, but swarthy and heavily muscled. Long black tresses displayed his Nordic heritage. He welcomed his long time friend with an embrace.

"Wonderful to see you again after so long. And no less pleased to find you well, Brenn Linderfell," said Andro, leaning close to the red-cheeked fellow opposite table.

"Is that all the welcome I get? A 'pleased to find you well,' while this blockhead gets along with a hug and a hello. I would have thought you a better judge of character than that, Master Rhine," quipped Brenn, who left his seat and properly bowed. He was a Mihtrir, and at five foot even, short for even his own.

"Forgive my insolence."

"You'll get no apologies from me, shorty," said Armond, shaking a fist, "I've put up with your antics all morning."

"...and I've tired of playing the nanny here, trying to keep this brute out of trouble when he can't hold his drink," jeered Brenn, who at twenty-four, held rank of eldest among the friends.

Andro couldn't help but laugh. "How long have I missed you both? Looks like Rogan and I came just in time."

"Just in time to watch me pull this shrimp up by his brown curls," growled Armond.

"Let me get my greeting in first," said Rogan. He placed a hand across his chest and bowed. "I am Rogan Pinehurst, Andro's neighbor from east of Logan. Leatherleaf Lane to be exact. This is my first time in Diegal's – or Thalon for that matter."

"Well, that calls for another round. Sit down you two, and never mind this ogre," replied Brenn, offering his seat. He promptly called over a barmaid: a quartet of pints was brought to table along with two small brown loaves, honey, and a slab of butter.

"*More hospitable that I imagined*," thought Rogan, first to finish a steaming roll.

"Armond, I understand Thalon is where you and Andro first met?" he asked, settling comfortably among friends.

"Indeed, at this very festival," replied Armond. "Andro and I have known each other since childhood when our fathers began bringing us to the city. We would play on the merchant streets while they gathered for some dull guild meeting. Those were some good times then."

"...when we avoided trouble," laughed Andro, interrupting. "Brenn was correct in saying it: one must keep an eye on this fellow – devilry runs in his veins."

"That is why I keep you near. No one has a better streak of luck than Andro – 'Rhine Luck' I call it. It is as if someone watches over his shoulder," replied Armond.

"You will have tell to me some stories when there's more time."

Armond chuckled. "Andro recounts them better: incidents with eggs and the city guard, sneaking into a parlor house, taking that old trader's wagon for a ride when we thought he was sleeping..."

"To name a few," said Andro, his cheeks blushing. "Now that

we have grown I hope opportunities for camaraderie will continue – not only at the festival, but abroad."

"Aye," said Armond, "maybe you'll find there is more to this land than just a Farrian forest to hang about."

"...and frost-bitten mountains. How did winter in the Vanadium's treat you this year?"

"The same as always – heavy snows, bitter winds, little movement for months. I too am glad for summer," answered Armond, resting thick arms upon the table. "But what I really want to learn is what news comes to Northern Gandol these days?"

Andro shrugged his shoulders.

"Oh, nothing out of the ordinary. My parents are well and my brother Aiden with his family. Logan never changes: boring, scheduled, the trees fall, and saws are kept sharp – business as usual," he replied.

"As far as forest news goes," interjected Rogan. He could not help but roll his eyes. "I keep reminding Andro to pay more attention to goings on beyond Logan and get his head out of the countryside and forest for a while. While local politics and neighborhood matters prove dull indeed, there are far greater dealings of interest coming out of the South."

"I have heard some of these things myself – war and siege," replied Armond. "That is more what I meant."

Andro blushed. He was ignorant to the talk of the day, so enamored to the simpler things in life; in contrast, Rogan Pinehurst learned from a young age that the world could be a tempest in one place, and a garden of tranquility in another. Edwin Pinehurst taught his son by his own dealings with the mayor and visiting dignitaries to Logan. Through his father, news came to young Rogan who devoured all curious talk concerning the Kingdoms of the West.

"What I have heard of late arrives from Fanael. Once again, Lokrey is held siege by Illutar and their Drukon overlords. Some say the tide comes like the battles of old," uttered Rogan in a hushed voice.

Armond glowered behind smeared fingers, taking the last

swallow of his beer. "Damn Illutar. I would like to learn more of this news."

Brenn laughed. "Well, if it's a report you want then you have come to the right place – scuttlebutt spreads like wildfire at the festival. Turrar and Kuirian are an anxious bunch when it comes to gossip, especially if that news concerns war, which to Nordhiem, is a paying sport."

"You would not say that if your cousins were here. Kuirian take an attack upon their kin seriously."

Brenn sighed, half for the empty flagon beneath his frowning lips, half for the talk of the moment. "It is true, Drago and Zerrin await the news. But what kind of fool seeks out war," he replied, stoking Armond's anger. Brenn pressed the issue:

"Don't let this ruffian fool you – he knows well the talk of late. Rumor spreads that King Kalwin seeks knowledge of the situation, and arrives tomorrow from Riccdare to join in Anor's council. This would be the first meeting of the kings in years. Also, they say an emissary from the south arrives tonight with a fresh report. That'll keep heads buzzing."

"All talk, no one is certain of anything," grumbled Armond. "But Brenn is correct in saying it – I *have* learned of these matters you speak, and not only me. Drago and Zerrin have come to the festival with us. They have plans to go to Fanael – to war if the need arises, as mercenaries. An attack on Lokrey is an attack on all Kuirian."

Armond leaned in close, staring deeply into Andro's eyes. "You know me well friend, and you know my mind – you will understand when I tell you that if Drago and Zerrin go to Fanael, I will go with them."

Andro felt a chill overtake him and his heart sank. He had seen Armond this way before – the look of determination despite the danger. He often feared this side of his friend, so much unlike himself. Armond read his silence until Brenn spoke up.

"And the fool I am would follow along, most likely to my own death. Who would pay mind to some bloke from Honodolch stumbling behind Armond and my two cousins into battle? Probably bring a laugh to those Drukon."

Armond grabbed Brenn by the neck, this time with affection. "I'll watch your back."

"And who will watch yours?"

Andro took a deep breath, raised his eyes and smiled. "I suppose that would fall to me."

"Aye, Andro, I knew you would come around!" bellowed Armond; the slam of his fist nearly flipped the table.

"You surprised me at first. This sounds like more adventure than we first bargained."

"We are capable fighters. Don't worry about sieges – we might never gaze upon Lokrey, even from a distance, for they are well fortified and an outlier. Nordic fighters have met their challenge upon the fields of Earlon instead where the Lord-Captains of Fanael respect a skilled sword."

"We never spoke of battle before, but I knew it lay heavily upon our hearts, cleaving drukon heads in the wake of a cavalry thrust. Still, you gave me a shock."

"Then I will give you another – I am joining the Tournament. Tomorrow I will fight at the competition."

Andro and Rogan nearly dropped their mugs in disbelief.

"This has indeed been a day of surprises. Let's get out of this place before we miss the festivities and talk more about it later," said Andro to the others approval. They left the tavern for the bright outdoors amid ringing trumpets and drums rolling in the distance.

They soon pressed along crowded Ardule Avenue as seemingly all Thalon turned out eager for a parade. The low drumming of wooden soles preceded a procession of flowing banners and flags from every city-state in Nordhiem, borne by squires of the Royal School dressed in red doublets of gossamer and coal black breeches: first came Thalon's pride, the flag of a great golden eagle held proudly in the warm breeze; proceeded by Vahar, the border city of the East, represented by a banner with an open gate guarded by silver swords; next came Huork's standard, a tall snow-capped mountain overlaid by a black sword, named *Ouracurs*, the doomed weapon of its lord, Turrar-Set; fourth proceeded Vanyor's proud symbol displaying a pick and axe crossed upon a checkered background of silver and gold, the sign of three-hundred years of mining and silverwork; the city of Rousk followed with a standard bearing a great horned stag set against a background of red satin, its lord and kinsmen lived upon the fringes of a great northern plain; and at last came the flag of northernmost Trungard, blue as twilight, bearing a white moon and the five stars of Turramirtel, Nordhiem's goddess of the North Wind. Trungard's renown came as an outpost town harboring the most rugged souls. This was the domain of a forbidding lord, Borgan the Black.

The traditional procession grew over the years as a display of unity and strength. By will of King Anor, all of Nordhiem brought forth representation, if only symbolic. The city-states each had their own concerns and quarrels, but for one week of the year all remained at peace in Nordhiem.

A festive line of musicians and performers arrived next, much to Andro's delight. A nudge in the ribs broke the spell, that and Armond's rousing cheer to the damsels who paraded before their eyes. Like pedals in the breeze, ribbons streamed from their hair, spinning dizzy circles as they went, symbols in hand and bright melodies upon soft lips. Andro felt his knees buckle.

Others filed in step, fifes and horns their song, just in front of a line of marching boys drumming a festive beat. These preceded a column of Thalon's legion guard, dressed in mail bearing round metal shields with heavy broad swords at their sides. They pounded towards the square, to Andro's estimation, two hundred strong. Once the procession ended, they followed in their wake.

An unorganized mass filed into the great Royal Square. Deep as it was wide, the grounds formed four perfect sides, several furlongs in each direction. The march ended before an empty dais, soon to become the seating platform for the King and Queen, the Lords of Nordhiem, and visiting dignitaries. Flowing in tapestries of red and gold, the stand provided the finest view of the square's centerpiece, the Forum of Tournament and its festivities. An arena sunk deep into the square, descending into a long grassy oval, built of stone and formed of twelve wide rows of stairs. Down a sloping bank, the marchers continued until the forum lined with banner-wavers, musicians, soldiers, and horsemen alike. Onlookers flocked the stairs ringing the arena until it was full, and more came only to wait above hoping for a vantage point. Once settled, a bell tolled high upon the castle ramparts and the clamor of horns and drums came to a sudden end.

All eyes turned north where upon a broad precipice Castle Rohbir loomed over the city and square, girding the hill with low thick walls. After a pause, a horn sounded within and the gate of the citadel opened, clanging with the roll of iron chains. A column of horsemen trotted out of the gate onto the winding stair of the hill, heralded by trumpeters who waited along its flanks. They crossed back and forth, descending in levels until they reached the square two hundred feet below. The Royal High-Calvary soon followed, their fair steeds of Bardol stock valiant and strong. Standing tall within their stirrups, they boasted breast-plated armor, silver mail, polished helms, and at their sides, long swords in scabbards of hardened black leather. Their shields bore an eagle of bronze in flight. The riders filed in a long line, halting in formation once upon the arena floor.

Cheers erupted in anticipation of the arrival of the Lords of Nordhiem, each preceded by his own horse-guard. And last, to the rousing approval of the masses, the emergence of King Anor II and Queen Darimeale in a carriage pulled by six white palfreys. The aging monarchs entered the square where retainers attended them.

The leaders of Nordhiem took their places upon the dais – the king and queen seated in its center upon lavish thrones. As if on queue, a bell peeled signaling the noon hour. King Anor officially began the festival, raising a sword into the air – the crowd offered its roaring approval. Musicians and performers marked the hour with dance and song followed by jugglers, acrobats, and jesters who performed deep into the afternoon. Afterwards came the traditional, yet rarely anticipated, oracles by Anor and other speakers of noble variety, including stately Lord Vesgar of Vanyor and Mayor Haggard of Barrith. Judging from the pain in Andro's neck, the seemingly overlong narrations ended none-too-soon. As the sun began its late summer descent, the lords returned to the castle and the crowds dispersed to make merry throughout the city.

    Andro and the others departed the plaza sun-brazen, tired, and thirsty. A large inn sat just off the common upon Ardule Avenue that fit the bill: the King's Inn, aptly named within shadow of the castle, lulled many with the smell of a roasting sow, the din of song, and clanking mugs of dark Thalon mead. With scant room indoors, the four found a spot of peace beneath a large porch, and stole away the heat of the day. With mugs at their sides and plates upon their knees, they sat content upon a row of round border stones.
    "This is what I like," said Brenn with a mouthful of food, "good people, the lights, the music…"
    "The food!" snapped Armond. "You have devoured more than the rest of us without a thought of trouble."
    Brenn blushed, staring down at his now empty plate. He could have eaten more.
    "Don't you fret, Mr. Linderfell. You're swift as any of us, even with a full belly," said Andro who relished his own dish of pork, potatoes, and cabbage.
    Andro cut his words short as three men stepped out of the manor. Two held large mugs and the other, a middle-aged balding fellow, wiped his hands across a beer-stained apron. They paused at the top step of the porch.

    "Ah, that's better. Some fresh air," said the eldest of the three, oblivious to the young men seated on the street below. "Rulle, I wanted to ask something of you earlier."
    "What is it?"
    "Do you think Baric is wise in wanting to leave so soon? After all, the old man knew many things concerning the southern road. Would it hurt to wait a while and see what kind of offer he brings to the table?"

"No Ashbarhe, I would not trust his kind at any price. Baric's offer is fair – he may be all puffed up, but I know I can trust him. Talk of war has many ready to take arms, for a price, but few have the nerve for it. It's a long way to Earlon, even on horseback," replied the man, Rulle, leaning his muscular frame against a white post.

"Baric wanted no part of him either, and that's good enough for me. Odd folk them Greyhoods, or what do some call 'em – Acolytes. They travel in secret and serve strange gods," said the broad shouldered third man, fairer than the other two.

"Perhaps, Carthain, but he is a Turrar and seems honest enough. They say his kind never lie, and this one may actually pay, not just promise a booty of battlefield spoils," replied Ashbarhe. "I listened in when the old man spoke to Baric and Reissing: he travels not to the war, but to another place – Asengard, although I had always thought that place deserted. All he seeks is an escort."

Rulle nicked the wood of the porch with the tip of his boot. "The offer is tempting."

Carthain found the matter uproarious. "Ha! You should know better than trust the whim of some strange bird. He might be a sorcerer for all we know. Baric and Reissing rejected his offer. He is old – he would only slow us down."

"You're probably right. All of Thalon talks of war these days, but few will go. Even the Kuirian speak of it, and their words are grim. But they have small chance of reaching Earlon before winter, even if they walked the whole distance without rest. I have no intention of crossing the Werithain Mountains in the snow," replied Ashbarhe.

"Baric's plan is fair enough, and that calls for men and horses. We will reach southern Fanael before the leaves change, and by then who will remember the Greyhood at all. Probably wander back to wherever he belongs," said Rulle.

"He's Vanyorian, that much I know, and steers clear of common men; that was, until now," replied Carthain.

Ashbarhe took the empty mugs from the men. "Then it is decided: Baric's riders will soon set their sights upon the southern road. I for one will be glad for the start. Now I must get back inside and tap another barrel. A few more nights and I can say farewell to this place."

"Until tomorrow then, at the tournament. Goodnight Ash," finished Rulle. He and Carthain left the porch and disappeared into the deepening dusk beyond the lampposts that were lit along the avenue. Ashbarhe tightened his smock and drifted back into the crowded tavern.

The four sat a moment in silence when suddenly Brenn rose to his feet.

"Well, what are you waiting for?" he asked. "You heard those men. Sounds like if you find this Baric, you find your party. They are fighters riding south, just like you…I mean us."

Armond sneered beneath the dancing firelight. "And what of Drago and Zerrin? They are a party to this decision."

"They will trust your choice."

"We all will," added Rogan.

"We? Are you sure Rogan? We've spoken of adventure in the past, but not this," asked Andro.

"I am no longer a child. I have heard the stories of valor and many times wondered how far the road lies in-between. There are dangers, yet glories ahead – perhaps a plunder for the taking. Wouldn't that be nice? Will you accept an undersized teenager in the party? I ride well and can handle a bow with some skill."

"No need for disclosures here, friend. We can use your bow and wits as well," replied Armond. Never one for flattery, the heaviness in his voice carried sincerity.

"And that makes six, Drago and Zerrin included," announced Brenn. "Now if everything is settled, let's go find this Baric and offer our services."

Andro considered a seventh, but kept his friend Leonin out of the conversation; after all, Farrian and Turrar make poor company.

Armond thought for a moment – then threw Andro a wink. "I'd like to try someone else before talking to this Baric, a name I know well from past tournaments. The Tall, they call him – a glory-hound if ever there was one. His head barely fits upon his shoulders. I have another ideal in mind," he announced with a grin somewhere between sly and sure.

"What are you talking about? What other ideal?" asked Brenn, now standing with hands planted firmly upon his hips.

"They mentioned a greyhood. One lives in the foothills above our city. I have never seen his face, but many old timers speak of him. Perhaps he is one and the same. I would like to find out."

Brenn's cheeks went flush and his jaw dropped in disbelief. "Did you not hear those men? Has the smell of strong drink made you drunk? He is a Greyhood – the one man called him a sorcerer. Perhaps he is. They are out of place in everyday affairs."

"I certainly doubt a man of magic walks Thalon. Maybe in the south where Whitehoods rule – their ways I do not know. But in Nordhiem, there is only a scattering of these grey sorts. I've heard very little aside from wive's tales to question their motives. They are mysterious, but worthy of a little trust. I'd like to find out if this old man is the one from home – the sage from the House upon the Hill," he replied.

"But what if those men spoke correctly? What if he leaves for ill-mannered reason? They said he travels not to war, but to another place," replied a defiant Brenn.

"We'll just have to judge for ourselves," answered Andro.

Despite Brenn's objections, they decided to try the greyhood first, if he could be found. Brenn followed behind, helpless to argue as they started up the stairs for the inn.

Never one for social grace, Armond pushed past sozzled patrons and mead-filled mugs on his way to the bar where Ashbarhe was busy pouring ales, rye, and spirits. No wine for this raucous crowd.

"Excuse me, may I have a word with you?" Armond shouted above the din. The man smoothed his black mustache and gave him a bothered look.

"What can I get you?"

"I overheard you outside just moments ago. You were speaking with two others."

Ashbarhe glinted at deceit. "What of it? Make it quick, my break is over."

"You mentioned a greyhood who seeks a traveling party. Do you know where we might find him?"

The barkeep laughed. "Looking for trouble, are you? Young fighters ready to stick their fingers in the pie? Rude awakenings are never pleasant," he replied.

"But he does seek an escort?"

"Yes, and he will pay. But he seeks experienced fighters. Talk to him if you can find him – I am not his keeper," replied the man. "You might consider speaking to Baric the Tall instead – he is assembling a Nordic cavalry; that is, if you can ride. Then you may learn the ropes of being mercenary."

"We will keep that option open. Do you recall anything about the greyhood?"

"He keeps to himself – they all do. This one goes by the name, Greynol, oddly enough. You might start by seeking the old Prelate House east of the square. Wetherton lives there. Now I've work to do, goodnight," he finished, abruptly ending the conversation to assist paying patrons.

Armond had enough to go on. He led the others back outside into a pleasant midsummer's night – a fair change from the heat of the day.

"At least we have a place to start," he said, turning east once his boots met the cobblestone of the avenue. The others hurried to keep pace.

Andro found it curious as they went: it seemed several heads in the manor turned at the mention of the name, Greynol. *"In a crowded place curiosities run high. They too must have heard of him,"* he thought. But more than once, he wondered if Brenn had a legitimate protest.

They entered the shadows of an emptied Royal Square; the rare light of beacons softened in the damp night air, illuminating the dais and casting an orange hue upon several guards who conversed beneath the stands. In the darkness, the castle Rohbir loomed, irreproachable and silent, floating upon a cloud of eventide above a disquiet city – the knoll it rest imperceptible, where torches upon its battlements exposed the keep's position. Small windows glowed with dim light, wherein royal halls even the nobility found it too much to rest this first night of celebration.

Silence overcame the young men as they crossed into the eastern quarter; the thrill of lights and song far behind them.

"No banners, no lamplight's, no happy sounds," muttered Brenn under his breath as they passed from the square onto a dark lane. A cat's mew and far off laughter gave him a start. Glancing down an alleyway, he saw only blackness.

"This is no street I would expect to find a person of trust. Let's go back."

"Brenn, you sound afraid of dark places. I imagine at daybreak this place is as pleasant as the rest of the city," replied Andro, without conviction. He had his own gnawing doubt to contend with.

The houses leaned upon the four as the road narrowed. Soot-covered windows frowned upon them; a feeling of unease all could sense, save Armond, intent on finding the Prelate's House.

"Which way now?" asked Rogan at a crossing of two gloomy lanes.

"My father brought me back here once to meet a merchant, but that was years ago," answered Armond. He pointed to a sign upon their right illuminated by the light of a single candle.

"This looks familiar."

They turned down a narrow street named simply, Gray Lane. Here the road bent to the left forming a narrow channel – the upper floors of buildings extended out beyond the lower in a crooked cavalcade. Little sign of life was seen or heard within, but Andro felt their presence known. Now in the darkest pocket of their search, where their only comforts came from a barking dog and distant singing, they approached upon their left a large estate.

There stood an old gray-stoned manor, its windows barred and dark, except upon the third floor that glowed with soft candlelight. After several paces, the house dropped away to form an overgrown courtyard guarded by a tall gate and palisade of black iron. A hedgerow bordered the yard's perimeter and rosy thorn bushes lined a walkway leading to the porch and front door. Narrow windows framed a scarlet oaken entryway, shut firm against the night.

"Who do you suppose lives here?" asked Brenn, leaning upon the gate beneath a burning lamp. He expected no answer.

"Wetherton," replied a voice from an alley across the lane. A cloaked figure stepped out of the darkness. Brenn nearly cried out.

"Who are you?" demanded Armond, a hand upon his dagger.

The individual paused once within the glow of the gate-lamp, drawing back the hood of his dove-gray frock.

"Well, I am not Wetherton, if you must know," replied the grey-bearded man, fair despite his age. "Unless you men have nothing better to do than stare through the gate like hungry dogs, I would like to go inside where my room awaits."

"Sorry to disturb you. We will be on our way," said Brenn, backing away until Armond grabbed him by the collar.

"Not another step, Linderfell," he whispered.

Armond straightened up and regained composure. "Pay no mind to my friend here. In truth, we came seeking information about an Acolyte named Greynol. You may have heard of him. We were told he has dealings in this part of town."

The old man hesitated, taken back by the question. "I recognize the name. What need have you of him?"

"We were told he seeks a traveling party – an armed escort, you might say. We came to offer our service."

The man stepped in closer. "You know these things for certain?" he asked cautiously.

"In truth, we overheard of his need at the King's Inn off the square."

"Well, word spreads quickly, even if spoken to a few," he said with a sigh. "I am Greynol, the one you seek. You caught me by happenstance; I was returning from an errand."

"The man at the inn mentioned your name and your need," said Andro, clearing his throat to ease the tension in his voice. "They spoke of a plan to journey south – an adventure perhaps."

"An adventure? I had not thought of it as such," he replied. "It seems my quiet planning has gone on ahead of me – much to my regret. I seek a traveling party, there you stand correct, but I require experienced fighters – sojourners who understand the road and its dangers. My body is old and my situation perilous; clearly, you men are too young. I am sorry to disappoint you."

They were quickly silenced, watching as he reached for the gate latch, but Armond was quick to speak up again.

"I know of your name sir. I too am Vanyorian. I am Armond, son of Baldor the Master Armorer."

Greynol listened politely. "The name sounds familiar, but faces fail me. He may have been a student of mine when Idarill House stood as a school for youth. But now I am told too old to teach. Until recent events, I had no choice save succumb to my retirement."

Next Andro and Rogan felt it proper to introduce themselves: each stepped forward with palms on their chests and heads bowed in proper Logander fashion. Brenn came last sporting a frown; he bowed slowly and with deliberate caution.

"Mister Linderfell, you have a suspecting eye," replied Greynol, clearly amused. "That is a useful quality. But you have nothing to fear in me."

Brenn remained stoic. "You are an Acolyte, and a mysterious one at that. I do not easily throw my trust to strange men," he replied to the others shock, and Armond's ire. He found the situation souring by the moment and pulled Brenn aside.

"Look, you had better pipe down. I'm trying to make good here."

Greynol shook his head, holding back a chuckle. "The wiles of youth, how easily forgotten. I fear old age has robbed me of such favor," he said, but the smile swiftly left his face. "The path I choose is a grim one, and I do not wish my plight upon innocent men. Go back to your good lives."

Words of wisdom held no sway to any save Brenn who wanted nothing more to do with the man. Armond held him in check with a glance.

Rogan's turn came to give a plea.

"I am eighteen and youngest in this company by two years. If I am the reason for any misgivings then send me away, but do not quell the hearts of my friends here whom are strong. Please understand Mister Greynol, I am ready for the road. I may not always feel the same when I am older. They say boys fight among men in the wars of the South. But I am no longer a child. Andro and I have prepared for such a chance with bow and arrow, tracking, hunting, and swordplay our schools of knowledge."

"Your knowledge goes beyond just those schools, my dear Rogan," replied Greynol. "Impressed I am with each of you by your sincerity and trustworthiness – I read it in your eyes when you speak. But like I said before, my path is perilous. Experienced fighters will guard my flank, and several more than four. I pay well for this service and I expect good value in return."

Armond took in a deep breath, fearing he might burst from eagerness to explain further:

"Sir, there are more than four of us," he replied with immediacy. "Drago and Zerrin stay with us in the city. Kuirian brothers and cousins of Brenn, they are capable fighters. They make up the remainder of our company."

Greynol grew pensive, fingers drumming over his folded hands. He glanced towards the window above the porch as if for guidance. "I am sorry, six is better than four, but I need to be certain I have a fighter of experience in my company, one whose sword rings true before the enemy."

Armond felt his pride swell within. "Sir, your concern is justifiable, and I can put your mind at ease if you give me time."

"What time do you need?"

"Just until tomorrow. Then I shall fight in the Tournament of Melee – watch then and decide. I have waited a long time for this opportunity. I *am* the fighter you seek."

"Have you prepared your entry? The number is set."

"I have."

Greynol glanced him up and down, like a master with an aspiring student. "You impress me, Armond, son of Baldor. The

Tournament is one event not to take lightly. Many of Nordhiem's fiercest combatants arrive in hopes of winning a bag of silverkrones. How can I refuse such an offer? I came to the festival to find swordsmen. If you prove to be one of worth, and provided there are at least six in your company, Drago and Zerrin included, then I will accept your offer. Now if all is settled, I am turning in for the evening. Until tomorrow."

"Thank you sir, goodnight," replied Armond with a bow. Greynol nodded and without further discussion passed through the gate and across the courtyard. He entered the house and disappeared within.

"Well, now you've put your foot into it this time. Do favorably in the fight and we go away with this odd man; get clobbered and go home mad. Which is the worse fate?" muttered Brenn, unhappy at the turn of events.

"I *will* fight hard. Let chance do it's part as well. Remember Brenn – no hire, no pay," replied a content Armond.

"I wish we knew more concerning his 'perilous way'," said Andro.

"I wish we never came here," added Brenn.

"Everything will work out for the best. I for one have confidence in Armond's ability and judgment: this Greynol may seem strange, but I trust him," replied Rogan with a yawn; "and since all that is finished it is time we go back to the camp and get some sleep. This has been an eventful day, indeed."

"The night is still young," protested Armond, "come back to the inn for a brew."

"...which will lead to many more," laughed Andro, who knew his friend all too well. "No, we will go on to our rest. So should you – tomorrow is a big day."

"All right, I'll give in – this once. Come along Brenn, back to the lodge where our party awaits; although things won't be less quiet."

The four ambled along the dark way, brightened now slightly by a rising moon, nearing full. They crossed the square and entered a lively western quarter before splitting company: Andro and Rogan down Ardule Avenue and out the gate to camp; and Armond and Brenn who found rest at a merchant street lodge where their bunks awaited them, but not before several rousing toasts among their own.

Greynol climbed the flight of stairs and found Prelate Wetherton standing at the hallway window.
"Have they gone?"
"They just turned the corner," replied Wetherton, an elderly balding fellow dressed in a simple white tunic. He leaned upon his cane and turned a cocked glance. "You spoke at length. Did they make any trouble?"
"No friend. They were seeking an old acolyte with a curious job to offer."
"Ha! cutthroats and mercenaries. Right you were to send them off."
"They are young men, nothing more, and may fill a need should nothing else materialize. Although inexperienced, they have good sense about them and appear honest. Where else might I find those qualities in Thalon?"
"Take my advice, go back and talk to Baric the Tall – his party will best suit your needs."
Greynol sighed, staring out the window to the gate light below. "Baric fears my age as a hindrance to his scheme: *A greyhood makes unsuitable company for Turrar and Kuirian warriors.* Now word spreads that I seek a party of my own. Before long my enemies will be at the doorstep."
"If only I could aid you, my friend, travel as in day's past; but my time of riding is long behind me," replied Wetherton, taking one of two chairs upon each side of the window. "An aging prelate is good for staying put, and an old acolyte should do the same. I am concerned over your decision to continue on this journey."
Greynol glanced down at a pack left beneath the stand with the scroll sticking out its top. He reached down to ensure it was safe.
"Don't worry, I kept an eye on it; although I wish you would

lose that accursed thing," said Wetherton.
    He reached into his pocket and pulled out a Timlet stone. Greynol did the same with the stone of his keeping. The orbs reflected the glow of the lamp: a yellow luminescence that calmed with kindly warmth. Wetherton opened a large book that rest upon the table between them, marked on its cover with the letter, *T*. Expertly versed, he found his place and read aloud until drowsiness overcame him – the words on the parchment a balm to ease disquiet minds to sleep:

    "...and in her hands, the sign of life, that brings to light, that burns all strife; gaze westward to the setting sun, the call to stay the rising storm."

Chapter Three – The Tournament

The morning of the Tournament came swiftly upon a warm southern breeze that soon died away. The air grew thick beneath a reddened sun and the day showed every sign of becoming a summer swelter. At the ninth hour, trumpets rang out along the castle ramparts signaling to all that the tournament would soon begin. Townspeople and visitors alike made their move towards the arena.

Andro and Rogan arrived in front of the King's Inn to find Armond, Brenn, and two others awaiting their arrival. Brenn stood with plate in hand loaded with bacon, honey cakes, cheese, and eggs.

"Have you eaten? They've plenty more inside," asked Brenn with a mouthful.

"We had a bite back at camp, thank you – wouldn't want be late after so much anticipation. I believe the whole city is about to boil over with excitement, myself included," replied Andro. He placed a hand upon his chest in a proper bow, turning to the two new faces. "Good morning, Drago. Good morning, Zerrin. Fine it is to see you again in good health."

A stout red-haired Kuirian bowed, his beard folding upon a ruddy shirt and brown suspenders. "A glad mornin' it tis, Master Rhine," replied Drago with a wink. "Now we witness the worthiness of our friend here. I understand the fate of our new company rests in Armond's hands."

Zerrin chuckled. Unlike Drago, he had black hair, a blue woolen shirt, and a beard two years less long. A Kuirian counted his years by the length of his beard. "I reckon it is in good hands;

besides, I tire of sparring against his mad ways. It'll be nice to watch him take out his wrath on somebody else."

Armond feigned a smile and looked away – silence in answer to their jest. He tensed thick shoulders that bulged from a sleeveless shirt, closing and opening his sword hand as he watched.

"He's been like that all morning, don't want to talk – butterflies or somethin'," said Brenn.

"No, just ignoring the likes of you," growled Armond, giving the brothers a good laugh. Bickering between their cousin and Armond a common occurrence back home in Vanyor.

Hasty introductions commenced: Rogan greeted Drago and Zerrin and they bowed in return; a brief moment for the young Logander to get acquainted. Andro knew the brothers from previous festivals.

"The six of us, eh. We may not be the most fearsome of warriors, but worthy of a little respect," said Zerrin with a generous grin. His cheerful nature made up for Drago's gruff disposition.

"But what of this Greynol, has anyone seen him today?" asked Drago.

"No, but he said he would show," replied Andro, nervously tapping his foot. "First things first. Are you ready, Armond? Fighters are entering the square now."

"Am I ready? Too ready. I've been awake for hours now," he answered, lifting a bundle off the ground. A padded leather vest for protection – all that is allowed.

Drago slapped him on the back. "You'll do fine. It'll be good practice for the road ahead."

"If we ever get there," replied Brenn, cleaning his plate with a piece of bread.

"What do you mean – *if?*" asked Andro.

"I *mean*, things out of our control. Baldor has already thrown a cog in the wheel, and knowing fathers and mothers, you youngsters will have your hands full trying to explain your way onto this journey. Don't think your parents will let things stand as they are."

Andro bit his tongue, for he knew the sentiments rang true. He held back news of the meeting with Greynol from his own father for fear of swift admonishment. *Why open up that can of worms*, he thought.

"It's not as you might think," replied Armond, eyes like burning blue embers focused on the trial ahead. "The problem lies in my responsibilities back home: there remains a list of heavy chores to finish before winter. If I am gone, my father and mother must go it alone, and the task is too much for them. Then they must hire help, which comes at a steep price."

"Then what solution is there?"

Drago crossed his thick arms before him. "Well Andro, that's what friends are for. Brenn, Zerrin, and I can accomplish in a few days of chopping wood and digging coal what takes one man weeks. The question remains – does this Acolyte have time to give us to ride to Vanyor and back again?"

Horns interrupted the dilemma, a warning for the participants to gather. Armond threw the bundle across his shoulder, motioning they start for the arena. "We can concern ourselves with these things when it is over."

With little time to spare, they hastened through the crowds, pausing at a ramp that led to the battlegrounds. Armond presented a token to the attendant, purchased the day before for one silver krone. Andro assisted him pulling the bulky padded-leather shirt over his shoulders and tightened the buckles across his waist. The others waited nearby, the assembly in their sights as it filled twelve ringed flights of the forum. Within the crowd watched Baldor and a group from Vanyor, and Audin and Aiden Rhine, Andro's older brother, with their own party from Logan. Greynol remained unseen.

"That would only make sense," grumbled Armond at the news, flexing his arms to loosen the tightness of the hardened leather. "Greynol had no confidence in us from the start."

Just then, several guards with spears came to chase all non-participants away. Andro and company settled in among the crowd and found a good vantage point along the steps directly across from the still empty dais. Armond found himself waiting in a long line of fighters who marched in file as directed to the arena floor. A trumpet blast announced the procession from Castle Rohbir, just as the day before: King Anor, Queen Darimeale, and the Nordic Lords arrived, each in their own manner, escorted by foot-soldiers and an armored cavalry. The royals and dignitaries promptly took their places upon the dais, for they, just like the raucous crowd below, anticipated a hard-fought contest.

Over two thousand participants waited their turn to best their opponent before king and countrymen. They huddled as those at attention, known and unknown, of varied ages and backgrounds – journeymen, foreign born, and common brawlers. Within their ranks stood men of notoriety who gained fame in battle or past tournaments, and these too arrived from across the northern realm.

The warriors stood fast at the blowing of a single horn upon the dais. Armond took a proud stance among the combatants, raising his right hand in the air in unison with the others, repeating the words of oath called out by the judges present: "For honor and service! To King and Country!"

The tournament was set – elimination down to the last man. Blunted weapons were doled out: swords, axes, spears, and wooden shields. The judges kept order and awarded victory at their determination of any blow of certainty to the head, neck, or heart. Eleven rounds separated the beginning rabble down to the one champion. The first two rounds, called 'the weeding out,' cut the number down to five hundred, eliminating the less deserving. Armond had no desire to join in their number.

In the end came the Champion's reward: two thousand forty-eight silver krones gathered from the fighters prior to the festival as presented by the king.

Sharp-edged spears pushed the participants to the edge of the circle. Armond took a seat upon the grass to watch as a spectator until called. Pairs were singled out, dozens at a time, and after hasty instructions, judges dropped their hands and the melee began. Armond witnessed a clash of arms: the fray appeared a clumsy orchestration as fighters stumbled and rushed, slashed and conquered. Some lay bleeding, bruised, moaning in pain, or red-faced and angered over a sudden loss. The melee continued. As one pair finished, another fight began. The arena was now awash with dueling combatants; the dust roiled and the crowd kept up its loud chorus. The winners of the first round received a white feather – the losers, jeers and a quick exit.

Armond glanced over his shoulder searching for his friends in the assembly, but the faces were many and noise drowned out their voices. After some time, an eternity in waiting it seemed, a large man in a traditional white tabard approached.

"You there – here!" he commanded, pointing Armond to a position upon the grass.

"And you, hurry it up," he called to another in wait.

An odd fellow lined up opposite Armond. Rangy arms tensed with hands folded at his waist and sweat beaded upon a cleaned-shaven head – the man looked strange even in Nordhiem.

"Choose!" bellowed the judge. Two young retainers stood near holding two swords, an axe, a spear, and two shields. Armond took a firm handled sword, its edge smoothed away, and a wooden shield. His opponent chose the second shield and a spear.

"Line up," called the judge once again. "The fight ends when I say, or my spearmen will end it for you. My judgment is final – now fight!"

With a drop of his hand, the contest began. Armond felt a flame surge in his heart, but it was met by the distraction of a roaring crowd and forty other fights going on simultaneously in the forum.

"Come boy, see what I have waiting," challenged the adversary, his accent thick and clever.

"Odd again," thought Armond, his mind drifting. *"Is he Noldarin? Perhaps from the western flanks..."*

A sudden attack ended the curiosity as Armond blocked a spear thrust with his shield. The man returned with slashes and drives, keeping him on the defensive. He came quickly on the attack, skilled with his weapon. Crouched low with spear in left hand and shield upon his right, he squatted ready to strike. Armond lunged forward hacking with the sword, but his blows were blocked and countered. The exchange continued until the man found an opportunity and swept low as if to strike a leg; then with a sudden dip and a deft twisting maneuver, he managed to get behind Armond's shield from below, blocking with his own shield and stabbing upward towards the heart. Armond reacted instinctively. He spun away from the near victorious strike, and with both shields knocked aside, struck a sword blow to the neck of his opponent. So sudden it came and it was done. Armond looked on as the strange man writhed in pain upon the ground, hand clutched upon a throbbing neck.

"The Victor!" called the judge. He raised Armond's hand above his head. He was given a white feather and walked back to where the victorious sat, waiting for round two. His opponent sent away cursing.

Armond retook his seat upon the grass in a large group of sweaty fighters. A boy came around to serve them water from a bucket. He graciously accepted, dunking a large dipping spoon to refresh his thirst.

"Nice move out there," called a husky man at his side. "You disappointed your opponent – he expected an easy tally."

"I wasn't about to give him one," replied Armond.

"He has used that maneuver before, with better results."

Armond looked at the fellow who seemed an overgrown Mihtrir with a red beard and bushy hair. "Do you know that man? He looked foreign."

The large man laughed.

"No, he is probably a renegade Gonar. I've seen his kind before, traveling alone, which is better, or in a group – that's when trouble starts. My party and I crossed the Fahrol Mountains east of here before arriving in Thalon from Vahar; that is where we ran across a number of them hiding near the pass, up to no good. They did not like the looks of our traveling party and kept away. Thieves and brigands, the marshals will flush them out to crawl into some other hole. I'm glad you beat this one," he replied, sticking out his large hand. "I am Orind."

"And I am Armond, son of Baldor of Vanyor."

"You seem young for this tournament, but a fighter, judging from the outcome. Are you military, or just a street scrapper?"

"Neither, I am the son of an armorer in a town wrought of iron. In Vanyor one swings a blade from childhood."

"Very well then, Armond of Vanyor," said the man. He pushed himself to his feet. "I am making my way up front to shorten the wait. Save your strength for round two. I myself have never earned more than three feathers, but take heart and stay alert."

"Thank you, may Hawe be with you," replied Armond, content to abide his time.

He looked on as fighters came and went throughout the hour, and sometime past noon was summoned again to fight.

"You, here!" came the call. Armond grabbed a sword and a shield. His opponent did the same. This time his adversary had equal brawn and height, but was stockier and less defined in the arms.

The fighter stepped forward. He had a thin unkempt beard and a long black braid behind his back. As soon as the judge's hand dropped, the man charged. He pushed the attack, hacking with his sword and bashing with his shield. Armond buffeted the blows. Another drive nearly pushed him off his feet, but after the next lunge, he leapt suddenly to the right and slammed his own shield against the man's head. Tempers raged. The two flailed against each other mercilessly. Chunks of wood flew as their makeshift bucklers broke apart. Another clash and both shields fell to ruin.

Armond swung wildly, but missed the mark, leaving himself vulnerable. The man drove a powerful shoulder into his chest and knocked him to the ground. Armond did all he could to fend off the man's attacks while on his back. He blocked several angry blows; then stabbed hard at his knees. Blunt weapons rarely cut, but can cause a hurt, evidenced by the man's wail. Armond seized the opportunity, and reached up to pull the fighter down by his braid, tripping him at the ankles. He sprung to his feet before his opponent could recover, pointing the sword at his chest.

"Kill!" shouted the judge. It was over.

Armond received feather number two, this time brown. He advanced out of the *weeding* and into the third round. The remaining fighters were treated to a late lunch of boiled eggs, a salted potato, and all the water they could drink. The pause was all too brief.

The sun reached its peak and the heat of the day became a growing fire. The wind died and the sky offered no cloud for relief. A cover of thick haze lay upon Thalon that stuck to the skin like a fine dust. Once the melee returned the fighters found weariness upon their limbs, but spirits did not dampen. Armond's time came and the young Turrar stood his ground: three times called, three times victorious until feathers of green, yellow, and blue joined the white and brown upon a leather strap that hung from his belt.

The competitors diminished until sixty-four of the beginning two thousand remained. The sixth round came as evening shadows fell across the forum. By chance, Armond's name was called first. He took his place upon the field, no longer shared with other combatants. There he stood alone beneath the dais and a sword wavered in his hand. The eyes of the city rest upon him for an unnerving moment, including King Anor, but not for the last time. A cheer arose from the crowd as his opponent was announced – onto the field walked Baric the Tall.

Baric brandished a broadsword with his right hand and a shield hung across his shoulder; a crafty fighter who held distinction with the manor crowd and Thalon's lower circles. Relishing in the attention, the Tall raised his arms to wild approval from the concourse. He shook his long brown mane and stroked a neatly groomed beard, winking at a group of watchful maidens as he went. Armond glowered over the display – he had seen Baric's act before, and it made his blood boil. The judge quieted the crowd and placed the two men opposite each other. Without further fanfare, his hand dropped.

"Welcome to the elite! You have done well...so far," exclaimed Baric as the two circled each other with swords extended. "I recall many faces, but know not yours."

"You will remember my blade," growled Armond, striking forcefully as Baric raised his shield. The Tall countered with a thump of his own and the two began a round of blows. The crowd started to chant as the battle heated up.

"Defeat will be your teacher today, boy," said Baric as a smirk crossed his lips. A hand taller than Armond, he used his long reach to an advantage, catching a piece of an arm or leg with nearly every swing – nothing detrimental, but enough to enrage his opponent.

Armond wasted little time and charged. He threw his body against Baric's chest, trying to force him off balance; but the Tall had experience on his side. He shifted his weight, causing Armond to stumble with back turned. A strike to the shoulder sent him to one knee, but he returned a blow to the hip and rolled aside. Baric came again striking down upon his shield. Armond tried to regain his footing, but here Baric took the advantage. He faked a lunge and put a boot to Armond's chest, bowling him over. Baric was upon him, but with a flash of speed Armond struck beneath his shield and into the ribs. The Tall reeled as a roar went up from the crowd.

The judge looked on but made no move. Armond hoped it was over, but the blow had not enough force and struck away from the heart. Baric came again, and Armond met the assault, driving headlong into his torso. They both tasted the earth. Baric was quick to push him away. Rolling to one side, he swung back with his long reach and landed a blow to the neck. The contest was over.

The dust settled and rose again as the melee continued until the end, but none of this mattered to young Armond. Some time passed before he would speak of the loss or Baric's arrogance in victory. Andro and the others left him to sulk in silence as they settled once again in front of the Royal Square Inn.

"If only I waited a moment longer...I could have regained my balance, then the strike would have landed home," muttered Armond, his voice thin from the heat and eyes red from sweat and dust.

"Don't be disappointed, you fared better than any of us imagined. To us you are a champion," replied a sympathetic Andro, glad the silence had left his friend.

"Come then, the competition keeps the crowds away. Let us go inside and get some food and drink – it will do us all good," said Brenn, expecting a jest from the Turrar, but it did not come. They found the Inn just what they needed to forget the distress of the turn of events. Beer, roasted beef, and a fresh loaf took the edge off and made the mood less somber. Talk came and thoughts of the Acolyte nearly forgotten. They made their way out of the place as night came in full; the crowds had begun to file out of the square since the tournament had ended. To their surprise, Greynol was waiting outside.

"Mister Greynol, how long have you been here?" asked Rogan. He greeted the Acolyte in the center of the avenue.

"Not overlong. The competition is over. Turraray bested Teonirr to retain the prize for another year and gain the silver as well as a golden quill from King Anor," he replied, throwing Armond a wink. "You might be pleased to know your adversary, Baric, lost in the seventh round to Teonirr – it was no contest."

"Good, Teonirr is from Vanyor and well respected back home. Baric holds no claim to one of his skill. My only wish is that it was by my sword."

"Look at it another way, you gave Baric the scare of his life – he nearly lost to an unknown before his own people," replied Greynol warmly. He placed a hand upon Armond's shoulder in a calming gesture. "Sometimes in defeat one gains victory. Take heart, each of you: the tournament plays out like actors on a stage, but out beyond these city walls comes the real test – away from your homes. That is where I go, far beyond Thalon, far from all save memory. My judgment remains clouded, but the die has been cast. My heart tells me you men are too young; yet, here you stand, as friends, faithful and with a sense of responsibility. Not lightly do I accept your services should your offer remain, to ride as my escort until Asenrael and Asengard. If your hearts lay further south in the boiling pot of Earlon, from there you can continue toward your goal. My contract is my word, and that being I will pay you a days labor for each day upon the road. When lodging and hot meals are possible, I will afford the charge."

"What of our pay, do we get half up front?" asked Drago, and it seemed a fair question.

"Half of what? The duration of my endeavor is unknown even to me. If provisions you require, I will pay you each five Krones until our start. Let this be an offering of fairness – I will not count it against your wages. If you so desire, keep the silver, even should you turn aside from my path, even now, and never speak of it again. If your minds have changed, then keep the silver and start sensible lives."

Brenn cleared his throat, the prospect of easy money easing his distrust of the Acolyte. "Greynol sir, are you rich? I don't ask to be rude, and five Krones doesn't make one rich, in the least, but no one gives money away to perfect strangers."

"As young men, you are far from perfect. If sense is what you need, and five bits of silver buys you each some sense, then it is money well spent," replied Greynol, reaching into his purse to remove a handful of coins. "These are the remains of my life – sold things and saved things. Acolytes have very little to hold on to as our own. We possess nothing save a robe and simple provisions. Idarill House was a fine hall for teaching, reading, and quiet, but I was only its resident – one of an old line. As for money, I have what I have, a small amount stored away for such an occasion. Old ways have returned to me, for I was not always an acolyte."

"Keep your money, sir, we will earn it later," replied Andro to the dismay of the Mihtrir who watched a handful of silver disappear into its pouch.

"Andro is right, we will earn it later," said Armond whose eyes lowered, "that is, if you can accept our new conditions."

"What did you say...conditions? Now it comes to bartering. Should disappointment overtake me? My offer was a fair one, but does it hold little sway. What do young men require for their services these days?"

"You misunderstand me, sir. My conditions have little to do with wages or payment – my situation is one of delay," replied Armond in frustration. "You see, my father, Baldor, is an armorer. I assist him when I can and have spent many hours learning the trade; but he too knows my desire to leave for a time, 'to become a man,' you might say. It's just that there remains unfinished business at home: chopping, digging, hauling, and a good deal of other preparations for the long winter. It is too much to ask my parents to go it alone without imposing on others. In fact, he might say it is unreasonable for me to leave him in such a state. The four of us from Vanyor can get it done in several days, but..."

"...but, you must ride back to Vanyor, a three days journey on horseback. I honor the responsibility you pay to your parent's need; how you leave them in a bind if unprepared for winter. I will consider these things carefully. But you must understand that I require haste – the longer I tarry, the more the danger grows. My whereabouts are sought, you should know, as men are so easily bought. Now this..."

Greynol pondered the situation, revealed by the burden across his brow. The young men, however, had made their decision: the Acolyte won their resolve, save Brenn whose distrust of the *greyhood* kept him weary. As for the rest, several chose Greynol for the promise of krones and possible glory; others, namely Andro, for a chance to see the lands of Turra Arrither. (*Wayward North* in the Common Tongue) A spirit of adventure and wanderlust found a home in his heart.

"I will allow your delay, Armond, Drago, Zerrin, and Brenn – go back to your households and prepare what is needed," announced Greynol after a brief deliberation.

"Do all you need to do. Leave first thing in the morning. I will give you ten days to return to me, not here, but in Barrith. That will save you a day, and confuse those who want to know more of my whereabouts. I will stay in the Briar's Inn on Riccdare Road. Can you manage this?"

"We can," answered Brenn, "I know the place well."

Armond thought hard. "If we leave tomorrow then we should have the time to do what is needed. Yes, this plan will work."

"Good, then this leaves Andro and Rogan the task of waiting out our arrival."

"An easy assignment compared to the rest," replied Andro. "Sorry I cannot help you, Armond, but we also have things to attend at home before departing."

"Repay us on the road then, the both of you. Start by showing up," laughed the Turrar in reply.

"Of course, but when and where?" asked Rogan.

Greynol played out the sequence: "Let's see now...ten days takes us to the twelfth of Gare, that is when Armond and company arrive in Barrith. By the fifteenth, we should make the crossing at Marist, west of Logan. I expect to find you both waiting and prepared."

"Indeed, you can count on us," replied Rogan.

Greynol gazed at the young faces of his new company; so brash, yet innocent in comparison to the typical mercenary. Uncertainty entered his mind – the weight of the scroll, which remained in Wetherton's keeping, and its secret burden. He desired once again to forget his plight and return to the simple enjoyments of life.

With a sigh, he left them a final warning:

"The responsibility you have undertaken is a solemn one. I call you each to obedience, and give word of my own reliance as a leader and confidant. My concern is for the well being of each man in this fellowship. I ask you to speak naught of me until our next meeting, except to your families. In their instance, be prudent in your speech. If others question you, say I have departed for whereabouts unknown, and speak nothing of our arrangement. Now I am retiring for the evening. Go with speed until we meet again, and Fawarra be with you."

The men bowed and after conversing together went their separate ways: Armond, Brenn, Zerrin, and Drago back to their places of rest before a long ride home in the morning; and Andro and Rogan, who returned to camp with hopes of explaining all that had transpired without alarming those who waited, namely Audin. But Andro quickly found trouble waited.

In the light of the moon and a robust fire, Audin and the others from Logan had a celebration of their own with Baldor and a crew of guildsmen from Vanyor to liven things up.

Andro's concern over facing his father with the truth did not delay Rogan's desire for sleep, deserting his friend for the peace of a pillow and blanket. Andro was left alone to explain everything, including the absence of Armond and the cousins, whom under normal circumstances might enjoy a night by the fire with several fresh pints. Upon entering their circle, Andro discovered Baldor already knew much concerning their decision – Armond had explained everything the night before. No longer could he ease the news to his own family, much to his dismay.

"So my son has chosen to go off with the old greyhood. He has made me proud with his performance tonight, and now his sword is in demand. Armond rushes into manhood, but without so much as a toast with his old man," joked Baldor with a glint of honor in his eyes. Sentiments unshared by Audin. The plan fresh in his ears, he pulled his son aside.

"Andro! Must you be so careless? How long were you going to hide this news from me? You wish to gallivant like some bandit into distant lands following a Gray Acolyte – and to drag Rogan with you! What have you gotten yourselves into?" chided the elder Rhine.

"An opportunity, father; a chance to see the world and earn my keep," answered Andro, but it did not help to ease tensions.

"This is foolishness – no less. You go against my best wishes," continued Audin, and he meant it. "You will learn in the long run, and with hope, live to look back on your decisions. You need to marry, settle down, work with your hands, and live off the land, just like your brother, Aiden."

But Andro stood firm on his decision and eventually his father's anger subsided.

Andro and Armond grew years in maturity that day: at the tournament, Armond learned what heart is taken to become a man of valor; and Andro, by choosing a difficult path despite his father's objections, stood on the unsure ground of freedom. Baldor, a stalwart man like his son, tried to set matters at ease with his Turrar wisdom and a spirit made light by several tankards of ale.

"Ah, my son is no armorer, but a fighter. May he find glory upon the road to war, like warriors before him. A father finds gladness in the courage of a brave son. Audin, your own son may one day prove your heart proud," he said kindly.

"Contrary, Andro will make the Hall family proud – his mother's people. He acts as they in most things; only his face is that of a Rhine," replied Audin, dissatisfied by spirited advice. Merrymaking was not in his nature, and he rarely drank strong drink.

Andro swallowed hard and spoke his heart: "Father, I am both a Rhine and Hall – nothing will ever change who I am. Why do you worry so and grow bitter?"

"He is bitter watching his youngest son grow up," answered Aiden who stepped in to assist his brother. Although ten years his senior, the eldest son of Audin understood what Andro was going through. "It is late. Worry no more about this thing. The time has come for my little brother to grow some wings of his own – let him finally leave the nest."

No other words were needed.

Andro spoke nothing more of the matter that night; grieved he was by the confrontation with his father. Doubt crept into his mind, but he remained firm of his choice – for the better or worse of it. That night he slept out in the open, disquiet beneath a warm summer night sky. Shadowy dreams swam between tosses and turns and made him wonder even more of what lay ahead.

"Is it finished?" asked Wetherton, waiting in the upper floor parlor of his east quarter home.

"Yes, everything is decided," answered Greynol. He reached for the railing at the top of the stairs, eyes dim with weariness and shoulders slumped as if from a great weight. He dropped onto the soft cushioned chair aside the window. Prelate Wetherton pitied him.

"I assume Baric has refused your offer."

"He has no need of an 'old greyhood' getting in the way."

Wetherton miffed at the response. "I do not like that term, *greyhood*, it is disrespectful, and so is his attitude towards your vitality. No better a man at eighty has ever looked."

Greynol laughed.

"And what of the boys?"

"They have a champion, but perhaps more than one will earn that distinction," replied Greynol. "Six boys – not the thirty or so horsemen whom ride with Baric the Tall – that is all I can muster to face the enemy."

"If only I had the strength of my youth," muttered Wetherton, staring down at his cane. "If only I could do more."

Greynol smiled placing his palm across his friend's withered hand.

"You have done enough already; yet, there might be a thing or two you could still accomplish."

"What do you mean?"

"As you know, my name has come up of late in Thalon, more than once, more than by chance. I fear spies were sent to read my movements, to learn of my departure and with what strength. All I can hope for is for is secrecy – that is my one chance at freeing Dariat," answered Greynol.

"I'll do what I can, but you hope against hope that your son remains anything but a soulless wretch, liken to a Raugulon. They have controlled him too long," replied Wetherton, turning to ponder his colleague's expression. Despite the warmth of the lamp upon his face, sadness entered Greynol's gaze.

"I must depart the morning after next," he said suddenly, removing the smooth stone from his pocket. He stared into its gentle radiance; blue eyes sparkled in its mild light.

"What I require from you, old friend, is a slight slip of the tongue," he continued. "Give word to whomever might be interested that I purpose to join Baric's party and have gone ahead to meet him on the road; to others say I am still in town; and others still that I have gone off alone. Some may be untruths, but I know of no other way."

"Spies they be, and no lie is too good for bad folk. But let us not take providence for granted – if we say it, then perhaps Fawarra makes it true in time. In any case, I will do what you say. A bit of confusion to aid your passage, yet it is a road I would avoid at all costs."

Greynol managed a smile as Wetherton opened the book, searching for a word to close the day. Then he read aloud:

"The tenth jewel, deemed least, became the reminder of transgression and greatest of treasures...and the Jewel of the Heart, used against Fasduen, turned from white to red, bathed with the iniquity of the people. Here the will of Fawarra scattered the high-race...and in confusion departed the people of Farria-Sire."

Chapter Four – Alliance

Andro charged quickly through the forest of the southern Lanfersi, driving hard upon Ambarr, his tawny, golden-maned stallion. In a flurry of hooves, leaves kicked high and mud splashed – the rush of wind brushed violently across his face. He tightened his grip upon the reins, knowing every bend in the trail by heart. He came upon a rise, and from the other side the sound of an onrushing rider.

"Let's go!" Andro cried.

Ambarr leapt forward with newfound speed.

Andro raised in his stirrups, his hair blown out of place and into his eyes. Just then, a second horseman appeared across the hill, charging fast towards the trail.

"This one will be close!" called Andro, rushing down a narrow ravine just in front of the rider. Andro leaned forward then veered suddenly to the right between scattered boulders onto an open patch of ground. He pulled the reins and leapt from the saddle just as the second came up from behind.

"Ha! I beat you square this time. I told you that shortcut wouldn't help," he laughed, running over to grab the bridle of the other steed, a chestnut steed named Courser. Her rider slid down to the loam incensed – it was Rogan.

"Are you mad? Just how fast were you going over that last hill?" he snapped, tucking in his shirt. "You'll get yourself killed with such a maneuver."

"Ambarr would never allow that to happen," replied Andro, a smile plastered across his face. "It looks as if you and Courser will work out fine together."

Rogan forgot his anger and ran a hand across the horse's sweat dampened neck. "She is an excellent steed – not your common hackney. I only wish I could purchase her from your uncle outright," he replied.

"Like I told you before, Courser is as good as yours. He will let you work it off later; that is, unless we earn enough keep along the way. Whatever happens, she is your ride for the journey."

"Uncle Breden is kind," said Rogan. "Now what do you say we go out to the Crook and have a look about? One last time before we leave."

They led their horses along a side-trail that continued onto Lake Lanfersi. An arm formed what locals called, 'the Crook', for its hook shape, and 'Crook's End', for the rocky point of the jetty. With blue water on either side of the narrow strip, they tied their steeds and climbed up a large boulder that formed the Crook's End. Once on top, a wide view of the lake spread out between the pine tops. Here they rested atop a steep ledge where in summer months the two, as boys, would leap into the deep cold waters for a swim. Neither Andro nor Rogan had a mind to go home dripping wet and cold that day, their time of youth behind them. They watched from above, content to take in the sights.

Across the lake, speckled sailboats flitted and danced like white feathers in the breeze. Other folk rowed dories into the calmer waters along the shore, several entering the placid bay of the Crook itself to fish a favorite hole. A well-crafted vessel slipped past tiny Elmhurst Island, and with full sail, began north towards Crook's End.

"Oh great, here comes Darius Ronen in his father's boat," muttered Rogan, casting stones into the lake. "That's enough to spoil my day."

"It only gets worse – guess who is with him."

The two sat dejected as the craft and its four riders passed by.

"There goes Randa Ostrom and her brother, Dane. Sarah Greenleaf looks nice today," remarked Andro. He raised a hand to shield his eyes; then tossed Rogan a look.

"At least Sarah waves back."

"Nice day, Darius. Hello Sarah, hello Randa!" called Andro, raising his voice to catch their ears. Sarah waved and yelled 'hello' in return.

"You two better see me tonight before you leave!" she said shouting.

The others offered polite, if not half-hearted, gestures before turning away. Lovely Randa managed to turn back; an elusive glance, but long enough to catch Andro's attention of such things.

"She looked back, Rogan. She held the stare," he said, a glint of hope in his eyes. "I knew she would come around. I told you there was something between us."

"Come on now, she rides with Darius. Who can compete with the mayor's son?"

"Dane rides with Darius; the girls go along for the ride."

Rogan became riled. "Now listen here, Rhine, tomorrow morning we leave for Fanael. I am not concerned over such silly things as girls. We may never return, so put these feelings aside."

"We will return," replied Andro. He stood long enough to watch the boat sail into the distance – a gleaming white canvas in full bloom. "Besides, who are you to talk? Sarah Greenleaf has eyes for you."

Rogan grimaced. "That is why she rides with Dane and Darius right now. I am in no mood for one of your fantasies, and I have no concern for Sarah or any girl at this time. I'm beginning to think you had me come out here so you can keep an eye on your interests."

"Now who's kidding who? At least we can let them see us off tonight. Sarah did say so."

"Whatever," Rogan grumbled.

Their argument ended abruptly as a tapping sound came from the direction of the horses below. They crept over for a look.

"That's odd. I thought I heard a noise over here; several taps, then a sound like someone climbing up," said Andro.

"Like this?" came a voice from behind and the rapping of a

stone against the rock. They turned to find a young man dressed in a pale gray cloak crouching at the opposite end of the boulder. He flitted an arrow to a bowstring before they could react.

"Now where does your guesswork leave you?" said the fair woodsman with a laugh.

"In a lot of trouble were you a foe. Leonin, you bested our senses again," replied Andro.

The slender built man stepped forward, his height even with Rogan, placing the shaft back into its quiver. He drew back the hood of a pale green cloak and a braid of flaxen hair dropped across his back. A thin smile broke across his face, which shone pale and bright, and gray-blue eyes gleamed, a mirror of the waters of the lake. His look was not at all like a Logander.

"So, have you made up your mind?" asked Andro.

"In the eyes of my people, the rite of manhood is a time not taken lightly. If I choose the difficult path, the trail that leads back to Orisduen, I cannot stray – or I shall fail. Their backs are turned now. I cannot return as anything less than a man. This is the way of a Farrian."

"Then you made your decision."

"Yes, I will join this Acolyte's band, should he have me."

"Should he have you!" exclaimed Rogan. "Someone of your considerable talent – Greynol will be delighted to take you in."

"Good, then it is settled," said Andro.

Leonin shrugged his shoulders. "I am glad for your optimism, but I have my doubts. Turrar and Kuirian, after all, have no love for my race. And the fact that the Acolyte knows nothing of me, or my want."

"Greynol seems a fair sort – more Acolyte than Turrar. As for the others, they are my friends, and my friends are your friends."

"Even Armond? He is not an Acolyte, and very much a Turrar."

"He will accept you. One cannot let race decide your friends," answered Andro assuredly.

"Then let us leave nothing else to worry. As long as Greynol welcomes me, that matters more than the rest – it is his party after all. My interests peaked ever since you spoke of Asenrael. I know of no man, common or Farrian, to have stepped foot in the land of my ancient brethren and speak of it."

"He did not say much about it," replied Andro as a westerly wind whipped off the lake, filling him new vigor. He placed two hands upon his friend's shoulders as eagerness for the road welled within.

"We are most alike, we three, and wanderlust lay heavy on our hearts, for the good or bad of it. I fear Greynol tried to worn us otherwise. Now let's get off this rock and finish our last night in Logan."

Andro and Rogan lived two houses apart on Leatherleaf Lane, within shadow of the forest where few Loganders live out of respect to the Farrian they befriend. Logan's pride came through its woodwork and timber; but as a logging town, they left the Lanfersi untouched, preferring younger woodlands such as Arel's Woods to the south, and the forests north of Hall – areas away from the sacred trees.

The roads of Logan ran bare and dusty, save in the town's center, where wooden planks lined the central avenues to make a dry place to tread. Leatherleaf Lane made its way off the lake flats east of town between Elmhurst Way, which paralleled the lake, and Logan Road, which ran from eastern Logan all the way to Ronen on the far western border of Northern Gandol. The first house on Logan Road, or last depending upon one's direction, belonged to Andro's favorite uncle, Breden Hall. Handed down from a long line of Halls, Breden's orchards and pastures ran from the beginning of Leatherleaf Lane, right up to the edge of the Lanfersi Forest where a fence shared its boundary.

Breden knelt upon the grass, mending a fence when the trio returned from the woods with their horses in tow. Leonin's gray steed pranced proudly in their wake.

"Ah, there you are. Go and stable your horses for the night," said the elder Hall, pulling himself to his feet, "then get back here and give me a hand…if you have the time."

"Of course, we all will. You shouldn't work so hard in the heat," replied Andro, tugging Ambarr by the reins. Breden greeted the others.

"Good afternoon, Rogan. And you, Leonin, glad I am to see you here again. Find a suitable stable for that fine beast of yours, white as silver she shines – a finer steed than many. Remember, the offer still stands should you ever wish to part with her."

"Thank you again, Mister Hall, but I found her alone as a foal on our borderlands near the Arrahurm, and I wish to never part with my Gairinrul – my silver runner."

"You have kept her well."

They did as Breden asked, penning their mounts in the stable: a long red barn with enough room for two-dozen horses. Afterwards, they helped mend the broken fence and replaced several rotting posts. They would have continued as long as needed, but he gave them their release.

"You have done enough. My nephew Andro insists that I cannot go on without him. Do you think my stable-hands and I incapable? My age slows, but never puts me down for long. Now you are ready to spread your wings, find out about yourselves and the world. I am glad for it. You have set your feet on the path – now complete the task," he said while resting upon the grass between the lane and the fence. He took out a kerchief and wiped his thinly haired scalp. The others took their rest with him, sitting against the posts and conversing while the day grew long.

Andro gazed westward down Logan Road: its path curved slightly south bordering a sparsely wooded grove of beeches in full leaf, then turned back towards Logan, becoming lost in a yellow horizon as the sun began its descent.

"How far does it go?" asked Andro.

"As long as necessary, if you read the signs correctly," replied Breden, guessing his thoughts. "Tarry a day too long and you may never return. I fear for you three, as do your parents, for into warring lands you go. But go you should. Strings have grown too long on my sister's apron, and it is time for my nephew to let go. I don't mean to embarrass you, Andro, but it takes a push to leave the nest. I realize you still have doubts; take heart and leave nothing to worry."

"Heart I *will* take, uncle. I wish to make you all proud."

Breden stood up and stretched. "It is getting late. You boys better make for dinner. I'll bet there's something special planned tonight."

"Will you not come and join us?" asked Andro. "I thought you might dine with the family tonight."

"No, I wish to eat on my own. The heat spoils my appetite until after dark – then I will put something on the fire. You should spend your last night with your parents and Aiden's clan. Leonin, I suppose you already said your goodbyes back home in the Lanfersi; keep Andro company at table should his mother leave her seat for the tears in her eyes. Rogan, you head home too. No Pinehurst worth his salt keeps his family long in waiting."

"Indeed, Mister Hall, I shall go. But before I forget, I wanted to thank you again for the use of Courser on our trip. I hope to repay you in full when we return," said Rogan with all sincerity.

"You're welcome, son. We can discuss the matter then. Go on now, get home to a good meal."

"Will we see you in the morning?" asked Leonin, standing to shake the grass off his cloak. Breden gave a nod and watched as the three started away, turning right onto Leatherleaf Lane. Then he too went in for the night.

They barely reached the Rhine homestead when Sarah Greenleaf came running out of her place of waiting across the road. She stomped towards them red-cheeked and angry.

"Look here Andro Rhine and Rogan Pinehurst. I told you to stop by and see me before you leave. Now it's dinner time and mother is already hollerin'," she said with a face all flushed, wagging her cinnamon-brown ponytail as she spoke.

"Then go, why did you wait for us anyway?" replied Rogan in a belligerent tone. "Go back home where you belong."

"You know very well why I waited. I should give you the boot for acting up. Just because I'm a girl you want to shove me aside while you go ambling about."

Rogan scoffed. "What is that supposed to mean? We don't have time for games, Sarah."

"He's right, and come morning we *will* go ambling – straight out of town," added Andro with a smirk.

Sarah's cheeks turned red as Carrinth apples as she fought back tears. "Andro, you will get the boot too. To think you head off for distant lands upsets me so – there's talk of war, you know."

"We heard the prattle long before your secondhand news," replied Rogan no less full of vitriol.

"I warned you once, Pinehurst. Why do you treat me so bad?"

"Go ask Dane, and what's his name – Darius. You had a good time on his boat today."

"Oh, that was Randa's ideal," said Sarah, "she could not wait to go for a ride on that thing. Boats scare me half to death. Darius brags about his father's all the time in front of Dane and Randa. Naturally I get dragged along."

Andro's mouth fell open as a bluegill upon hearing the name, Randa. He stumbled over his next question. "By chance did she mention any name…I mean my name? I mean to say, did she have anything to say about me, or us? About our leaving?"

"She asked a little about it. I told her you were followin' some holy man for pay," replied Sarah, then her eyes grew wide. "You do have feelings for her. I knew it all along. Well, she didn't ask anymore about it once I mentioned your leaving."

"I don't have feelings for her. I was just wondering, that's all," muttered Andro, turning red in the ears with embarrassment.

"Oh, there goes mother calling again, just like I told you. Now I've got to go home," she said sobbingly. She kissed each of them on the cheek, including Leonin whom she barely knew.

"If I wake early, I will come to see you boys off. Goodbye."

Rogan wiped his face as Sarah ran back up the lane and turned left onto Elmhurst Way towards her home. "I wish she would warn us first before doing that," he said. "I'm heading in before I get stopped again. See you both at sunup."

He gave a wave and departed for his family home: a rather tidy yellow cottage with two floors and a tall thatched roof. A last night of comfort surrounded by family.

Andro and Leonin entered the Rhine household, crossing the

flush oaken boards of a homely front porch; Audin's skill evident in every fixture, furnishing, and nook within. Belma Rhine greeted them from the kitchen with all the warmth she could offer. Neatly adorned in a long blue summer dress with a white apron tied behind her back, she kept a wary eye on her Andro as he conversed earlier outside the dining room window. Andro lived a long comfortable childhood under those watchful eyes that now hid a tear.

As evening approached the house came alive: Andro's brother, Aiden, conversed at table with Audin; while his wife, Molly, as sweet as she was comely, kept busy with Andro's two nieces, Rachel and Dinia, who ran between the kitchen and dining room, circling the table where their father and grandfather discussed the work of the day. Leonin took his baggage to a side bedroom where a small down bed once belonging to Aiden was his for the night. The Lanfersi he left behind that day, and while the sun was setting, he wondered about home. Andro had doubts of his own, and he was glad Rogan had departed before detecting it and leave him with an earful.

The family gathered for one last meal of Andro's favorites: turkey, dressing, corn, potatoes, and a steaming bowl of gravy that graced the ornate dining table. The aroma alone carried everyone to his or her place setting. Afterwards, the adults moved to the front porch where Belma served cider and warm apple pie to top off a grand meal. Andro and Leonin ate their fill as twilight settled and the song of a whippoorwill came to greet the night.

"Listen, the Nightjar, she sings her summer evensong," said Leonin, laying an empty plate aside. He placed his elbows upon the armrests of a Rhine-built chair. "I believe I shall miss the remainder of summer in the fair Lernahurn. The nights have grown calm and the stars shine brightly."

"Those same stars you will see upon the road, just as fair. Maybe then you will think of home," said Audin, puffing on his after-dinner pipe.

"I expect we will think of it often," replied Andro.

"Aye, you will — and I shall often wonder about this Greynol.

Baldor speaks well of him, as do you young ones, whom I hold little trust in such matters. But I judge on my own terms. Acolytes and Prelates don't hold well in Logan: fanatics some say, mages others, then those who claim them righteous men. Who is right and who is wrong? How am I to believe?"

"You can begin by leaving that decision to Andro, Rogan, and Leonin," answered Belma, untying her apron and taking a seat between Audin and Molly. "The boys know what they are doing."

"Of course we do," replied Andro, knowing full well he had no idea.

By nightfall the air cooled and grew quite comfortable. After the others went off to bed Andro and Belma sat alone, speaking in low voices as clouds overtook a starry night sky.

"Mother, is father angry with me?" asked Andro. "I don't want to hurt his feelings."

"He is not angry with you – he fears for you. Tomorrow you leave on a long journey, and that gives him reason for worry. We are concerned parents after all; we have our misgivings."

"I wish it were easier. Armond's father seemed so glad to hear the news of our adventure," replied Andro, hands fumbling with a small carving Audin had set aside.

"Armond and Baldor live a life among soldiers and warriors," replied Belma. "We think less about warring things in Logan, buffered as we are. Baldor may show outward approval, but I feel certain his heart breaks at the thought of losing his only son."

Trembling, she placed her hand on Andro's arm.

"You do what you need to do. I'm happy to see you so free – I can't have two Aidens now. Aiden is a Rhine, through and through; you my son are a Hall, just like those long ago whose steps you will retrace before they came to this land. I am sad, but grateful to Fawarra to find my son a man ready to face the world."

Andro leaned over and kissed Belma on the forehead. "Thank you, Mother."

"Goodnight, Andro," she returned, standing from her chair.

She wiped away a tear and stepped inside the darkened house for bed.

An early morning breeze swept across the lake and into the city of Logan. Warm currents swayed branches and sweetened the air after a night shower, which gave way to clearer skies and the vermillion sun of daybreak. The day had come, Gare the fifteenth, and it arrived on a Sunday, a pleasant day for riding. Andro, Rogan, and Leonin busied themselves in Uncle Breden's stable, their bags nearly packed, hoping to forget nothing.

"I am finished here," said Andro, buckling Ambarr's saddle straps. "Tent, clothing, food, flint, and an extra quiver. Do we need anything else?"

"A little more room," answered Breden at his back. He tugged the reigns of a sturdy brown cob removed from the yard. "Your steeds are loaded down. You could use a pack animal."

They thanked him for his kindness.

"I know a thing or two about the road. Aside from a cart, a sturdy packhorse can take some of the burden from the rest."

"We shall return him promptly...I mean to say, as soon as we return," replied Rogan. He broke a nervous smile, realizing the time had come to depart.

Footsteps approached from outside the stable. They turned to find Audin and Belma rounding the corner. "You are you still here, good," said Audin, a long bundle in his hands. Belma carried a steaming basket that gave off the unmistakable aroma of fresh biscuits and honey.

"You knew we hadn't left yet," replied Andro, "not without saying goodbye."

"Better to get off to an early start. Do you remember where to meet the others?"

"At the Crossing, just as planned."

"That is, if all goes as *planned*," said Rogan to Andro's displeasure. He wanted no doubts, at least as long as his father stood near.

"And if they don't show, then what?" asked Audin – a fair question. "I guess you'll be coming home early."

"Now, get off on the right track, all of you, and quit talking about 'what if'," said Belma, chiming in. "You boys will work things out in a pinch. We came by because your father has something to give you, Andro."

Audin unwrapped the blanket to expose a sword and scabbard. He handed it to Andro and stepped back wanting to see how it looked upon his son. The elder Rhine glanced him over; a stroke of the beard and thorough scrutiny, just as he had so many times before.

"We were never fighters in this family, but a good blade is worth keeping around," he said. "Your grandfather gave me this years ago. I have no use for it now. It feels sturdy enough, and it has a keen edge – old Kuirian workmanship, I believe. When and where Grandpa Aldrin bought it, I have no ideal."

"Maybe he held back some stories of his own, eh?" chuckled Andro. He unsheathed the blade and held it up at eyelevel.

"It is plain – yet beautiful. Well crafted, if Armond has taught me anything about swords. I remember now: it use to hang above the fireplace in the old house."

"Your grandfather did all he could to keep you little ones away from it," replied Audin. "He gave it to me for safekeeping. Back then you and your cousins had mischief on your minds. Now I wonder what kind of mischief you three might be getting into today." Belma responded with a slap on the shoulder.

"Come along, old man. Let us leave these men to finish their work," she said, turning to give Andro a hug and a kiss. "Farewell son, return home safely and soon." Her voice cracked as she went to embrace Rogan and Leonin.

Audin came next with a firm round of handshakes. "Take care of yourself, Rogan Pinehurst, your family worries over you too," he said, "and perhaps a certain young lady, Sarah Greenleaf. She will wait for you. And Leonin, you are eldest here – watch out for these boys."

Then Uncle Breden made the last turn with an offer of well wishes. He left them as Audin and Belma walked slowly away.

A new pain overtook Andro's heart, a feeling he had never quite known before. "Greynol spoke the truth: we are too young for this journey," he uttered, swallowing hard to suppress the lump in his throat. Rogan kept silent, for he felt a chill in his own being. The time had come to leave.

Andro offered a sigh to the skies above – a sapphire jewel that gleamed and gave his heart the will to begin. He fixed the scabbard of his new sword to his belt and tossed the other aside; a shoddy short blade that was worthy of little more than slicing butter.
"Come now. Let's get it together and finish up here – we've friends to meet," he said at last.
They loaded all they could onto the packhorse and readjusted the baggage on their own steeds, devouring the fresh biscuits and honey in-between. Andro climbed atop Ambarr, leading the packhorse in tow. The others followed behind. With a kick and a splash, they cleared the puddles in Breden Hall's courtyard and started away.
The Lanfersi Forest watched at their backs shrouded in mist and shadow – a friend that would wait to greet them another day. One last look about put them upon Leatherleaf Lane, waving to their families as they passed; Audin and Belma watched from their porch, as did the Pinehurst's, Edmund and Mary, and sisters Lynne and Rhea. Across the lane, Aiden Rhine poked his head out of the shop behind their home where wife Molly waited to see them off.
Another turn placed them west upon Elmhurst Way, close to the lake. Here they increased their gait, minds full of fond memories: familiar houses of friends and relatives they passed; most notably the Greenleaf residence with its hedgerow and tall thatched roof where sparrows took their delight. Sarah rushed out into the yard, waking later than she hoped, but just in time to watch the three ride on by. She said her goodbyes, calling each by name, lastly Rogan, and once outside earshot, she put her hands to her face and wept.

Tarrying no longer, the trio swept along the quiet lanes of East Logan, riding the length of Maple Street and entering tree-lined

Logan Road just outside of town. The sun rose upon their backs with a satisfying breeze before them – Andro's sorrow diminished with every mile. Next came the city of Logan with its trader shops and manors, all in neat rows, and the whitewashed city dwellings where dogs barked and children roused from their slumber. Here they crossed noisily upon the wooden-planked avenues of Logan's celebrated merchant district – noisy but dry, without puddles.

Gazing north between the lanes rest the deep blue waters of Lake Lanfersi, and tracing a line westward along its opposite shore stood the town of Hall, named after Nevander Hall, a long and distant relative of Breden and Belma, whom founded the city in 1245. Eastward rolled the dark green folds of the North Forest, rising and falling upon rounded hills that increased in height until reaching the crest of a rocky crag, and just beyond, the Vale of the Lanfersi. Leonin gave pause to gaze one last time upon his homeland, lowering his head in honor of the Orisduen, the Blessed Jewel that rest beneath a steep stony bluff named, Pallias Hill.

Before long, with the last house of Logan well behind them, the road formed a westward leading swath through fields of clover and wild-grass, interrupted at times by crops from outlying farms. Logan Road stayed its course close to the Ronen River, which paralleled their path as it branched off the lake, still blue in the distance. The thoroughfare remained a level, well-traveled route; good, save for furrows from stout-wheeled tree-wagons – wains that bore the tall white-pine logs destined for cities throughout the kingdom, as far as Lyle, where ship masts were built.

Twelve leagues and seemingly a long distance from home, they came upon the Crossing. Here they met suddenly with the King's Road, a swift riding passage that began in Thalon and journeyed far into southern Gandol. Logan Road continued west, following a course aside the river, changing only its name to Ronen Road. But they would go no further that day.

The Crossing featured a hamlet, named Marist; if one would call an inn, blacksmith, and a scattering of homes, anything more than a ham. A grove of elms lined the crossroads just north of the

Marist Inn, an old manor owned and operated by Barre Marist, one of a long line of keepers who resided in the village. By midday, the trio made their way onto the crossroads, but to their dismay, Greynol was not there. The Hamlet seemed in a summer slumber, and the roads in each direction were barren. To the north, a long wooden bridge crossed the Ronen River, now hidden in a deep basin. All lay quiet.

They decided to first check the manor. Andro secured the horses beside an open trough next to the inn, and once inside found Barre, his wife, and an elderly villager seated about a common table. Otherwise, the place was empty.

"No, haven't seen any riding party today, 'cept you," replied Barre in answer to Andro's question, hastening over to greet the day's first customers. "Been a slow mornin', Sunday after all, no one in a hurry. Things will pick up in the 'eve, usually do. Your friends will show when you least expect it – that's the way it goes."

"Strange, I assumed they might be here by now, guessing they left Barrith yesterday," said Andro, met with a nudge by Rogan's elbow.

"Don't give anything away," he whispered under his breath. Rogan did not care for the curious look in the keeper's eye.

"Its a long ride to Noll, if your headed south. Might I satisfy your thirst? We have the local best, brewed just down river. And how 'bout a nice slice of beef, you couldn't 'ave had lunch, yet," called Barre with a voice more prying than his glance.

"A bucket will do, for the three of us. We will wait on the food," replied Rogan, tossing him two bits. "As for where we go, that is our business alone."

"Certainly! Yours alone," he bellowed. "But judgin' you have a Lanfersian with you, a rare sight these days indeed, and you await a northern party, I'd just assume you might be headed for Noll – or further south, perhaps?"

"You are a meddling sort, Barre Marist. My friend is wise to keep his tongue, or you might find out everyone's business and throw it to the four winds," laughed Andro, drawing a huff from the keeper. Barre tightened his fists and planted them upon wide hips, like a crow ready to squawk.

"Just who do you think you're talkin' to, Logander? I saw you from far off, riding up out of the east. You dress like a green wearin' Farrian. Am I such a dotard? How's this one: you come out of Logan, east of Logan to be exact, near the lake, near the woods. I might even come up with names if I had the time. I'll drop one for now – the tall one looks like a Rhinehurst."

"Close enough, Mr. Marist. I am a Rhine – Rhinehursts are cousins," replied Andro, finding another elbow to the ribs thanks to Rogan.

"Too much information," he strained as Barre chortled.

"Your friend worries too much, Master Rhine. But you should know me better than to assume so little of my intentions. Your kin comes this way now and again, headed to the festival up in Thalon, or on a merchant round. You should also know that I am a Marist from a long line of Marists – a caretaker of sorts and the lord of this humble village. And I watch closely what kind of rabble travel through my kingdom. We had a nasty bunch come through lately – thieves, plunderers, or worse. Night folk, and they won't be stopping in 'ere for a drink any time soon. Marist holds to the fire longer 'n most. This village may look small, but in the lore of the Lernahurn, it ranks above 'em all."

Barre's wife marched off to pour the ale, knowing full well the telling of Marist lore takes some time, as long as her husband did the telling. Barre leaned back, drumming thick fingers across the dark-stained counter, and began to explain the historical significance of his village, from its original settlement by Bardolites in 1240, to the building of the bridge by men of Hall in 1350, to the arrival of Gandol's King Gregory II six years later as a means to unite Northern Gandol and dissuade war with Nordhiem. Even Rogan was impressed by Barre's knowledge of many things. Bucket poured, they left the inn with heads full of story and hopes of finding their friends riding down to greet them, but only a farmer and an ox-lead cart was met upon the crossing. They decided to relax beneath the shadow of the elms and wait.

The sun waned in the deepening blue of early evening. Andro and Rogan awoke from a nap, hungry and discouraged to find their friends had yet to arrive. Leonin remained vigilant, watching in silence beneath the crossing trees. He greeted them from their slumber with a report.

"Travelers have picked up the pace a little," he said calmly, back against a sturdy elm. His yew-green shoes, like leaf-covered slippers, drew his knees to his chin. "Several farmers came and went, and a north-bound messenger, but he ignored the village altogether. A man of noble dress rode up from the south and stopped at the manor, as did several locals. Judging from the aroma there's lamb on the rack, and some pie..."

"Say no more, friend, I'm starving. I'll fetch us some dinner; then we can discuss the plan since our awaited party seems nowhere to be found," said Rogan who jumped to his feet and ran off for the inn. He reappeared shortly after with a hunk of meat upon a metal platter and a raspberry pie still warm in its pan. "Forget the vegetables – look at this pie."

They looked, briefly, and consumed everything in efficient fashion. Soon as mouths were wiped and drinks drained, Leonin asked the obvious question:

"Well, how long do we wait? We could start north to meet them."

"No, that sounds too risky, and it's getting late for a ride," replied Andro. "I think we should stay right here. They will show up soon enough."

Rogan tapped an impatient foot, gazing northward beyond the river where a thin line of forest crossed the horizon. "Andro is right. Three leagues separate us from the North Forest. Night would be upon us by the time we reach it. Since it has come to waiting, I'll wager a room in the manor more comfortable than these roots against our backs," he said after a quick check of his money pouch.

"You can waste your silver if you wish. But it's a nice enough evening for sleeping outdoors, and we better get used to it if the Acolyte materializes," replied Andro. He removed a heavy blanket from his saddlebag and unrolled it upon the grass, and prepared to settle down for the evening. "If only we knew where they where."

The night remained warm. The stars above shone brightly between the boughs of the tall crossing trees. Leonin awoke at midnight, startled by the sound of hooves upon the bridge. Gazing north, only the feint glow of beacons gave away the span's position. In the moonless black, shadows moved swiftly and the unmistakable clomp of hooves upon wooden beams revealed the approach of several riders.

"*Could it be them?*" he wondered, jumping to his feet. The others slept soundly nearby.

The horsemen reached the last pair of lamps, lit each night by Barre himself so no poor soul might take a wrong step and fall headlong into the river, and once upon solid ground spurred their steeds into a full gallop. Leonin ran to the roadside for a look, but they showed no sign of stopping. He narrowly avoided being run down.

"I am looking for five; yet these are six and dressed like bandits," he muttered. The riders continued through Marist unabated. He watched them disappear into the night, and then returned to his place of rest to wait in silence.

The next morning, Andro woke to the sound of voices. The day was already bright and his eyes shot open wide.

"Rogan, wake up someone is coming," he said, kicking the foot of his friend who lay near. Rogan groaned and managed to roll over, knocking a daddy longlegs off his shirt.

"Sleeping late today, are we?" asked a familiar voice.

Andro rubbed his eyes. Looking up he realized it was Greynol.

"You've made it!" he called out, surprised to find the Acolyte waiting beneath the elms. Greynol's smile was generous, and Andro felt a sense of calm from the old man, stilling his apprehension.

Armond, Drago, Zerrin, and Brenn came up from behind, ruffled and muddied from several days of riding. Leonin kept his distance, unsure of the situation, securing their horses at roadside.

"Now, now, it is after seven, you know. I should complain about your oversleeping, yet here we are a day late with little room to speak," said Greynol with a laugh more pleasant than his usual demeanor allowed; "but I am pleased just the same to find you diligent and waiting. You have passed the first test."

"But what kept you?" asked Andro.

"That fault remains mine alone," replied Armond in a dejected voice. "The list of chores my father left kept us going for a while."

"Aye, Baldor is set for the next two winters," added Drago, crossing his arms before him.

"No blame on either party then. But since when is seven in the morning sleeping late?" asked Rogan. The others took the comment in jest.

"You will find out for yourself," replied Brenn with a chuckle. "Been with this fellow three days now, and he keeps a tight schedule. Time to wake, time to eat, time to move on – not unlike those mine bosses back home."

"Well, we are all together now."

Andro threw a look toward Leonin who watched nearby, uncomfortable while awaiting his fate. "Greynol, as you can see, I bring another with us. This is my friend Leonin of the Lanfersi."

The Farrian, who looked clearly different than the others in appearance and dress, straightened up and gave a proper bow. Drago returned a grunt, which could have meant any number of responses, while Brenn and Zerrin nodded in return. But it was Armond's purposeful stare, somewhere between disgust and disbelief, which angered Andro.

"Leonin greeted us as we arrived," replied Greynol. "If not for his diligence, we may have missed your sleeping bodies altogether. The horses are fine where they stand, son. Come over and join us."

Leonin left the reins to Rogan and strode forward, bowing again. "Let no one hold any animosity toward my friends. It was I who wished to come along once told of the your need – an escort and passage to Asenrael. My hope is that you might accept my services. I am of a strange race, this I recognize, and I hold no ill favor should you sent me away."

"You speak of hasty judgments, friend. First, I need to hear an account of what you offer before making a decision," replied Greynol in his polite manner.

"If I may, I can attest to Leonin's abilities," said Andro, quick to jump in. "He handles the finest bow in all the Lanfersi, and his skill in the forest stands alone."

"I can second these things," added Rogan.

"The need for an archer holds a pressing need in my company, and if you can track and hunt, I might put your talent to good use in the wilderness," replied Greynol thoughtfully. "My road is a long one. I have my mountain lords in Armond, Drago, and Zerrin; and Rogan and Andro hold talents suitable for such a journey, but remain quite green when it comes to experience; Brenn is my right hand man, whether he understands it or not, and his eyes and ears will guide us through the city marches, and perhaps a thick plot or two. Leonin, a place for your skills may exist in this party, and I see it plain: like Brenn in the city, you can be my eyes and ears in the wild. Yet, I have my misgivings..."

"And well you should!" interrupted Drago who could no longer hold back. "This man is a Farrian, after all. How do we know he can be trusted?"

"No less trustworthy than Mihtrir, Turrar, or Loganders. I have taken a chance in accepting this company, not my first choice mind you – and eight sounds better than seven," replied Greynol in a firm voice that silenced their doubts. All save one.

Armond bit his lip and walked away, swallowing hard so not to express his disdain, which was obvious. He leaned against Calhurg, his sable war-horse, and listened while Greynol addressed the others.

"If there remains a legitimate concern in my choice of Leonin, and I see no reason to dismiss this man, then bring it out before us all," he implored.

"Your pardon, sir," replied Drago, now humbled. "I spoke ill words of Andro's friend and I am ashamed for it. But my new concern has merit, if you will hear me out."

"Go on."

"I fear his presence may put us in a difficult way. At first, your detractors will not look for such a party, one with a Farrian in the lead, but once known, how easy for them to find you out..."

Leonin waited in silence as the debate continued. He leaned back, breathing deep the windswept mien of the plain, so different than the woodland silence of his Lanfersi home. His thoughts drifted away from the others, dreaming of new lands, sights, and smells. "If not with these men, then perhaps alone," he considered, until the mention of his name brought him back to the present.

"The choice of Leonin is mine alone, right you are Rogan; but the risk remains – this is also true. I have already accepted the risk of taking on each one of you. I am pleased now to have all the races of the 'Good North' represented in my party; yet, hardly a party at all. We make an Alliance now – more than what meets the eye, if I read things correctly," said Greynol, as the men circled around.

"An Alliance as in the days of old when Mihtrir befriended the Farrian and barbarian alike – the days before leaving the Waulhern," said Drago thoughtfully. "An Alliance we shall be then, Master Greynol."

"Then do we have consensus?" he asked, taking a deliberate turn toward Armond. "What have you to say, young warrior? My need for a Champion remains."

Armond cleared his throat, eyes downcast and voice full of grit. "I have no quarrel with the Farrian, although our forefathers left much unsettled between the races. Hard pressed we stand to settle things here and now. Since each man has a part in this Alliance, let him keep his piece of the bargain," he replied coldly.

"Then everything is settled," said Greynol. He threw his bag over a shoulder and smiled. "Time to push on."

Chapter Five – the Vinery of Ristle

At mid-morning they departed Marist Crossing. Andro turned back as if to say goodbye to an old friend. Greynol resumed the lead he held with the others, putting a charge put in Toryche's gait. The plains of the Lernahurn spread wide before them where summer breezes, sweet and fresh, danced across fields of wheat and young corn. The King's Road ran pin-straight, save in small villages called *thorps* or *wicks* that emerged like an oasis across a vast desert. A Thorp would consist of a tavern, merchant, and several well-kept cottages encircling a central well where any person could retrieve water during daylight hours. Upon their occurrence, they took their rests, only to have Greynol push them on soon after.

Rolling grasslands and pockets of forests blanketed their path, and herds of cattle and goats that roamed freely about the countryside. The road now carried a scattered lot of travelers; farmers and herdsmen mostly, each going about his business, looking on as the strange company passed their way.

By day's end, they approached of the town of Noll with its eloquent homes and grand estates. Finely groomed lawns, flowerbeds, and tea gardens framed the yards of the noble-class, where hedgerows divided the city from the fields and farms of the north. Common houses were neatly spaced west of the King's Road, brightly painted, with thick lawns and dividing walls of stone. Order was the theme of this most southerly town in Northern Gandol, its end marked by a dark forest.

Dusk brought quiet upon the city as families settled down for supper, edging the men's hunger. They settled for a lesser meal beneath the apple-laden boughs of orchard trees where they set camp. No watch was set that clear night. Tired and out of plain sight, Andro slept his last evening in the Lernahurn at peace.

"Our welcome awaits!" called Greynol to start new the day.

Andro scrambled to his feet, barely awake, eyes mere slits in the emerging dawn. The town of Noll rest peacefully across the fields beneath a blanket of cloud and wisps of chimney smoke. Clothes wet with dew, he drank deeply the early morning air, his heart glad to be on the road with friends.

Greynol was quick with instructions.

"Suspicion grows in Gandol. We will be stopped and questioned at the forest-gate. Hold your tongues – I will speak for all of us," he said, drawing his cloak to put a shadow across his brow. Andro found him imposing now – the urgency in his voice strange and slightly alarming.

They hastened through morning preparations, and crossed into the unlit forest south of the city where the road ran wide and even. Greynol pondered his words carefully as they came within sight of the sentry keep: an unimpressive fortress of spiked logs that marked the border of Central Gandol, and the King's Road ran straight through its gate. There was no *legal* way but through.

"There was a time when the border welcomed its own," whispered Rogan as they approached. "My father warned me of this: Gandol fears the North more than ever – even Logan."

Greynol silenced him as a tall silver-mailed guardian stepped out from the gate. He wore a pallium of verdant green that bore the crested lion of Gandol. Two others of similar dress joined him, bearing long pikes, and archers watched from above.

He raised his hand defiantly, calling out. "Halt, in the name of Raeletin, King and Ruler!" Beneath the rim of his pointy helm, he scrutinized them severely. "State your business with Gandol."

"We ride south to Barame," answered Greynol unmoved.

"Strange men indeed. Where do you hail?"

"The Lernahurn and Nordhiem."

"*Lernahurn* is an insult to my ears. You have no claim of your own save to the King. When will you log-haulers get some sense put to you? Your land is Northern Gandol, nothing more," retorted the guard. He placed his hands at his side, giving no ground.

"As for Nordhiem, you are the second party within a week's time claiming that distinction, although the first numbered over thirty riders. I'll wager you go beyond Barame; revelers looking for a good fight and money. You should have stayed home – Fanael isn't paying. Maybe you are in league with those spies that tried to skirt our watch last night, taking to the forest to avoid our spears."

"No sir, we head for Barame – nothing more have we to do with Gandol," returned Greynol.

The guard noted their swords and bows.

"Do Nordic Acolytes fly also into battle? Perhaps war against Gandol? I can summon fifty men-in-arms at my command. Like I told the other Turrar, the border will soon be closed to your kind. I for one will be glad see to it. Nordic men dressed for war left to ride our fair vales, searching for a house to rob or a poor soul to plunder, but no longer."

Greynol was not amused. He understood the game afoot.

"What does it take to appease your concern?"

"The same I charged the others: two-hundred florin – two silver krones will do."

As if knowing beforehand, Greynol flipped two silver coins to the guard who caught them greedily. The others held their tongues, but each thought the same thing: *"That was four days pay."*

"You may enter," said the guard with a mocking bow, pleased at his take. Greynol hurried them through.

Andro lowered his eyes and bit his tongue; he had not the strength to face down a Gandol Captain. Not until they put the fort well behind them did his resentment fade.

Beneath a ring of woodland, a welcome of pale-green leaves brought a smile to Andro's face. Sweet birch, beech, and hackberry offered swift passage into the Central Valley. By mid-day the thoroughfare left the forest to enter a green valley where steep-sided hills rolled down to greet a wide plodding river. From its northern home, the Brodden River began a courtship with the highway that continued south for leagues, like old friends, journeying towards the sea.

Andro soon discovered the road was less than isolated. Glancing this way and that, he found sheep trails greeted the highway; like lost souls, these earthen ribbons wandered through gullies, or climbed fast towards unseen pastures. Eyes were upon them, and Andro felt more than just a shepherd's curiosity.

The passage narrowed and the day's heat was upon them. When rest came, the horses were treated to the Brodden's cool waters. Southward, the land grew less hilly and sharp: expansive domaines drew straight lines for leagues on end, laden with grapes. Within sight of Ristle, the Governor's seat of Central Gandol, the river took a sudden turn to the east, away from the highway, soon to wind its way back through the fair city and rejoin it further along. But Greynol did not go to the city, deciding upon a little used path north of town, and set camp upon a western valley hillock aside the vineyards of Gandol fame. The young men lifted several fragrant green clusters to sample, but Greynol was quick to rebuke them of Ristle's intolerance for thieves among its renowned trade – the pride of Central Valley wine. The men tucked what they had into their pockets and hid out of sight of the road to enjoy the savory yield.

Just west of their watch, a meadow formed a sloping bowl fed by a spring where the horses drank freely. Andro settled down to campfire fare – a steaming bowl of potato stew and day-old bread. He ate his fill and assisted Brenn in cleaning the pots and plates. At dusk they relaxed in relative comfort, taking advantage of the wide view: Ristle lay a mile to the south, spread evenly along the valley floor, and just beneath its perch, by a hundred feet or so, the King's Road ran in silence. Brenn lay nearby upon the damp grass full from dinner as the emerging stars danced in his thoughts.

"This place seems as fair as any other, but few say anything good about Gandol back home. Is this really the kingdom

Nordhiem hates?"

Greynol chuckled at the question.

"From a certain perspective, Brenn, the answer is *yes*. This is Gandol, and neither they nor Nordhiem consider themselves allies. But these are discussions best left for aging monarchs to ponder. Let those who rule worry over old feuds."

Armond countered, eager to defend his homeland. "Begging your pardon, sir, the rivalry has merit in the history of my people. The Kings of Gandol have pushed the brink of open war – foolish minds like that of the keep guard. If not for the hedges in-between of the Lernahurn and Sindelware, the stroke may have already fallen."

"Perhaps, but war remains a grievous choice," replied Greynol. He turned his gaze toward the lamplights of the city. "Despite age-old disputes, both sides profit nicely in their quiet dealings. I assure you, Governor Raynor Lolle the Third sleeps in his Ristle estate tonight with Nordic Steel in his armory, fine tapestries from Barrith in his halls, and Bardol steeds in his livery. And seldom a banquet passes in Anor's court without the finest vintage of the Central Valley to sample."

"Should we have anything to fear then, aside from the guard from this morning? Why did you pay him anyway?" asked Rogan. He leaned back upon the grass, elbows propped and legs extended. "There must be many comfortable beds in the city tonight."

"Aye, the boy is right," said Drago, taking the pipe from his mouth. "Besides, the stars have clouded over in the south and the wind has shifted. I fear we shall have rain come the morn'."

"In different circumstances I would agree, but even in Ristle there are spying eyes. The peril increases closer to Lyle," replied Greynol in a low voice.

As he spoke, three riders started north out of the city and into the empty gloom, swiftly passing beneath the hill and the men's uncomfortable stares.

"Who rides so mad in the twilight?" wondered Andro, startled by the timing of Greynol's words. "Do you think they can they see us?"

Leonin strode to the edge of the tall bank for a look, for his eyes were keenest in the party. "The fire is concealed from the road – they gave us no notice. But a northern approach would betray our position."

"Should we snuff out the fire?" asked Zerrin.

"Yes, and quickly," answered Greynol, the others held by his reaction. "We will do without a fire tonight."

He watched carefully as Drago and Zerrin used a bucket and small shovel to cover the flames; his attention drawn between their actions and the now distant riders.

"They could have been anyone," muttered Zerrin.

"In these parts, as in many lands, the night belongs to thieves. But I fear our paths shall soon intertwine," replied the Acolyte in a cold tone, straining to gain the purplish dusk. He breathed deep, as if trying to learn the mind of the enemy upon the wind.

"They would take full advantage knowing my whereabouts, setting their plan for my demise. A final escort to see I am properly served for the feast. I know with some reliability that spies sought me in Thalon, but I set traps for them to buy time."

Armond yawned and stretched, unmoved by the prospect of the enemy so near. "I say a taste of Nordic steel solves the problem of night insurgents," he replied, patting the hilt of his sword.

"Let us avoid that prospect as long as possible."

Andro drew his hood to block out a stiff breeze that fell across the meadow. The talk of the moment gave him much to ponder – too much to leave for his dreams to answer. With great curiosity, he watched the Acolyte's hand drop slowly into the wide pocket of his frock. He did not reveal its contents, but Andro caught glimpse of a sudden glow within his closed hand, and how he seemed to still his distress by it. But Andro was not at peace, and offered his fresh concern:

"Greynol, you mentioned something earlier about the peril increasing as we near Lyle. It is a long way still, but I was wondering what you suggest we do to avoid trouble in the King's City?"

"Simple. Our path lies not through Lyle. We shall take another path instead," answered Greynol matter-of-factly, hoping to avoid any further questions of the matter. It did not work.

"Beggin' your pardon, sir," replied Drago, "I am well versed in map lore, and I understand well that the only way this far south is through Brodden and the crossing near Lyle; or else we must double back and cross into Bardol. There is no other road leading into Fanael save through southern Gandol – unless we travel the wilderness."

"And there you have it. Drago, you thought it out correctly," said Greynol.

"Now what are you talking about? Unless that scroll you've been carrying is some map of rare value, then I am at a loss."

Greynol glanced down at his haversack that lay unguarded upon the grass; the scroll stuck out of the side pocket within its deerskin canister. He threw his mantle over the bag, which did nothing to quell their curiosity.

"That is a personal message and of no consequence to you," he replied, and his look held warning. He then addressed the Kuirian's question. "What I am talking about, Drago, *is* another road. You will find it on few maps as it is forgotten by most. The way was called the Arrither Road, the Wayward Road, for in older times it was a way into the unsettled Central Valley from the east."

Drago wasted no time. He lit a lamp and held its light above a map he pulled from a leather pouch. With a finger he traced the route they followed; from the meeting in Barrith, down through the southern plains of Nordhiem, then Northern Gandol and into the Central Valley.

"We Kuirian have many maps, and if knowledge of an ancient roads exist, it is recorded," said Drago with a curious glance. "The King's Road is plain enough, but aside from these barest marked trails, there are no other paths south."

"Your finger points to the answer, friend," said Greynol. He took his own hand and traced a crooked dotted line that ran from Baramc into the eastern wilderness, ending abruptly several leagues away. "See here, Kuirian maps do not forget. This line *is* our road."

"But it is only a trail, as far as I can tell from these markings," replied Zerrin, leaning in for a glimpse.

"And what of the horses and speed? Begging your pardon, sir, but this seems no common route, only a path to an unmarked spot in the wilderness. The wilds are a dangerous place to find yourself lost," added Drago.

Greynol leaned back out of the light, concealing the slightest grin. "Your map is incomplete, son. The Arrither Road is suitable for horses, last I traveled it, and time will be on our side. At its end we will find ourselves on the southern fringes of Bardol, a week further along than if we had gone through Lyle."

"Then why is it forsaken if one can save so much time?" asked a suspicious Brenn.

They eagerly awaited an answer to soothe their concerns, but Greynol had no words to comfort them; that is, if he had a chance to speak. Rogan interrupted him, adding fuel to the other's discontent.

"I remember now," he said excitedly, "I know this place. The East Wilds where men forsake. Legend surrounds it. My father used to tell me stories of *the Haunted Road*."

Brenn's jaw dropped. He stammered from the tightness in his throat.

"What do you mean by, *Haunted*? No one said anything about haunted places," he uttered, wide-eyed and cheeks a fish-white.

Mihtrir had strong reservations concerning such things, and Brenn was no exception. He pulled the hood of his own brown cloak over his head. "I'd prefer to travel to Lyle instead and take our chances, thank you."

Drago and Zerrin nodded in firm agreement with their cousin.

Greynol ruffled his forehead. His reply rippled from tense lips: "Rumors, stories, a travelers tale – that is what you fear. I hoped for courage from this party. Is it from your mother's arms that I bring you here? I may have been wrong in my selection."

Armond had no such reservations and put things in quick order. "Don't you worry over us, Mister Greynol. Be it haunted or no, we will go upon this Arrither Road, or whatever road you require. Your choice remains sound," he answered with a hand planted firmly upon Brenn's shoulder – a friendly reminder to keep his mouth shut, which the he did reluctantly.

The others shook off their misgiving and came around, save Brenn who kept his silent protest.

A headstrong breeze blew up from the south as night set in full. Greynol stared into the dark skies and walked off silent and alone for a while. The others watched him from a distance, offering a moment of repose.

"Stake your tents if you hope to get some rest. Tomorrow we leave at dawn. We may find better lodgings by nightfall," he said, finally breaking his silence. The others did as he instructed, and once done, drifted off one-by-one beneath a restless gray sky.

Drago made sure to gather some dry embers and damp woodchips prior to dousing the fire. He layered each within a canister he kept beside his blanket. "I will bear the fire. Flints are good for nothin' in wet weather. These will keep a few days should the need arise," he said, making a bed upon the grass. A blanket covered him up to his beard where he munched his remaining grapes in solace.

Andro too wrestled with sleep that night, for he too had heard rumors of the Arrither Road, although he did not reveal it. "We really are in for an adventure – should we get that far," he thought to himself, drifting off into an uneasy dream.

Chapter Six – A House in the Green

The forth morning since Andro stepped out of his Logan home arrived upon dark shapeless clouds. Drago's expectations from the night before were spot-on as rain began to fall, first as an airy mist, then in steady sheets across the valley. The company hastened to pack their baggage and put things in order. Mounting their steeds, they entered the highway beneath a deepening sky and the drizzle soon became a downpour. Eight pitiful riders splashed through sleeping Ristle with little notice; its townsfolk preferring the warmth of their beds to the early morning spate. By Greynol's design, they split into two groups of four, crossing the lanes of the sleepy town, and regrouped once far from sight. And at their flank, the Brodden stirred in a sullen mood.

South of Ristle, the valley grew wide with low-shouldered hills that bounded both east and west and deep forests framed their heights. The woodland lay behind a vale of rain, tall and dark above the green slopes of Central Gandol. The deluge ever increased and the men were drenched by the minute. Heads bowed and covered, they shielded their eyes to keep the rain off their faces; even the spare cloths packed away in saddlebags had small chance of escaping it.

Andro and Armond rode side by side, watching the leagues pass, each in their own miserable state. Armond placed a shield over the hindquarters of his warhorse to protect his baggage. Andro heard the clink of metal chain and tried to catch a glimpse what lay beneath: a glint of tightly woven mail appeared from time to time within the rain-soaked opening of a leather pouch.

He wondered if the concealment contained Armond's work of winter's labor, but kept quiet so not to spoil the surprise.

"The weather worsens!" shouted Drago from the rear sometime past noon, although the time of day was only a guess. "Greynol, how long until shelter? I don't know how much more of this we can take."

"No refuge or dry places until we near Barame. We must press on," he replied, and no one found pleasure in his words.

Greynol never wavered, seemingly unaffected by the elements. He hid beneath the brow of his cloak and buried the fix of his gaze upon the road ahead, however far-sighted his thoughts would take him. He offered only the briefest rests: a simple meal within the embrace of a river-fed willow, or the frame of a long abandoned farmhouse – nothing more.

The sky grayed and evening descended on a day of distress. Thoughts of Barame entered the young men's minds; a fair city, larger than Ristle, with several large inns to warm tired bones. Waking dreams of glowing hearths, roasted lamb, and cups of hot cider kept their thoughts alive. Greynol raised his hand, and with a sudden stop, wiped the vision from their eyes.

"Too many years," he muttered with arms crossed and a hand upon his chin, rankled over some unknown concern. "Paths change. Roads disappear. Memories fail..."

Greynol paused at the beginning of a muddy trail that left the King's Road and dropped towards the river. Desperate eyes searched back and forth with indecision; then a smile broke across his face. He whispered into Toryche's ear and veered onto the trail, heading straight for the Brodden. The men were bound to follow. Around a bend and a down slippery slope, they came upon a swollen ford.

"Surely you don't expect us to cross here?" growled Drago, already out of sorts. "I am a miner, not a horse-lord."

"We must make for the eastern bank, and quickly before the river worsens," answered Greynol above the rush of the water. Without hesitation, he and Toryche started into the river. "The Brodden has been a more gracious host, but not this day. Move along now."

Andro and Armond came next, their steeds thrust into barrel deep water after only a few paces. Then with careful steps, Rogan and Leonin's horses took to the current. The last three brought up the rear, finding the ford a great struggle: Drago's brown cob, Arkenoak, pushed forward, angry but steady as was its rider; and so marched Zerrin with a tight grip on the reins, but his horses footfalls plodded along slowly in the mud. Brenn found himself last, his pony timid in the brown swirling rapids.

"She won't budge!" he cried.

Rogan spun Courser around after making the opposite side. He started back once he heard the call. "Hold on, Mister Linderfell, I will help you!"

Rogan passed Drago and Zerrin mid-stream, and soon came upon Brenn's pony; Leonin and Gairinrul were quickly at his back. Rogan stretched out to grab the cob's reigns, but it reared back, spilling Brenn into the river.

"Steady the horse, I will get our friend," shouted Leonin, nearly amused to see poor Brenn swallowed up in the froth, throwing shouts and curses as he rolled with the current. The Farrian understood haste, and in half-a-moment's time had Brenn by the hood, sputtering and soused.

"Where are you headed Mister Linderfell, to the ocean?" he asked in jest.

Brenn scrambled to his feet, a firm grasp of the Farrian's arm, and managed to crawl upon the back of his silvery mare.

"Thank you, friend," he gasped, "just get me away from this river."

Greynol waited upon the shore as they brought Brenn and his unhappy pony to safety out of the rapids. "Are you all right? Stay with Leonin for the remainder of the ride if you wish. Let us waste no more time here," he said in a disconcerting mood. Drago could stand no more.

"Mister Greynol, you are a hard man – tougher than any thick-necked Vanadium mine-steward. What next? A drowning won't do for today?" he asked candidly, cheeks smoldering above the red of his beard. "I must insist, after everything that has happened, and this weather, we need to stop."

"He is right, sir. We shall surely catch our deaths if we continue," added Zerrin.

Greynol sighed, but he understood more than the rest where they had to go. "I am sorry to press you like this, but a little further still. Trust me this last time," he replied.

A last bit of resolve pushed them forward, despite Drago's grumbling. Lack of direction made them wary – they had only the Acolyte to trust. In file, they rode up a grassy bank along a path that climbed the eastern slope.

Greynol brought them higher, leaving the Brodden River behind for good. Soon a tree line emerged from the mists, brooding and silent; an invitation they did not seek. A few miles down the valley lay the desired city of Barame, but they would never glimpse it. A wider path came up from the south in the direction of the city and entered the darkened forest after joining with their trail.

A covering of trees dripped upon the unhappy file. Heavy raindrops turned into cascades poured through openings in the leafy canopy. Mire-filled puddles streamed together to form pools that the horses sloshed with every step, and the gloom was overshadowing. Night fell across the forest and hopeless thoughts of rest crept over them. But Greynol knew the way. Upon their right came a low wall and gateless opening where he took a sudden turn upon a wet, leaf-strewn path.

"Someone has been here," said Rogan, searching the darkness. "Look, wood piles cut and neatly stacked, and over here I see a wheel-barrel."

"Never mind those," replied Andro, "look ahead, there is a light."

They soon came upon a white gate and paused. A squat house of log stood obscured from the main trail in the middle of a level treed lot. A lamp glowed in one window and smoke rose from the chimney despite a shifting wind.

"From the look of things someone is home," said Brenn,

wiping the grime from his face with a wet kerchief.

"But is it a friendly house?" asked Zerrin. An answer came swiftly as two large dogs dashed from the rear, separated only by the fence.

"Thank goodness they can't jump higher."

Greynol returned a smile to their snarls and paws upon the gate. "Well, here is our doorbell."

Within moments, the front door of the house flew open and a voice boomed from within. "Fendor, Scout – come!" The dogs obeyed at once and ran to back greet their master who stepped out onto the porch.

"Who goes there? State your business!"

"An old friend," answered Greynol gladly. "My men and I could use shelter this foul night."

The man stepped forward, lamp in hand, ducking his tall head for a better look. His long black beard and ample girth came into view.

"Arowen?" he gasped. "Is it really you, or am I seeing a ghost?"

Greynol laughed. "I am no ghost, but still alive after so many years away. My men and I come out of the lower valley after crossing the river. I hoped you might be home."

"Very well, then. Just like old times!" he boomed, and his voice rang out like a trumpet. "Come along! Friends of Arowen are always welcome here. I am Harifin Tardane and my home is yours. Put your mounts in the barn out back where there is hay, then come around and join us. Don't worry about the dogs, they are harmless."

The others did as he said, leaving Greynol who took his friend by the sleeve. Fendor and Scout looked on. "Excuse the hounds, friend, been uneasy these days. Vagabonds are on the road of late…suspicious folk," said Harifin. "The Arrither Road has grown useful once again, but only spies and thieves ride it now. It is enough that I am alone here with only the dogs and my old bones to fend them off."

"Alone? What of Lena, and your sons?"

Harifin lowered his gaze. A gray-streaked beard fell across a green woolen shirt.

"She is gone, dear friend, passed on three winters ago. And the boys have moved into the city since they are now grown. I live here alone, save the animals and an occasional visitor. I am glad to see you once again."

Greynol took Harifin's immense hand in his own.

"May she have peace, and may it fall also to you. I am sorry for your grief."

"This sorrow will never completely pass, not until I go on to join her," he said thoughtfully. "But now I see it is time for you to get out of those wet clothes before you find yourself ill. We'll see what's left in the oak chest in the boy's old bedroom – something warm for the night. Now come on inside and tell me, what brings an old acolyte this far from home?"

The others found the barn in the dark and lit two lamps within, surprising an old nag, a sow, and a brown heifer with their company. Andro removed the bit from Ambarr's muzzle and caressed his faithful companion of the road, rewarding each of the horses with hay and a dry place to rest. He removed the extra clothes from his saddlebag and headed back to the house with the others, and with any luck, to a warm meal.

The first thing Andro noticed when he entered the home was the smell of a seasoned fire. Built of solid oak, like his home back in Logan, Harifin's was a squat, deep-rooted lodge, seemingly carved out of the forest itself. There were furs, of course, upon the floor and along the walls, and homely things about the mantle and unstained shelves – reminders of Lena that Harifin could never depart with. And there was humor.

Greynol changed from his soaked frock into long johns that were red and too short, and a buttoned shirt that hung loosely about his waist; while Harifin went off to fetch a teapot and toss several more logs upon the fire. The others were left to fend for themselves, soaked to the bone, arms piled with clothes from their packs that were no less wet. The dogs greeted them with sniffs and tail wags, but Scout gave a growl when Andro bent low to pat its head.

"That's all right, get to know me first," he said.

Harifin gathered them in. "Warm your bones, then we can settle around the table. In the meantime, I shall fix something for your stomachs – I heard their rumblings from the kitchen. Perhaps the smallest one of you, a Mihtrir if I ever saw one, might assist me. Take no offense – you may stand closer to the mud, as evidenced by your clothing, but at least you don't burst at the seams like I do," he chuckled, placing two hands upon his round belly.

"My name is Brenn Linderfell from the village of Honodolch, and I don't mind being called short, as I am often reminded. I am happy to help – if only there where drier clothes to change into," replied Brenn as he swung his arms into the air, spraying the room with water.

Harifin laughed so loudly it nearly shook the mugs and plates off the kitchen shelf.

"A rain-soaked rag you make, Mister Linderfell. I will set you up with a towel and fresh clothes. You may find some younger garments in the bedroom drawers, long outgrown by my two boys who are now my size. The others will have to do their drying by the fire. Now hurry along, let us not keep these hungry men waiting."

Andro found it strange, even more uproarious, as the six of them removed their pants and shirts, lining them across the mantle and upon chairs placed in front of the hearth. Barechested and barelegged they squatted upon the warm stone threshold, and with swords and sticks held their soaked garb above the fire, like campers roasting apples. The scene of the steam rising off of his favorite shirt in the middle of their embarrassed huddle stuck in Andro's memory for some time to come.

A rare wall clock struck nine by the time the men were dressed and somewhat dry – the room's blaze fed for a night out of the damp and cold. Harifin showed them to two rear bedrooms, seldom used for anything save storing things.

"You will find two small beds in each room and furs you might want to shake off first, they are a bit dusty for those who must take to the floor. How good it is to have someone sleep in here again," he said, lighting an oil-lamp in the hall.

"Come along now, my nose tells me the biscuits are ready. Your Brenn is putting a pot on the table as we speak," he said, sporting a generous smile.

Two tables were joined in the hearth-room laden with a kettle of venison and potato stew, roasted carrots, fresh brown biscuits, and beer. Chairs placed in tight accommodated nine hungry men, and no one complained. Fendor and Scout lay nearby, waiting for scraps to be thrown their way.

"You were fortunate I cut a larger roast tonight. You can thank Brenn for preparing the vegetables and bread in quick order. Sorry I have no honey, but there is fresh butter and milk," said Harifin, given to occupy the largest chair at the table's head. He seemed a curious fellow for Gandol folk, who tend to be neat as a pin and all 'skin and bones'. Harifin sat ruffled and plump, beard dipping into his bowl more than once. He looked the part of a large Kuirian, straight out of a Vanadium mine; or so thought Drago and Zerrin who felt right at home with the woodsman. Before his playful glance, they spoke openly in the firelight:

"Mister Tardane, we can't thank you enough for your hospitality. We were at wits end, stuck in the rain since sunup," said Zerrin, cleaning his plate with a piece of bread.

"Truly, friend. We will recompense you for the trouble. I hope we left something in your pantry," added Greynol.

"Nonsense," replied Harifin, "I have more than I need. Offer nothing more than your company – whatever else is required can be taken care of in the morning. And since you men nearly caught your deaths out in the rain, I suggest some hearty wine to warm your bones."

Harifin went over to a shelf and grabbed a strange round flask of a dark vintage. He poured them each a glass and insisted they raise a toast. With glasses held high, including Armond, who had no fondness for wine, Harifin offered a blessing:

"To my fine guests – to health and long life. Finish your glasses and good fortune is yours...that is what we say in the Central Valley. You cannot stay near without tasting of her bounty."

They toasted Harifin as he continued. "I am very happy to have you all here. So many years have passed since Arowen last came to my house, I believed him dead. That was until recently when his name returned to me. I began to grow suspicious – I was not wholly surprised to find you at my gate."

"Someone has been asking about Greynol...I mean, Arowen?" asked Rogan, lifting a spoonful of stew to his lips.

"A man came out of Barame claiming to be a messenger of Lord Durn. As I recall, that was sometime in late spring. Someone in town recalled that Arowen and I were friends, and this fellow assumed I would know of his whereabouts. 'How should I know where he's been?' I told him, 'haven't seen the bloke in years'."

"Could this be the same man who came to my door early in Orist?" wondered Greynol. "A messenger arrived at Idarill from Barame bearing a scroll – the same scroll that carries me south. The man's name was Caron, an emissary of Lord Durn."

"Well," thought Harifin, placing his elbows upon the table. "I am not so good with names, but this one was no emissary. Any messenger of Durn knows his place and manner of dress – I would sooner call my messenger a tramp. I sent him away empty-handed."

"You are keen, my friend. An emissary has no need to knock on doors in a search."

Andro's interest peaked, for all things were news to his ears. "But what of this man? And what of this scroll?" he asked.

Harifin lit a pipe to gather his thoughts, sharing his pouch with the Kuirian who filled their own. "A message I know nothing about; but concerning the visitor, there *is* more to tell. Although my eyes and memory fail me, I do have help. The man who came to my door appeared alone, but others in his company hid in wait. Since then, men of his ilk, the most devious kind, have returned to the Arrither Road. They were not many, six at one time, five the next, watching the road, watching me at times. But I have a watcher of my own," he said with a wink.

"Yes, they'll think twice before returning here. If my dogs and bow aren't enough to put a scare in them, the *men in hiding* they will fear. Spies won't pass this way again – they found another trail, a path off the Arrither a day's ride or so to the east. That way brings them out north of Ristle, although it is harder going. And they bestride stolen horses, preferring to travel in darkness; but once in the wilds, they go by day."

Brenn gasped. "Mister Harifin, how do you know these things?" he asked. The others were no less intrigued. Greynol, however, understood much on his own and tried to buffer the young men from learning too much.

"You need not indulge our young friends. I will speak to them of these matters another time," said the Acolyte with a wink.

"I do not mind at all," replied Harifin, mistaking the forewarning for good manners, which he was never well versed. "Friends, I have dwelt in these woods for most of my long life, reared in a small cabin just beyond the forest edge. But that house has long fallen to ruin. Now I am caretaker of this forest, from the hilltop down into the gully of the eastern rill is my own. Others claim the woodland from that point eastward – folk who lord over the East-wilds south of the Arrither Road, and nothing escapes their watch. One of these *fellow's* in hiding is known to me and speaks of goings on about the woods."

"Is this the 'watcher' you mentioned earlier?" asked Andro.

"Yes, and if I am correct, if actions mean anything, one of his kin sits at table with us."

Harifin took a long puff of his pipe turning his gaze toward Leonin whom sat quietly at the far end of the table. The Farrian stood at once and bowed. "At your service Mister Tardane. Is it I whom you speak?"

Harifin gave a chuckle from his belly that shook like a jar of warm honey.

"Yes, and you talk in a similar polite fashion, unlike city-folk who push this way and that. Take no offense you others – I mean to say my forest friend knows only his woodland home, caring little for the ways of common men. Strange that he would fancy speaking to me, but for a long time it has been so."

Leonin smiled. "He trusts you as a member of the forest, not a trespasser. But if a Farrian, he and his people are unknown to the Lanfersi. There are those once akin to the my race known as *Laichenrowe*, 'the unseen', a lost tribe that remains an enigma to my people."

"He never used that word, *Laichenrowe*, but I feel he is somehow akin to the Farrian."

"Well, what does he look like? Does he appear like Leonin with ashen hair and fair features? Or perhaps a dark-haired Sindelwarian – fair but dour?" asked Rogan.

"I do not know for certain."

"You cannot describe him?"

"Actually, I have never seen him," replied Harifin quite plainly. "On certain days I walk down to the rill where the gully forms and follow a stream to a series of falls. I do not cross the bank, for that is their land. Instead, I wait at the bottom. The east bank is higher, and when my friend comes, he will speak to me from above. I have never looked upon his face for he remains hidden."

"Odd that you've never seen him once," remarked Armond, somewhat skeptical.

"One time at dusk, as the sun was setting behind the hill, I caught a glimpse of his shadow upon the trees as he started away."

Brenn shuddered, shaking his head. "Mysterious folk."

Talk died away and dishes and bowls were cleared – everyone helped put things back in order. The men were tired and longed for nothing but sleep beneath the soft woolen blankets of the bedroom. Harifin pulled Greynol aside before he too turned in for the night upon a warm bench in the hearth room.

"Friend, I am planning a ride into Barame in the morning. There is room on my wagon if you wish to accompany me."

"I told you we were eating you out of house and home. I planned on departing at daybreak."

Harifin miffed at the ideal. "Haven't you recalled our travels? After today's ride, you and your men could use an extra day off the road — not to mention the horses. And I could use a hand here. Don't worry, I'll put them to work before we leave for town."

"You are still insistent, friend, and trusting. You hardly know these men to leave them here all alone."

"If they ride with you, I can trust them. You would have told me otherwise."

"I find them worthy of most things, and I claim responsibility for them," replied Greynol, "but they are young, immature, and inexperienced. Only out of necessity do I bring them here."

Harifin lowered a brow. "There you go again with talk of necessity. No more beating around the bush. What of this message that leads you south? And why are there marauders at my door asking your name? So far you have held back," he said.

Greynol turned to see if any eavesdroppers had revealed themselves, but the hall was empty. "Come with me to the stable. I will speak of it there."

A lamp was lit to pierce the fog as the rain had ended. Fendor and Scout followed behind, entering the stable before them. Toryche was found at rest within a large stall, sharing its space with Leonin's Gairinrul. Harifin's eyes grew wide as he looked upon the silver mare munching hay.

"A fine creature, this one," he said, lifting a hand to its muzzle. He turned his attention to the older steed as it lifted its eyes from sleep, giving a bray that sounded more like laughter.

"And here is ol' Toryche, just a youthful stallion when I saw him last. Greynol, you have stayed away too long."

"A dozen years, and in times less desperate," he replied.

"What is it, friend? I hear the heaviness in your voice."

Greynol reached into the saddlebag that hung from a peg upon the wall, removing the scroll from its pouch. "Here is the reason for my journey and why men seek me. I will show you its torn seal, but not its contents, for I fear darkness troubles the reader."

The Acolyte's hands trembled as he removed the scroll from its sleeve, displaying it before Harifin's waiting eyes.

"The message came to me from Gunkar, and passed from hand to hand until reaching Barame where Lord Durn received it. Finally, it came north by emissary to my home. The seal was opened along the way. Friend or foe, the unknown reader has complicated my thoughts."

"What of this thing? Why does a scroll trouble you so?" asked Harifin, unhappy to look upon his friend so grim. The lightness of the mood at table was soon forgotten.

"The name on the letter belongs to a man called Fauglir, but its authorship is uncertain. The script is penned in blood and enchanted by an evil spell – I feel its heaviness in my hands," he replied coldly.

"You know my story, friend, tales told before the fire while Lena served hot cider on autumn nights. You know how once I fought as a soldier, not unlike the young men with me now. Resolve carried me, and in Earlon I made my made my mark – and met my match. Nary a day goes by that I fail to rethink those events of forty years ago. If only I had known the trap was laid, Aliane would never have been lost...and furthermore, my son."

"Arowen? In all the years I have known you never is made mention of a son," said Harifin, this time shaken.

"Many questions of those days have been answered by this message, for unknown to me, Aliane was with child the day the village was taken. I feared her dead, as you know, exhausting every attempt to find her. But still she lived. How can a peaceful woman and a child survive a life as slaves of Illutar? Fauglir, whose name claims authorship of this scroll, also claims to be my son."

Harifin's face paled. "Then you go to meet your son – this much is clear. But it does nothing to remove the questions. Why the secrecy? Why these questions from foul men?"

"I fear my son is no longer my son," replied Greynol, "his life is controlled by a Raugulon now. One directs his every move and trains him in the arts of the Black Coven. These men who search for me have orders from Fauglir, or another who wishes me ill. They come for me – a bounty to learn the whereabouts of the 'Old Acolyte'. Fauglir and his lord have a plan for my demise."

"And you have a plan to save your son. I know you well enough, Arowen, and I know your heart. Leave this one go. You have friends who will take you in, protect you. I will protect you."

"Most fortunate I am to include you in that number," replied Greynol, "but to hide is futility – they would find me and kill those in the way. The enemy is strong now: they advance boldly into places once thought unreachable. By means untold, Fauglir is a warlord of Illutar, and his next move is to bring ruin to more than just his father."

Harifin placed a large boot upon an overturned bucket, and it creaked as he leaned in close. The lamp exposed the wonder in his deep brown eyes. "Who is this old man whose heart knows not fear? You spoke to me once of standing within sight of Toure, the fell-city of Illutar, searching for your dear Aliane. How bold you are."

"Not bold enough to keep from running away," returned Greynol. "I fled that place for fear of death, a land beneath Ezzakar's rule. The Black Queen shows no mercy to her enemies. If I knew then what has been revealed today, I would have searched until the end."

"Friend, do not succumb to pride. One man cannot break a kingdom."

Greynol placed the scroll back in its pouch.

"My party knows precious little concerning these things – it is for their own good. I seek only their help, as far as Asengard. Then they can go on their way, which will probably end as mercenaries in Earlon – their first destination. Why do young hearts desire what brings most harm?" he said wondering, tossing a glance towards the house through the stall opening.

"I recall several such boys, myself included. You led us well as fighters then – you will lead these men better as an acolyte," replied Harifin.

"Time will tell their worth," said Greynol, returning his gaze. "The time is late and my bones ache for sleep…despite the scrutiny of prying eyes. Look, they watch us from the bedroom window."

"Curious boys," laughed Harifin, "they mean no harm".

"Boys indeed."

Once finished, they started indoors for the night. The dogs followed close behind.

"Look! They are talking in the stable so we can't hear them," said Rogan with a nose pressed against the bedroom window. Andro and Leonin attempted to settle in for the night, while the others preferred a room across the hall, being slightly larger. But for the moment, they all gathered in one place.

"Now, now, Rogan. They are old friends who haven't a chance to speak alone with us hanging about," replied Zerrin.

"I overheard Mister Tardane earlier. He and Greynol head into town in the morning," said Andro, pushing down Rogan's head for a look. "Instead of a morning ride we may have chores ahead of us. At least the horses get a day of rest."

Drago grunted. "My saddle-sores will attest to it."

"Look now," called Rogan, interrupting them; "Greynol has taken that scroll out of his pack, but he keeps Harifin from reading it, or even touch it. I wonder what it says."

"Whatever it is, he keeps it a secret," said Armond.

"There is something strange about that thing and how he treats it," added Brenn. "It seems dark to me, like magic. I wish no part of that thing."

"They're coming back. We should get to our beds," said Andro.

Warning heeded, they went off to their places of slumber. Rogan took one last look out the window; from his view, he could see Greynol's saddlebag hanging inside the stall with the scroll sticking out its pouch, partially covered. He laid back in bed wondering what mysteries it might contain.

Thursday morning began splendid and bright, spring-like in the dawn hours; the woodland still wet from an earlier rain. Greynol and Harifin roused the men early; save Leonin, who woke before the others. The Master of the House wished to see the men before departing and prepared a simple but plentiful breakfast of bacon, biscuits, and eggs – the eggs from his chickens cooped outside the stable.

Harifin settled down at table, this time in the bright front kitchen where he insisted eating the first meal of the day. The others gathered in, finding room to squeeze their chairs around an oaken table, eating until their belly's were full. Harifin enjoyed the discourse and the young men delighted in his company. They exchanged news of the North, and he, tales of the East-Wilds and Central Gandol. No mention was made of Greynol's revelation from the night before as the conversation continued:

"You sound disappointed over bypassing Lyle, our King-city – worthy of the title in better times," replied Harifin to the others gathered around. "The city has aged like her master, King Raeletin. His rule grows corrupt by those seeking power, giving bad advice and forsaking wise counsel. Even in Barame, Lord Durn governs and taxes like an overlord, busying himself over the concerns of Lyle, he forgets his own. Prince Galin is the future hope of Gandol now, nephew and heir to the throne. We, *the good people of the green meadow*, await his kingdom: a fair time, as in days gone by. My sons tell me only the prince can restore what goodness has been lost – the past glories of the Sea-Kings of old."

Greynol shook his head. "Now, now, never rush the demise of an old man."

"You are correct in saying it," chuckled Harifin, "Raeletin may have some good years left."

"Please, tell us more about the East-Wilds, since that is our destination, and not Lyle," requested Andro.

Harifin nodded, as it was his pleasure, first taking a puff of his morning pipe:

"In the days of King Edarin, about five-hundred years ago and prior to the slaying of his son, Prince Randall, upon the throne, Barame existed only as an outpost along a little used trading route going by the name of Heriton. My forefathers settled in this region and Central Gandol began to grow. They widened the meadow and tilled the land allowing sheep room to roam and vines to grow hardily."

"Not far from here, within a half-days ride by mount, the men of Heriton found a strange people residing in the hills of the East-

Wilds: these folk came from a small kingdom to the east, named Dagoraust, and built a road extending west to where they settled. One day long ago these folk forsook Dagoraust, leaving its stone edifices – but not all departed. Preferring lives of seclusion, they formed their own settlement in the hills where my forefathers encountered them. They dressed in odd garments, long tunics of red silk, and adorned themselves in gold. At first my people considered them Turrar, since in those days Nordhiem remain unsettled and northern races seldom encountered."

Harifin stared out the window into the forest, as if witnessing it firsthand. He continued: "Gandolites were curious about these new folk. They found them articulate and inventive; their language odd, yet similar to the western tongue. They spoke of things beyond the realm of reason; they foretold future events, and honored relics unknown to Gandol. Trade was exchanged: our wine, furs, and fine foods for ornate tokens and cleaver devices to tell time. From their knowledge craftsmen gained the understanding to build such intricacies."

In the other room, as if on queue, the clock upon the hearth's mantle chimed, signaling the hour, eight o'clock. Brenn nearly leapt out of his chair. Harifin laughed.

"It's a nice trinket, the old clock, given to me by my father. But I find as much satisfaction reading the sun as it rises and falls – it is a gentler cycle. That is how the seasons and days are planned, and they do not complain. Little do I care to plot my days hour by hour, moment by moment; a trinket to tell me when to lie down, when to rise."

"Unfortunately, time is the world's heartbeat, and the clock is telling us it is time to get along to Barame," said Greynol.

"But what became of this strange race? And what of the hidden friends who live near your land now? Will you at least allow Mister Tardane to finish his story?" asked Rogan. Greynol nodded, reluctantly.

Harifin raised his eyes in retrospect, the tale a source of pride and wonder:

"For a brief period of years the polite discourse continued, until one day, upon returning to the village, visitors from Barame found the place in ruins and its inhabitants gone. Nary a soul was found, nor body, nor drop of blood. They simply vanished," he said, leaning back in his chair as the last puff of his pipe drifted from a satisfied grin into the rafters.

"And as for the Watchers in the Wood, Master Rogan, they play little part in the tale. Once I asked my hidden friend concerning the matter; all he would tell me came from the lore of his own people, that at one time a greater force pervaded the East-Wilds, emanating from Dagoraust, and from this new presence his people recoiled, drawing deeper into the wilderness. They did not return until the presence diminished. He spoke no more about the subject."

"Does all this have to do with the name given to the Arrither Road? Rogan called it, 'the Haunted road'," asked Brenn whose curiosity peaked in the safe comfort of friends.

Harifin searched out an answer, but none would suffice that would make circumstances better. "I have no stories to answer that one, Brenn. The name, 'Haunt', is an old one too; but given the strange circumstances of the East-Wilds and men's imaginations, it is reasonable to assume why men use such titles."

Brenn opened his mouth again but Greynol saved Harifin from further questioning. "Let us leave the past to the past, where it belongs," replied the Acolyte. By his tone they knew the discussion had ended, and so was breakfast.

Soon after, Greynol and Harifin rode out upon a small horse-drawn wagon. A trail began at the rear of the house, which ran westward towards a thick meadow; there they came upon a larger trail and headed south over the hills towards Barame where markets and merchants abound. The others had business of their own to attend as Harifin left a note to detail his needs. Brenn read the directives aloud to the others:

"First, I want fresh cut cabbage and carrots pulled from the meadow garden; then till the ground and add some manure from the barn; secondly, cut a bushel of hay for the animals; use a cart, just go out the way you came yesterday, down my front path and back towards the open fields. Then it's a short walk south."

"Third, sweep the house and wash the dishes left over from the breakfast meal."

"Forth, clean the stables, and if any mending you find, do so; also check over my ladders and tools."

"Fifth, if you come across any game, bring it back dressed for supper."

"...and not even a thank you?" finished Brenn, lowering the note.

"Well, we better get moving, or else there may be no supper tonight," replied Drago accustomed to a day of labor.

The tasks were divided: Brenn, a farmer by nature, dirtied his hands in the moist earth of a garden plot; Drago and Zerrin, who farmed little and tilled less, helped as best as they could. They worked the soil, as instructed, filling a bushel basket with heads of firm cabbage and bright, sweet-smelling carrots. Andro, Armond, Rogan, and Leonin took scythes and a pair of rakes from the barn and cleared a patch of tall grass, piling a sizable mound in the field. Afterwards, they filled a cart pulled grudgingly by Ambarr.

By noon, their chores brought them to the stable, which meant the dirty work of cleaning after the animals. Besides Harifin's cow and chickens, the stalls were full with the nine horses of Greynol's Alliance. Andro and Rogan felt too much at home, or Uncle Breden's stable to be exact. Pitch forks in hand, they added considerably to Harifin's manure heap. The others performed other much-needed labors: repairing a broken ladder, mending a bridle, and straightening bent tools. Armond played the apprentice blacksmith with hammer and tongs in hand.

"That's it for this old axe – not so dull anymore," he said, wearing only a sleeveless shirt and rolled up breeches.

Drago looked things over and nodded, lighting his pipe from a fire pot. "It must be nearing two o'clock and no sign of them. What is there left to do?"

"Harifin asked for game – I spotted some pheasant earlier in the fields," answered Leonin. He inspected the string of his bow and numbered the arrows in his quiver. "You are all welcome to join me in the meadow."

"That and housekeeping are what remains," replied Andro.

"Hunting sounds better than cleaning, any day," said Zerrin.

"We can't all go chasing game. Mister Tardane will expect everything to be in proper order."

Rogan sniffed and glanced out the stable door. "Looks like we still have some time before he and Greynol return; or should I call him the name Harifin gives him – Arowen?"

"He does seem to know our master better than any of us," replied Drago.

"Well, I for one would like to know more."

"What do you have in mind, Rogan?" asked Armond, returning a pair of sharpened shears where they previously hung.

Rogan threw another glance outside; then, feeling somewhat safe, stepped into the stall where Gairinrul and Toryche rested. He placed a hand upon the brown leather saddlebag that now contained the scroll.

"Perhaps it's time we had a look," he said, "since this message has something to do with Greynol's journey, and we have promised to follow. He showed it to Harifin last night. We deserve to know more."

"But he did not reveal its contents," replied Leonin. "If he wanted us to see it, he would have shown us by now."

"Come to think of it, he never said much about it," said Drago.

Rogan did not wait for a resolution to the debate. He slowly slid the scroll from its pouch, then with a deliberate snap, he removed it completely.

"What are you doing?" choked Andro, not at all comfortable with the situation. But as the emblem emerged, it caught everyone's attention.

"Look, a blood seal!"

"Illutarian," mumbled Drago. "Why does Greynol carry such a thing?"

Brenn practically leapt back. "It is evil. And if you wish to look at it, count me out. I'll just stand by the door – or better yet, you may find Leonin and me out in the meadow searching for game. I will signal you when they return."

Rogan ignored the warning. He stared boldly at the insignia as one determined to master its hidden power; curiosity took hold, and after a slight hesitation, he unrolled the scroll.

Leonin started away to join Brenn in the hunt, but Rogan called out to him. "There is mention of Asenrael – and war."

He paused, Farrian curiosity waning. "This is what I waited to hear," muttered Leonin under his breath. His expression changed and a shadow came over his brow.

"Only a moment, friend...only a moment. I shall join you in the field," he said, turning back to join the others. Brenn hung his head and walked away alone.

The day grew clear and warm and a breeze swayed the grass as it rolled across the valley. A flock of sparrows chased white flies in the open, but no game bird came near Brenn who waited with bow in hand. Greynol and Harifin returned to find him wading across the meadow near the forest edge.

"What goes friend, no luck?" hollered Harifin, firmly seated behind his gray steed with reins in hand, "no matter, we brought enough for dinner at the market."

"Leonin bagged two pheasants earlier. They are in the oven as we speak – a few hours more and they will be ready," replied Brenn somberly.

"Good then, two birds will do just fine. You no longer need to stay out here and away from the others."

Brenn lowered his eyes, trying to hold back his distress. Greynol found the look odd for the young Mihtrir.

"Brenn, is everything all right?" he asked.

"Fine, sir. Just fine."

"Come along then."

Harifin made his way into the stable, undoing the bridles and leading the palfrey back to its stall, leaving it with fresh water. Greynol waited behind while Brenn ran indoors to alert the others.

"Looks like work's been done around here, and the chimney has smoke. I approve of these men of yours – they are hard workers," said Harifin.

"We shall see what kind of men they be," exclaimed Greynol, his mood turning. The saddlebag upon its peg was void of one glaring article – the scroll was missing. "Where there's smoke, there's fire."

Harifin threw up his shoulders. "They had time to return it. I wouldn't yet call them thieves."

"I call them young and foolish. Brenn alone seems innocent in this matter. Say nothing until I address the others," replied Greynol, starting at once for the house.

Warmth filled the kitchen where a fancy wood-burning stove gave the aroma of fresh bread and roasting pheasants. Brenn inspected everything, his orders followed close to perfection: the birds were browned and salted, steaming in a pan with chopped cabbage. Into a boiling pot, he added carrots, leaks, and a dash of sage to flavor fresh turnips. The others watched him work – like men awaiting their sentence. Through a polished oaken door, whose tint matched the oversized kitchen cabinets, once the pride and joy of Lena Tardane, entered Harifin and Greynol.

"Good afternoon, gentlemen. I see we have dinner on the boil, excellent. There are provisions in the wagon; you men can bring them into the pantry when time allows. And before I forget, thank you each for your labors, my list was well managed," announced Harifin, trying hard to be polite, but faces remained sullen.

"I shall clean up a bit, then see what's going on under these pots."

Harifin threw a floppy red hat upon a wall-peg and marched off to his bedroom to wash up, closing the door firmly behind him. The others remained silent with heads lowered. Andro gave up his chair to Greynol, taking a spot against the kitchen door beside Leonin.

"We had no ideal when you might return. Was everything is in order?" asked Andro quick to realize his choice of words untimely.

"*Everything*, Andro?"

"Well, what I mean to say is..."

"Never mind, the fault here is mine alone," said Rogan, promptly interrupting. "I will explain, sir. There is something of grave importance here."

With a slow hand, Rogan revealed the scroll he held beneath the kitchen table. Greynol's eyes darkened, but he remained silent.

"I removed this from your baggage. I knew it was of consequence to you, and when I saw how you discussed it with Harifin in the stable last evening, my heart grew suspicious. I am burdened to have read it, and sorry to have done you any wrong. I should have returned it, but I could not. Why have you hid so much from us? Why is it that you found no need to tell your own alliance of these terrible things?" he asked, voice filled with remorse.

Greynol did not speak. His gaze went from one of pity for Rogan, to one of dismay as his eyes came to rest upon the scroll. He scanned the others faces – all guilty save Brenn.

"Sir, why did you keep this from us? We ride as your escort upon this journey and have offered you our swords. There is much here that should be explained," added Drago, snuffing out his pipe and sliding it into a shirt pocket.

Greynol's lips tightened in his anger. "Why did I keep this from you? For your protection, that is why. Brenn alone I can trust in this matter. And what shall I call the rest of you: thieves, fools, or traitors worse still?"

"Sir, please, we meant no betrayal. We only wanted to help. All of this is my fault. I wanted to know more about this quest, about what we face," replied Rogan.

"But what of this Fauglir, the Illutarian markings, an attack upon Asenrael, and blood-letters?" Zerrin asked.

"And what of your name: are we to call you Greynol or Arowen? Is this Fauglir really your son?" added Armond, animated as he spoke. He could no longer hold back.

"One thing at a time," called Greynol, raising a hand to still their tongues. "To answer Drago first: you were kept in the dark to keep you in the light, but it seems you prefer darkness. Why is it one must burn his fingers to discover the danger of fire? An

Illutarian seal and blood-letters clearly speaks of dark magic. Signs of sorcery are omens one should avoid; whomever reads them becomes entangled in its purpose – a sticky web for a fly to break."

"Oh, I told them not to read it. I was curious myself...until seeing that Dragon-seal. No charms for me, thank you," said Brenn with a shudder. He glanced over to Leonin who lowered his head in shame.

Greynol removed the scroll from Rogan's hand – he would ever touch it again. "I hoped to keep these things from you," said the Acolyte, "for your own sake, not mine. I cannot hide the message like some hand note in my pocket, and I bid not destroy it for the ill that might come of it. Another's eyes have looked upon this, one I do not know, and I wish to find out who."

"I do not understand," said Brenn as he returned to the stove to check a boiling pot. "Why not burn the thing if it brings so much trouble?"

"Burning does not break a spell and may bring harm to those infected by its design. These things are fell and best left for *the Sons of Perdition*. A great price has been paid for this enchantment, and a greater repayment is demanded. The course has begun, my passage, and must continue until completion," Greynol replied. He took the scroll from their sight, placing it beneath his chair to trouble them no longer.

Harifin returned after a deliberate respite and joined Brenn at the stove, although his intentions had more to do with curiosity. Greynol held everyone's fullest attention as he continued:

"I am not angry with any of you, for your honest words, your openness, brings me hope," he said calmly. "But still, your actions have compromised your positions. Your actions have linked you to my plight by the blood upon the scroll; now you must remain with me until your roles are played out, save Brenn who alone remains unburdened. You, my friend, are still free to choose."

Brenn threw up is shoulders. "Free to choose what? I had my misgivings from the start. But I am a fool and friendship means much more to me than the danger ahead. I want to help these blokes – if I can," he replied.

Armond gave him a wink as if to say, "Well spoken, friend."

Greynol's spirit lightened a little as he explained his lifelong tale. "It was a humble beginning as a swordsman, journeying to the southlands far from Nordhiem. I was Arowen then, seeking glory and wanting to learn more of my mother's lineage, for she was of a rare race from Tuirowe that long ago departed Acrindian for Turra Arrither."

"My skills as a fighter grew and I fought in the highlands as a cavalryman, near the Kuirian ruins of Llorky when Earlon tried in vain to recapture the fortress lost to Illutar. In the Earlon Valley near Ralderon, we drove off Drukon armies, and brought peace to the land. There I met a beautiful young maiden named Aliane, daughter of an alderman from Tier. Ten years her senior, we wed in the spring of 1610."

"We settled in Tier where I held the title of Champion, leading the militia against an Illutarian threat that pressed ever nearer. The menace grew: Drukon armies broke the strong defenses of southern Earlon, taking the fortress of Ralderon; a hoard that threatened Tier and all surrounding lands. Given warning, I assembled the horsemen to stave off an enemy attack, killing their Raugulon leader. With victory in our wake, and fresh reports from field sentinels, I lead a hearty group of riders, including Aram, the father of murdered Sahr, whose slain body bore the scroll, into the western hills held by Illutar. We charged to stave off a mountain push by the enemy, believing that a second Raugulon led an army into the bluffs south of the Asen Lainar, but it was a ruse. The spectre remained, and with a force greater than before, swept over Tier and its insufficient defenses."

"Once word came to us, Tier was already lost and the remaining armies of Earlon devastated; those were Earlon's last days and nevermore did the fair kingdom rise, its good people killed, enslaved, or scattered, taking refuge in nearby Lokrey or Fanael. Aliane was gone, and unknown to me, my son. That is how Dariat ended up in Illutar, born into slavery. And although this revelation remained hidden from me until the arrival of the scroll, in my heart I knew it to be true," finished Greynol, his pain sufficient to hold off further questioning.

Harifin, who stood listening at the doorway, gathered the others help to finish supper and prepare the dining table. Dinner came and soon trails of pipe-smoke drifted into dark rafters; casual talk flowed into the evening hours and darkness ended their day of respite. That night they took full advantage of the dry homey comforts, for while they slept another rain fell, ending hours before dawn where the Arrither Road waited.

Chapter Seven – the Arrither Road

Sunlight through the bedroom window warmed the bed where Andro lay. Noises from the stable roused him from a pleasant slumber as Greynol and Harifin were already hard at work outside; seen from the window, they set Toryche's bridle and saddle, and filled packs for the long trek into the wilderness. Andro rubbed his eyes and watched intently, as if expecting some magical surprise, aside from the enchanted scroll, which in his mind seemed less like magic and more of a watchful presence. And it gave him the strangest dreams.

Rogan and Leonin heard the commotion outside, tossing their covers once they realized the time. Loud snoring in the bedroom across the hall promised to be more of a challenge. With prompting, Armond and the cousins crawled out of their beds, or in Brenn and Zerrin's case, off the floor where rugs and furs made for comfortable berths.

"Rise and shine!" called Greynol entering the kitchen, glad to find several of them dressed and ready. "Harifin was kind enough to have breakfast prepared. Move along now, it will be your last home-cooked meal for some time."

Breakfast could not have tasted better nor disappear faster. The master of the house was well pleased, but sad just the same. With a wave of dismissal, their conversations ended – it was time for the Alliance to make their departure. They thanked Mister Tardane for his hospitality – he could do no more. This time he insisted they leave the dirty plates behind.

"No gents, I'll take care of the chores from here. You get along now; daytime is for riding. Come back one day…if you can manage it."

Their belongings were gathered and the horses, now rested, assembled in a line. Greynol anticipated the passage, and it made his heart young again. The others wished to remain a little longer in the Fair House of the Green Wood, so homely it felt, but their hopes were squashed. Once ready, they gathered outside the front-gate where Fendor and Scout barked at the commotion of so many riders. Greynol stood beside Toryche, a hand upon its reins; Harifin strode down the walkway towards him.

"Thank you again, friend. We were graced to find to your home in our time of need. Since you accept no repayment, a blessing I will leave in return," said Greynol warmly.

"The pleasure was all mine. Now be off with you. Make good speed upon the 'Old Arrither'. The pack horse is loaded with fresh provisions – just a gift for your journey," replied Harifin, returning a smile.

He took Greynol by the hand. "May Fawarra bless you, friend. I pray that you return to visit me again – this time on better terms."

Greynol lowered his eyes. "Let us reside ourselves to the will of Fawarra; but meet again we shall, and that day will seem all the brighter."

The others said their good-byes as they passed; following Greynol who climbed upon the saddle, heeling Toryche down the lane in the direction they first arrived. Harifin waved, a smoking pipe clenched between his teeth. "Farewell friends, keep together, and remember always, leave the land south of the road alone – it is not yours to venture."

With that last bit of advice to guide them, Greynol approached the stone wall marking the end of Harifin's property. They turned eastward to face the sun between the trees and entered the Arrither Road.

Greynol was glad for the start, although later than he first hoped. The men, satisfied from their time of rest, felt content to ride out the day. The beginning of the East-wilds arrived as a pleasant forest saunter met with ease by horse and rider alike: tall broad-leafed trees shaded the company, and a feeling of welcome edged them on. The Arrither, once a wide much-traveled route, cut a straight swath through the timberland. As mid-day approached, the damp earth warmed and the air grew thick; a haze hung in the leaves turning dappled sunlight into a golden shroud where it penetrated the trees. At times thickets crept onto the path that made riding single file necessary – they were forced to dismount to cut brambles with sword strokes, or move aside felled trees.

After several miles, the trail dropped away from the plateau marking the approach of smaller hills. Along an uneven slope, they encountered long abandoned homes of gray-colored brick; houses deteriorated long past usefulness as shelter. They navigated sections of a broken thoroughfare that once ran through a thriving village.

"How old is this place?" asked Brenn, gazing about the emptiness.

"Hard to say," answered Greynol, hands planted firmly against the pommel of his saddle. "Harifin spoke of a lost race that once flourished in the east; these were its descendants whom, for a short time, befriended the inhabitants of the Central Valley. Four-hundred years ago the people of the Dagoraust disappeared – what Harifin did not tell you is that a remnant of that race claim to reside in Fallis, not far from here upon the north-east folds. They remain a quiet, humble people, rarely straying from their hills. Evidence of their claim is disputed and unclear, but what is known is that this village found its end several centuries ago, about the time of Llorkey's fall."

Zerrin and Drago lowered their heads at the mention of the once great Kuirian fortress.

"I hope Logan fares better in future days," said Andro, reminded of his own city among the trees. "Proud is our homeland and heritage, but if some kingdoms fail, what keeps others from the same fate."

Armond dismissed the thought. "What had these people in times of full glory in comparison to Logan or Vanyor? Isolation brought this place to ruin – and perhaps fear."

"Why do you say that?" asked Greynol.

"Well, if Harifin spoke correctly, these folk came from a greater realm. Why did they desert their old homes? For fear, or to escape an imposition – perhaps both."

"This was always thought a queer place," replied Drago. "If only trees could talk."

Drago realized his choice of words, and turned to find Leonin fixated upon flowing vines that tangled between what seemed twin pillars – his attention held fast by the curious landscape.

"Is it true what they say, that the Farrian can read the trees?" asked Drago.

Leonin gave him a discerning look, and then found a chuckle escape his throat. "We do not read the trees, Drago, but signs in the forest. There is little mystery to it."

"Well, what signs do you read here?"

"I am no seer, but my impressions here are many. Concerning a lost race, I sense they tried to control what could not be controlled. Foremost, they lost an attempt to tame the East-Wilds."

"Maybe the *Laichenrowe* in hiding chased them out," said Brenn, quickly drawing Greynol's ire.

"Nonsense! Speak no ill of those you know nothing about," snapped the Acolyte, "or not only spies will find this road a peril. Time to move on. Control your tongues while you can."

Beyond the village, the Arrither turned less kind: steep climbs and sudden falls belabored the horses every step. They came upon an arched bridge where a ravine divided the road. Beneath its heavy beams, a stone chute roared with water from recent rains, dropping away into an unseen series of falls. The horses' hoof-falls echoed against the rock gully as they passed, and from it, a narrow southeastern view appeared between the trees, exposing a densely wooded valley far below. A ridge lay opposite the vale, running north to south – its crest clearly the highest point along the way. A short distance more and the path began to wind its way skyward.

Twelve miles from Harifin's home, roughly four leagues on foot, they reached the summit where a stand of pitch pine crowned a natural wall of stone, guarded below by chestnut, oak, and maple dressed in their summer array. At the crest, Greynol afforded them a longer rest. A late lunch upon the rocks found welcome indeed; although the men softened their hunger along the way with apples and grapes stowed in their packs.

Andro delighted in high places, curious why no person had ever settled in that particular spot. Climbing the wall a wide view spread out in every direction before him. He surveyed the surrounding landscape with the others: to the west, a deep and dense valley fell sharply below, obscured by the tops of trees that circled the crest, and beyond, the eastern forest lay in green folds far into the horizon. Further still, as seen through keen eyes, a pale glimpse of the grassy western slopes of the Brodden Valley from which they came.

"Harifin's house is out there, somewhere in the trees," said Zerrin, staring into the distance.

"He is a good man, like my Uncle Breden," added Andro. "Greynol, how long have you known him?"

The Acolyte smiled in recollection. "Many, many years. Forty years ago, Harifin knew these trails by heart, but now he cannot travel far. And you are correct in saying it – he is a good man."

Turning their gaze to the east, they shielded their eyes beneath the mid-day sun, but the sky cast a haze concealing the distant horizon: towards the south and east, the ridge dropped swiftly away and smaller hills continued in descending order until fading into a mist. In their eagerness, Rogan and Andro climbed along the sharp stones of the ridge hoping for an unobstructed view north where the sky remained clear and unspoiled, and several leagues away the forest ended and green hills appeared. To the northeast grasslands spread wide, and Rogan heard, only for a moment, the ringing of bells and a young woman's song.

"Andro, did you hear that? A heavenly voice, and it drifts up out of the plain. I wonder who it could be," he said with a hand cupped to an ear.

Andro just shook his head – he heard nothing.

"Greynol, what lie beyond the forest edge? Is it Bardol?" asked Rogan when the others approached.

"Out in the green and open roll the Fallis Hills," he answered. "There you will find sheep and fields and farms aplenty, and a maze of trails and quiet villages scattered in-between. I walked there in younger days – mile upon mile. If you lose your way, hours turn into days."

"I would like to see it one day," said Rogan.

"One day, Master Pinehurst, but save that for your own travels. Our destination is not so hospitable."

Down into a steep wooded descent they withdrew, continuing their push into the East-wilds. The road took cautious turns as a shear cliff dropped suddenly away with only a narrow space left to tread. The men left little to chance and lead their horses until a gentler grade returned.

"This is the price we pay for taking in the view – it's a long way down," said Andro, "and my legs burn."

Armond laughed. "Only a mere foothill. Return with me to Vanyor and I will show you how high the sky climbs," he replied with a wink and a grin.

Soon they came upon a rocky landing, like a ridge between the hills, and entered a steep-sided hollow. The wall of the valley deepened, frowning upon the party now cast in the shadow of a tall and silent forest. A stream ran aside their path, beating against the rocks of the gorge as it went. Again, they took to their mounts.

Andro gazed about this new place, dark despite the mid-day sun. Reminded of the Lanfersi, he found the lull of the wilderness inviting. He knew of none to compare, save the forest of his

homeland. Andro felt content cradled in this new beauty; a silent strength he felt in his bones.
"*If only I were Farrian,*" he thought quietly.
Once upon the valley floor the air grew thick and hot. The creek bed widened to form a glade where the horses took water. The men gazed longingly for relief.
"We will rest here," said Greynol to their delight. "Just long enough to refresh yourselves."

Trees of ash and linden formed shadows beneath a sapphire sky, dimming the hour well before dusk. Sunlight pierced thru a filter of branches; a pallet of colors for the eye's delight: the white and slate grays of brook stones, and reflections of emerald leaves that crossed the mirror of the brook. A sudden breeze blew down from the ridge they came, whose summit remained obscured from the deep glen, refreshing the men from the swelter. Armond wasted no time. He marched over to the stream and dropped to a knee to dunk his head.
"Ah, this beats the weather," he said laying back against the rocks. Long strands of black hair dripped onto his shoulders.
"Southern heat already getting to you?" asked Rogan.
"What are you saying? When the wind dies, the Vanyor Valley steams like an oven in the summer. But this place feels just as hot today."
"I have to admit, the water might kill the heat," said Andro, leaning forward to splash his face.
Greynol broke a smile as he watched, filling his flask with water while snacking on dried fruit and nuts. "Come along, all of you, eat something. There's dried venison, bread and wine…all compliments of Harifin."
The others took seats upon the rocks that filled the stream's basin. Brenn finished his small meal, small by his standards, and munched an apple while tossing pebbles into the brook. Like a scheming child, he plunked Armond in the back of the head, a hand over his mouth to conceal his laugher.
"One more and you'll be swimming with the minnows,"

growled Armond.

Brenn could not resist the taunt, and as Armond returned a look, a stone smacked square off his forehead. With a shout, he charged his antagonist, grabbing Brenn's heel before he could scuttle away. Brenn was lifted into the air kicking and screaming, his shouts muffled by a mouthful of water as his head went under.

"Take that pebble thrower!" bellowed Armond, standing in knee-deep water. A round of laughter erupted, for as soon as Brenn emerged from the stream and opened his mouth in rebuttal, an apple was stuffed in.

"Wet again, Mister Linderfell? I believe you might be part fish," chuckled Andro.

"That will teach you not to take threats so lightly," added Drago.

Brenn crawled out the brook shaking water everywhere as he passed. "Oh, I was hot anyway."

Greynol could not help but laugh, shaking his head. "I am among boys once again."

Leonin drifted away from the others, indifferent to the frivolity. The trees of the southern slope held his attention as he ran his hand in smooth strokes across Gairinrul's mane, listening for noises much too silent for any raucous commoner.

Andro, who became aware of his friend's distraction, joined him on the road. "What is it, friend?" he asked.

"There are noises about the southern forest…curious sounds."

"Probably some animal – a deer or a bird. I find birds can make a racket in the brush, enough to make one think a larger animal is near," replied Andro, eyes darting back and forth between the trees of the long slope.

"They are not animals."

"Then what?"

"Harifin was right about *Watchers* in the wood."

"Really? Perhaps we could meet them."

"Easier to chase shadows, Master Rhine," replied Greynol from behind as the others approached. "These ones avoid contact with common men and Farrian alike."

Leonin finally relented his watch and turned back. "You recall Harifin's advice not to enter the south-wood. We are at the border of their land," he added.

"Then you must be quite a sight to their eyes – a Farrian traveling with common men. The *Laichenrowe* might recognize you as one of their kin," said Rogan.

"What are you saying? Do not use that word here. It is not a name of honor, but of condemnation. They are not my kin – a true Farrian has no dealings with this kind," returned Leonin, suddenly out of sorts.

"Have an open mind, friend. Your brethren, the Sindelwarian to be sure, condemn most of us for one reason or another. And seeing you now would scandalize them, traveling abroad on an adventure with commoners," said Andro, but his words were ill timed and lacked wisdom. In a rare expression, Leonin eyes flashed with anger; yet, his voice remained controlled.

"Andro, even you misunderstand? Who do I cause scandal by going abroad? My people are free as anyone else. We only choose not to trample noisily upon open roads for all to see. But yes, my actions *might* prove foolishness indeed, that I do not doubt."

Armond found Leonin's tone struck a nerve. He strode confidently towards the Farrian, making sure the rattle of his sword in its scabbard was obvious.

"What of common men? Do we seem fools also to you?" he asked, pausing with only Andro between them.

"Our differences are obvious: Kuirian and Turrar have no love for my race, and many of my own return the same indignation. Farrian live by different means, different principles. Neither way should be considered wrong or foolish – it is what separates us."

"More than that separates us," muttered Armond, catching Leonin's gaze.

Armond's eyes burned hot. His pride went before him and his look shown of 'quick to the hilt' rashness. Leonin, on the other hand, returned no provocation and remained composed. What Armond found in his appearance was a lack of fear, and it tore at him. Traditional ways made him slow to accept an adversary of his people, which Farrian were considered since centuries past. Hard fought would be their friendship to ever exist. Armond walked away mumbling under his breath, "Farrian."

Greynol insisted on one last push until evening. Curiosity of the southern forest held them on edge as they went: a quick glimpse into the trees showed no trace of onlookers, but they thought otherwise. The horses grew uneasy, biting at their legs in anger; they veered off the trail to avoid trees that leaned in to snag them as they passed, save Gairinrul who remained calm. Once out of the valley, the stream crossed suddenly beneath their feet, and disappeared into the wilderness. Soon the feelings of unease lifted and the road wound its way along a wide basin where the trees began to thin. Rangy hills rose upon their left and smaller hillocks lined their right; the sun sank in an orange glow in the direction they came, bright against the ridge from earlier that day, now several leagues away. Once dusk settled, the darkness set in like a storm.

They approached the rise of a tall hill that stood in their path. The Arrither Road bent to the south to skirt its flank. Rising like a black mound against the deep blue of twilight, the riders entered its shadow. "There is a small clearing within sight of the road – it will give us cover for the night," said Greynol, turning off the path and into the forest at the foot of the hummock.

The woods turned to black as bright stars opened in a moonless sky. A fire was set and tents pitched upon a level spot between the trees. The remaining wine and cheese were consumed, along with day old bread and salted bacon. The horses were watered in a nearby brook and fed on wild-grass and some packed away oats. They were tethered behind the tents for the night.

Once settled, Andro found Leonin seated alone beside the horses. "The ponies had a long day, but they are fit for several more," said Leonin like a sentry giving a report.

"I gave them a good checking over earlier. You need not stay here with the animals, come and join us," replied Andro with a curious look, trying to discern his friend's mood. "I wanted to apologize for my words earlier at the stream – I am ignorant of so many things."

"You are not to blame. You spoke in truth. Many of my people fall into rash judgments; I am trying to avoid having such a mind," he replied. "There was something about that place, so familiar to the Lanfersi wilderness. I perceived our *Watchers*; their eyes were upon me as I them, but their gaze I did not understand. I felt judged, pitied, and feared at once. They are unlike any of the Phullan tribes: *the People of the Jewels* they no longer remain."

"Then it is good we left that place."

"Yes, and it troubles me. If I were to approach they would not allow it; but still, I would like to know more about them," replied Leonin, throwing sideways glances towards the others gathered about the fire. "Andro, this ride may prove too much to bear out. My presence alone infuriates everyone. I hoped the situation would prove better, but it has only worsened."

"Friend, take heart in what I say – do not underestimate my friends."

Supper was unremarkable, and once finished the camp prepared for sleep. First watch was set: Drago and Zerrin placed crossbows at their feet as the others sunk swiftly into their dreams. A small fire to warm them, the brothers sat back, struggling against sleep as the hours drifted past. At midnight, a hoot owl roused Zerrin from his thoughts, and his neck lurched.

"I dunno, Drago."

"Dunno what?"

"Do you think we are cut out for this sort of thing? I mean adventure and all?" asked Zerrin, his voice groggy with sleep.

"You talk nonsense. Why wouldn't we be fit?" replied Drago, poking a branch into the fire.

"Well, speaking for myself, I'd like to keep my wits about me.

You know how the mines affect some of those hole-diggers back home: they withdraw from the open, seeking greater riches, deeper treasure. They treat summer as winter, all holed up waiting for the next day's labor; the chance at larger booty in the next vein."

Drago gave a grunt, waving his hand as if swatting flies. "Bah, you worry over growing old, just like our brothers – old before their time in the silver lode. Perhaps chance has taken us this far for a reason. Yaldarra looks upon us with favor."

"…or Greynol's Fawarra," replied Zerrin. "Strange that common men would follow a Farrian god. But aside from those things of which we know little, I still hope to keep my wits from failing."

"Now why do you keep saying that?" growled Drago, growing annoyed as he tossed the stick into the fire.

"Well, for starters, I keep hearing voices."

"Voices?" asked Drago. He quickly stood and cupped a hand to his ear. "You fool, that's not your imagination. Now I hear it too. Light the lamp with an ember while I cover the fire."

Drago stood outside the lamplight listening, but was startled as Leonin came up from behind. "My, you *do* sleep light," said the Kuirian, spinning around. "We heard chatter somewhere in the woods."

"I hear it too," replied Leonin, "there are men upon the hilltop."

"Are they the Watchers from before?" asked Zerrin.

"No, these are careless voices, loud and full of drink," he answered. By this time the others were roused over the commotion and came out to join them, looking to Leonin for answers.

"What now do we do? Friend or foe, our camp is too near to trust they won't stumble upon us?" asked Rogan.

"They seem to gather in one place for now, at the crest of the hill," replied Leonin whose senses were keen.

Armond took a heavy crossbow from his tent and started ahead. "It is clear what is needed here. Anyone care to back me up while I figure out this riddle?" he asked, but Greynol shook him by the arm.

"No Armond, you are too anxious. I want Leonin and Brenn to go, just close enough to find out to whom they belong," replied Greynol.

"What are you saying? Brenn is no fighter. You wish to send him alone to face an adversary?"

"You forgot about Leonin," answered Greynol. "Together, they are the stealthiest in our group. They will get only as near as needed, but close enough to decide friend or foe."

"Then I will not be far behind," grumbled Armond.

Brenn swallowed hard. Bow in hand he traced Leonin's footsteps up the hill, glad that Greynol felt sure of his skills. The others marched fifty paces behind with Armond at the lead, weapon ready and a fire in his eyes.

The two crept along a dry gully that ran the length of the hill ending near the crest where there was a treeless opening; Leonin's footfalls were silent, while Brenn's but slight. Hiding behind thickets that lined the rounded hilltop the voices became clear. Arrows flitted, they went as far as they dared to go; staring between the brambles a large fire came into view surrounded by several men.

Brenn slunk behind a tree and bent low. "I count five," he whispered.

The men sat in full view dressed in dusky cloaks with hoods pulled back, save one; and boots, mud splattered and leather worn. Seven horses stood tied on the opposite side. The men drank and laughed, spat and cursed in a loud conversation:

"...I'm wearin' thin in waitin'. I need to get my hands on that promised booty – you know, a deal's a deal," said one, bearing a thick black beard and a long braid that twisted about his tattooed neck.

"What do you plan to do with yer share?" sniffed another with crimson locks and scars on his face.

"It's all planned, Red. I'm gonna buy me a woman up in Barrimir, and some choice swill, not this rotgut Gandol wine."

"Go back to yer own wife, fool Narm. How many do you need anyhow?".

"Maybe I'll go to Barrimir wit' you. They'll buy those nag cobs from us, then we'll snag some hard stuff, eh," slurred the third, a huge unkempt man with a flask in hand. He stumbled forward into the firelight – Brenn found his look sinister.

"Good plan, eh, Cedric? An' you Red…mind yer manners. I'll take as many wives as I choose, lessin' one tries to rope me down for good."

"Bah, yer both drunken fools."

A forth man, an older balding brigand with a look no less threatening, started up with a mocking cackle. "That's sayin' we get paid at all. This ol' sneak 'ere keeps us reassured, but his word sounds no differ' than what we've 'eard before," he laughed, pointing to a hooded fellow seated with his back to Leonin and Brenn. "We don't need promises – gold speaks truth 'ere."

The hooded man let his black-handled dagger settle into a gloved hand. "I don't care what you have heard before; if my benefactor's plans go forward, as discussed, you will each be justly compensated," he replied in a thick accent.

"Bah, too much left to chance, isn't there?" mocked the older bandit. "Back in Thalon, Ubar's cronies thought they were chasing ghosts. Why waste time floating after a rumor – we've other jobs to do. They have a need for fresh horses in Brodden, or even Roallin if we're careful."

"If we ain't careful that bleedin' Bardol guard might put the clamps on us for good," returned Cedric, spilling part of his mug on an already stained shirt. "It's bad enough to be playin' against the border again. I'd rather steal from that friend of yers since we're fixin' to go all the way to see him. Take his booty, then we can hang low in Lyle."

"You fear the Bardol guard more than my associate's power?" asked the cloaked man, a sardonic smile hidden within his hood.

"Then I must ride with fools. Rather you should live out in this wilderness and eat bark than cross a sorcerer. You choose death, my friend, and I can make it happen sooner."

The man's grip tightened on his dagger, causing Red to shake and stutter.

"Now...now, let-let's not get all upset. Cedrics just talkin' 'cause he's drunk," he replied, rubbing his forehead. "We've got nothin' against yer associate."

"Then why do you go against his desires by stealing horses when you have a job to do? We have a short time to get back into Ainiald and make our move. Or should I take care of business alone?"

"Hold on now, we ain't gonna let good pickins' go by. We're low on money as it is, and there are plenty of ripe steeds over those hills. Yer boss is just gonna have to wait his turn," replied the massive Narm, jumping to his feet. The tattoos upon his neck bulged as he pointed in the face of the hooded man who returned no motion.

"Now this is all wrong. Sit down Narm!" called Red, worried about a confrontation.

"We all took an oath – a blood oath."

"Yes, Raugulon blood, no turning back now. Our friend is here for a reason, Narm, let him speak; or maybe I should give you a boot of my own," said the older fellow, concerned more over losing a paying job than actual bloodshed. With a homely smile, he slid nearer the hooded man upon the log they shared.

"Now friend, when do we make our move? And where?"

The man slid his dagger back into its hidden sheath. Leonin caught a glimpse of his black mustache and goatee as he turned, and dark eyes that glowed like embers beneath his cloak.

"Wait and see. If the one we seek rides among the mercenaries, Ubar's men will let us know; although our meeting in Ristle brought no news. Ubar has spies following the company, and perhaps another who is closer to the situation. But I have my doubts since our pursuant friend spoke to more than one party up north. If this turns out to be true and he travels alone or with others, we shall await them in Roallin — there you can kill them all, save the one we seek."

Cedric flopped down upon a stump and raised his flask. "I hope you're right, Dorrish-man, it's been too long and I ain't killed since Larin last winter..."

Brenn muffled a gasp.

"I've heard enough," whispered Leonin.

"Thieves and cutthroats of the worst kind," muttered Brenn, backing out of the thicket.

They scrambled back down to meet the others waiting just below the crest. Armond stood by anxiously, crossbow in hand and sword dangling now upon a ring at his side. Greynol signaled they all come lower, well out of earshot, where he waited.

"Speak to us. Who are they?" asked an impatient Armond.

"Five men, just like the visitors Harifin described that came to his door. They were coarse and talked as thieves and murderers, and they spoke of looking for someone from 'up north'. 'Our pursuant friend,' the sneaky one said," answered Brenn.

Greynol glanced towards the crest. "Harifin mentioned a thieves road near here, one to avoid the Arrither and skirt the East-Wilds. We must be near it now. You both have done well," he said, placing a hand on Brenn's shoulder to calm him.

"Let us waste no more time, we can take them by surprise," said Armond, his foot upon the slope. Greynol quelled his charge.

"No, Armond, you do not understand the enemy. Darkness is their home — theirs is the advantage here," said Greynol in a low, but firm tone.

"But there are only five, and we have crossbows and arrows," replied Zerrin.

Greynol turned to Leonin. "How many horses did you see?"

"Seven were tethered on the north crest — saddled and ready to depart. I understand now your asking."

"Yes, there are seven men: two must wait out of sight just in case of ambush, and possibly with poisoned darts. Trust what I tell you, we must return to camp."

"And just leave them be? Even you called them the enemy," pleaded Armond, unmoved by the threat. But the sound of poison weapons made them all think twice.

"Nothing is certain; even so, just men cannot move upon another unprovoked."

"But they are planning evil," replied Brenn.

"Undoubtedly, but wisdom speaks of its own justice. Leave them to fate for now," finished Greynol, the certainty in his voice convincing enough to send them back to camp, although grudgingly. Only the small light of Drago's lamp was permitted, and then only concealed behind a tree so not to be seen from above. Leonin continued to explain what they had witnessed:

"Brenn was correct in calling them thieves and cutthroats, for they spoke of such things. There seemed a leader among them, one cloaked in black; he handled an assassin's dagger and his accent ran thick – one of the others called him *Dorrishman*. He has sought another since Thalon, but he said not who or why. These foul men hope to take him and kill the others in his party."

"This is grave talk indeed," replied Greynol, "but not our concern."

Rogan nearly jumped out of his skin. "What are you saying? They must be speaking of you – and us! Your capture and our deaths," he cried, flustered and pink in the cheeks.

"We must leave them alone, for now. The night is for evil, and I am against risking my men and this journey for petty scoundrels. The road ahead brings peril enough. Add a man to the watch tonight while the others rest. I am certain our visitors will soon depart to ride out the night, only to steal away the daylight hours hiding elsewhere. Such is the way of the thief."

"We may regret passing this opportunity," said Drago.

"Rest your thoughts;" replied Greynol, "we go by the light of day."

Leonin, Brenn, and Greynol took over the watch while the others slept. Brenn was far too awake to try and rest, and Greynol had much to ponder; otherwise, it was unusual that he would take a turn beside the fire. His decision to remain where they were upset the others, but he had concerns about a further movement east at night, and the southern forest remained an option no one favored. Through the early hours of morning, they could hear calls and drunken rants from above; at one point Leonin caught the sound of hooves that seemed to circle the knoll then fade away, and afterwards, silence.

Morning arrived to find Andro, Armond, and Drago sound asleep and leaning against each other. It was Saturday and the seventh day since Andro left his home, and it was home he dreamed of that night: Audin and Belma, Uncle Breden, Randa, and all the joys of summer in Logan. Then he felt alone, at once standing upon the crest of a high hill. A cold wind wrapped about his body, and he could not shake the chill. He sought a fire, but there was none to bring him comfort. Andro awoke to find the others gathered in discussion: he learned quickly of the decision to search the crest in daylight. What they discovered were only the charred embers of a fire and a broken keg of ale. Leonin found the tracks of horses following a northern path.

"They departed the same direction they came; northward and away from the Arrither Road," he said, examining fresh hoofprints. He led them to a landing beneath the crest where the horses were tied, kneeling before fresh boot-prints in the earth. "Greynol was correct. At least two waited here out of sight. There are scatterings of pipe-leaf and wood shavings to show they remained a while."

"Odd, they seemed concerned with only the northern approach, ignoring the Arrither altogether," said Andro who kicked through the leaves looking for more traces.

"They were concerned with their own kind. Thieves have few loyalties, even out in the wild," replied Greynol.

Armond sniffed. "Why do we trek where they do not?"

"We are not thieves. We have less to fear."

"I hope letting them go won't prove a mistake."

"Like I told you earlier, leave these men to providence. Now pack your things and prepare to ride – the day awaits," Greynol replied, starting away.

A second day upon the Arrither Road bore them deeper into the wilderness. East of the knoll, they entered a wide valley with hills skirting each side. A dense forest overtook the trail overshadowing the sun above, but offered small relief from the heat. The path narrowed and the pace slowed: rocks, roots, and furrows made every misstep unforgiving. The men kept a wary eye out for the thieves; their ears strained to hear the sound of advancing hooves. A strange new feeling of watchfulness came over them, and it offered little comfort; although Leonin was certain they no longer traversed Laichenrowe land.

Along a wider stretch of forest, Armond pulled beside Andro and his ride, Ambarr, which appeared like bronze in sunlight. Armond's black giant, Calhurg, found little welcome as the two bit and kicked at each other, strangely disturbed by the heat, the bumpy trail, and pervasive feelings of threat even the horses could sense.

"Calm down now, Ambarr, what's gotten into you? Calhurg is going to bite back," called Andro, stroking his steed's smooth neck.

"Shall I pull back?" asked Armond.

"No, stay put, he'll get over it. Ambarr is a warm-blood, but seldom acts this way. Gairinrul and Toryche have calmer dispositions – the other horses no better. I don't know what is wrong with them today."

"I was going to ask the same thing about you. You have said little since breakfast."

"I'm tired and sore," replied Andro, flexing his tense back. "I've traveled before, but never on so hard a trail."

"Is that it?"

Andro sighed. "No, not all. After last night's events I was caught by surprise; my guard was let down and I feared the worst. I never expected to find an enemy out here in the wilderness."

"You are not in Logan anymore," reminded Armond, but his

smile was full of reassurance. "Overcome your fears, just as I do. I will fight at your side, and together we will get out of any scrape put upon us. Our swords will ring with the pride of the North."

Armond sat tall in the saddle as a breeze swept through his long hair: he resembled the valiant Turrar warriors of northern lore riding off into battle. Andro drew upon his friend's courage.

After several leagues, the road grew wide and even and the horse's pace picked up. By days end they climbed out of the nameless lower valley and entered a rugged land of hollows and steep-walled glens. As the sun set against a burning red sky, they found themselves winding along the floor of a tucked away gully where boulders hung upon stone cliffs supported by the broad cedars and hemlocks that scattered beneath. Here the Arrither cut a twisted path, climbing through a land formed of stone and forest. The aroma of pine needles rose up from the earth; the horse's hooves where muted upon its carpet.

Greynol was cautious now in the twilight, searching for a familiar sight. The others felt unease as they went, if not for the simple fact that it was the perfect spot for an ambush.

"Greynol, will we find a place to stop soon, or else we might ride off of the trail in the dark?" called Drago from the rear.

"I remember now, just a moment or two more. Light your lantern if you wish. The years have changed some things, but not all," replied the Acolyte.

Brenn rode in the middle of the pack. Gazing about his anxiety gave way. "Leonin, how are those eyes of yours working? I get the feeling we are being watched; in fact, I've felt it much of the day," he said oddly enough, except for the fact that they all sensed the same thing.

Leonin looked about and took a deep breath.

"I do not know. It feels as if we are being scrutinized, searched indiscriminately; but nothing has shown itself."

"...I stand corrected, here we are," interrupted Greynol, who paid no attention to their concerns. He led them off the road onto a narrow trail where they came suddenly upon a shear rock wall.

Along its base, they found a wide gap, and within, a natural open space framed between twelve-meter tall cliffs.

Drago entered first, lantern in hand burning brightly. The gap was skinny at first, allowing one at a time, and then opened to form a large oval-shaped shelter. The floor was made of coarse sand with a natural fire-pit in its center. To the rear of the grotto was a narrower exit; a tight squeeze for a horse, but passable if the necessity arose.

"Small relief should it rain; otherwise, this is as good a place as any to set camp," said Greynol with a smile of recollection. "Our light will remain hidden from the road, so you need not worry about last night's interruption."

Drago held up his lamp so that it reflected against the periphery – a bright glow against the yellow rock wall. "So you have been here before?" he asked.

"Yes Drago, but not for many years. I judge from recent fires it still is known."

Andro spread his blanket upon the ground; a layer pine needles to carpet the sand. The warmth of the fire removed any need for cover. The others did likewise, filling the enclosure, but few were ready for sleep. The night sky opened overhead, but the feeling of discontent grew.

"Greynol, how do you know we are safe here? It is so dark away from the fire," asked Brenn, shivering as if a cold wind were upon his back.

"Because you are with me and my time of challenge is yet to arrive. Be at peace, Mister Linderfell – all of you." But Greynol's advice fell on deaf ears.

A dreadful black seemed to descend outside the firelight. Leonin was alerted to something behind the trees upon the cliff. He started for his bow, but Greynol signaled him to be still. A strange growl came out of the shadows, but none could tell its position.

"Whatever it is, we are without cover down here. Shall I douse the fire?" asked Drago in a whisper, clearly startled.

"Leave it alone," replied Greynol in a calm voice. "Now, all of you gather about."

The Acolyte reached into his pocket and pulled out a smooth round stone that glowed in the firelight.

"What is it?" they each asked.

"A Timlet Stone, an ancient relic held sacred by those given over to Fasduen," he replied, holding it out in his open hand. "Allow me to speak of its origin."

They listened as he told the story of the treble-blessed stones, frequently distracted by the sound of growls and scratching out in the black. Yellow eyes scrutinized them above the cliff, searching from the darkness.

They marveled as the once opaque stone turned translucent, burning orange in reflectance of the blaze. As if in rebellion, the noises from the shadows increased. The stone then turned white with an inner fire of its own, and soon the light permeated every niche of the shelter walls, flashing even unto the trees atop the cliff. Andro imagined a star came to rest in Greynol's palm, swallowed within its magnificent light.

A sudden wail arose outside its radiance, which swiftly fell away. Then came the sound of a great rushing wind, like that of powerful wings that slowly faded into the distance. The stone returned to its normal state and the light dissipated, leaving only the crackle and glow of the fire. Greynol smiled and placed the stone back into his pocket without saying another word, and so ended their second day upon the Arrither Road.

Chapter Eight – the Haunt of Dagoraust

Andro awoke early to find to Greynol and Leonin conversing in low voices beside the fire. The others slept soundly nearby out in the open upon unrolled blankets. The sky above had grown shapeless and gray, hinting of rain – Andro frowned at the prospect of a wet ride. Reaching for his water flask, he took a seat between the two.

"Sleep well, son?" asked Greynol in a warm voice, reminding Andro of home and his father Audin.

"Very well, thank you. Almost as if we never left Harifin's," he replied, turning his gaze towards Leonin. To Andro's surprise, he held the Timlet Stone in his hand.

"What were you both talking about?"

"Many things, Andro. The past, the future, our journey so far, and what may be to come," replied Greynol, receiving the artifact back from Leonin.

"Last night remains fresh in my mind – I felt frightened and calm all at once. The stone chased off whatever came out of the darkness."

"There are evil powers in this world and they are combated by the good. Such battles occur in the heart as well," replied Greynol, speaking as a thoughtful teacher.

Andro lowered his eyes. "I understand what you are saying, and that reminds me of something I hoped to speak to you about, but had not the chance."

"What burdens you?"

"Since Harifin's house I meant to bring up the occasion of the scroll, to apologize once more for going behind your back to look at it. My actions were wrong...I am certain we all feel this way now," replied Andro with sincerity, but his eyes showed doubt at the last.

"I explained to Greynol my own feelings concerning the matter — how fear of the unknown drove me to err," added Leonin.

Greynol understood well the effect of the spell upon the young men. "May your contrition bring you peace and mitigate the darkness of this curse; for just as the scroll is wrought in evil, the power of the stone is from light, which is greater," he replied.

"What of its power? Can it help to us help fight the enemy later on?" asked Andro.

"Timlet Stones are not weapons; on the contrary, they are a sign of Fawarra. Like any holy relic, they are a reminder, not created for misuse. They remind one of solemnity in daily life," answered the Acolyte, but Andro did not understand.

Reading his thoughts, Greynol handed Andro the smooth stone. He graciously accepted, examining the opaque artifact that shone with an inner light, as if the sun were behind it. And it felt warm in his hands.

"I have never seen one of these before yesterday."

"They are a rare find; a forgotten vestige of days long past," replied Greynol. "Prelates hold some within their possession, but we acolytes favor their graces most since they carry well within our frocks. We believe firmly in the tradition I spoke of last evening, that the stones be thrice blessed by Fawarra himself: first, by the words of Fawarra in an age called *Durronduen Sire*; secondly, by the blood swollen waters of the Tuirowan Straights that claimed the slain Fasduen who was cast into the sea; and thirdly, by Fasduen himself, who arose from the depths and first set foot upon the Tuirowan shore. This comes from the faith of the Patriarchs and is handed down to us through the Tuirowan observance."

"This is a whole world of which I know little. In Logan, such outward signs are mainly shunned, but I do not know why. Loganders have good hearts – good but reserved," replied Andro.

"My race rejects the claim of the Fasduen story," muttered Leonin with a downward glance; "the Lay of Tuirowe disturbs my people greatly. *Durronduen Sire*, the Age of the Gifts of Fawarra, remains a time shrouded in suffering. Farrian have languished far from their homeland, exiled from the Farria-Sire to search for the *Jewels of Firdom* – the wise gifts of Fawarra. The greatest of these remain in our keeping, divided between the four Farrian realms, and thus we serve in obedience. I await my call to serve the Orisduen, the Gift of the Lanfersi; to become its guardian is one of our greatest honors."

"But my people are divided," he continued, "and some lost as with the Laichenrowe and Farilliare. There is a growing disquiet between the Lanfersi, Sindelware, and Falliscade, those whom bear the greatest of the Jewels, that Asenrael may forsake their charge and also become lost."

"You spoke of this before, but I did not understand what you meant by it. Would war drive Asenrael into hiding?" asked Andro.

"Not into hiding, but lost indeed," Leonin answered, and his appearance turned grave. "There is a growing concern that the King of Asenrael usurps ownership over the great jewel, the Rindurron, which no one man can claim. Troubled is the rule of King Halphun."

Greynol stood in readiness to wake the others and begin their ride. "The answers to these questions must await another day. Let us rouse these slumbering warriors – I hope to be far along by mornings end," he said, throwing a precarious glance to the gray skies. Soon the camp came alive as the others greeted the new day.

A third morning's ride into the wilderness began early as Greynol's Alliance moved in haste for fear of a storm: the sky darkened as they went, but the rain never came. In short order the hill country disappeared behind them with its rocks and glens, giving way to a flat plain scattered with groves of dark trees separated by fields of wild-grass and thicket. A mile to the north ran low mounds paralleling the road, covered in forest; and to the south, a chain of bare crags like boulders piled upon each other, more distant, yet ominous to look upon.

Greynol continued his eastern push – a destination known by him alone. The road ran slightly higher that the land about it, and by mid-day warm dank air rose up from marshes and bogs they crossed. The air smelled of rot and swarmed with flies. In the sullen sky above, ravens took wing and vultures circled searching for a meal.

"I hope we are clear of this stink by day's end," grumbled Andro to his riding partner.

"Damn these flies, too!" cursed Armond. "I slept at peace last night, waking much too soon. Any hope Greynol might find some new magic to help us tonight?"

Andro threw him a glance of irony. "Magic? Greynol is an Acolyte, not a magician. If you refer to last night's events, there was no sorcery involved at all, just the faith of one holy man and a blessed stone."

"You understand these things better than me. Greyhoods have a place in Nordhiem, always have, but never were their actions anything less than peculiar. Greynol serves his Fawarra, but Turrar have gods too; although I never seen one do anything like I saw last evening."

Andro returned a smirk.

To no one's delight, they crossed from the marsh into a grove of black-barked trees – leaves like ivy displayed a brown underside that stung the nose with their reek. There was a strange ugliness about them, old and onerous; Andro found it strange, for the first time in his young life, he loathed the forest. Just beyond a pair of white pillars flanked the road on either side: a marked entrance into a strange place.

"We are here men, Dagoraust. Stay together and I will see if lodging awaits," called Greynol to strange looks from the company. They found his humor rare and quite odd. Gazing north, there were heaps of crumbled buildings and once proud ancient walls, and to the south, a green bog.

"You will find only broken homesteads closest the road," he continued, "but over this rise there is solid shelter. They are good enough for a night's stay, although thoroughly plundered. And a word of warning: the dead held prominent rank in 'Old Dagoraust'."

"We am not sure what you mean, but lead on sage. And a suitable well would be nice, unless swamp water is all we have to drink aside from our flasks," replied Drago, too hot and tired to worry over the unknown. Greynol turned off the Arrither Road and headed northward onto a wide broken thoroughfare.

Armond hesitated, letting the others pass into the ruins. A strange sight caught his eye in the distance, although it disappeared as soon as it came. He dismounted and turned towards the southern mountains in hopes it would appear again.

"What are you looking at?" asked Andro from behind. He broke off from the others to join his friend. He did not like the ideal of leaving anyone alone in that place.

"There it is, I saw it again. Something strange roams that mountain," replied Armond, pointing to the southernmost peak, which was tallest of the crags and completely barren of vegetation. Andro watched at his side, wondering what he was supposed to look for, when it came again.

"I see it now, a firelight moving back and forth upon that bald ridge – first in one place, then other. Now it is gone again."

Armond smacked his fist in frustration. "If only we had the time to investigate: it is much too large for torch-fire, and too quick for a man. Maybe give us an answer to last night's mystery."

"It is more than a league away," replied Andro, returning to his mount. He was relieved when Armond did the same. "Come along before the others forget about us."

Greynol led them into the heart of a dead city. Beyond a small climb houses became numerous, each broken and worn, overgrown with thorny weeds and ivy. The street veered to the right where a monument of ebony stone awaited them, like a brooding sentinel. The four-sided monolith raised to a height no less than forty feet, set thick at the base, tapering to a broad point; its north-east facing corner was cut at the top, forming an angle in the shape of a diamond. They passed slowly beneath its shadow, entering a wide avenue framed by massive stone buildings: rows of windowless structures supported by broad columns, well intact, culminated at road's end by a blue-domed pantheon.

Acting with one mind, they hastened towards the domed building, the tallest of any structure in Dagoraust. Formed of a perfect square, granite stairs rose to an encircling portico where six columns flanked each side: one hundred feet in height, the columns supported the massive sky-blue dome. Doors of solid bronze sealed the front portal, its only entrance, save a strange hole in the roof of the dome, barely two meters across that looked ill made. On each end of the building stood conical shaped bunkers, three on a side, with a single opening in the front, barely large enough for a man to enter.

"These were once grain silos, but the doors have been broken away," said Greynol as they approached the Great Dome. "I have spent more than one night inside these. They make for a clean dry shelter in a pinch."

"Surely you don't expect us to sleep in one of those things; we do have horses to keep," replied Brenn in disbelief.

"Do not fret, Mister Linderfell, a pen makes for a poor berth. Look, there is a wooden shelter nearby, between those silos and the foundation of the next edifice. A well house once stood there, now destroyed as it once was. From the look of things, someone tried to built it back up – another failed attempt to resettle 'Old Dagoraust'," replied Greynol. He dismounted, making a deliberate move toward the opposite side where a plank-walled shanty stood. The others looked at it with bewilderment, for it was but a shack among palaces.

"But what of these other places?" asked Zerrin, "they look like solid shelter to me, just by their size alone."

"And how about that domed building?" added Armond.

"No!" snapped Greynol suddenly. "Of all the places in Dagoraust, the Grand Dome is its own. They sealed it long ago, those who crafted such doors that regarded burglars as nothing, and they have never been opened since. No man has ever entered that place and returned to speak of it. There is a hole in the dome, as you can see, caused by means beyond my learning; but if your desire is to climb those sheer columns and towering dome, only to drop inside by rope, then I cannot help you. As for the other buildings, thieves have tried them all with minimal success – my advice is to stay right here in the well house."

Greynol's recommendation felt more a consternation, and the party gave in to his wishes. But the young men had better ideals in mind: Brenn for one wanted nothing more than to leave that place; he felt a storm brewing in the air, but it was the dome he feared most.

"It is empty now and a bit cramped; not much room to lay out blankets about the cistern. But the waters smell clean and there is a chimney for a fire," said Leonin, returning after a quick peek inside. "There is also a makeshift stable out back – an open porch attached to the rear with a trough and some hay for the horses."

"Then we have it. Several hours of daylight remain and there is work to be done; so before we settle in let us get things secure. You will find stormy weather a frequent occurrence in Dagoraust after dark," replied Greynol. He immediately began doling out chores.

"Drago and Zerrin find some buckets or earthenware and fetch us water in the pool below, there you can dip your buckets; Leonin and Rogan, prepare the stable for the horses – you say there is ample hay, then someone planned on keeping livestock and provisions here; as for Brenn, he and I will prepare a fire and clean our 'living space'; and lastly, Andro and Armond will tend the horses. There is a lawn behind the well house. Follow the wall to an opening where you will find grass and a pond out in the graveyard."

Not even Greynol thought he could get away with mention of such a place, but he tried.

"Graveyard, sir? We do have them in Honodolch, unlike Vanyor, whose pyres give me the butterflies. But with everything that's been mentioned already – I mean to say, how can we remain here, this place is called *the Haunt* after all?" asked Brenn who could barely contain his anxiety. Greynol did not ease his fears.

"Where shall we go, friend? Beyond the city, the swamps are thick with flies and stench. Or do we ride 'till evening and stay out in the open? I told you about the storms."

"We'll stay put right here, or perhaps Brenn needs some convincing," growled Armond, shaking a fist in his face.

"Just find me a broom," he muttered.

A short time and several chores later found Armond seated upon a fractured stone column in the middle of an ancient overgrown necropolis. Andro paced nearby, searching the granite markers and gray worn crypts, now broken and looted of their contents. The horses grazed at peace near an iron fence that circled the burial ground, having first sated their thirst in a nearby brook.

Andro took great intrigue in the place, running his hand across the gravestones and their odd writings, none that he could interpret: inscriptions were worn, but many featured runes and detailed drawings of the sun, moon, and stars. Crypts remained as they were with steel gates pried away, littered with clothing, tapestries, and in some instances, bone.

"You should see this one, Armond," called Andro, sticking his head inside a large vault. "If I had a torch I'd be able to make out the body inside. Someone has broken the stone and robbed it of everything of value."

"That's alright," mumbled a dejected Armond, turning his head in disgust. "Why are you snooping there anyway?"

"Nothing to fear here," replied Andro, making his way back. "It's an impressive place, quite unlike like the crowded plots in Logan. Big stones to honor Nevander Hall and some of the founders, but nothing so grand as these."

"And nothing at all like what we have in Vanyor. Strange people lived here in Dagoraust, and if you ask me, graveyards are bad luck. From the looks of it, bad luck *had* befallen them."

Andro shrugged his shoulders, returning a glance to the largest mausoleum that stood in the center of the graveyard hill. "Greynol was right – they put at lot of thought towards the dead. Whomever visited this place since its demise had no trouble stealing what they could."

"Burning is better, better than being disgraced by thieves. The ashes of our dead rise to the arms of Turramitral where we too become the stars of heaven, if found worthy," replied Armond.

Andro turned towards the gate. "Ah, here come Rogan and Leonin now. Hopefully to relieve us, or gather us for supper."

"I'm not so sure, it is still early for dinner and they carry their bows."

Rogan and Leonin strode up the hill in their direction, seemingly ready for a hunt.

"Everything is finished below – everything except dinner. And some fresh meat would be nice," said Rogan with his hunting bow in hand and a quiver of arrows on his back.

"As long as we get back by dusk. That was Greynol's warning," added Leonin.

Armond leaned on his fist dejected. "And that leaves us here watching the horses…not that Andro's been much company," he muttered. "He's spent most of his time talking to the dead, and I'm left here to fend for myself. But I'm not moving. This is where I'll stay – right here until dinner is ready,"

"Oh, never mind Armond and his exaggerations. I find this place intriguing, and very strange. I believe these crypts once contained treasure, but anything of value has long been removed by grave-robbers," replied Andro.

"Can you blame them, a lost kingdom and no one to claim ownership," said Rogan. "I for one would like to find something of value."

Leonin was less venturesome. "Leave things be, that is my advice. Who knows if anything in Dagoraust can be claimed," he said in reply. Armond agreed, looking over his shoulder towards the well house.

"There's chimney smoke; maybe they found something worth cooking besides boiled potatoes."

"Come on, Leonin, let's scare up something for the pot. You said you heard a turkey calling earlier in the backwoods," said Rogan.

"And now I just saw them, creeping in a line along the hillside brush. Follow me, Rogan, quiet as housecats if you want any luck in the hunt. Turkeys have an odd sense about them, but the wind is in our favor," he replied. They jogged down through the northern gate and slipped silently into the forest.

Leonin climbed over a fallen portion a wall: a granite portal set between the black iron bars of the fence. He followed along a stream bank until reaching the base of the pantheon, which was near; its blue vault hidden high above the massive columns. Rogan tried to match his stealth from behind. A wooded gully ran away from the place into the hillside where Leonin first spotted the birds.

"Our game should be near; watch for them behind the thicket," he whispered with an arrow notched and ready. Crouching low, they marched up a steep slope. The call of a tom roused their attention. And suddenly, behind a hedgerow, appeared a dozen birds marching in a line between the bayberry and winter-bush.

"Don't wait for me," said Rogan, fumbling with his weapon.

Leonin fired, bringing down a large tom before it could react. In a flurry of wings, Rogan managed a shot of his own, felling a hen that dropped away behind a thicket – the rest scattered in every direction.

"Excellent! and enough time to get one on the fire tonight," called a joyous Rogan.

"A late meal, perhaps," replied Leonin, "now get your kill. It flew straight back over the brush."

Rogan stumbled through the bracken like a hound on a scent trail. His vision obscured, he tripped over a stone and rolled down a steep bank, ending with a loud thump. Leonin left his catch to find him seated at the bottom of a muddy landing. "Are you alright?" he called.

"Yes, I'm fine...I think. Lucky to avoid falling in," he replied, brushing the leaves off his shirt. "I don't know what this stone is, but it might have killed me had I struck it."

Leonin glanced over the edge to find a tree uprooted and leaning to one side, a victim of a recent storm; its great roots pulled away the earth to expose a stone slab halfway ajar from the opening it covered.

Rogan ran his hand along its smooth edge. "Rain has washed the dirt away. It seems to have exposed a cave," he said.

Leonin leapt down for a look, and found the entrance much too uniform to be natural.

"This is no cave, but a hewn-out tunnel," he said, hand held flat against the slab as he peered in. "It seems wide enough for one to enter at a time; a place as old as the rest of Dagoraust. But why is it apart?"

"Only one way to find out," answered Rogan as he slipped through the crack.

"Be careful. You don't know what is in there."

"Treasure, I hope."

He unsheathed his sword, standing within a small vault that disappeared into a blackened corridor. He stepped forward and stumbled over something in the shadows. Reaching out his hand he let out a shout.

"What is wrong?" called Leonin as he leapt through the opening, dagger in hand.

Rogan knelt upon the stone floor, examining a corrupt skeleton that guarded the entrance; its tattered red tunic covered in cobwebs, as were the sandals upon its boney feet. There were others similarly dressed, lying in state along niches that lined the low tunnel. In the dim light of the opening, they could see tarnished swords upon their breasts and arms folded beneath.

"Most have been looted, but not all," said Rogan.

"The barrow has been opened only a short time. The outside air has begun to deteriorate what centuries had preserved," said Leonin at his back.

"I would like to have a look about first – find a keepsake of a forgotten realm."

"Do as you please. I for one will touch nothing that belongs to the dead."

Rogan turned and smiled. "But Leonin, that's what adventures are for."

Rogan found an extinguished torch on the floor and held it as Leonin struck a flint; an orange flame rose up giving the tunnel an ominous glow while pushing away the shadows.

"It's not long. I can see the rear wall, or so it seems, no more than fifty paces ahead," said Rogan, searching this way and that, careful to avoid the remains of a man lying halfway off its niche and onto the floor.

At the end of the passage, they found a small circular room without exit: there, upon two marble thresholds, were the resting places for its pair of inhabitants. Upon the right a smaller body lay dressed in a long blue gown, the hue of the cities dome, laced with golden-thread; the dress was torn in several places and the figure now lay upon its side, skeletal arms hanging off its berth. The corpse upon the left, thoroughly violated, lay upon the floor, headless and unclothed; a rusted helmet placed where the head should be, and broken links of silver chain were strewn about the chamber.

"Someone had difficulty removing its adornment. What a pity to witness such defilement," said Leonin gravely. "This one was a man, that much is plain; the other his wife. If royalty, these others must have been a sworn guard. We of the Lanfersi have a similar custom of burial, although our King and Queen reside in the distant Falliscade. Our men, those honored to the of service of guarding our great jewel, await burial within one of the common vaults that surround the Orisduen, forever to guard her flanks."

Rogan noticed the manner the Farrian spoke of his heritage, with fullness of respect, bowing his head at the mention of the *Orisduen*.

"In the name of honor, if this man and woman were once a king and queen, they have been disgraced – their crowns are gone," he continued.

"As well as *his* head," smirked Rogan with disregard. "Anything of value here is long gone. I will take a guard's sword, if you don't mind. It will only turn to rust now."

Leonin shrugged his shoulders and returned to the entrance.

Rogan paused at the first body nearest the Royal Chamber, and removed a gleaming blade from where it sat across the dead man's chest. Then he unbuckled the belt and scabbard from its waist. In the struggle of pulling the belt away, a key fell to the floor from its closed hand, previously hidden. Rogan picked it up and stuffed it into a pocket, then ran out of the tunnel to catch up.

By dusk the party settled into meager comforts within the well house: the smell of wild turkey set to roast on a spit above the fire, despite its gaminess, was the one true comfort of home in that strange place. The horses grazed in the makeshift stable on hay piled along a stone trough: they stamped and neighed, tethered to a fence rail, uneasy at the approach of night.

Munching on crusty bread between slurps of a watery potato soup, the men listened to Rogan and Leonin tell their tale of the hillside chamber and the finding of Rogan's new sword, which passed with great interest between them: a broad-bladed weapon of fair design, inscribed with a blazing sun and half-moon, it tapered down to a deadly point. Armond admired its ancient handiwork, possibly Kuirian in design, which he wondered. Rogan made no mention of the key.

Night came on deep and disquieting. Swallows that earlier

flitted the great buildings where now gone from sight and sound. The wind picked up from the west upon billowing clouds that mingled with the sound of thunder. Lanterns were hung to offer light: one in the well house and the other in the stable entry where it rocked back and forth in a swirling wind. The darkness brought an undesired change to Dagoraust, where earlier they walked about unabated in curiosity, desiring nothing more than to explore a lost realm; but night carried disquiet as the world outside turned to black.

"I apologize, there is no door to shut out the night," said Greynol in his thoughtful manner," but look at it this way, we could have remained out on the trail without shelter." His words did nothing to still the other's anxiety as the storm closed in.

Brays and whinnies revealed the beasts were just as fearful. Andro jumped to his feet. "The horses like this weather no better than me. I'll go and calm them."

He ran quickly to the stable, a gentle hand and whispers to still their fears. Peels of thunder drew close; the steeds paced and neighed in protest, save Gairinrul who stood firm. Andro shivered despite the warmth of its breath against his neck. The open stable gave a clear view of the graveyard, where the trees atop the cemetery mound danced like skeletons in a tempest, and within the shadows of the crypts lurked wild eyes, or Andro thought it so.

The rain came suddenly and a strong wind blew through the open door and stable: every loose article was shaken free and sparks were tossed from the hearth. The wind carried upon it strange disquieting sounds; whispers and howls that echoed throughout Dagoraust, filled with menace. Calls came out of the darkness, but none would dare go out and learn its source. The party huddled together against the far wall, save Andro who remained in the stable, but not for long.

Rogan ignored it all. With great satisfaction, he gazed at his newfound sword. His mind drifted into a waking dream with thoughts of the dead bodies within the chamber. He closed his eyes for a moment, trying to glimpse it better. "The weather worsens, but I am too tired to care. I wish to turn in for now; leave me a later watch if it is for the choosing," he said groggily.

He pulled a cloak over his head and curled up in a corner with a blanket, the sword in its scabbard at his side upon the stone floor.

The others looked on dumbfounded until Greynol spoke up. "Well, that settles that. Choose your watch, by twos; the others should try to get some sleep. We will leave before sunrise."

Andro and Armond volunteered for the first watch and settled beside the fire. "Who can sleep in this weather anyway?" asked Andro. "If my father could see me now, stuck in a most unhappy place with a storm of souls outside – he might say he was right about a lot of things."

"Don't let the elements get to you: there are a lot worse things in Turra Arrither to concern yourself over," replied Armond, stoking the fire with a brand.

"You are no comforter."

"Come now, the rain softens. Let us leave the others to their slumber and sit in the quiet of the night."

Andro wrapped himself in his mantle. "I suppose you are right. The whispers have left us, and that brings me a bit of comfort," he replied.

"Contrary friend. The hunter is quietest when he nears his prey."

With that bit of Turrar wisdom in mind, Andro sat his watch wide-eyed and weary.

One by one, the others drifted off to sleep. Rogan was already deep within an uneasy dream: in his mind the city came alive again, its streets filled with citizens dressed in long robes and sandaled feet; their attention focused upon the domed pantheon with its bronze doors opened wide. Tall men with red tunics bearing golden helms stood guard between the pillars, in their hands bright broadswords and rounded shields painted with the crescent moon. Above, the blue dome stood polished and bright without any sight of damage or opening.

"Come and see," said a voice, and Rogan followed.

Into the Great Dome he went, pausing in the central hall that shone with the light of many fires. An assembly gathered before him, their attention held by a strange glow upon the steps of gilded thrones. Rogan came nearer. There sat a man clothed in crimson and gold, and beside him a woman in a gown of blue – the color of the outer dome. The light of the object shone white upon their faces with indescribable brilliance. The king's look was impassioned, as one brooding over a great treasure.

A man entered the hall from an unseen entrance, a blood-red robe trailing in his wake. The sound of his black staff tapping upon the marble floor drew everyone's notice. The king and queen turned towards the figure, their expressions grave. The crowd backed away from the object of their desire.

"So it is true," called the man in a voice that carried to the roof of the chamber, "you have betrayed the *Corih Thair!* You have dealt with the demon, and the price is death."

Rogan strode forward, as one summoned, seeing as through another's eyes. A broadsword flashed in his hands as he approached the throne. The king recoiled in terror as his blade struck again and again. The king's body fell, devoured by savage wounds.

"Rogan, wake up," came a call with a hand upon his shoulder. He opened his eyes to find Andro standing near. "What were you doing? Do you want to stab yourself?"

Rogan realized at once his arms were crossed over his chest with the sword pointed just below his chin, the same position as the bodies in the catacomb. He immediately shoved the weapon away and it clanged upon the floor.

"What hour is it?"

"About midnight, and time for the second watch – Brenn and you. That is when I noticed the sword. Are you alright?" asked Andro unsure of what to make of it.

"Yes, I'm fine...just cold. I must have caught a chill."

"Well, the fire is still hot and there is a flask to warm your bones," replied Armond with less concern, collapsing on the floor himself. "I'm beat. Do us a favor and wake 'the shrimp'. He can be a handful when he is out cold and snoring."

"I'll manage it. Get some sleep, both of you. I see the rain has ended."

Rogan watched them settle in, still wary over his dream – so real it seemed. He tried to gather his thoughts and wake Brenn whom he found snoring away in a corner.

"Brenn, rise and shine – second watch," he said with a hard shake. Brenn sat up, briefly, with eyes like slits; then he drifted sideways against the wall, propped up and still snoring.

"Don't that beat all? Forget about it, sleep away," whispered Rogan as he reached for the flask of wine that sat in front of the fire; too warm from the heated slab. He managed a long drink and wondered aloud. "What was I dreaming about, anyway?"

Rogan thought for a moment. He lifted the ancient sword off the ground and slid it into the scabbard upon his belt. He stepped out into the street where rainwater filled the cracks of the brick avenue, leftover from the storm. The sky was clearing in the west and a quarter-moon appeared from behind the clouds; its pale light tossed ghostly shadows across the street. The pantheon stood before him, unlike his dream, dark with ivy-covered stairs and bronze doors tarnished and shut. Then he recalled something cold in his pocket.

Rogan fumbled within his pants and removed the large rusted key. As he examined its design, a chill wind blew across his face, waking his senses. "Let's see if this thing works."

He strode towards the prominent structure, looking about to see if eyes were upon him. Satisfied, he strode up the stairs, pausing before the large metal doors. Years of effort proved unsuccessful, for none had crossed the threshold of the Great Dome since it was last shut. A strange magic held the door, but something urged Rogan on. He slid the key into a fine-crafted mechanism – a perfect fit; and then, with a firm twist and a loud clang, he proceeded to unlock the portal. The key became like ice in his hand, and he swiftly stowed it away.

"A spell bound this door; that can be the only explanation," he thought, tugging upon the handle, which gave way and opened for the first time in centuries.

Rogan faced a wall of black. His first uneasy step echoed within the cavernous hall; a floor of polished marble gave away his every movement. The hole of the dome was evident now as a beam of moonlight formed a pale circle in the center of the great room, giving a faint glow. He started forward, the same direction as his dream, towards two thrones in the shadows upon the opposite side. Rogan's mind was set awhirl, he felt awake, yet still within a dream. The hall was empty now: the once spotless floor littered with pieces of rock and rainwater that dripped from the opening above. Mold-covered chairs and a stone table turned on its side blocked his way. Behind the throne, once locked doors, were now broken and set aside; and upon his left, twin-doors nearly flat with the floor, barred the passage below. As one entranced, his attention was drawn to the stairwell.

His movements were contrived, feeling both controlled and in control. Rogan's eyes adjusted to the black. Gazing above, he could see the slight reflections of a gilded dome set with a myriad of golden stars, and in its center, a great crescent moon. The strange hole seemed out of place, off center and not made by deft hands, but by force. Scorch marks spread unevenly about it; likewise, the inside of the bronzed doors had a look of being put to flame. Rogan gripped the new sword, pulling it from its ornate scabbard, and it shone in the feint light that reflected off the floor. He tried the doors to the stairs below, but they would not budge. Instinctively, he slid the sword in-between to pry them open, but they were thrown aside, dropping back on their own as if by unseen hands. A darkened stairway led straight down some twenty-one steps to the bottom. He followed them to the blackness below.

A strange glow met his eyes, emitting from a room within a curved corridor. It was dimly lit, but offered a better invitation than the blackened passages to his left and right. Rogan felt as if eyes watched his every move. He walked slowly towards the chamber and the light seemed to grow; but turning the corner, he jumped back, lifting his sword to strike.

"I thought it was a man," he muttered under his breath, but a second look proved otherwise.

In the room's center stood a rough pedestal covered with cobwebs and dust, and upon it sat a stone that gave off a resonant amethyst glow. Forgetting his fears, Rogan felt compelled to approach the object. No taller than an arrow shaft and as wide as a butcher's knife at its base, the stone tapered to a rough point, cut at the corners and angled on one face in a diamond pattern – it was a match for the monolith they passed when entering the city. But the stone was unique: opaque in translucence, it was as simple as quartz and precious as gemstone. Rogan drew close; the purplish hue reflected off his face. He examined it closely, especially the strange dagger-like mark that pierced its diamond face.

"What a find. I wonder how long has it been here?" he thought. Rogan's mind ran fast with thoughts of grandeur, yet he was apprehensive. "I could carry it out of here, fit it in my large pack. But look, only before a king is it fit, if anyone at all."

In a move that gave him much to think about in times to come, Rogan reached out his left hand to lightly touch its surface. Trembling fingers met with the stone, and it felt strangely warm against his skin, but a sudden jolt sent his arm back as a surge ran throughout his body. Then a strange sigh echoed from a darkened room opposite the entrance.

"Who's there?" whispered Rogan, trying to catch his breath. A murmuring sound returned from the darkness that caused his heart to shudder.

"Who is it?" he asked. He did not expect an answer.

"*Calli-Shurba*," returned a voice from the shadows.

A shrouded figure formed out of the black, taking shape from emptiness. Rogan's heart leapt in his chest, and the sword from the chamber trembled in his hand.

"Who are you?" he gasped.

The figure approached. His robe was crimson, like fresh-spilt blood; the staff he leaned upon gnarled and black. Behind a veil, he hid his face – only a slit remained for terrible dark eyes.

"Archinius, you have returned to me bearing your bane," hissed the specter with a voice that rent Rogan through the heart. "They said you took your life. I knew better. Your will was weak, but faithful to the *Corih Thair*, faithful enough to slay the King with the sword you now bear – a killing sword. Do you await my next command?"

"I...I am not the one you seek. My name is Rogan Pinehurst of Logan," answered Rogan, the words choking in his throat.

"Archinius, no longer shall you deceive me. Whose sword do you hold and whose key is in your pocket? Only the Captain of the Royal Guard bears the key to the outer door."

"You are a shrewd one," he continued. "How is it you escaped the end? The Chamber of the Dead was your home, sealed until the appointed time. Your bane and key your only possessions."

The figure moved forward as it spoke, the stone between he and Rogan, who perceived this was no mere man: its voice struck like a winter's wind, its eyes like a bitter storm, wearing a robe that shimmered as though dipped in blood. In Rogan's mind, the man seemed real and unreal at once.

"Sir, I am not the one you say. I found these items only this afternoon in the barrow along the hillside – I can return them if you wish," he said, lowering his weapon.

"Silence, Archinius! You are a crafty devil, to wait until all was forgotten. Did you think my eyes would yield to sleep? That your transgression is forgotten? You abided your time only to return in disguise. Where is your long hair, your beard? What of this strange tongue? You have returned to steal the jewel, and so your crime remains the same as King Olarius – you have dealt with the demon."

The figure paced around the pedestal as he spoke. Rogan kept his distance, leaving the stone to divide them. He noticed how the specter avoided getting too near it.

"Was it not Olarius whom first desired the *Corih Thair*? Indeed. I read it in his wicked heart. His queen sought a new treasure to hoard; her death was too merciful, as were the others," he spoke again.

"I will leave you be, sir. You have no reason to worry over me – I'll just be going now," replied Rogan, but to no avail.

"*Calli-Shurba!*" the man called out. "You shall remain in my sight, for infidels must be dealt with severely. No man shall remove the *Corih Thair* until the appointed time – the fateful star must wait."

"What do you mean?"

"Do you play against me, Archinius? In what year is it that you return to me like a common thief?"

"What year? It is the summer of 1653, of course."

The specter looked away for a moment to collect its thoughts; Rogan felt the grip of its enchantment relax.

"...Four-hundred years. What is the time? What is the time? Tell me, are the rival kings without heir?" he rattled on maddeningly.

"I do not know what you are talking about," cried Rogan, sweat beading upon his brow. He tried to flee, but he could not move. The sword fell from his hand.

"You have dealt with the demon. You have sold the secret of the Jewel. The *Corih Thair* remains – and so shall you," he said, approaching. The figure tapped his staff upon the floor and suddenly Rogan was clad in the red tunic of the royal guard.

"*Shurba-Kalil!*" he commanded, and Rogan felt his life give way. He dropped to the floor, whispering with his last breath the name, *Greynol*.

The others were fast asleep when Greynol awoke with a start. "What is it?" he asked. "Who called my name?"

He stood up to look about. The night was strangely calm, yet unnerving. Leonin stirred upon hearing his movements.

"Is something wrong, sir?" he asked.

"I do not know. Someone called my name outside of a

dream," answered Greynol now perplexed in the midst of the sleeping men.

"I heard nothing. But since I'm awake, it might be a good time to start the third watch."

"Yes, but who has the second?"

Greynol found Brenn still fast asleep along the wall. He began searching between the sleeping bodies, indiscriminately waking the others as he went. He peered down the cistern, reaching for a lamp to illuminate the deep well.

"What are you looking for? Where is Rogan?" asked Leonin.

Greynol did not answer. He stepped out into the empty street, glancing one way, then towards the Great Dome. Then his face went flush. Leonin saw what the Acolyte feared most: the doors of the Pantheon were open. Greynol's reaction was enough to send a chill into the Farrian's heart. "Be quick, gather the others. Something very wrong has happened."

Soon the party huddled out in the street, disturbed from their rest. But no one cared for sleep once they learned of Rogan's disappearance. "Who saw him last?" asked Armond tightening the belt upon his waist.

"We both did," replied Andro. "Before his watch I awoke him. Remember how he looked as one dead with arms crossed, the sword he found upon his chest. We left him to rouse Brenn, but I assume he never did."

Brenn looked up with tears in his eyes. "I believe he tried, but he left me to sleep, and I did. This is all my fault, I shall go find him."

"No Brenn, something strange has happened here, and before long I expect to hear a full account," replied Greynol, quick to comfort the Mihtrir. "You and Leonin were sent two nights ago upon the hill. This time you both shall remain while the rest of us search for Rogan."

Greynol and the others wasted no time and hastened up the stairs of the Great Dome. "How is it he opened these doors?" asked Andro, barely able to contain his distress.

"I do not know. I have stood at this very threshold while others tried without success. To my knowledge, never have they moved," replied Greynol, lightly pressing his hand against the bronzed entry.

Once inside the main hall, they began searching in every direction. Drago's lantern shed light upon the floor and grime-covered walls. He walked quickly between the broken pieces of furnishings, kicking aside a chair on his way to the rear of the chamber.

"There is a doorway in the back. Should we go through?" he asked.

At that point, Andro found the stairwell on the other side. "No, over here!" he called. "There is a way below. And I hear strange noises – like a great wind blowing."

Greynol was the first to join him at the opening.

"Stay behind me," he warned.

He then led them down the stairwell, retracing Rogan's steps. The strange sounds, like a raging tempest, subsided once they set foot in the corridor. Here they discovered the empty chamber with the stone upon its pedestal, a purplish hue emitting within and about it. The sight gave them awe, but none more than the Kuirian, despite the fact that Rogan was not there.

"What a find! Amethyst of the rarest quality," gasped Drago, approaching it.

"Do not touch it," rebuked Greynol, "we know nothing of its nature or place."

That moment came a sound like a heavy sigh out of the small room opposite the entrance, now lit by candlelight. They rushed to investigate. Upon a small bed lay Rogan, dressed in a red tunic with arms crossed and palms flat upon his chest. The burial sword lay flat across his arms, its point just beneath his chin. His face lost all of its color, and a strange crimson mist hovered above.

"This is how he looked when I woke him earlier," gasped Andro, touching the red tunic. "But what is he wearing?"

Greynol waved aside the heavy mist. "He has been prepared as one dead. Help me to wake him. Prop him up while I attend to this malady."

Armond and Andro gingerly lifted Rogan by the shoulders.

"What afflicts him so?" asked Andro.

"Death," replied Greynol, "a killing spell lay heavy upon him."

He pulled a small vial of oil from his pouch, and upon opening it, released a pervasive scent that cleared the air. He touched Rogan's forehead with the oil, his lips, and then pulling down the tunic, rubbed some on his chest.

"Is there life left in the boy?" asked Drago, sadness in his eyes.

"Yes, but death closes in. Perhaps none of us are safe. Now take this garment off and throw aside that sword."

They did as he asked, then Greynol removed a second vial from his pouch containing small white clumps. Taking a pinch, he placed it on Rogan's tongue.

"That looks like salt – if ever I saw it," remarked Zerrin.

"Blessed salt to stimulate his senses and heal his mind. Prelate Wetherton was good enough to give me some before I departed Thalon," replied Greynol.

Rogan's face grew flush and lifeblood rushed into his frozen limbs. His body began to shake uncontrollably. Suddenly, his eyes opened and he turned to gaze at the others.

"Greynol – friends, so glad am I to find you here in my nightmare. I thought this was the end," he said weeping.

"I heard your call. But we are not out of trouble just yet. I fear there is no other way out, save through the chamber. Then you can tell us how this came to be."

They helped Rogan to his feet when came another noise, like the sound of a rushing wind. A brilliant luminance circled the podium and a spectrum of color swirled about the chamber upon a mist that increased once they stepped through; only the stone remained unaffected. The men proceeded to the exit, but the spell increased even more. The doorway vanished from sight and the room seemed to transform into another place and time.

From the mists a ghost-like figure appeared, and the men stood, as it seemed, upon the shore of a stormy sea with the roar of wind and clouds of orange, crimson, and gray twisting about. The stone remained before them as the figure become whole: a man dressed in a scarlet robe approached with a ebony staff in his hands, and from within the blackness of his cloak emerged a face like bronze and a beard black as jet.

"Red Coven!" gasped Greynol, entranced by the power of the image.

The man's eyes were mad, worse than the tempest itself. He began to age before them. His hair turned long and gray, like his beard, and soon they were white. He withered and grew old as the party trembled at the sight. Again, he changed, aging beyond that of natural years. His skin wore thin and bones were exposed. A deathly face became that of a skeleton with only a thin covering of gray, and hair turned ashen with white patches, matted and encrusted with filth. Only his eyes remained the same: coals that reflected the burning sky, like a nightmare from the grave. The specter came towards them, floating upon the wind.

"Accomplices to your plot, Archinius? I bring you all to doom – the doom that awaits a thief," it hissed in a rage, its robe now tattered and blowing in a fiery wind.

They could only watch as their limbs froze, including Rogan, who muttered, "Not again."

Greynol managed to pull the Timlet Stone from his pocket, but it dropped from his paralyzed hand: it fell away unaffected and out of reach.

"Thieves and demons, one in the same; both have come to take the Stone. But the *Corih Thair* will remain. I am its only protector now, and I know its place. The demon earns nothing from me," he uttered, watching them struggle to find release from the spell.

The figure leaned upon its staff and power seemed to channel through it. Armond was the last to drop his weapon, and when he did, the sorcerer smiled with satisfaction.

"There is no escaping me, Archinius. The King tried his hand at deception; even more, inviting a demon into the sacred place – a treasure in exchange for his own doom. But the demon could not escape me, save by returning to the abyss where the secret cannot leave. Here the secret remains. Now you must suffer the same fate…"

"I can wait no longer. This is all my fault and now I must help find Rogan," said Brenn who stood at the entrance of the well house.
Leonin waited pensively in the street. "You heard Greynol – we are to wait here. There is no telling what is afoot, and our horses and supplies need guarded."
"You stay and watch over things. I will see what is happening inside. Holler if you need me."
Leonin gave way. "Go on then, and be careful." With that sendoff, Brenn rushed into the pantheon.
Mister Linderfell, as the others would call him in happier times, circled the main hall searching up and down, and wondered aloud. "Where can they be?" But noises from the lower floor gave him a start. He ran over for a look.
"Now I'm in a fix; it sounds like all heck's broke loose down below. Whatever it is I have to find out, for I am sure they heard it too," he said, swallowing hard. Brenn gripped his sword and started for the stairs.
He found the darkness outside the chamber bitterly cold, but no less disconcerting the strange light that poured out of the room. Daring to look, he nearly cried out in disbelief: there stood his six friends caught in the grip of a storm of color and sound. At first he did not see the figure that stood before them, leaning upon his staff, eyes closed within the focus of its spell. Brenn bent low, noticing a white glow upon the floor – the Timlet Stone dropped from Greynol's hand.
"This is no good. He must have lost it in the commotion. But now they are caught in a strange trap," he muttered.
Brenn crawled slowly into the room; the stone only a short reach away. Swirls of cloud swam about him like thick smoke. He tried to avoid its touch – unsuccessfully. His head became like a block of ice, his mind lost in a mire. Once he grasped the Timlet Stone, the spell relented.

"I must help them," he muttered, "and quickly."

Brenn reached up at Greynol, who was closest, and with a fistful of frock, pulled him backwards until he fell. He was now out of the heaviest mists, but still within the grip of the spell.

"Can't you move at all?" cried Brenn, taking hold of the Acolyte, careful to rest his head against the wall. It was then he felt eyes upon his back. Brenn turned to find the specter approaching.

Brenn gasped. "What are you?" His knees buckled beneath its terrible gaze. The stone nearly fell from his hand.

As if claimed from a Dagoraust crypt, the sorcerer drew near, his skeletal appearance far from any earthly human quality. "How dare you disturb my justice!" it shrieked, a tattered robe streaming in an unearthly wind. The light of the Timlet Stone caught his attention, and made him curious and fearful at once.

"What do you hold before you?" it asked.

Brenn could not find words to answer.

The Timlet Stone was bright now and overcame much of the scattered light, dividing the streams of color — the light from the black. Brenn saw uncertainty in the sorcerer's eyes; if only he would back away.

"Greynol, what should I do?" asked Brenn hurriedly. The Acolyte began to regain some of his strength, but could not speak.

The figure approached, tapping its staff upon the ground as it went. Brenn was caught, and retreated until he felt his back against the wall — there was no room for escape. In desperation, he thrust the stone forward, causing it to reel from its light. In anger, the specter gripped its staff with both hands, and with a howl, raised it to strike. But Brenn was swifter and leapt aside, and like a boy throwing at a target, whipped the stone as hard as he could muster, striking its hand. It disappeared at once and all light dissipated, save that of the *Corih Thair* and the soft glow of the Timlet Stone, which Brenn picked up and handed back to its owner who smiled.

"In a fix, weren't we?" whispered Greynol, struggling to ward off the effects of the spell. "Let us help the others before more trouble starts."

Before long, the party gathered around Brenn.

"Only a moment more," said Armond, lifting his sword off the floor, "and that thing would have learned a lesson in steel. But you did just fine, shorty."

Brenn winked. "I know, you were just waiting your next move."

"Yes, right out the door, if he had a chance," replied Andro, "and that's where I'm headed before it returns."

"But what of this thing?" asked Rogan, pointing to the *Corih Thair*. He rubbed his left arm, which felt numb and lifeless. The temptation of the stone nearly faded from his mind, but not entirely.

"Don't be a fool, Rogan Pinehurst," replied Greynol. "I assume this is where the trouble started."

Rogan nodded reluctantly.

Without a word of debate, they departed that place, closing the bronze doors that locked behind them. Leonin awaited them in the street.

"What happened in there? I heard strange sounds and voices," he asked.

"There is much to tell, but not here," answered Greynol. "I fear the danger remains if we stay in Dagoraust. Our visit must be cut short."

"You'll get no argument from me," said Brenn.

"The horses are ready, that I can tell you. They have been in a panic ever since you went inside," replied Leonin.

Greynol turned to glimpse the hole in the dome that flashed with lightening and rang with unearthly howls. "Everyone, grab your things, someone is displeased over our escape."

"I'd like to show him some wrath of my own," replied Armond, patting the hilt of his sword, "but leaving sounds better."

Greynol's warning urged them on: they packed their blankets

and odd things, and with horses saddled, rode out of Dagoraust into the night, leaving an angered soul behind them.

Chapter Nine – Three's a Charm

They rode out the night under cover of darkness, grateful that the Arrither Road stayed an even, unobstructed course. The men, now exhausted, watched as stars disappeared one by one, giving way to the sudden glow of daybreak. They went without rest, riding at a slow pace, happy to put any distance between they and the Haunt of Dagoraust. The broken ridge Armond glimpsed the day before ended in a steep wall just south of the road. To the north lay the familiar wooded hills that formed the border of the East-Wilds and Fallis. Armond kept a watchful eye on the stone crags, searching for a sign of the fire he saw earlier, wary of more trouble. A league further the road bent southward following the backside of the ridge into a green valley filled with shade trees, verdant glades, and a lively brook. Greynol felt content to end their ride and take a well-deserved rest.

"Thank you, sir. So long a push after so little rest, I feared for falling headlong off my mount sound asleep, and that might not have roused me," said Drago as he dropped like a sack from his saddle to the ground.

"It was necessary to put some distance between us and Dagoraust. Now we can afford a brief rest," replied Greynol, dismounting more slowly, clearly pained by the night's events. "You men must be tired; eat something, then get some rest."

"Gladly. But now that we have escaped danger, can you tell us anything about the wizard in that terrible chamber?" asked Brenn, tying his pony to a dogwood tree along the bank of the stream.

"I will tell what I can. The man was indeed a sorcerer, even more, and from his dress he had the look of a Red Coven wizard, like those whom rule Egenol. But why he remains in the Great Dome, and in his deathly state, I do not know. The menace that once existed in Dagoraust clearly remains," replied Greynol.

"Rogan was there first – perhaps he knows more," said Andro in a suspicious tone, but Rogan held his silence. "I know you are weary of questions, but I found you with the sword pointed beneath your chin, the same way we all saw you in the chamber – you looked dead. And how is it you entered that place, anyway?"

Rogan sat down upon the grass beneath the trees of the grove – his eyes gave the look of intense torment at the recollection. "There is little to tell you," he replied, gazing blankly into the distance. He removed the key from his pocket. "I found this in the barrow along with the sword, and it I wish to keep – a token from Dagoraust which stole part of my soul. I don't know why the specter drew me in, or how, but you saw its power. The pain is too great to speak of it now."

"Sleep Rogan. No more questions until later," said Greynol, removing the others from his side. Once alone, Rogan lay back on the grass and closed his eyes, trying to forget all that happened in the chamber.

Once away, Greynol tried to relieve the others. "These questions may never have an adequate answer," he said in a low voice, "we must reside ourselves with this prospect."

"A jewel was mentioned. If only I could have seen it," said Leonin.

"That may not have helped us – let us be content with what we know. Speaking of these things at present does little to help Rogan, for he has been wounded beyond the craft of any sword," replied Greynol. He insisted the others take a respite. They needed little prodding.

Rogan slept until about noon; that is when Andro woke him from a strange dream about a small boat crossing a rough sea. A lunch of dried venison, stale biscuits, and blackberries from underbrush about the stream were the order of the day. Rogan sat and ate quietly, his mind reeling in dark thought. He desired to speak of the ordeal, but another ailment brought discomfort: a pain returned to his left arm, the same sensation that incurred after first touching the stone, which crept like fire from his hand, down the arm and into his shoulder. He bit his lip to conceal the throes until they subsided. Once relieved, Rogan put aside his silence, gaining everyone's attention as they gathered nearby.

"The sword and key belonged to the Captain of the Royal Guard. His name was Archinius – the same name the wizard gave me," he said, sweat beading on his blanched forehead with the recollection. "It was Archinius, who by his order, killed their king and perhaps many others with the very sword I found. I witnessed this and felt it in my mind while I slept that night."

"Why would he want the king dead?" asked Drago.

"The King and Queen of Dagoraust desired the Stone for their own pleasure. I saw in their eyes a look of corruption."

"And you saw these things in your sleep? That explains why I found you as you were, caught in a trance," replied Andro.

"It seemed hardly a dream."

Drago laughed it off. "We all might be dreaming still if Brenn hadn't found us."

"Looks like we have two champions in this party," replied Greynol, watching for Armond's reaction. A frown of disapproval soon turned to a chuckle from the proud Turrar.

"We all owe you one, shrimp," he laughed, "but I contend it wasn't settled yet. That wizard hadn't killed me, and as long as life-blood flowed in my veins, there was a chance of retaliation. That's twice now that we run instead of fight."

"You wish to be back in Dagoraust? Your sword against a powerful wizard?"

"I don't like to run, sir, but I am glad to be here instead of that chamber."

Leonin listened intently, the only member of the party not to enter the Great Dome. Mention of a jewel grabbed his curiosity.

"Forgive my asking, Rogan, but I would like to learn more about this thing you found. A stone of Amethyst from Drago's description," he said.

Rogan looked up, thoughts of the jewel reminded him of the pain. "I think it found me," he replied sordidly. "What the wizard protected was ancient, yet veiled: he called it the *Corih Thair*, but I know not what it means."

"We each saw it. Purplish in color and of the same design as the monolith in the town's center," added Drago.

"Then he asked me strange questions," continued Rogan, "something about the present year, and he was taken aback when I told him. Then he muttered something about four hundred years passing and a strange question concerning rival kings without heir. Greynol, do you understand these things?"

Greynol leaned back and scratched his bare head. "Well, as I recall the saying is an old prophecy concerning rival monarchs: both are childless – without heir. Their passing would signal the coming of great trials," he replied.

"My father's father spoke of such things when I was young. It's all nonsense, right?" asked Brenn.

"Not necessarily. Many tales are born out of common sense: if rival kings and kingdoms have no one to claim their throne, then difficult times are certain to arise with those seeking power."

"But are not both the monarchies of Nordhiem and Gandol childless? They are surely rivals, are they not?" asked Andro, concerned over the unknown, and that included soothsaying.

"The Prophecy could be applied to this day, but have these things not happened in the past?"

"I agree with Greynol – it is common sense: if two kingdoms have not king or queen to rule, then many trials should come, namely war," replied Armond.

"But you miss a crucial fact concerning this prophecy: King Raeletin and Queen Elizabeth have an heir – Raeletin's nephew, Prince Galin," replied Rogan.

Greynol nodded, untying Toryche's lead from the stump that held him. "An astute observation, and enough to clear the air while we ride. Now let us put some leagues behind us – Bardol is near."

They formed a line of riding pairs, and this time Armond and Andro brought up the rear. Armond felt the urge to look again upon the mountains at his back, and in an instant, saw the flame return upon its northernmost peak, closer than the day before. He sighed in frustration because he knew he could not investigate, and heeled his black mount forward to catch up to the others.

Several leagues carried them into a gentle stretch of forest where the grade ran even and strong. But weariness soon overcame Rogan, and the others no less, as the battle with the wizard weakened their spirits. They managed frequent rests, and with the approach of dusk, found little desire to push further. As darkness settled in, they encamped within the shadow of twin columns marking the border of Bardol. Andro was pleased to be in friendlier territory.

By the morning's first light, they were pounding the Arrither once more, driving southeast along the lonesome road. Riding in order, Armond would glance over his shoulder now and again to glimpse the rocky ridge in the distance, but no more did he find a trace of fire.

At this time, Rogan felt the pain in his arm return. A fire traveled down his shoulder and into the fingertips, the intensity more than he could bear, only to have it depart once again. The sensation pulsated throughout his body and he swooned, nearly falling him from Courser in distress. He and Leonin now took the rear position, by Rogan's design, to hide his discomfort from the others.

"Are you alright?" asked Leonin, grabbing him by the cloak.

"I'll be fine," he said with a gasp. "Please don't tell Greynol."

"What is it?"

"In Dagoraust I touched the strange stone, only slightly, and now it brings me great pain."

Leonin looked at him strangely. *"If only I could have seen it,"* he thought. He was a Farrian, one of 'the People of the Jewels'. The matter intrigued him deeply.

Rogan's infirmity increased as they went: he managed to secure his arm, held it as still as he could, pressing it against his lap to fight the pain. The pathway changed now, from a stony narrow lane into a wide and open road. Just ahead, they saw a crossing and a welcome end to the Arrither. Rogan began to feel his arm as though put to flame; his tendons jolted as one struck by lightning.

"Oh, when will it end?" he cried with Leonin looking on, deeply concerned and not sure what to do.

They approached the crossing, a highroad linking Bardol to Ainiald, when Rogan, reeling with pain, lost his grip upon the reigns of his steed. Leonin saved him from a terrible fall, and in doing so, missed the movements of a solitary rider racing through the forest just beyond the crossroads – a man he had seen before.

They entered Bardol Road, and immediately, Greynol gave the signal to stop. Leonin's hand grasped Rogan's shirtsleeve, holding him upright as he swooned. When their steeds left the Arrither behind, the pain ceased instantly.

"It is gone, Leonin, just like that. The spell has departed – one last pinch from that awful place," he said, wiping the tears from his eyes.

The others were alerted to Rogan's odd behavior, including a suspicious Greynol. That is when the sound of hooves and a clashing of arms turned their attention away. Gazing north, the Bardol Road ran wide between soft shoulders of woodland hills. Onto the road spilled a group of hurried riders, six men and ten horses in all; they readied a southward charge into the path of the Alliance. Once they realized the way was blocked, the riders swerved east upon the forest slope, but not before loosing several errant shafts.

"How's that for a greeting, one should find out friend or foe before firing a round!" called Drago, reaching for his shield.

"Those are the men from the hill the other night," gasped Leonin, "but the cloaked fellow is not with them."

Armond drew his crossbow and loaded an iron bolt. The glint in his eye made Andro cringe. "Now what do you say, Greynol? Twice we left the enemy at our back, but 'third times a charm', just like we say at home," he said with a laugh.

But before Greynol could utter a word of protest, several new riders came out of the woods in pursuit: six from the same path used by the bandits; two others appeared upon the Arrither Road from an unseen trail. Both groups rode at speed towards the Alliance, and converged at the crossing with bows and arrows notched and drawn.

"Be quick!" called Greynol to the others. "Lower your weapons – these are the wardens of Bardol."

Armond yielded with reluctance, setting the bow across his lap, trigger cocked and ready.

The horsemen charged forward, halting suddenly only paces before Greynol's raised hand. Skilled riders clad in gray mail, they bore long swords, iron helms, and squared shields painted red about the edge with a black stallion upon a background of verdant green.

"Hark! Make no advance or we shall strike swiftly," called one of their number, a woman dressed similar to the others, save that her helm that was red and gilded in fine lines about the edge and center. Armond stirred at the flash of her angry brown eyes.

"Remain as you are or you will test Bardol darts against your own skins – I can assure you the darts will prevail," she commanded.

"Others have taken to the forest – those whom you pursue. They came upon us by chance," said Rogan, rubbing his forearm as normal feeling returned.

"We will deal with the horse-thieves. They have chosen an errant path that leads to a sudden end," replied the woman. Her face was hardened and tawny from the sun, matching the long pleats of brown hair clasped behind her neck. "I am Warden-lord of the border watch. What business do you have upon a thief's road? Perhaps waiting to payoff the others for fresh horses?"

Greynol bowed. "Lady, we have no dealings with such men. I am Acolyte Greynol from Vanyor, and these men are my escort. I chose to travel *the Wayward Road* out of necessity and haste – the Arrither was not always a path for thieves."

The woman rode forward upon a fiery black stallion; her gaze softened to one of curiosity now. She let the crossbow in her hands drop to her lap. "Now that you have entered Bardol I seek a full account of your intentions, while there is time; for yes, this was not always a way for thieves, but shunned none-the-less," she replied, signaling two of her riders to go further down the road and wait. They watched closely the hillside as they went.

"My choice is one of speed – the Arrither Road brings this to me. In two days I hope to be in Larin," returned Greynol.

"I know little about Greyhoods, save they do not lie. Prudent as your choice seems, to travel a dangerous road with a group of young lads at your side might…encourage the enemy?" she said with a wry look and a round of laughs from the guards at her back.

"They are capable and I can vouch for them," replied Greynol, trying to save the others from further embarrassment. "Four nights ago we spied these brigands in the hills of the East-wilds – they have been hired for more than just petty thievery. I offer my men at your service should you require it; otherwise, we wish to pass through to the border…that is, if the way remains open."

"The way is open – to allies."

Armond ignored the backhanded comments, enamored by the beauty in her strength. He struggled to steal her glance, addressing her in a most unwise fashion: "Woman, we *are* allies and brothers of Bardol. Are not the sons of Nordhiem and Bardol kin?"

"…as well as their daughters. Now remove your finger off the trigger of your crossbow, or this conversation will come to a swift end," she replied with a smile that meant much more than it conveyed.

Armond relented.

"I am Tanna, call me *Woman* again and be prepared to receive a dart of my own. You say you are kin, but not all of you are Nordic."

"You are correct, my party comes from several kingdom's of the North," answered Greynol, interrupted by a call from the two waiting riders.

"We must go," said a guard at the captain's back, whose features closely resembled Tanna's.

"Yes, Thain, prepare for a confrontation," she said, turning to the others of her company. "Greynol, you may depart – go swiftly now. The bridge marks the end of our land and the entry into Ainiald."

"But will you not accept our swords instead?" asked Armond. "There are six or seven against your eight, and they are backed into a corner. These bandits are crafty and dangerous."

"I have others, but they remain behind. A string of trouble your friends left us to repair – a wounded landowner and stolen horses in their wake. If you wish to aid us, then guard our flanks. Remain on the road in case one slips through. Nothing more."

Armond scowled at the thought of being left behind, but waited grudgingly at the forest edge. Tanna and her companions entered the trail where the thieves galloped moments before; the two guards down the road had already entered from a different path.

"I don't like the feel of this: Tanna seems to know the land, but not these spies. They might have a trick or two up their sleeves before all is over," uttered Armond, staring intently into the forest.

"This is their watch," replied Greynol. "The warden rides too proud to accept our help. I fear she may be grateful for it when it is over."

"But what of poison? You told us that night upon the hill, southern spies use it in their weapons," asked Andro.

"A bitter tree grows in the Khuldark where a poison is harvested, but only the most cunning can keep it. It is used in darts and dirks, but rarely would one find it so far north: great skill is needed to keep the dosage fresh for so long. Only the keenest assassins craft daggers to contain such venom," replied Greynol who learned the habits of the enemy many years before.

"How deadly is it?" wondered Brenn.

"Very deadly when fresh, but that is impossible here. With skill, even old poisons can kill, but the effects take longer."

"What of an antidote?" asked Andro, but he was interrupted by noises in the forest.

They awaited news from the wood, perched like birds of prey seeking a victim. "Something is happening," said Leonin, his ear trained to far off sounds. "I hear horses and shouting over the hill; and now closer, in the direction where the two guards entered, I heard a strange sound."

Greynol barely gave a nod of consent when Armond charged beneath the trees with the others close behind. He slashed through the thicket until standing upon a deer trail that ran parallel with the road, fifty paces from the tree line.

"To the south," called Leonin, easily keeping pace, "that is where the noises came."

In a crooked line, they followed the trail as it curved along the contour of the hill and away from the road, when suddenly two bare-saddled horses came into view. As they neared, they discovered two prone bodies lying on the ground.

"Aye, there!" called Armond. "Two men are down. Get Greynol up here."

Before Brenn could turn back, Greynol came riding up from below upon the trail used by the injured guards. He anticipated trouble. "I'm already here," he said, quickly dismounting with bag in hand. He knelt between the two guards now trembling and pale.

"Just as I feared," Greynol said. He propped one of the men against a tree exposing the dart that pierced his neck. He tore it out at once. "They were taken by surprise – a skilled attack."

He shifted over to the second guard whose leg was punctured.

Black oil mingled with blood that oozed down his thigh.

"There is no dart here," said Andro.

"A deadly blade laced with poison did the trick. His injury is less, but both are in dire need. Be quick with a clean rag and some spirits before dressing their wounds. At least one of those spies is a skilled assassin," said Greynol, dividing his attention between the two.

Armond paced nearby, tightly gripping the stock of his crossbow; his eyes darted between the injured and the surrounding forest.

"The one who did this has slipped by and he should be hunted down; but I hear other voices across this hill, not those of the guards. Greynol, can anything be done for these two?"

"Andro asked about an antidote: it is called Heartweed, and yes, I have some oil in my possession – but precious little."

"Do what you can. I sense there is trouble brewing nearby and I am going to find out what. Who will join me?" asked Armond.

"He is right, the Bardol Company is down by two. I will go if someone stays here to help," said Andro, summoning his courage. Rogan and Leonin were most comfortable in the forest and chose to accompany them.

"I will not stop you, but look at these poor men and remember the danger," replied Greynol. "You will do best to find first Tanna and tell her what has happened."

Armond hurried away and led the others east along the curve of the trail, wary of a sudden attack. Each bore a shield, save Leonin: Armond a full metal round, and the Logander's, plain circular bucklers of wood framed with steel. Each carried a sword and dagger, and all held bows – Armond's crossbow to the other's wooden bows. They scuttled between the trees, dodging rocks that scattered the hillside. A new trail emerged upon their right that brought them aside a steep drop into a gorge where a river played far below in the sun – the ragged border of Ainiald.

"I see what Tanna meant by the thieves being caught in a trap – there is no climbing down these cliffs," said Armond, to the others at his back.

"Stay alert. Someone calls in the forest ahead," said Leonin, "I fear the trap is set."

The forest smoothed out into a small plateau covered with woody fern and broken boulders. Andro never forgot the setting of his first skirmish. Tanna and the Bardol guard were nowhere to be seen as they went from stone to stone, keeping their cover. A man's voice sounded clear over a small rise:

"Where are you filthy riders? I'll take you on. Some Bardol wench ain't no match for an ol' scrapper," hollered the largest ruffian. Leonin recalled him from four nights ago. "Now if we could get our hands on that cloaker and his 'black bite'."

"I told you he'd ditch as soon as trouble hit," said another, the oldest of the group. "He's been a shady of late."

"I'll teach 'em once we're out of this spot."

"You'd better watch yerself, he's got a sting to match. Now be quiet, I hear someone coming."

Armond slid around a boulder and crept up a rise to see. The others followed behind, several paces apart, finding their own cover. Andro and Leonin slipped behind a large flat rock, while Armond and Rogan used the broad trunks of oaks as a blind. Four men stood fifty paces from their watch in dark muddied garments, backed into a corner: two held bows while the other pair raised long pipes to their mouths, and each had a scimitar upon their belts. They watched and waited, facing an unseen opponent from the opposite direction. Ten horses waited nearby scattered upon a landing pressed against the cliff edge – six wore saddles.

"We saw six men earlier, now there are only four," whispered Leonin.

"That means two are unaccounted for," replied Andro. They readied their bows for a quick strike when a commotion arose – a rush of hooves from the opposite rise. Tanna and her men made their move from the north, sending several arrows overhead, but none landed home. The thieves returned fire.

"Damn, they're too close!" snapped Armond, lowering his crossbow. He relinquished his position and charged towards Tanna who leapt from her steed to match swords with the largest ruffian.

Out of the corner of his eye, Armond caught a glimpse of the plan: a lurker waited upon the lower landing to strike. With a bow pulled taut, he prepared to strike down Tanna. Armond reacted at once, loosing his crossbow, which fired bolts strong enough to pierce armor; but the shot fell short of its mark, kicking up earth and leaves in front of the adversary. The man returned the favor, sending an arrow past Armond as he dove, striking a nearby tree.

"Now you're mine!" called Armond, scrambling to his feet. He charged the thief, who had only enough time to brandish a sword of his own. A clash of swords reminded Armond of the tournament, but a nicked hand spoke clearly that the days of blunted weapons were behind him.

Armond parried then drove his shield into the man's chest, knocking him backwards. His Turrar spirit kindled, he felt as if the king and crowds watched his every move. Ready to pounce, he caught a glimpse of a concealed pipe rising to the man's mouth; he dove aside just as a dart flew past his neck. Armond reacted quickly, squatting down like a cat poised to strike. With every sinew in his body he lunged at the man – a sudden sword thrust that pierced flesh, organ, and bone.

Armond froze where he stood. The feel of the blade as he pulled it from his opponent's flesh hard to shake. "No longer do I stand upon a field of melee – far from it," he muttered as the fellow died at his feet.

Andro and Leonin caught a similar trap higher up the rocky slope. This time a hidden archer found two Lanfersian arrows in his side before he could react. Leonin's shot was sure; Andro, on the other hand, missed his mark.

Rogan settled for backing up the Bardol guard, who handled their opponents with skill, as one by one they fell. Tanna's battled against the largest of the thieves, and found the struggle greatest: strong in her own right, the combatant stood a foot taller and bore considerable weight. The warden was a seasoned fighter, matching the scoundrel blow for blow; she bled from the arm, and he, the forearms and legs. He bore down upon her shield arm, striking again and again with brutish force. Witnessing her struggle, Rogan rushed to her aid.

The man took a mighty swing at Tanna, who blocked with her sword, causing it to shatter. "Now you die, woman," he growled, striking wildly against her shield. She stood firm with a dagger her only weapon.

Rogan charged from behind, but too fast to escape notice. The man turned to take a swing that Rogan ducked just in time. Tanna reacted, smashing her shield against the ruffian's head and stabbing her knife into his shoulder. He toppled over onto Rogan. Tanna leapt in for the attack, pressing her knife to his neck for submission, but the man resisted. By the look in his eyes, there would be no surrender.

"Never will you take me!" he shouted, pulling a knife from his belt. He went to thrust its curved point into her side, but a sudden shrill cry made even the most seasoned fighter turn away. Tanna slit his throat.

The bodies of six dead thieves were laid out upon the hillside. "They fought as those doomed to die – none willing to surrender when it was over," muttered one of the guards, searching the fallen men.

"I saw five men several nights ago, four of whom are here now. But two I do not recognize," said Leonin somberly.

"They are the enemy and they get no sympathy from me; nor shall you, should I find your reason for being here insufficient," replied Tanna unmoved by events save the tremble of her sword-hand.

"Two of your men lay injured in the woods," answered Armond, stepping forward. "They were taken by surprise by the last thief whom I fear has escaped, and now poison is in their veins. The Acolyte tends their injuries at this moment; he carries an antidote for just such a need."

"Heartweed, a necessity in dealing with those sent by the enemy," said Tanna distressed over the news. "Thain, make haste and bring their possessions. We will deal with burning these fools later – I want to see our fallen brothers."

On the road, they found Greynol and the others gathered with two bandaged horsemen, each swooning with sickness from the toxin in their blood. Heartweed removed them from sudden danger, but healing would take time. Their wounds were soaked with oil and bandaged with clean rags, and a small amount of the elixir was placed in their mouths.

"They would do better with fresh water or tea, even milk; nothing of which we have here, as we are in need of fresh supplies ourselves," said Greynol, attending to their needs with the skill of a physician. "I am glad to find you all safe with only minor wounds. Warden Tanna, I will give a full account of what has transpired here, and the reason for my men's indiscretion by entering the forest against your command."

"The matter has been resolved. Your men fought bravely," replied Tanna.

"But one has escaped. I'm afraid he was the most cunning of the group," replied Greynol.

Thain tossed the thieves' possessions upon the road. "If only fate brought them into our hands earlier. Two days ago I saw seven riders along the forest edge; they came into the fields ready to loot and plunder. I summoned my sister and the rest of the company to assemble a search, discovering six men sneaking about Gerimal's stable. A seventh man watched from a distance nearest the woods. But they managed to escape with several horses, only after injuring Gerimal's stable hand and two of our number, felling them with darts. Our comrades were taken into town, which is why we ride shorthanded. The daylong we pursued these cutthroats, discovering them in the woods – then we gave chase."

"We might discover something of their plan in those articles," said Rogan, pointing to pile at their feet. Thain leafed through scraps of parchment and several ragged maps of Gandol and Nordhiem.

"There is nothing worth noting: rubbish and a small amount of money – Gandol shillings mostly."

"What of the thieves? None were taken prisoner?" asked Greynol.

"They are all dead. Strange as it was, they fought without attempt at surrender. We will burn them were they lay," replied Tanna. "Whatever secrets they carried remain with them."

"This is good news, is it not? Six are dead and only one of your searchers remain," said Zerrin. But Greynol found no joy over the news.

"Long gone are the years that I gloated over a fallen enemy. These men, wherever they hail, fell into deceit – an offer they could not refuse. The seduction of the enemy claims many that are unprepared. As for my company, I say find no delight in the death of a foe, save drukon or durag, whom have no place among creatures of 'good'," replied Greynol, his mood now solemn. His thoughts drifted to the unknown, leafing through a black rag that contained the thieves' goods.

Tanna mended her wounds, the worst a ragged cut across her bicep that dripped with fresh blood; but her concern drew her to her injured brethren, assisting their every need. She pondered in silence, reserved in recollection of events and whether every choice taken was sound, as any leader is apt to do. Soon they all returned to the dead to set a pyre. The bodies were stacked upon a hastily made brier and doused with oil – Greynol whispered words of prayer as the wood was set ablaze. Upon returning to the road, with black smoke rising over the hill at their backs, the parties were ready to move on.

"Lady-warden, which way do you ride?" asked Armond, hoping in some manner to gain her respect. He was jealous. After all, Rogan came to her aid and not he.

"We ride to the southern border and Ainar River crossing. Perhaps the last thief lurks that way still."

"We saw the river from the ridge, it cannot be far," said Andro.

"The Ainar travels due south from here for about a league, then shifts west beneath the road," replied Thain. "Twenty-five leagues remain until Roallin, if that is your direction?"

"Indeed it is. We shall rest at the border and enter Ainiald in the morning," replied Greynol.

Tanna mounted her fine black steed, a Bardol stallion known for their fire. "Very well, I am sending Ulran and Kant back with Fedorim to recover fully from their wounds. The rest of us will set watch at the bridge tonight. With hope we will find that last scoundrel," she said.

They watched as Fedorim rode north to an unseen place, returning shortly after with a small cart for the two injured guards whom were too ill to ride their own steeds. They were soon departed for Oakview, where great care would be allotted them. Afterwards Greynol and Tanna led their companies south.

A short ride later they came upon a deep river valley and a bridged crossing: the Ainar River swept swiftly beneath the tall span bordered by stony gray cliffs. Here the Bardol guard kept a log hut overlooking the river with an open shelter for their horses in the rear. Greynol's Alliance settled down upon the soft turf beside the road, a short distance from the cabin, which was small and contained only the barest necessities. Glad to find a comfortable spot and fresh breezes to cool the day, they laid out their beds and prepared a fire. Tanna and her men shared bread, cheese, and stout Bardol mead with them, speaking at length of the fight and the latest news of the day.

"We ride by day, other times by night; always close to the borderlands. There is much to be watchful for these days and our numbers are short," said Tanna in the glow of the evening fire. Her look was hardened, but beautiful in the twilight. "The war in Earlon demands many of our best riders – Bardol has always supported her allies. A thousand spears on horseback departed for the southern plains not two months ago."

"What of the North, do they come to the aid of Fanael?" asked Thain.

"King Anor has taken council on such matters. If the need grows, Nordhiem will come," replied Armond with an uncomfortable attempt at diplomacy. "We go in advance of others..."

"Go on," said Tanna. "What others?"

Armond feared he gave away too much and hesitated, but Greynol saved him. "My young champion fears only in words these days. What he means to say are men of the North *may* come, as mercenaries, since the offer for field-pay spreads to Thalon."

"And what of you?"

"We also venture south, beyond Ainiald, but to what final destination remains untold here. We may yet see war."

"These *boys* are your hirelings?" asked Tanna with a smug look.

"Do not call them mercenary or verily young, for they are entrusted to more than just wielding a sword."

"Very well then, if there is anything more we can do for you, speak up. I owe you a dept of gratitude for assisting my two riders."

"Our needs shall be mended in Roallin."

"And our attention remains with Bardol," replied Tanna, excusing herself. "Your missing friend seems to have eluded our grasp; but fear not, we have watches set for the night, so feel free to sleep at ease. We rise with the sun, goodnight."

Later in the evening, they drifted off beside the fire, blankets and stars for cover. Greynol approached Armond who attempted to rub away the crimson smudge upon his sword. "Best not to let it dry," he said gazing down at the bloodstained blade.

"I thought I had done so after the fight, but things were in a rush," replied the Turrar, and his look was solemn.

Greynol read his thoughts. "This was your first kill?"

"Indeed. Is it true what they say about lifeblood, that a man's soul flows through it?"

"Blood is part of the whole, but it is not the soul – that takes more care than the rest, and a sword cannot pierce it."

"The man died. I watched him die. The bodies were burnt; he cannot still live."

"There is no returning from the dead. Imagine the caged bird instead: a door is now opened for it to fly. But in the case of men sworn to dishonor, I would rather not speak of it."

Satisfied, Armond placed his weapon back into its scabbard, laying it at his feet. He tossed the bloodied rag into the fire and gazed up at Greynol. There was uncertainty in his voice. "It was necessary, wasn't it? The fault is not ours. Tanna was correct in saying they showed no surrender."

"Something more compelled them; oaths taken that no man should utter. Do you feel different about your position in this company?"

"No, sir. My resolve does not waver," he answered.

Greynol touched his shoulder. "I know what happened upon that hill – you and Leonin were left no choice. Should the day come after such action that your heart show no remorse, then my son, you should trouble."

Armond nodded and found a soft spot upon the ground to lay. *Sleep might bring rest to this racing mind.* Worry gave way to weariness and he drifted off into sweeter dreams.

Chapter Ten – Ainiald

The first thing Armond saw the next morning was Tanna's face as a knee nudged him from sleep – he awoke at once. Greynol sipped tea nearby with Leonin at his side, and the others were scattered in various stages of waking. Armond, for one, slept soundly that night, only after re-playing the events of the day before many times in his head. Then he heard a jealous sound.

"Here is my hero! I might have been laid up in a comfortable sickbed if this boy hadn't come to my aid," called Tanna with an arm around a stunned Rogan. He shook the sleep from his eyes and shrugged it off blushing. She paid him a kiss on the cheek and walked off with a droll grin.

"What was that all about?" asked Andro.

"I dunno. Who can figure out girls, even if she ain't quite a girl anymore," he mumbled, rubbing his cheek.

"Maybe she likes you," laughed Brenn from the grass where he sat. Armond grunted in disbelief, quick to pull Andro aside.

"If only she knew what I had done for her."

"Then what? Come on Armond, she must be ten years older than you. She's just having fun anyway."

"Tanna is what a woman should be."

"You'll get yours in time," replied Andro, leaning in close. "Shall I kiss your cheek and make it better?"

Andro nearly fell to the ground snickering at his own words, and from Armond's shove. But he too found the matter humorous.

Soon the horses stood packed and ready. The companies of Greynol and the Bardol guard bowed to each other and prepared to part ways. Tanna sat proud upon her steed.

"This is the end of our meeting, friends. Farewell in the southlands, or wherever you ride," she said in a stately manner.

"Indeed, may our paths cross again," replied Armond, in an odd last attempt to gain her attention.

"Should they not, I once again owe this company a debt of gratitude: to Greynol for his healing oils; to Leonin and Andro for their proud bows; and to Rogan Pinehurst for his bravery against that troll of a man," she exclaimed, her hardened expression smoothing away into a smile.

They bowed again.

"Oh yes, and to Armond of Vanyor, whom I owe my life should that poisoned dart found its mark. I do not forget, but I will not pay him a kiss as I did Rogan, for I am wary this one might kiss back."

They finished their meeting with a round of laugher, and this time Armond blushed. He was delighted for the recognition.

"I was certain she missed it," he whispered to Andro as the companies started each their own direction. The border-guard galloped northward, and the Alliance south, crossing the bridge into Ainiald.

"Seems she misses very little," replied Andro. He urged Ambarr forward to match the pace of their leader.

The remaining day passed swiftly as they entered the Ainiald backcountry; the trade route ran an even stretch between wooded hills and bright open fields. Andro enjoyed a placid ride, keeping to his thoughts, speaking now and again of the change from wilderness into a fertile upland. The nearness of the coast he could feel in a warm invigorating breeze.

Armond said little; his heart remained in Bardol with Tanna. Andro read the feelings his friend bore:

"I'll leave him alone for now. Armond is young and easily smitten," he thought, slow to recognize the same affinity he held for Randa

back home.

Come evening, they camped upon a grassy mead where the lamplights of distant dwellings emerged above pastures flanking the eastern hills, lifted as it were upon a pillow of fog. A fire was lit with twilight settling in, gentle now, like a fine Logan summer. Five days since departing Harifin's house, the wilds were finally behind them.

Their second morning in Ainiald began before sunrise with the feint glow of amber-yellow flowering in the eastern sky. In nearby groves, birds awakened to greet the new day, singing their melodies to the heavens as they tested their wings between the trees. A cool mist hung about the meadow and a breath of calm lay upon the land. Andro gave no thought to worry, not even to the lone spy whom failed to materialize along the way. Greynol promised a rewarding end to the day with hopes of reaching Roallin before nightfall.

"...an accommodating town indeed, and certain to be bustling on a Thursday night. We shall rest in comfort and tidy up before reaching Larin," said Greynol, his eyes bright with thoughts of rest and comfort. The others were delighted to hear the news, but wondered what he meant by, *tidied up*.

The land opened wide as they went. Farmsteads and tidy hamlets dotted the countryside isolated from all attention, seen across the rolling distance where wisps of chimney smoke made trails upon a heady breeze. The road now bustled in contrast to the loneliness of the Arrither. Solitary farmers, tanners, and a lone pig herder made their homes within reach of the men's noses, but much of the populace avoided the highroad and its history of odd travelers – the Alliance being no exception. As the sun rose, orchards and fields emerged from the shadows, and along the southern horizon, the thin purple line of a mountain range, still two day's ride away. The sight took the Kuirians' breath away.

"Look!" cried Zerrin, "a sight liken to the Vanadium's back home. I feel as if we ride through Carrinth, or even Thalon, gazing west."

"The great Werithain Range – gateway to the South. A sight King Taladra looked upon ages ago, and it stole his heart," replied Drago. "I am anxious to set my feet upon her paths."

"We have Larin first as her footstool," said Greynol, "then you will get your fill of the mountains."

They took delight upon hearing it.

The day waned and a wispy sky drifted past a lowering sun. Andro felt glad as a swath of forest opened into a vineyards flanked by fields of corn, wheat, and rye. Common folk stopped to stare at the riders as they went, bowing at the sight of Greynol, and Andro took notice. After a short rest, they approached a grove of white oaks, and just beyond, clover fields and the city of Roallin. A sigh of relief left them, the first town to greet the party since Ristle eight days earlier.

Roallin looked every part the accommodating city Greynol described: without battlement or heavy guard, the city grew from its early days as a farmer's post and resting spot for wary travelers. The Werithain and Bardol Roads met at town's center. Roallin lie a day's ride from Larin, Ainiald's Capital, and three from Ainar on the western border – a fortress on the brink of Gandol. Distant sea winds carried over meadow and pastureland, and in Roallin, the air was fresh and clean. Greynol led the men onto an east-west running thoroughfare; their hearts gladdened at the sight of a cobblestone avenue lined with several inviting inns.

Greynol knew exactly where to go, pausing in front of a green two-storied manor that featured white shuttered windows and spacious rooms. Smoke from several chimneys made it known that dinner was ready.

"This is the place, Rengal's Manor, an old standby for tired bones. With luck they will have accommodations for eight," he said, gazing up at a wooden sign above the door sporting a boar's head. "I fondly recall soft beds and plentiful suppers. One may have a bath drawn and clothes cleaned for a small price. And we shall, for our appearance has already drawn attention."

The young men looked at each other and realized the toll a

week in the wilderness took upon their façade – a stark comparison to the properly dressed townsfolk. In fact, they were downright filthy.

"Also mind your manners – respect for proper things holds sway here. Even the farmer holds dignity aside the noble in Ainiald: it is his harvest that feeds the armies headed south," said Greynol.

He stepped inside to secure a room, and reappeared soon after with two men, alike in appearance, one young and the other older and dressed like a butler. They bowed in unison as the elder fellow greeted them.

"Welcome travelers, pleased we are that you should stay with us tonight," he said in a voice that put all at ease. "A visit from an old friend is welcome news. Like we say in Roallin, 'the company of a friend is good company indeed'. You have traveled far – in from the wilds from all accounts. Make yourselves comfortable; we are at your service."

"Thank you again, Rinigel, son of Rengal, your house has welcomed many a weary soul – myself included. Tonight is no exception. Aside from lodging, we require baths drawn, clothes cleaned, and supper, of course," replied Greynol with a wink.

"All will be tended to in proper order, Acolyte Arowen, a name that came to us not so long ago – enough to waken distant memories. The Wandering Acolyte we would call him. They were fair visits indeed, and always in good company. But that was many years ago. I have a way with faces more than names, an inheritance from my old sire who passed on several years ago. And here is my own son, also named Rengal, and he is gifted more than the both of us together."

"I too am at your fullest service," added Rengal with second bow, a mirror image of his father without the tinges of gray.

With a clap of his hands, Rengal summoned several young matrons who led the party to an upper room consisting of ten beds set apart by a dining table, while male servants took the horses to a rear stable. Baggage was placed at the foot of each bed and clothes separated for a good washing. The men were treated to wine and cider while they reclined upon their berths. Baths were prepared in a room at the end of the hall – a bit of luxury they were altogether unaccustomed; but a welcome sight for many a road-worn traveler. Eight oval-shaped tubs, some wood, others brass, steamed with warm soapy water.

"Now Greynol sir, is this really necessary? I mean to say, fancy baths are for proper folk, ladies mostly, those of nobility," protested Armond, curling his nose at the soapy water. "Is that perfume?"

"A bucket will do us miners," added Drago, head cocked as one looking over a stockyard steer, not a brass tub.

Greynol laughed loudly. "These my friends are a luxury to ease the road from your bones, not to mention the smell of your horses, whom will be washed and groomed with less objection."

"Come on now, we faced the Wizard of Dagoraust with less argument," said Andro undoing his shoes and belt. "I for one am going to soak a bit and relax before supper."

Armond shook his head, but soon gave in and removed the woolen vest off his back. "To think what they might say back home – a tournament-tested fighter bathing like some silk-stocking," he muttered. Ending his protest, he eased his sore body into the suds.

This was an evening of ease for Andro and friends – a rare treat in times to come. They were each cleaned, groomed, and shaven, save Greynol and the Kuirian brothers who kept their beards, and Andro his mustache – neatly trimmed. Dinner was of the common variety: groundnut stew, kidney pie, turnips, and fresh rye in the first floor dining room. They were content to relax in the company of others, rather than remain in their lonely chamber. The cherry-wood columns and walls matched the color of its mead, which Andro sipped beneath the dim manor lamps.

"You'll have to excuse me, gentlemen," said Greynol, a half-empty bowl before him. "I wish return to our room for some quiet before bed."

He dismissed himself, but not before speaking to proprietor

Rinigel who busied himself setting mugs behind the bar.

"Pardon my intrusion, friend. I wanted to ask a question of you," said Greynol from an isolated corner, trying to keep his needs from curious ears. Rinigel drew near. "You mentioned my name coming up earlier. Do you recall the nature of the conversation?"

"As I think of it, the occurrence took place in springtime; I remember it well since it seemed to occur after a long cold spell," he answered. "We housed a certain messenger dispatched for Lyle bearing a peculiar message. Roallin is a gathering place for emissaries fielding articles from Ainiald and places south – it is commonplace to find several waiting here before their next run. This rider had a note pertaining to you, and I found it quite curious. Begging your pardon, my head is filled with many names and curiosity gets the best of me. I found it odd to learn of a message destined for so far north and bearing a familiar title. I do hope it arrived."

"Indeed, a scroll came to my door several months ago, sent from Fanael. But the seal was broken."

"I do not recall seeing the actual message, but I could find out more," replied Rinigel, lying a dap towel upon the bar. "Thonas is the messenger's name, and he can be found in Roallin between routes. Shall I seek him out?"

"Yes, if it is no trouble, but speak of it discreetly. I wish to keep private matters to myself," Greynol replied.

Rinigel gave him a dubious look, but nodded in compliance. "Indeed, give me until morning then."

"Of course," answered Greynol.

He started at once for the stairs and bed, understanding well his caution offered no assurances. Rinigel put out word of the request to his assistants who worked with less caution: the name of Greynol would soon catch the ears of an anxious few.

Leonin too sought a little time for himself – a precious moment to one unused to the ways of city folk. He decided some night air might clear away the smoke and noise of the tavern. Poised in front of the inn he spied the moon, still in its first quarter, and the bright southern stars, many new to his eyes. A steady stream of persons walked the streets before him: well-to-do travelers and city-folk alike, aside from drunkards stumbling from tavern to tavern in the dark. He sought not to arouse suspicion and drifted into the shadows beneath the eaves of the inn; after all, from what he could tell, he was the only Farrian within fifty leagues of that place.

As the crowds thinned, a cloaked man stepped out of a small post a stone's throw east of Rengel's. The building drew Leonin's notice for the first time: uncomfortably dark and cramped if an inn, and noticeably shunned by others as they hurried past its entrance. A second man appeared, speaking with hurried motions to the first. He pointed out Rengal's as if giving directions. Leonin watched without moving as the first man started his way.

Fully cloaked and face hidden, the fellow drew near. He glanced furtively towards the second floor trying to steal a glimpse inside. His steps were careful and light, and as he approached the light of the manor, his eyes came into view, dark with purpose. With a long black mustache that dripped past the corners of his mouth, he walked like a cat stalking its prey.

Instinctively, he stopped in his tracks. Lowering his eyes, he discovered he was not alone – Leonin had spied him all along. He paused, a hand frozen in place upon his belt, gripping the handle of an unseen weapon. Several patrons exited the door speaking in loud voices and the man reeled back out of its light. He turned aside to flee. Then Leonin saw the dagger in his hand – the same black-handled assassin's dirk he spied upon the hill that first night on the Arrither Road.

"That is the seventh man who escaped the Bardol guard," muttered Leonin. He started forward, unsure of the choice to give chase or stay, for none of his party was in sight, still at ale within the manor. Leonin turned in pursuit, but in hesitating, gave the fellow time to slip down a blackened alleyway.

"I cannot follow him. They might never find me down here in the dark should a dart strike," he said, pausing at the entry of a side street. He could hear the sound of soft shoes running in the distance. The man was gone.

Leonin hurried back inside and straight for the stairs. He found Greynol reading silently in the candlelight of their room, and quickly explained everything that had happened:

"Worry not over our lone transgressor – not tonight, at least. I gather our friend will make no more appearances in Roallin," replied Greynol without alarm. "You were wise to not pursue. Tomorrow we will tell the others of the news – no use having Armond run through the streets tonight in search of a ghost. Now if you could, gather the men before they drink themselves into trouble of their own making. We must rest up for our ride into Larin in the morning."

"I was wondering about that, sir. How will they accept one of my kind there? I only ask since Larin is the House of the White Religion."

Greynol smiled. "No less than I accept you."

Leonin nodded graciously and ran off to summon the others. He convinced them to end their diversion, but not without some prodding. Armond was last to arrive, dropping like a sack of potatoes upon his bed. Without worries, the men slept the night hours away at peace, save Leonin, who could not help but wonder where the spy lurked next.

Morning comes quickly when uninvited, especially for those who spent long hours that night merrymaking. Breakfast consisted of boiled eggs and fresh rolls, a luxury offered to travelers – but seldom of importance in Roallin whose inhabitants afforded three meals a day – and it softened the mood for a ride into Larin. Andro anticipated his visit to the capital of Ainiald; her beauty and regality held his imagination ever since Uncle Breden first described it to him as a boy. But peaceful thoughts soon changed. Prior to setting out, the tale of Leonin's encounter made everyone anxious.

"That last thief will get his," growled Armond. "Since he is so determined, let him try and cross my path."

"He is crafty and has an assassin's blade. I wouldn't get too hasty," replied Andro, trying to still his friend's anger.

Greynol appealed to such wisdom. "At least there is one of you, aside from Leonin, who knows not to rush into trouble."

Preparations in order, Greynol sought out Rinigel and son, who greeted them at the rear door adjacent the stable. He was met with pleasant smiles.

"Good morning to you both. Any news of our conversation last night regarding the messenger, Thonas?" he asked of the keepers.

"Yes, and no," replied Rinigel. "I queried several emissaries about town, and it seems we missed the elusive Thonas by a week. I was assured he would never break the seal of a message in his care. I fear there is no other information to offer."

Greynol realized their intentions were honest, but misguided, and thanked them. The time had come to depart. He gathered the others and they rode out of Roallin entering upon the great Werithain Road, the Road of the West.

The sun rose upon their faces — a bright flame against an azure sky. They delighted in the breezy warmth of the Ainiald countryside. A broad plain became before them a canvas of farmed fields and wild rolling grassland. Far beyond a ridge of low grassy hills broke the once smooth upland as the heavily traveled road veered from east to south. Green strips of forest separated hill and vale in an embroidery of village, plain, and pastureland that rolled gently in broad ripples. The southern mountains grew steadily upon the horizon. The men decided to rest upon a hilltop to take in the view, a last pause before the capital city.

"Look, the mountains are more pronounced now, but less like our Vanadiums," said Zerrin. He removed a fresh pear out of his pack — one of several bought for a penny along the way.

"The Nordic Range is abrupt as a sudden storm, but here green foothills rise to support the taller peaks. The ridgebacks look more brown and red, unlike the steel-gray of home," replied Armond, standing on the verge of the road with a hand to shield his eyes. Drago beside him drew in a long breathless look.

"Kuirian have mined the Werithain for ages, as long as the North," he said. "Our ore is better, but here they find larger veins of gold, platinum, and precious stone. Copper is more abundant in the south, and their silver nearly equals ours in purity. This sight makes me anxious to see her; never before have I gone so long without the mountains beneath my feet."

"And you shall, Drago," replied Greynol nearby. "This is only the beginning of a chain that stretches deep into Fanael. But Larin is first, and I see the great city from here: its twin citadels gleam upon the crest of a lesser hill – Mont Eldalard."

"From now on, let caution be our guide," he continued, slowly scrutinizing each of them. "The time has come where secrecy is no longer possible. Only one road remains, through Larin, beyond the mountain passes, and on to Rintar. Today my concern lay only with the Citadel, the Temple of Dawn and realm of High-Exarch Eathadur. There the servants of Fawarra reside: Exarchs Livarian, Ondolowne, and Suor rule with the Patriarch – each considered wise and blessed. In Rintar we will find the sister temple, Oriscane, where Belhuor and Quoraine lead."

Armond shrugged his shoulders. "I never made sense of the make-up of this kingdom," he said. "Ainiald has a ruler, King Emeraith, yet you speak of the High-Exarch's power. Is it possible that a king shares his throne? This is the fear your sect brings to Nordhiem – a desire to take a share of the realm. Few back home understand the White Religion."

Greynol looked at him thoughtfully. "You will find the Exarchs seek no such power: their authority deals with the unseen, the mystical, the wiles of the heart. The teaching and belief of Fasduen is a vessel the king's of the South would reluctantly do without. *The White Religion*, as you call it, has authority, but not of this world. At coronation, every Ainurian King places his crown at the feet of the Patriarch, swearing allegiance to Fawarra. He calls out the words, 'the Kingdom and Fawarra are one'. In time you may understand these things in full."

Armond shook his head and started back to his mount.

They turned their attention to the last leg of the ride, hoping to finish in time for an early dinner. They rode hard across the mounds until reaching a fair village at the foot of a solitary knoll just north of Larin, named Borinarth, after the great Ainiald King born in the town in 1341 AE.

"We have entered the birthplace of a king of renown, Borinarth. He reigned for seventy years until the blessed age of 108," called Greynol, recalling his history lessons. "This is the gateway into Larin. Expect a fair question or two before entering."

At the first gate they were stopped, just as predicted, and allowed entry after a short inquiry pertaining to destination and pertinence of stay. The guards displayed great respect towards the Acolyte, leaving Andro to wonder what kind of treatment they would have received alone, and how would that scoundrel thief escape their notice. No toll was exacted upon entry.

Greynol answered the guards obediently, being that the citadel was their destination. At his answer, two riders in red were summoned as an escort.

"They will lead you to the Larin city-gate," said the commander of the guard. "We are a kingdom at war; your men must leave their weapons at their sides – swords sheathed."

Reasonable terms accepted, they followed their lead from the north-gate, through town and up the slope of a tall grassy hill. They paused at its crest. Andro let out a gasp as Larin fanned out before his searching eyes:

Ainiald's capital spread wide across a myriad of avenues and lanes, each formed of uniform circles that extended out from the twin citadels; here the King and Patriarch took their respective seats upon a prominence that ran through the heart of the city, cut off from the north by the Larin Rivar. Along the flanks of its eastern slope rose vast mansions and opulent residences – schools and housing for prelate and dignitary alike. At its tabled crest stood, first, the Temple of the Dawn, with a tall spire that rose from its center, gilded and bright in the sun with layers of gold and bronze, tapering down to the wide shoulders of the main chamber that gleamed with a cascade of glass. The palace of the king and queen flanked the temple with walls that towered high above the river upon a sheer cliff; less striking in appearance, yet grand indeed with its broad tower and many layered chambers, like brownish-red steps unevenly laid about the monticule.

"What a sight, worthy of all expectation," thought Andro, wondering what his parents might think of him now in such a place.

His trance was broken, pressed on by the escort, and they proceeded to the bottom of the hill where they were halted again. At a large open gate the two red riders were replaced by four wearing silver mail, gleaming helms, and squared shields, beveled at the bottom, which displayed Ainiald's four-squared standard, matching that of the beacons that hung above the city walls: the top right square was blue, as the bottom left green, the colors of the kingdom; the second of the top squares bore three crowns, one gold, one white, and one red; and the last square, upon the bottom right, bore the crested lion of the king. The rider's bore long-swords and crossbows, one had a morning star flail, another a mace.

"We are instructed to escort you to the to the Rilgirand Bridge – from there you shall be led onto the Mont," said one of the guards, bowing to Greynol.

"Thank you, sir. We will follow," he replied, although he knew the way. He also understood that no townsperson desired unchecked foreigners loosed upon their city, at least none of their sort; but he kept this from the young party who felt rather important at that moment.

They proceeded in file, two deep, along cobblestone avenues, passing homes, shops, and garden parks with fountains – no more did they feel as in a northern city with their saloons and gritty districts, for Larin's effect gave way to repose and cleanliness. Andro found the distance deceiving from the knoll to the city's center, and by the time they reached the watercourse, cressets were being lit about the curve of the river lane. High above, the castle mount stood brazen in the late sun with flags flitted in the wind and the play of larks that danced across ivory cliffs. The reflection of the Mont drifted like a picture upon the still moving waters below.

The escort came upon a heavy stone bridge that allowed entry onto the citadel grounds. A number of guardsmen alerted to their approach lined up with pikes in hand. The company drew to a sudden halt.

"Send word, Acolyte Arowen and company of seven men wish to board at the Common House for the evening, and possibly a second," said the lead man to the bridge captain who was dressed in similar fashion, except for the tall blue plume on his helmet.

"Very well then. I'll alert Lord Chamberlain," he replied, sending a runner across the span through a gateway beyond. With that, the four-guard escort departed.

The tall captain set his hands upon his hips, gruff compared to the other guards, inspecting Greynol and the Alliance with dark narrow-set eyes. He nodded to a footman who waved a standard to another upon the opposite side.

"I am Torisil, captain of the watch upon Rilgirand and the outer walls. Check your weapons here before you enter within; they shall remain safe within our stockade until your departure," he said, but not without protest.

"Captain Torisil, sir, our weapons are our livelihood – hard pressed we find ourselves to replace them," replied Drago to the request, climbing off his saddle as a guard held Arkenoak's reins.

"These are Vanadium Steel, the pride of Turra Arrither. We prefer to hold on to them ourselves," added Armond.

"Understand young Kuirian and Nordic, no weapon shall be brandished anywhere in the city; and none, save the arms of Eldalard's sworn guard, are permitted on the Mont. Ainiald is a Kingdom at war: Prince Duihirr and his men fight at Daehronn this very day. Vanadium Steel or no, the citadel remains secure."

Greynol pulled them aside for a quick reproach. "Listen, all of you. You must trust our fine captain here, or enjoy sleeping out in the countryside. I plan on no such thing. These are the grounds of King Emeraith – the honor is ours to stay here. My needs lay within."

His look meant far more than words allowed. One by one, weapons were piled onto a ramshackle cart, the last being Armond who dropped his prized sword into the pile – a gift from his father years before. They followed the cart, pulled by two attendants, across the famed bridge.

After a short wait, the doors of the greater gate opened allowing the men entrance. With horses in tow, they came to a portcullis, then a second and third gate that remained open. A stately gentleman awaited them on the other side, dressed as a noble in a green tabard bearing three intertwining circles of gold. He greeted them with a welcome smile, and a cheerful clean-shaven face that matched his hairless head.

"Greetings men of the North. And how long has it been since Acolyte Arowen walked these halls?" he asked with a formal bow.

"Too long, Lord Corsey. But I do not wish to trouble you at this hour."

"Nonsense. What trouble can an acolyte and old friend of the citadel bring?" he replied, taking Greynol's outstretched hand into his own. He turned his attention to the others. "My friends, I am Lord Chamberlain Corsey, and I am in the care and charge of the House you will reside this night. And perhaps a second?"

"I am inclined to stay a second day and rest up for the mountain ride."

"We will play it by ear, then," replied Corsey with a curious look. "A further trip south takes you into Fanael – there the war has taken its toll."

"I understand, friend, but that is our direction."

"Very well. Come along and be at peace, you are now at Mont Eldalard."

Stable hands relieved them of their steeds, escorting nine tired beasts through an alley towards the common stable. Their weapons followed, taken into the armory in the basement of the bridge-warden's quarters. Armond watched that great care was taken each step of the way until the swords, axes, and bows were securely stowed away and locked firm behind an iron door.

Afterwards, Lord Corsey led them along a wide lane that followed the spine of the hill, ascending gradually across the eastern slope with great mansions upon either side. Andro marched behind in wide-eyed astonishment, pausing at the threshold of a grand house on the south side of the avenue that boasted three tall stories of whitewashed stone and high arching breezeways above each corridor. A marble canopied bridge connected the house to an equally large manor up slope – home for many of the prelates and acolyte novices residing in Larin. The wall of the twin citadels lie west of the quarters taking in the full height of the Mont; an immense black gate at the end of the lane exposed the Ainurian Castle grounds from which they were excluded.

Before he could utter a word of protest, Andro's bags were removed from his hands. Then he and the others were escorted through marble halls and breezy stairwells to third floor accommodations, although, to Andro, the pace seemed altogether rushed. A corner guestroom at the end of a long row of open rooms was theirs; windowless and simple, but spacious enough with comfortable beds and clean linens. He was drawn to the arches along the outer corridor where a grand view of southern Larin appeared: a purplish hue fell across the city from the setting sun, and below, within the walls, terraced gardens and the lower stables whose yard was illuminated by lamplight.

Lord Corsey, who disappeared without their knowing, returned to check on their progress. He joined them for dinner in the grand hall located near the entrance of the house where a small number of visitors, servants, and guards ate quietly upon long common tables. A meatless supper disappointed the young men, for flesh was rationed in times of war. Elderly women dressed in gray and blue habits offered them wine and mead, along with bread served in wooden bowls. They ate until satisfied, honored by those in attendance, while others gazed at them with curious glances, especially Leonin, for his appearance on the Mont was strange indeed.

Corsey did not eat, but enjoyed himself in the conversation.

"You seem refreshed after so long a journey. Not so ragged as some who drop in for a spell – even those in pompous carriages," he said, accepting a cup and saucer from an attendant. He was quite comfortable in their company.

"The road does take a toll, but a hot Roallin bath dispels the hurt," replied Greynol. "I allowed for a later start this morning, otherwise we would have arrived earlier."

"But they are young. At fifty, my bones ache at the thought of such a sojourn. How have you faired, old friend?"

"I gather strength, for I was not helpless in my retirement. And purpose drives me all the more."

Corsey smiled in his astute manner, reading the Acolyte's thoughts: he saw plainly the struggle held within, but did not press him on the issue. Instead, he turned his attention to Andro and the others. "I am pleased in these difficult times to welcome such a fine gathering under my roof. Many days have passed since last the northern realms were brought into my service, and longer still since a Logander had visited, let alone two. Are my assumptions correct?"

Andro and Rogan stood at once. "Indeed you are, Lord Corsey," replied Andro who nearly knocked over his chair, delighted at the acknowledgement. "I am Andro Rhine and this is Rogan Pinehurst. We are happy to be at your service."

"...as are Drago, Zerrin, Brenn, and myself," added Armond across the table. "I am Armond, son of Baldor, and we hail from Vanyor, although Brenn was raised in Carrinth. What of Nordics arriving in Larin? I would have expected others before us."

"Some may have come, Armond, but not in my service – nor of this house," replied Corsey. "As Lord Chamberlain, my responsibilities include only a small portion of Mont Eldalard, and once outside these walls I hold no authority. Nordic ambassadors have visited King Emeraith in the past, and I know only a little of the goings on within city confines. Multitudes enter Larin's gates each season, staying in local manors or hostels, for Mont Eldalard is reserved for the noble and consecrated...and their companions.

You see, this is my home and refuge, and to many an opinion, my prison. But I would trade nothing for the honor of my post."

Corsey leaned in close beneath the light of candelabrum lit at both ends of the table. He was happy to have an eager audience. "Let me speak to you of my home," he continued:

"In the ninth century, the Annicrin came to Fanael from across the straights – the end of a long-suffering exile. They settled in Earlon and flourished among allies; that was until Maarkun's hoards arrived and took the southlands, driving them out. The wrath of Ninterat fell across the land and dragons came to bring destruction. Rintar fell to fire, only to rise again. Those were hard days indeed. The Annicrin drove north and settled here, out of the mountains, forming a kingdom of their own – Ainiald."

"Larin's first king, Eldalard, was crowned in 959, and he and son Rilgirand ruled through the turn of the first millennium; they were strong rulers by every account of history. In all, six lines have ruled Ainiald: the most treacherous, Irudian, overthrown in 1274; and the most beloved, Borinarth, father of the fifth line of rulers, who sat upon the throne for seventy years. Now Emeraith comes to us out of the line of Duihirr, his grand-sire and distant kin to the Borinarth family, with Prince Duihirr II, his beloved son and future king."

"Now you have come to this grand residence, named Merthanir House. Although no placard mentions it, books and memory do not forget. Merthanir was a fair king of the third ruling line. You will find many past monarchs honored in the 'White City'."

"What a wonderful place is Mont Eldalard, so rich in history," said Andro in a manner that made his twenty years seem more like ten.

"It is a fair people that remembers its past," replied Greynol with a smile. "I understand your time is pressed, Lord Corsey, but one last favor I need to ask of you."

"What do you require, friend?"

"Not a small thing in the least," he replied. "What I seek is a meeting with the Patriarch, or perhaps one of the Exarchs, for I greatly desire their council."

Corsey drew a thoughtful look, but it seemed more of a grimace. "You might have better luck at the Prelate House, for they are closer to the rulers. But I will see what I can do. The temple hour brings the holy lords together, and afterwards you may try to speak with one of them: Ondolowne might be the better choice, for Eathadur remains under tremendous conflict and Queen Fania prefers him near."

"What does the Queen require of the Patriarch?" asked Rogan, intrigued by the mention of royalty.

Corsey set down the spoon he used to stir his tea – thoughts of better days evaporating like the steam above his cup.

"Day and night she labors under the weight of war, praying for the safe return of her son and the riders under his command. A dour mood fills the castle grounds, and news of late bears account of great Illutarian armies – Drukon, men, and new terrors on the border near Rottian, even west towards Asenrael," answered Corsey. Mention of the Farrian kingdom caught Leonin unaware.

"I pray my words cause no distress, friend who has not yet been introduced. News of Asenrael and the great Rindurron comes rare these days; yet, I wish it otherwise. It must be the spirit of Merthanir himself, for the king and his sons were the last vestiges of an alliance Ainiald and Asenrael once held. That was four centuries ago and a time forgotten by most. My friend, you are Lanfersian and not from Asenrael, but I am glad you are here with us just the same."

"Thank you, Lord Corsey, your are very kind. I am Leonin, son of Lenin, and I hope that one day every race joins in such an alliance," he replied respectfully. King Merthanir held favor in Lanfersian lore, and Leonin recognized the name. His mind was put at ease to reside in the house of his notoriety.

Corsey stood to excuse himself. "The sun is setting and that calls for an early rest, although my dear wife must suffer through my snores. Arowen, shall I expect your men to join us for the temple hour at sunrise?"

Greynol shrugged his shoulders; he never gave it a thought. "I leave it in their hands. If you chose to come, the upper floor is for visitors and proselytes. There you will find a place to observe — in silence, mind you."

"At the break of dawn?" quipped Drago. "We've been doing that for two weeks now. Go ahead to your ritual — I for one will keep on sleeping."

"As you wish. You are all welcome should you change your minds," replied Greynol, but he was unsure of the ideal himself.

Collectively they turned in early for a night of rest — no barrels to tap here. Greynol left the decision in their hands to be ready before the break of day should they come along. Excited at the opportunity, Andro insisted that he would be prepared.

Andro's eyes flew open in the darkness before dawn. The bells heard in his dreams were suddenly real. "Hold on, Greynol, I'm coming!" he called still half asleep.

"He's not here. Greynol left for the temple not long ago," said Leonin, seated quietly nearby upon his bed.

"He must have tried to wake me, that I can remember, but I fell back asleep. Is it too late?"

"There may still be time — the sun has not risen."

Andro scrambled about like an excited child. Leonin thought it odd, he had not realized the importance of such an event to his friend. Andro tried waking the others, just as Greynol did earlier. Only Rogan accepted the invitation.

"You men go on; it is in your tradition. Allow us a bit more rest if you may," said a drowsy but polite Zerrin, the most coherent of the remaining four.

"He is right," replied Rogan who dressed quickly. "Let's hurry to the citadel before it is too late. How about you, Leonin, are you coming? This is a once in a lifetime chance since the doors are not always open to outsiders, and tomorrow we will be gone."

"I had not given it much thought," he replied. "Will they allow a Farrian to enter; after all, the White Religion holds my people in contempt."

Andro took him by the shoulder. "I do not believe it is how

you say, but let us speak of it later while there is time."

They ran out of the house and straight up the slope towards the citadel gate. The eastern sky was clear and a bright orange glow blazed across a line of silhouetted hills. In moments, the sun would climb the skies.

"It is late. They will shut us out for sure," puffed Rogan, jogging up to the gate where soldiers stood at attention. A small line of people filed in – nobles, knights, dignitaries, and several common-looking folk. Most were workers and visitors residing in Merthanir or one of several houses upon the Mont. Many passed through the portal unabated, but that was not the case with the three.

"Just a moment, please," called a guardsman with a bright sword upon a ring at his side. "From whence do you come, and under whose care?"

"We are from the Lernahurn, but I think you mean to ask where do we stay – that would be Merthanir House, under Lord Corsey's care. Acolyte Greynol...I mean, Acolyte Arowen, is our steward," replied Rogan plainly.

Andro gave him a wink that meant. *"Well said."*

Another guard checked over a written roster and nodded. "You may enter, and be quick about it – the time is short," he replied, stepping aside to allow them entrance.

They stepped out into a decorated yard, last in a line that had nearly entered the temple. Andro had little time to notice the colored walkways and bushes of manicured rose, lilac, and juniper. But none of them could escape the beauty of the Temple of the Dawn, the sun already gleaming upon its lofty spire. The body of the cathedral, wrought of iron and glass, formed huge shoulders until it reached a base of granite. Beside its towering entrance, a bell tower rang its last peels. They entered the chamber just its doors began to close.

They crossed a large foyer, whose height dizzied their senses; and there, upon a floor of polished marble, stood the figure of a giant winged man bearing a sword lifted high into the air.

Beneath its stare they stumbled, realizing it was only a statue. Andro glanced down at its base and read the markings, *Anavah – Sword of Fawarra*, written in each the Annicrin, Farria-Sirien, and western tongues.

They were chased away from twin doors of oak that remained closed and guarded on the opposite end of the room, since that entrance belonged to the consecrated. They were instead directed along with many others up a set of marble stairs onto a cavernous loft where a gathering of men and women gazed over a railing to the floor below. A young novice arranged the host as best he could.

"Silence now, it is beginning," he said with a finger to his lips.

Andro stood upon his toes in the back of the gallery, but he still could not see. He listened for a moment as all fell quiet. A murmur of silent prayers drifted out of the main chamber – a strange anticipation for what he could not imagine. Their backs were against the rear wall, so they drifted to one side where the crowd thinned. A narrow strip of footing remained between several white pillars and the stone railing – a place unintended for spectators, yet still protected from below. No one complained, and none of the crowd in the lower chamber gave notice.

Andro gazed above: the stained glass of the outer wall leaned over the western shoulder of the temple where they stood, rising to a lofty height. Incised upon the glass were the familiar intertwining crowns of Ainiald that gave hint of the coming day. Upon the eastern wall, across what seemed a dim candlelit gulf, a narrow band of polished glass and several small windows, stained green and blue, ran the full length of the temple, from the top of the shoulder to the floor. Along the floor, Andro saw a gathering of a great number of prelates in white as they came into view, and those dressed in a variety of colored cloaks behind them. They filed silently before what seemed a large flat stone borne upon an ancient oak frame.

A horn rang out and the people gathered above and below became at once silent and still. At that moment, as if on queue, the sun broke through the thin opening: a narrow shaft of light shone onto the rock, turning it from slate-gray to an opaque white with shades of amber. A deep red hue seemed to wash over it at times, and to Andro, the stone seemed a living thing.

"The day is nigh! The firstborn has come from out of the depths: Fasduen, our brother, has come ashore to claim a new land where the darkness conquers no more!" called one dressed in brilliant white with his cloak pulled back and a band of gold about his forehead. The aged man bowed slowly, frail as he was, a gray beard pressed against white vestments.

"Humility and prayer are servants of the free!" he sang in a voice that echoed about the chamber walls.

The Prelate climbed a small flight behind the wooden altar, kneeling before the stone where the sunbeam shone brightest and its surface appeared a translucent gold. Andro noticed from above how much it reminded him of the Timlet Stone. Following the prompting of the consecrated below, he dropped to his knees.

A song arose from the floor: a low melodic chant familiar to those of the Annicrin Tongue, of which Andro knew a few words. Like fine incense, the melody climbed to the heavens, supported by the consecrated who wore cloaks of ivory, browns, and gray, and stranger still, women dressed in blue and roan. And the old man in white was their leader – the Patriarch Eathadur.

Rogan caught a curious sight of his own. He leaned over the railing for a better look, risking discovery from those accustomed to regal sights, and unfamiliar with an over-eager foreigner. With bowed archers near and knights at their side, a richly dressed man and two women sat upon thrones against the lower wall, crowns resting upon pillows at their feet.

"King Emeraith, Queen Daria, and the princess!" gasped Rogan, but fortunately, only a few heard him.

"What are you doing?" asked Andro, giving him a tug.

Rogan pushed back from the railing. "Sorry, but I never expected to find royalty on this journey."

"We'll see the dungeon if you are not careful."

After a time of prayer and preparation, Eathadur began a new song, and upon hearing it, the people stood and joined in the verse:

"...*to the waters he has risen, to the sleeping he calls to rise; from the one who sends, he shall come again.*"

Quietly it came. At the height of the temple a mist formed, and fell over the chamber like a slow descending cloud until it met the stone; then it flowed out into the crowd, gentle upon the skin, overtaking the sunlight with its subtle presence. Andro felt it pass over him, for only a moment before spreading out of the temple into the morning air.

"*Emiarra calls – the spirit of Fawarra! Peace to the hearts of upright men; ascend to the heights where eagles dare,*" called Eathadur in a robust voice, seemingly renewed by the passing spirit. He closed the book from where he read. "Go now. Continue upon the path of watchfulness and hope."

The crowd was dismissed and departed the temple in orderly fashion while the Patriarch and consecrated remained behind, entering into a litany of supplication in the language of ancient Tuirowe. Andro, Rogan, and Leonin hurried out into the bright of day, and once outside the gate a wide view of Larin opened before their eyes. To their astonishment, the mist that began in the temple had spread out into the city in an ever-widening circle, lingering in places it previously crossed.

They watched as it swept across the city plain, beyond the northern hill and into Borinarth and the plains towards Roallin; and to the south, across the Faubourg and southern foothills. But even there it did not stop. The cloud climbed the mountain slopes entering its deep vales where others awaited its blessing. To Andro's wonder, townspeople stood along the avenues and across the river lane, kneeling to receive the blessing when it passed. As soon as it came it was gone, and the people were once again back to their regular lives, glad to accept the grace given their fair land.

"How did they know?" asked Andro in disbelief. "Never had I heard of such a thing in all the tales my mother spoke."

"Perhaps they do not boast for fear of losing what they have received," replied Leonin, hardly himself, astonished and fearful over what he had witnessed. Rogan could only manage a shrug. They waited outside Merthanir House for a time, taking in what had overtaken them, unprepared to start a day of normalcy with the others having just experienced heaven on earth.

Chapter Eleven – A Thief in the Night

Greynol entered the temple before the dawn hour and assembled with his brother acolytes, ladyhoods, and prelates, gathered each according to order, designated by colored cassock – brown and gray, blue and white. Consecrated woman formed their own body, wearing every color but white, reserved for the prelates alone. Greynol tried to glimpse every face, recognizing a few from memory, and fewer recalled his name. His last entreaty from the citadel, where the superiors of every order resided, was a letter to Prelate Wetherton three years prior announcing the request for Arowen's immediate retirement, which he submitted to with reluctance.

The Holy Exarchs entered the temple from a set of south-end doors dawning white vestments and gold; they proceeded to gather before the stone led by Patriarch Eathadur, who used a cane to walk until the ceremony began. Their role, along with the prelates, was to call down a blessing upon the land.

Greynol participated in solemnity, unknowing if any of his party arrived or even arose from their beds. The blessing fell upon him as it did the others: a quiet thing that strengthened his resolve and prepared him for what he hoped to accomplish that morning – to hold a meeting with the High Exarch. The holy hour became a second filled with prayer and supplication; the participants upon the second level were gone now and only the consecrated remained. After the allotted time, Eathadur departed with a small entourage through the west door, the same used by the royal family earlier.

"*Corsey was correct, the Patriarch has many concerns above my own,*" thought Greynol, the weight of his plight felt small in comparison to the needs of the kingdom. When the time of supplication ended, the gray acolytes, as a group, went back to their residence just outside the citadel walls. Only blue-hooded minions remained within the temple: their charge of constant vigilance before the 'Rock of Fasduen' was shared by consecrated women who otherwise resided in a house within the walls.

The Acolytes ate their first meal together, a late breakfast they referred to as the *Fourchette*. Greynol delighted in the company of his associates, quick to find confidants to entrust his questions; but a greyhood's call meant to scatter the countryside, some to settle, some to wander, leaving mainly novices and those of special calling at the Mont. Only a few had the understanding to help, and none had answers to the mystery of the scroll. Soon after, a novice brought Greynol hopeful news:

"Please, come to the High Prelate's chamber. Lord Ondolowne takes council before the noon hour – I have inquired of his schedule. May you find an answer to your questions and help besides."

"Thank you," replied Greynol. He followed the young man across a covered bridge, entering the Ainurian citadel through a lesser-known passage. After several winding corridors, they came to a bright and narrow hall.

"Wait here and the Exarch will be with you shortly," said the novice with a bow before departing.

Greynol took his seat aside a long black table that could seat thirty in comfort. Bright light entered the hall from several white-stained windows that covered the greater portion of a steeply slanted ceiling. Across the eastern wall a row of stained-glass windows, tilted open, exposed a manicured yard and garden of decorated shrubs and sweetly fragrant blossoms. He waited patiently, pouch at his feet, hands folded upon the table. From the far end of the room, a lock unlatched and twin-doors opened – a mature man entered. Greynol stood at once.

The man's step was brisk; a white mantle edged with blue silk fluttered at his back, and beneath it a coarse ivory tunic common to a steward. An inner strength emanated from his being, and like Greynol, his appearance defied his age.

"Lord Ondolowne," said Greynol with a bow.

"Greetings brother. I am told you seek my council," he replied in a warm voice, signaling with a hand for both to take a seat.

"Your pardon, lord. I understand your time is valuable, and I would never impose, but my need is great and I seek advice. My name is Greynol Arowen of Idarill House in Vanyor, and..."

Ondolowne raised a hand to still Greynol's apparent anxiety. "I know who you are Greynol Arowen, and I am glad you keep both the name of your upbringing and that given you by the Nordic people: Greynol, or *Greyhood* is how they identify you. Yours is humility to accept it."

"They are hard to change, but easy to accept a friend. Still, I am one of their own."

"You are like a father among many sons. The countryside is scattered with the influence of the acolyte, treating every man as equal," replied Ondolowne. His peaceful demeanor put Greynol at ease. "I am glad that you have come – now speak to me of this need."

Greynol swallowed hard and removed the scroll from its pouch, placing it on the table. "In all honesty, I hoped my arrival in Larin more anticipated," he answered, fingers resting atop the parchment. He held it close, almost embarrassed to reveal it. "Last spring this message came to my door from southern Fanael. Within in it you would learn that not all of my past acquaintances call me 'friend'. The seal was broken prior to my receiving it, and I hoped one of my superiors may have looked at it under suspicion, for the sender is evil."

Ondolowne took the scroll from Greynol's hands before he could protest. "Never have I seen this before, nor would I expect a prelate to open what is not his. This seal is Illutarian in design, but a Raugulon has left the real impression."

"I feared as much," replied Greynol, eyes lowering. "Forgive my intrusion. I shall take it away. Do not read it, for I fear a dark spell permeates the message."

"There is no reason for fear here, Arowen – darkness has no power so near the temple. But my eyes are open to its design, and more than one person's blood mingles upon the parchment."

Ondolowne spoke clearly, drawing knowledge from the scroll without unrolling it. He closed his eyes. "There is the blood of one who died, innocent of the fate he received. But his life mingles with the blood of another whom lives in death. The seal itself brings ruin, for the Raugulon fused its own fell blood into it – not lifeblood, mind you, for a Raugulon no longer has life in it. Only death fills its heart. Now tell me in your own words, what is the meaning of these things?"

The Exarch listened empathetically as Greynol gave account of his life's journey. Ondolowne looked into his eyes as if peering into a soul. "Long ago I heard your story, the tale of the fighter turned acolyte; that was before I became Exarch to the Acolytes whose care and attention are my calling. Many times I searched the maps in my room, uniting my thoughts to the consecrated who have gone off into the present world, carrying the message of Fawarra and Fasduen."

"Such as Idarill and Maxius in Nordhiem," said Greynol.

"Their courage and resolve is imitated today by gray-soldiers across the land: into Bardol, Rorrahiem, Kahrihiem, and Sorreign-Aln they tread. Today I find such resolve in the venerable man before me now; but your pain brings my heart to breaking, for the questions of your wife were never answered, save one – the son whom darkness has claimed."

Ondolowne continued, and his expression grew dour: "I recall well those days when I was a prelate in Ainar. How many souls were lost at Tier and throughout Earlon? That threat exists this day, although defenses have been greatly strengthened. War pulls at the very spirit of Ainiald and Fanael, and how heavily does this weigh upon the Patriarch Eathadur – our Holy Father. Only the support of prayer can sustain him now."

He handed the scroll back to Greynol. "How do you discern this man named, Dariat-Fauglir?"

"I believe he *is* my son. Aliane carried a child at the time Tier was destroyed, but she spoke naught of it, and I withheld my suspicions. The time of her expectancy still early, she may have kept the news from me in her doubt. But she was taken and bore the child in enemy lands. She named him Dariat, after her father, fearing my name, which bears the Raugulon curse, for one of their number we slew in battle. Revenge is the soul of a blackheart. Now I return to war with hope he can still be saved," replied Greynol.

"The path of faith is dark," replied Ondolowne after a pause. "Future days will be dominated by Urrgath and his legions in Ninterat and Illutar, and he has other lands still his own. Men, even the most clever, cannot engage in the conflict against evil. Fawarra acts through those whom empty themselves the most to ensure victory. We empty ourselves of everything in time: poverty is the call of the consecrated."

Greynol understood. "Long have I prepared myself to face this bitterness. I keep little, only enough to get my party and I to Asengard. But now I doubt the choices I have made, for there are others less deserving involved; the young men I bring with me, a buffer against the trials of the road. They too face the dangers that come to me – dangers that belong to me alone. It is not my intention to bring them to harm."

Ondolowne smiled in consolation.

"Arowen, your passage is a difficult one: no man need endure it. The endgame might bring death alone in enemy lands – no number of warriors could help you there. I propose you remain here on Mont Eldalard in safety, for as long as you require it."

Greynol broke a smile of his own, but it quickly faded. "Thank you, your Excellency. But if I were to perform a great evil, one that would consume my soul forever, how would you act?"

"I would do whatever possible to stop you in order to save you," replied the Exarch, leaning back in his chair. "But Fauglir is consumed by the darkness of the enemy. His greatest evil might be in killing you, his own father, to seal his fate and become lost forever — as a Raugulon himself. Stay here and live in peace, brother."

"My own life I forfeit — that concerns me little. I feel there is no other way but to face him and what controls his mind. If I stay here, difficulties will it bring and much hardship: evil will come to defile what is pure. This is not Rintar whose trials have made them warlike in vigilance. Let us leave Larin in peace."

"Not a true peace, Arowen, for war still comes to us through our prince and sons. Now tell me more of this party you bring. What of them?"

"They are immature and undeserving of such a fate. They have brought themselves to err due to my own ignorance: once I left the scroll unguarded to their tempting, and they took it upon themselves to read it, save one who resisted out of fear. The spell might hold sway over them in time, just as the unknown reader who first broke the seal somewhere between Gunkar and here."

"Now I understand your earlier question: you hoped a trusted soul broke the seal," replied Ondolowne. "This unknown reader, be he friend or foe, cannot be determined now, but your fellowship I hold most in regard. Tell me; did any go to the Temple for the Blessing? It may mitigate part of the spell."

"Alas, no," answered Greynol with remorse, for he did not know about Andro, Rogan, and Leonin's arrival. "They chose to sleep — rest is a luxury on the long road. I should have insisted, but they come from various backgrounds — Turrar, Kuirian, Mihtrir, Loganders, and a Lanfersian."

"A Lanfersian, here? Unusual indeed," remarked Ondolowne, the palm of his hand flat against the smooth table. "There seems more to your company than meets the eye — they represent the northern kingdoms in a rare alliance. Trust fully in the hope you bear, Greynol Arowen, the time of trial is nigh. But to go forward alone is imprudent. There might be something more I can do for you, perhaps arrange an escort to the borders of Asenrael, although I am not sure how long it might take to manage it. Queen Fania could be swayed..."

"You cannot afford such an offer in times like these. You require soldiers here since so many have gone off to the southlands."

"Then I will give you this in their stead," he replied. He reached beneath his mantle and removed a long silver chain from around his neck. "This is a relic of Anavah, sword of Fawarra. I have worn it since becoming Exarch. It will protect you from many evils."

He held out the chain upon which a large burnished gold metal hung, designed with the figure of a winged warrior similar to the statue in the temple. Greynol folded his hands in humility. "I cannot accept such a gift – I am not worthy to take it," he exclaimed.

Ondolowne stretched out his arm in insistence. "I give it freely, and with it the prayers of the Temple." Greynol relented, and opened his hand to receive the medallion, which covered most of his palm. "Wear it from now on. And as for the scroll, keep it near for the spell upon it is powerful. What it contains can be used against you if found in corrupt hands."

Greynol put the chain on and hid it beneath his cloak. He stood and bowed low. "I am grateful."

The Holy Prelate rose and placed both hands upon Greynol's lowered forehead. "May Fawarra bless you and Emiarra guide you. May Fasduen be your strength. Fare well my bother and friend."

"Thank you, your holiness. May Fawarra bless you and all whom you love," replied Greynol, holding back tears. With a call, the doors opened and the Exarch returned to his chambers, while Greynol was escorted back to the Prelate House. He desired to spend some time alone in thought before returning to the others.

Lord Chamberlain Corsey entered the third floor chamber a short time after lunch; Greynol had yet to return and the others rested leisurely upon their beds or stood out along the breezeway gazing into a fair summer vista.

"Good afternoon. How have you managed your first afternoon

in Larin?" he asked, beaming his familiar handsome smile. "I missed you at lunch – much to do today. I understand several of you enjoyed the holy hour. A remarkable blessing this morning; it is seldom a visible thing, in fact, quite rare. I hadn't a chance to greet you there, trying to keep things in order down below. Then my services were required at the castle."

Andro's attention peaked at the telling.

"The castle?" he replied with boyish wonder. "How I would have enjoyed seeing that too. We were just abiding our time since Greynol hasn't come back."

"He has business with his masters today. He will return when he can."

"But what sort of business takes you to the citadel? Did you meet with royalty?" asked Rogan with curiosity all his own.

"Indeed, Rogan Pinehurst. King Emeraith requests a council of House Chamberlains and the Marquis' of both Larin and Borinarth. He gathers us every Saturday after temple hour to learn of goings on here and there; news we pick up from visitors and the rumor of the day, you might say."

"Sounds like messenger work," laughed Zerrin.

"Yes, but due to unreliable reporting the king prefers trusted sources. He seeks all information possible to still his anxiety. The monarchs and Princess Ginette worry day and night over Prince Duihirr, but I told you this before. You may enjoy knowing I spoke with him briefly of your company. He was interested to learn of a northern party on the Mont."

Their young hearts leapt. They stumbled over each other with the next round of questions, puerile in their actions:

"What did he say about us?" asked Andro.

"And what of King Anor? Did he speak well of Nordhiem?" questioned Armond.

"And what news of the battle in Earlon?" added Drago, all in order.

Corsey put up a hand with a laugh. "One at a time, please. You remind me of my daughter, Lora – so many questions. First,

King Emeraith spoke nothing of your company, save he welcomed the news of your arrival; secondly, he speaks highly of King Anor, but he did not mention him today; and thirdly, news from the south brings fair tidings from the northern anvil, but the battle rages fiercest near Rottian."

"Any other news you could tell us? It seems we are always kept in the dark," asked Brenn, a bit more reserved than the rest.

"There were some things worth telling. King Emeraith did trust that the North would respond to Fanael's call for aid; and that coincided with news brought to us by Alvan, Marquis of Borinarth, of a report that a Nordic cavalry was seen upon the road west of Roallin. There were no other details given," replied Lord Corsey, holding court against the onslaught of queries. His attention turned at the howling wind that streamed down the corridor.

Corsey left his chair to gaze out one of the arched windows along the gallery. "The breeze picks up," he said, staring long into the horizon. "Clouds in the west and south, bright on top, but shadows underneath. We shall see a storm before evening. I suggest you take advantage of the day. Go on outdoors before the weather changes – there are garden terraces below, and you can sample our wine cellars."

"We are not gardeners here, save Brenn," replied Armond, "and wine does little for Turrar and Kuirian tastes. But I would enjoy a look at your armory."

"The Armory? I should have guessed it by your hands – you have bent steel before. Very well, find Cleotin and he will take you where you need to go; then you can judge for yourself the skill of Ainiald smithies. The rest of you may do as you wish. Your master shall return soon enough," finished Lord Corsey who departed with a bow.

They took his advice and went off to explore the wealth of Mont Eldalard. A young retainer, Cleotin, was happy to show them the weapon housing and smithy, much to Armond's delight. He and the others took in the sights and smells of iron and leather, while Leonin and Brenn stayed behind to enjoy the seeming peace of the gardens.

"My father would have called this heaven. Good earth here," said Brenn with the sun on his face. He and Leonin found the hillside terrace a bounty of flowering trees and flora, where bees danced between tall hedgerows, wisteria laced grottos, and stone ponds complete with fish and terrapin. Acolytes and ladyhoods, each dressed in woolen brown frocks, pressed new plants into the freshly turned loam and trimmed grass along red-bricked walkways. A level area close to the Prelate House was kept for food crops, and brimmed with cabbage, ripened tomatoes, and beans on the vine. Brenn smiled at a flat of freshly picked carrots and beats – a glimpse of dinner to come.

"Strange as it sounds, this place reminds me of home."

Leonin laughed. "We are a long way from Carrinth, but I see you have an eye for working the land."

"A hand-me-down from my father."

"Have both your parents passed on?"

"Indeed, yes. Dad first, back in Honodolch, then mother three years ago this winter. I had an older brother who died as a boy, but I hardly remember him. I am the only Linderfell now. I tried to make it alone, but land and seed cost more than a poor man can manage. The family plot had long been sold after my father's death – mother thought she knew what she was doing. Others work the fields now; soil that my father broke with the sweat of his brow. But it is gone. If not for my mother's kin in Vanyor, I'd be in a sorry state today."

Leonin forced a frown, nicking the stones that lined the trail with his shoe as they walked. "Sad to hear of such hardship. These things do not happen in the Lanfersi. No one is left outside the family – orphaned you might say."

"Orphaned? Not at my age," replied Brenn. "I'll land on my own two feet – and soon. I suppose we work for Greynol now, although it doesn't feel like work. As far as the Lanfersi is concerned, your people must be the nicest in all Turra Arrither. If only I was a Farrian."

"We are just, and at times kind. But our burden remains, that of a sad race torn apart. The Blessed Jewels have scattered a once proud people," replied Leonin, eying a line of stairs that led down to the rear yard, the stables, and the main wall. "Come along, let us go to bottom. There is a well. Let us have a drink and sit in the sun; something I like to do when out of the forest."

The deep waters of the cistern stilled the heat of the day. They found a bench to rest upon, watching as clouds drifted past, throwing shadows across the hill.

"Lord Corsey may be right, the warm air stirs and the wind has kicked up. Just the recipe for a storm," said Leonin, shielding his eyes from the dust that blew out of the stable-yard. "I think I'll go check on the horses before we head back."

"I'll take another drink and wait here," replied Brenn, enjoying a rare moment of solitude.

An attendant led Leonin to the horses at his request. He found the steeds resting in comfort among the many-stalled stable housing, which actually consisted of twin stables, a smithy in the rear, and several smaller storehouses; one near the well that overlooked the yard. It was within the storehouse that Brenn, while quaffing water from a bucket, saw a strange sight. A figure hid in the shadows in the back of the shed, seemingly a cloak that hung upon a peg, if Brenn had a guess; but then it turned suddenly, gazing in the direction of Leonin and the servant as they rounded the corner.

"Is that a worker or a figment of my imagination?" thought Brenn, shielding his eyes to see. The motionless silhouette seemed only a statue until Leonin returned, and then it backed away and fell out of sight.

"The horses are happily munching hay, although not so glad to see my face. They thought their time of rest had ended early," said Leonin with a grin. He noticed Brenn's strange expression as he looked towards the shed.

"Is something wrong?"

"Oh nothing I suppose. I thought I saw something, or

someone, in the storeroom over there. Must have been another worker," replied Brenn, waving off the concern.

Leonin turned to look, but saw nothing. "Whoever it was has left," he said.

"And so should we. Let's go back before it gets late."

Both groups returned to their chamber to find Greynol waiting, happy to learn his men enjoyed the humbler sights of Mont Eldalard. Brenn and Leonin entered the room just after the others who returned from the noteworthy armory. Armond and the Kuirian held their visit with particular interest, marveling at a broad selection of weaponry, some too delicate and ornate for anything but parading and pageantry. Their discussion was brief, for their stomachs and noses told them dinner was ready.

"Lord Corsey has family plans, so we are on our own for supper," said Andro as the roll of distant thunder entered the house.

"On our own? Corsey must have taken a liking to you – don't assume he dines with every guest of the house, or bothers explaining himself in small matters," replied Greynol at the ringing of the early dinner bell. They did not wait for a second.

They made their way to the dining room, only to wait as pompously dressed visitors filed in before them. In comparison, they seemed more like paupers, and it would not have missed the mark by far.

"Judging from the company he keeps, Corsey must find us a welcome change," whispered Brenn.

"It shows where his roots lie: the chamberlain accepts his role as if a servant, but his rank rises above those here born to privilege," replied Greynol. He found an empty table, taking the first seat as a strong breeze cleared the staleness from of the room.

The storm blew in while dinner was served; a minor inconvenience to the staff that doled out bowls of thick potage. Shutters were closed along the west side windows as a thunderclap sounded just above the Mont; tables' shook and plates rattled beneath the patron's refined slurps. Alarmed guests and attendants jumped with each flash of lightning and toll of thunder, all save Greynol and company who ate cheerfully and laughed as if nothing happened. They had seen worse storms before.

"So three of you came to the temple this morning. What were your impressions?" asked Greynol once he learned of their whereabouts.

"I for one found it wonderful indeed," answered Andro, "it seemed that all of Larin was touched."

"All of Ainiald, Andro. The Breath of Emiarra brings life into these very hills, and today it was made manifest – a special blessing."

The men understood little of the matter; their attention drawn to the lone open window facing the avenue. A hard rain began to fall, instantly turning the brick lane into a torrent, and steam began to rise. Lightning burst again just above the hill.

"A common summer storm, mind you. They come often to these parts, rolling in from the ocean," said Greynol.

"Storms like this might hamper us on the road," said Rogan.

"Beyond the valley wall lie the Werithain Range; rain is the least of our concerns there."

"And when might we take to the mountains?" asked Drago, anxious to enter the peaks he saw from afar.

"Prepare for a morning departure."

Brenn put a hand upon his belly, seemingly searching for room to stuff another roll. He turned to flag down a matron when he noticed a waterlogged stable-hand entered the room from the rear. "There is the young man who escorted Leonin at the stable. We should inform him of our intention to leave at daybreak, since Corsey is not here to do it," he said, waving to get the fellow's attention. "Looks like he didn't beat the weather."

The young man approached, rain dripping from the brim of his hood. He drew it back to avoid drenching the others.

"Sorry to disturb you in your state," remarked Brenn like a

snobbish patron with an overwhelmed waiter, "but I wanted to inform you that we will be riding out come morning."

"Very well, sir," he replied with a nod. "When the weather breaks, I will inform the steward of your intentions. Your mounts will be saddled and ready tomorrow by the seventh bell."

"Excellent. And how did the horses handle the storm?" asked Andro in a more polite tone. "I am a stableman myself and know how excitable they can get in the elements."

"Well, nervous as horses and thunderstorms go, but calm enough to entrust them to the night-steward without assistance. We maintain several workers during the day, and come evening we keep a hand around to watch over things. He is experienced – you've no need to worry."

"Oh yes, I believe I saw him in the storehouse earlier. He was watching from the building near the well," said Brenn, recalling the odd person in the shadows.

"Saw who? I left the stable moments ago, as soon my replacement arrived, and he rushed to his post right after supper. There should be no one else on the stable grounds. We try to keep the curious folk in view; some like to visit the horses or inspect the livery, but no one should be left there on their own."

All eyes fell upon Brenn who shrugged his shoulders. "Well, I did see someone or something inside the storehouse, shortly before the storm."

The stableman gave a sigh and drew his wet hood. "I will go and take a look. We do find a stray soul now and again; those whom wander where they ought not," he replied, but the consideration in his eyes gave Armond a new concern.

"Hold on now. Just what did you see, Brenn?"

"I...I'm not sure. It was just a lone figure in the shadows of the shed. I thought it only a mantle on a peg, but it backed away when Leonin returned with this fellow from inspecting the horses."

"A cloaked man in hiding? Brenn, you fool, that could be the spy from the woods!" growled Armond.

"But we are within a grand fortress. No one could enter here without passing the guard post. Could they?"

The stable hand opened his mouth to speak, but held his tongue. The others read the answer in his eyes – there was another way inside the walls.

Leonin jumped to his feet. "Armond is right. Brenn, you should have said something earlier. I will go with this man and have a look about."

"Now, now, Leonin. Who is being hasty now?" asked Greynol, breaking in to interject some common sense. "What good is there in stirring a hornets nest of trouble alone. Brenn, take *all* of us to the place you saw this person."

Outside the air was thick, the rain ended as suddenly as it came. Large stray drops fell from a purplish-grey cloud that rolled eastward with flashes of lightning. The party filed down the hillside at the rear of the house along a maze of garden hedgerows, flowerbeds, and rosebushes. The cloudburst caused furrows in the dirt all the way down to the bottom of the hill, settling about the well in a mud-filled mire. The sun re-emerged only to disappear once again across the horizon of a clearing western sky – a banner of scarlet upon the vista of the west.

Brenn marched towards the open shed, pausing at the stable entrance. The night-steward met them at the gate, startled at the sight of a crowd.

"Is something wrong?" he asked with a freshly lit lantern in hand.

"I saw the strange person in there," replied Brenn, pointing towards the storehouse.

"Our guest here noticed someone lurking about earlier. Have you seen anyone wandering about the grounds?" asked the first worker, opening the gate to allow them entrance.

"I have seen no one – not in this weather."

Armond wasted little time and began searching the storehouse. He lifted a pitched fork and walked slowly about the room.

"There's nothing in here but farming tools and bridling," he said turning to Brenn. "You spoke too late."

"Well, this *was* the place."

Leonin decided to recheck the horses, entering a long white building with open stalls where the animals took in the air. He was quick to find the baggage and saddling checked earlier now disheveled and searched through.

"Over here, all of you, and be quick!" he called.

Splashing through puddles about the soaked yard the others ran to his side, save Armond who tarried about unsatisfied.

"Someone has picked this through," exclaimed Rogan, opening his saddlebag wide for Greynol to see. "Our remaining food and extra clothes have been worked over, but nothing seems taken. Somebody was in a rush to find something."

"Perhaps a worker came in here looking for something to eat," replied Andro, clearly out of line.

"With due respect, sir, we value our positions on Mont Eldalard. We are forbidden to touch of any of our guest's property, let alone remove items," replied the first servant, displeased and shaken by the turn of events that were soon to worsen. They took their leave to alert a superior of the possibility of a thief on the premises. Armond returned to meet the others in front of Toryche's stall, a scowl upon his lips.

"Nothing at all. You should have spoken earlier, Brenn, we might have caught him in the act," he snarled, smacking his fist in anger.

"I know, I am sorry. I was thinking of supper, and then the storm came."

"Fret not about it, either of you," said Greynol. He placed a hand upon the pouch containing the scroll, ever present at his side. "Nothing of value is missing."

As they spoke, Leonin strode to the rear of the stall that butted against the lower wall of the Mont, crouching low to examine a loose board at the bottom. He discovered a small gap separated the building from the stone bulwark.

"There is an opening behind these boards," he called.

Brenn came and knelt beside him. "I could easily slip inside there."

"That is unnecessary," replied Greynol, aware that the danger could still be near. Just then a shuffling sound was heard further along the wall.

Andro crept down the aisle following the noise. "There must be a crawlspace in-between, and from the sound of it, someone is still there," he whispered.

"Quick, find another opening."

The others ducked their heads in and out of the stalls until they came to the end where the noises stopped.

"End of the line. The space must lead all the way outside – that might explain his elusiveness. Armond, be quick. Grab something and..."

Greynol cut his words short for Armond was gone: he had already figured out the plan and rushed to confront the transgressor as he emerged from his hiding place.

Armond ran to a spot outside where the back of the stable met the city wall. Several boards concealed the space in-between. Suddenly as he came, the bottom plank slid aside from within, and out from the shadows a figure emerged crawling upon hands and knees onto the wet grass.

"Hold on there! Stay put or I'll stay you myself," called Armond, his knuckles bone-white with a hoe held high to strike. In times to come, he would often ask himself, *why did I open my mouth first?*

"Yes, yes," returned a startled voice within a black hood. The figure paused, stooping on all fours. "A Turrar...why, yes. Please sir, offer me no harm."

"What were you doing in there?"

The man lifted his gaze, but in the darkness, Armond could not tell if this was the spy from Leonin's description. *Why did I hesitate to strike?* Armond's second question rang in his ears in later times to come. He stepped closer, but paused, for the man gave no indication of resistance.

But an instant was all that was needed – just enough time for a reaction. A deft hand from a hidden pocket and a toss of powder flashed before Armond's eyes, blinding him as it singed his hair.

"Was it lightning?" he cried, fists buried into burning eyes. Suddenly, a deep pain sank into his chest just below the right collarbone, and it sent a surge throughout his body.

Armond let out a shout. Blinded and staggering, he swung his arms wildly against an invisible foe. By the time footsteps of his party came near, he stood bent against the wall. The shadowy figure leapt a fence and ran off into the darkness beneath the ramparts, a bloodied dagger gleaming in his hand.

Armond's shirt was now stained red and he tried to shake off the effects of the dark wound. "I...I will be fine. It's only a cut," he stammered, and then suddenly dropped to a knee. His head swam within shadow.

By now, guards were alerted to the commotion and arrived in a small group. Rogan and Leonin led them away to find the attacker. Greynol and the others struggled to pull Armond to his feet.

"It is just as I feared," said Greynol, trying to get a firm hold under his shoulder, "there is poison in his wound. We must take him to the house, immediately."

Andro and Drago pulled him up, supporting him under each arm.

"What of your ointment – the salve you used on the Bardol guards?" sobbed Brenn from behind as they dragged his weakened body away.

"I used the last precious drops that day upon the road," replied Greynol in the lead, marching up the stairs as quickly as they could follow.

"Will he die?"

"Pray not, Brenn. But we must act quickly, just as with the others. This is another foolish turn indeed!"

They reached the house, met at once by several alarmed attendants who hastened them to a first floor infirmity. Armond was laid upon a small white bed and drifted off into unconsciousness.

"We have alerted the Lord Chamberlain and the nurses," said an elder woman at the door. She watched in horror as Greynol prepared the wound with a soiled rag. His directives were firm:

"Woman, bring me some hot water and a clean cloth. Brenn, hand me my bag. Andro, help me remove Armond's shirt," he commanded in order.

All items were brought quickly and Greynol prepared the deep knife-wound for what came next. Two women dressed in long blue robes entered the room with Corsey and a slender girl at his side – unmistakably his daughter from the shape and hue of her brown eyes and thin waiting smile.

"Arowen, I am sorry. I do not know how this could happen," said Corsey, deeply troubled at the sight of Armond pale and lifeless before him. "Has his attacker been found?"

"Leonin and Rogan took off after him with several guards," replied Zerrin, the hope in his eyes falling once again upon Greynol. "Can Armond be saved?"

"This man who has followed us since Roallin, if the same as the spy we encountered upon the Arrither Road, carries the poison of the Khuldark. Armond's wound is strong with its peril; perhaps not as fresh, and that will give us time. But an antidote we need, the Arrowroot, and I have no more," he replied.

"Nor have we what you seek. I will place a bitter root in his mouth and hallowed salt on his tongue; next will come an ointment and dressing for the wound," said one of the blue-dressed nurses, displeased more at the sight of a Turrar bleeding on her clean sheets than the injury itself. The second nurse smeared a pungent gray balm over the gash as she held it open. Armond's eyes flew open, delirious with pain. The women held him down until he lost consciousness.

"What is happening?" cried Andro, fearing the worst.

"The ointment is a strong calomel to root out the infection, but its affect against such a poison may be small," she replied plainly. "You have only to hope he survives the night."

Andro gave Greynol a sudden tug. "Surely there must be

something else we can do."

Despite the tears in his eyes, Greynol had no answer.

A young brownhood came to the door shortly after the nurses finished dressing the wound: an attaché from the Prelate House. He bowed low as a spirit of deep despondency poured cold over his flesh.

"Acolyte Arowen, I am Neville. News of the attack on your friend has come to my superiors. Might there be some way to offer assistance?"

"Unless you have Arrowroot in your possession, or rarer still, a Lygerian plant, we are short on hope," replied Greynol as weariness stole his voice. "Someone go and find Leonin. By some odd chance he may have some in his possession – the High Race cherish it."

Neville placed a hand to his chin. "I fear we have no such items outside the royal store, and none save the king's physician can administer those. They are reserved for the royal family alone," he replied.

"This is absurd, my friend lay dying. If Arrowroot or some other healing plant rots in a storeroom up the hill and Armond loses his fight, then what good is there in Larin?" asked Andro. He was displeased at the reply.

"There is an assassin on the city plain – nothing will leave the royal store this day."

Leonin and Rogan returned during the exchange. The exhilaration of the chase departed once they saw Armond upon the berth, pale and wet with perspiration. Leonin was immediately interrogated for the requested items.

"Lygerian foil? I have none. Good it is for so many things, but quite rare," he replied, stepping into the chamber, cautious that even his footfalls might disturb the injured Turrar.

"What news of the spy, then?" asked Drago.

"We lost him along the wall; he escaped through a narrow passage, just a crack along the rocks below the garden. I never would have suspected it to be more than some loose stones, but he slipped right through. Small though it might seem, the guards say tunnels like these run beneath the city and deep below the Mont. Only a few know the way."

"They are called 'ratholes' by the guards, and like a rat the attacker slipped through," added Rogan. "No one could follow without difficulty, for the danger is greater in the darkness beneath the earth where he could lurk. The guards summoned a mason to brick the hole instead, and hope to find him when he surfaces again."

"Waiting for an assassin to *turn up* will prove fruitless indeed. He is somehow linked to this passage of mine – our paths are intertwined," replied Greynol, now dejected. He removed the Timlet stone from his pocket and placed it in Armond's hand before exiting the room. The others followed him into the hall. The nurses protested his actions between themselves, bickering in the Ainurian tongue about holy objects given to a pagan. A look from Neville silenced their petty concerns.

"What now? Our friend lay dying," asked Drago grimly, eyes downcast, burying his red beard into his chest.

Greynol stared blankly out an open window, arms crossed before him. "His blood is tainted by the poison root; I smelled its pungency while cleaning his wound. Arrowroot would be our greatest hope now, aside from the hand of Fawarra himself."

"Surely, in this whole place, in some garden plot, there must be a remedy," muttered Brenn.

Corsey felt Brenn's desperation. He wanted to offer hope, as best he could. "The remaining arrowroot traveled south with Prince Duihirr's retainers should his cavalry require it. The soldiers of Ainiald are entitled to every good provision; nevertheless, we will search up and down until something turns...what is it Lora? You have elbowed me twice now."

Lord Corsey turned to his daughter who listened at his side; a bright fifteen-year old, she pondered the situation. Shyly, she leaned in to explain, gazing nervously with all eyes upon her. She softly spoke:

"What is known of the Lygerian plant, and what of its appearance?"

"Well, it is the great healer of the Farrian realm, and quite precious. I have seen it only in pale dried fronds," answered Greynol. Leonin had a better description to offer.

"It is a treasure back home in the Vale of Orisduen, and it is beautiful to behold," he added. "The Lygerian is a well-rooted plant, loving wet places and deep shady hollows: bell-shaped are its leaves, thick and sturdy, forming a deep pitcher containing a sweet fragrant liquid; from it a long stem grows bearing a cluster of small pearl-like flowers. These my people grow with great care and reverence, for it is a healing plant – I will always regret not begging for some before departing. The plant must be destroyed in the process of removing its liquid, for only a fresh draught heals; even had I brought a vial with me, its properties would have been greatly reduced."

Lora's bright cinnamon-brown eyes grew wide. "Sir, I believe I have seen this plant."

She stepped from her father's side, gazing with folded hands into her memory. "Acolyte Hawthorne's garden – in his dark garden within the hidden alcove. There are many wondrous things there, including the plant called Lygerian. I recall the name from Hawthorne himself."

The Lord Chamberlain cleared his throat, unsure and embarrassed by the false hope of one so young.

"Lora spends much time in the gardens when away from her studies," replied Corsey, voicing doubt. "You must be mistaken about *this* plant, dear." But she insisted.

"Acolyte Hawthorne is away with the others of his province – this is their time of retreat in the mountains," said Neville, listening in. "But I shall gather the key from a caretaker and we will have a look. If this Lygerian plant is what you require, then by all means do as needed."

"Lora, are you certain of what you say? Can you find this plant in the dark?" asked Corsey gently.

"Yes father, I know just where to look."

"Good then," replied Neville. "Bring a light and meet me at the garden gate. Should any ask you of your intentions, tell them you await my return."

Lanterns were gathered. Corsey, Andro, Rogan, and Leonin followed behind young Lora to the outer porch, down a flight of stairs and across an upper garden. Greynol and the Mihtrir waited behind.

They found a stone path parallel to the foundation of Merthanir House, and made their way in the darkness beneath a bridge that linked it to the prelate residence. The Ainurian Citadel and Temple of the Dawn lie opposite the house behind a massive wall seated atop a sheer ledge ten meters above the upper gardens. In the gap beneath a blackened alcove formed, guarded by an iron-barred fence and a gate draped with wisteria and framed with granite columns and a stone archway. Compared to the other gardens of Mont Eldalard, this one felt secluded and forgotten, locked away from the rest; the blackness within was impenetrable, save for only a few meters. A bricked path wound back into a cool, deep cove between raised beds of stone. The outer darkness of twilight became a moonless midnight in the depths of the alcove; the glow of a lantern exposed ivy-covered walls that disappeared into shadow, and deeper within, the sound of falling water.

"Here is the dark garden of Acolyte Hawthorne. The plants here care little for sun, and the acolyte loves them as if they were his own children," said Lora; staring deeply into the blackness, she very much called home. "Out on the terraces, I help the gardeners with their chores; but here, Acolyte Hawthorne never calls for assistance. This is his place. He is happy to show me around and let me sit in its quiet."

Neville returned bearing a ring of keys.

"I hope I have not kept you long. Many of the caretakers have gone to bed, although news of the attack upon your friend spreads rapidly throughout the Mont," he said once catching his breath.

With a twist of a long iron key, he unlocked the gate.

"Acolyte Hawthorne loves quiet places. He seems to understand plants better than people," said Lora, proceeding onto the dark path. Leonin and Andro followed closely behind.

Andro held the lantern high, illuminating the cliff-wall. "These ferns and vines are most peculiar. They seem deep forest plants. How did Hawthorne come upon them?" he wondered.

"Acolytes have a place of retreat in the Werithain. Hawthorne finds plants for his garden in deep mountain vales and brings them back here to cultivate," replied Corsey from behind.

"This Hawthorne finds treasures indeed," marveled Leonin, glimpsing strange fragrant flowers across the cliff-wall, snowy white upon thick vines, as large as an opened hand.

Lora walked along, her fingertips brushing gently across the leafy plant tops. "They say there are places only he knows — hollows where the rains play daily and the sun seen only in a shroud."

"Yes dear, but can you find what we came here for?" asked Corsey, not soon to forget their need.

Lora quickened her pace and came to the end of the path where a stream of water trickled out from the cliff-side, dropping into a small pool that brimmed with lily pads and speckled fish. Ferns and broad-leafed sylvan plants filled every nook of the earthen bed. Andro felt as if he were thrust into a deep-forest glen.

"I trust this is what you seek," she said, leaning upon a stone where several long-stemmed fronds spiked out between plantain lilies.

"Please be right, Lora," she whispered, sifting through the under layer with careful hands. "Here, beside these plants they call Heartweed, there are several bells and tiny blooms of small white flowers, just as you described."

Leonin bent low as the others pressed around. He ran his hand back to examine the well-rooted plant, one of several grouped in the bed. Heavy green veins ran upwards to form a narrow cup bearing a clear liquid, and beside it, a thin stemmed shoot bearing small white flowers and heart-shaped leaves. Leonin let out a laugh that rang throughout the cove.

"May you be blessed, Lora, your father and mother, too."

Lora blushed, unsure of what to say.

"What is it, Leonin?" asked Andro on her behalf. "Is this the plant we seek?"

"This, my friend, is the Lygerian," explained Leonin, "never would I have hoped to find one outside the Lanfersi. Undersized, but hardy indeed."

He lifted gently the neighboring stalk, displaying its odd leaves.

"And this is not Heartweed, but the Arrowroot itself. Greynol would have a chuckle indeed – both cures in the same garden plot."

"Then let us take one of each," said Neville. "How odd, how clever Hawthorne hid them under our noses."

"And under lock and key, no less. I suppose only the Acolyte knows what treasures lie in his garden," added Rogan. "Now be quick with a knife and let's get it back to the infirmary."

Armond dreamed an uneasy dream: first a flash of light, then the bite of a knife. An attempt to give chase proved impossible with legs so heavy and the world set to spin about his head. "What is wrong with me? Where are they taking me? My shoulder burns with fire and it spreads throughout my limbs," he gasped.

His thoughts ran wild for a time, and then came darkness; the smoke of death entered his heart, lungs, and bones. Then came a new pain as the nurse applied a healing balm to the wound – his eyes flew upon, but he recalled none of it. Then he drifted off into a long painful dream; his mind swam back into unconsciousness. A struggle welled up within and it seemed as if fire surrounded his flesh. Armond fought as though against an unseen foe; sword in hand, he descended into darkness, the weapon his only light. He heard voices – far off echoes that increased over time, and it brought him faint hope. But he could not find a way to escape the darkness.

"Awake Armond, awake and drink," said a soothing voice he did not recognize as Greynol's. A warm liquid was poured into his mouth. "Do not struggle...drink slowly."

He choked, spewing much of his first sip of tea, but it was enough to lift the dark veil from his eyes.

"Drink Armond, finish it all," he repeated.

Armond obeyed, trying to swallow the foul elixir that soon covered his face and clothes. New warmth entered his blood and flowed throughout his limbs, and the blindness began to fade. Before long, he managed to speak.

"Let me sleep a little...talk later," he muttered.

"All right, friend. Rest for now," replied Greynol. "Let us allow the Lygerian tea to do its work."

A group had gathered around his bed: the Alliance, Corsey and Lora, Neville and one other — a white prelate and assistant of Lord Ondolowne, who brought with him healing oils from the Exarch himself. Once Armond drifted into a peaceful dream, they dispersed for the evening, except Greynol and Andro who refused to depart, taking their rest within the infirmary. The nurses in blue returned time and again to check upon the injured Turrar until morning.

Andro awoke sharply at the seven o'clock bell, shocked to find Armond conscious and seated on his bed, head lowered and feet upon the floor. Andro jumped up with a start.

"Glory be, you are awake! We thought we lost you," he cried, running to Armond's side. "How do you feel, my friend?"

"Like I've been through a battle," he answered with a groan. "How long did I sleep?"

"It seems like such a long time now, but you were only out the night."

Armond lifted the bandages from his shoulder for a look. "Strange, I never felt the stitches go in."

"Your senses were put down at that point: balms and healing oils pungent enough to cause us all to stagger," replied Andro just as Greynol came to the door. Corsey and the company were with him.

"Ah, you are up," said the Acolyte. "You've been tossing and turning the last couple hours. I figured you would wake on your own before long."

"I could have slept longer, but why lay about – I've had hangovers worse than this scratch," mused Armond with a painful laugh. "How is it this little stick under the collar gave me so much trouble?"

"Poison from the Khuldark," answered Drago, "the same used against the Bardol guards."

"I figured as much. Now we know the attacker is one in the same as the spy from the Arrither Road. Greynol, we should have grabbed him when we had a chance."

"And to what result? For better or worse? There were several in hiding that day."

"Well, did anyone catch him?"

"No," answered Brenn, "the sneak got away."

"Good, leave him for me. I'll be prepared next time," replied Armond with a devious smirk. He turned to Corsey. "Lord Chamberlain, tell your attendants to gather our weapons and ready the horses."

"Surely you don't expect to leave so soon?" he asked in disbelief. "You are in no shape to travel."

"All due respect, and with Greynol's blessing, I'd prefer to leave today as planned."

Greynol glanced him over and gave a nod. He understood the spirit of the warrior more than they realized. "Armond, you know my pressing need for haste. Are you certain you have the strength to ride?"

Armond stood, warily at first, walked over to a chamber pot and vomited.

"Now I'm ready."

"Just like a night on the townie, eh?" roared Zerrin. Armond splashed his face in a water bowl and gave him a wink.

Greynol shrugged his shoulders and sighed, unfortunate that the chamberlain had to witness such brashness in his own house.

Corsey just smiled and shrugged it off.

"If this is your decision, everything shall be prepared in short order – right after breakfast," he replied.

Greynol nodded, turning to Armond. "And you, my foolish warrior, owe much thanks to Lord Corsey and his House – especially his daughter, Lora. It was she who found the Lygerian plant and Arrowroot besides, which may aid us on the road ahead; although I hope we have no further need of either."

"How fortunate indeed that she found it here," added Leonin.

"Yes, one might say the alliances of old bear fruit long unforeseen: when old King Merthanir reigned, his love extended to Asenrael, bearing many good things for both Kingdoms. Lygerian was given as one of many great tokens of friendship, and unknown to many, this gift had been cultivated over the years; for I feel this is one plant Hawthorne did not find in his secret vale. He and master gardeners before him learned the art of growing the plant of great healing. Long forgotten were its properties," replied Corsey.

Leonin's heart sprang to life upon hearing it. "Mention of old alliances between Farrian and common men brings me great hope, whether these plants are the fruit of this friendship or not."

"A plant gives hope? Now I know I am no longer in Nordhiem," laughed Brenn.

Armond crossed his arms before him. "The poison hadn't done me in yet. Plant or no, there still remained fight in these bones."

"You won't admit that there are things even you can't defeat?" asked Brenn.

"Not without a fight. But I do recognize when to offer my appreciation: to the Lord Chamberlain I offer my gratitude, and to your daughter if she were here."

"You can tell her soon enough. I expect her to come around after breakfast, which I suggest you all attend while the hour is upon us," replied Corsey.

"All save Armond," said Greynol. "Even if you tried to eat, food would give more trouble than it is worth."

Armond nodded, fighting to walk on his own despite a swooning head. He waved off assistance and followed the others to the dining hall. Sight of him drew many in the residence to wonder if he were the man spoken of that evening, for many thought him dead. He tolerated suspicion for a while, if not enjoy entirely the mystery behind 'the undead barbarian'.

Pride became nausea; the very smell of food turned his stomach. Armond pushed away from the table and went off to pack his things alone. Once finished, he took his leave and hobbled off for the stables to await the others and prepare his rested war-horse, Calhurg. Greynol and company arrived to find him finished and securing his saddlebags and riding articles, but one heavy item he left covered in his hands. He pulled Andro aside to reveal its secret:

"I learned one important fact of life last night, Rhine," he said with a wink; "that is, how to keep alive in desperate times."

"What are you talking about?" asked Andro, staring at the large bundle.

"Being always prepared," he said, throwing aside the blanket to reveal a chain-metal hauberk. Armond held it up so they could both look it over. "Well, what do you think? I worked all winter long making it."

"I knew you kept something in hiding."

"Yes, but too late to turn last nights events. Now grab me a cloth to cover my bandages while I put it on."

Andro lifted the metal shirt over his head, careful to press a folded piece of cloth underneath as it settled. "It is certainly strong enough – your skill has grown."

"Pretty good, eh," laughed Armond who placed a horned helmet on his head, an old relic from his father. "Come, let us show the others."

Corsey arrived at the stable with Lora and the Brown Acolyte, Neville. The horses were lined in a row outside the stalls while Greynol and company made final preparations. Andro rounded the corner with Armond beside him in his glinting mail, and it gave the others quite a shock.

"Are all fighters from Nordhiem as resolute as you, Armond of Vanyor, for to see you now I would have never imagined the state you were in last evening," said Corsey, raising a brow.

"Cold is the heart of the North – slow to die," he replied in a sober, yet respectable tone.

"Rest assured, the hunt for your assailant will continue," said Neville.

"No matter. He will turn up again, and I look forward to it," said Armond, turning his gaze upon the shy girl who avoided his stare. "Lord, might this be the daughter I owe much thanks?"

"This is Lora. She insisted on seeing you men off," replied Corsey. Instinctively, he kept himself between she and the young fighter.

Armond bowed, his face grim, but voice sincere. "Lora, I am indebted to you most – by your efforts I am well again."

"I am glad to have assisted you, sir. You are welcome at the house under my father's care. May Merthanir bless you," she replied in a proper manner.

"I have little I can give you in repayment."

She swallowed hard in reply, raising her eyes to meet his stare, which softened. "You can repay us all by defeating the enemy in Earlon. Prince Duihirr is there, should you ride in his wake."

"I will take your blessing, young lady. And now that I think of it, I do have something I can give you," replied Armond. He reached into his saddlebag and pulled out a thin brown strap that held five colored feathers – the tokens of victory won at the tournament.

"Here's a little color for you: my winnings from earlier this summer at the King's Festival in Thalon, although that seems long ago now."

Lora took them in her frail hand and touched each feather lightly, running from white, brown, green, yellow, and blue at the end of the strap. "Thank you, sir. You must be a great champion."

Armond smiled, but it turned sour with Brenn's snickering.

"Well, now that is over, I too bid you farewell. May Fawarra bless the road at your feet. Lora was correct in saying you are welcome to stay here upon your return," replied Corsey with a smile of relief.

"Thank you for your graciousness," answered Greynol for them all. "The time has come to leave this hospitable place, but I fear my heart will remain."

Greynol led the party into the open where several stable-stewards waited. He dropped a few copper coins into waiting hands: Ainiald tradition called for silent service, where the benefactor was trusted to compensate without asking.

Following Corsey and four guards, they marched through a wide alley to the lower eastern slope of the Mont – an earthen path with broad steps for the horses to trod. Lora remained behind watching in curiosity; her attention drawn between the Alliance and Armond's gift that she held gently in her hand. She witnessed many leavings that summer, from the regal departure of Prince Duihirr to the quiet exit of Greynol's fellowship. For reasons her heart could not tell, the pain within felt the same.

Beneath the long stair, a path merged from an unseen lower garden bordering the city wall. Here they waited at a portcullis where two new guards brought their weapons from the storeroom. They took their swords, axes, and dirks, garbing themselves as fighters eager for battle: as a rule, bow and arrows were withheld until crossing the bridge. Quivers were filled and missing darts replaced – a reward for their troubles. Here Lord Corsey left them, making certain every provision was addressed. Once outside the side-gate, they passed a fountain and statue of Anavah, similar to the larger one inside the temple.

"What king of Ainiald is known to fly, for that statue has wings?" asked Drago loudly.

"That is *Anavah*, defender of the holy gate," replied Greynol.

"Looks like Hawe: winged, powerful, with a great sword in

hand. Perhaps there is hope for this White religion of yours," laughed Armond, drawing the Acolyte's stare, but he did not reply. A high tolling bell sent them far away from Mont Eldalard, but the memory would remain.

Chapter Twelve – Fire in the Night

"Now comes the time," said Greynol, feet planted firmly in Toryche's stirrups, "to take on the Werithain Road; an old friend indeed in better times indeed." The day was the twenty-ninth of Gare, the middle of summer and an excellent season to enter the great passage to the South.

The hours passed slowly on their long ascent above the plain of Larin: the highway cut a swath through the foothills and forest leaving a clear view of the city, and beyond, the northern fields they traversed two days earlier. They rose steadily in a series of wide sweeping turns. A shoulder of pine covered the length of a slender ridge, seen from the Ainurian citadel as a green wave set to roll over the lower foothills of mixed forest and meadow. Fall would bring further contrast of color when the lower woodland blazed with color before the unchanging evergreen – a footstool beneath the chiseled mountain peaks.

The road took a steep turn south into a stone-filled gorge, dividing the pine stand. At the end of the climb, the forest closed in sheltering them from a chill western breeze. Here they caught a final glimpse of Larin. Greynol turned back, like one who gazes upon his homeland before sailing off to far away shores.

"What is it, sir? Is something wrong?" asked Rogan.

"I wanted to look upon her one last time," he replied with eyes fixed upon the distant, yet clearly distinguishable temple and citadel. He bowed his head, striking his heart with a closed hand. Then with a tug of the reins, he circled Toryche southward and turned back no more.

The day waned and horses tired. A pass lay before them above the timberline, guarded on each side by tall, rust-colored peaks. Andro breathed deep the new air, throwing a mantle over his cloak as they entered the shadow of a mountain vale.

Daylight ended early. The sun faded into a deep-blue dusk. They entered a stony gap beneath rows of jutting peaks, the tallest with snow dusting its northern face. Camp was set upon a flat piece of grassy earth – too hard to Andro's liking. The area proved a common resting place with a spring and large fire-scarred pit. Throughout the day travelers passed their way, but that night the encampment was all their own.

Armond excused himself from the chores: the pain beneath his shoulder and weariness of his limbs intensified during the daylong ride. Seated upon a log beside the pit, he stared into a glad fire, sipping from Drago's flask to still the hurt. He removed his mail, only long enough to examine the stitches; his body was numb and head felt like a block of ice. A cup of spirited cider warmed his bones. Normally at home in the cold, Armond felt great distress, for the poison that remained gripped his flesh with new malice.

"If I cannot kill him, then let him suffer," he mumbled under his breath. Andro heard it more than once that day.

"Friend, allow me to redress your wound," replied Andro, pretending not to hear. He stripped away the yellow-stained rags, replacing them with fresh ones.

"Mercy brother. Throw my mail back on as soon you have finished – never may I be removed of it again, nor my sword, until by Hawe I fail to rise again," exclaimed Armond.

"Don't speak that way. Let me get you something to eat – it'll give you strength. Corsey made sure we had plenty of provisions for the road: rich breads, dried meats, and Brenn is fixing us beef stew. Finally some meat!" said Andro excitedly. He helped Armond recline upon the ground, a woolen blanket for cover. Sleep lay heavy in his eyes.

Armond began to drift off, and the clouds lifted from his mind. He saw the surrounding mountains, heartened to feel a little more at home – then he saw it. High upon a solitary southern peak, its face darkened against the twilight sky, flashed an orange light. A flame, it seemed, flickered high above the vale. He had seen it before.

"By Hawe, there it comes again, the fire from Dagoraust," he muttered. "What on earth can it be?"

"It's stew," answered Andro with a steaming bowl in hand and a hunk of Larin *pain*. "Maybe a bit watery, but the bread will soak it up. It needs more potatoes, but try to tell that to Brenn and then you know what happens…"

But Armond heard none of it. He stared straight away towards the mountain…waiting. Then it returned. A distant fire moved along what seemed a shear rock face. Andro turned to look, but it disappeared as soon as he caught a glimpse.

"Did you see that? Like the fire we witnessed near Dagoraust – unless there are two of them," said Armond. Together they watched and waited, but the fire did not return.

The next morning brought a deeper push into the high valleys of the Werithain. The mountains increased, impenetrable from the road, snow capped and varying in color from red and pale brown to silver-gray. The passage followed the easiest course, but not without its difficulties: throughout the day, they scaled the mountain roots or slipped into deep glens where the turf was soft and streams cold as ice.

At dusk, the road took a southeasterly turn, the horizon before them dominated by massive twin peaks: Mount Kairn in the forefront, with great black shoulders like a giant's cape in the wind; and Mount Sorindon, slightly taller, with steep-sided slopes forming a sharp peak capped with snow. Wisps of frozen cloud shrouded each, held aloft by strong western winds. The mountains were the grandest of all Ainiald.

Drago and Zerrin gazed in awe, recalling many a traveler tale that spoke of the revered peaks. Kuirian of old laid no shovel or pick to their roots, accepting not their riches in homage to the mountains they considered sacred. Zerrin sung of their glory:

PASSAGE OF THE ACOLYTE

Kairn the Great with shadows long, Mother of the Werithain song;
South her spouse reigns with his crown, Sorindon, King of Kings renown...

    They settled within a clearing beneath a shear ridge that leaned out like an uneven wall, protecting them from the wind. In the deepening dusk, Mount Kairn turned its frown upon the Alliance who huddled about a small fire – a look that carried royal contempt. Night came on and brought a feeling of solitude. The moon gleamed, nearing full, and cast long shadows about the craggy landscape; the face of Kairn now shone like a giant dreamed of in a Nordic legend, giving off a soft light of its own that fell like a veil about the glen. They felt a strange peace at the sight, a feeling of home, especially the Kuirian brothers and Armond – lighthearted that the strange firelight made paid no visit that night. Cold entered the camp and so came sleep; the next day would prove an arduous one indeed, for the pass of Mount Sorindon waited. Greynol kept it from their minds and let them rest a while.
    Rogan's first step outside his tent the next morning was barefoot onto a frost-covered patch of grass. He jumped back and finished getting dressed inside. After a hasty breakfast and hastier packing, they were back upon their mounts; steam wafting from their muzzles, the horses resumed the wearisome passage.
    Before they were comfortable in their saddles, the road began to climb: quick crooked bends lifted them out of the valley until they topped a narrow ledge across Kairn's knees, and the early sun was in their eyes. Looking back, they surveyed their encampment from above; only a small bare patch aside the ribbon of highway framed between yawning walls of rock. After a short rest the climb continued, skyward it seemed, the mountain's face keen to their every move.
    The Werithain Road remained an excellent passage, the pride of Kuirian labor; but not without its difficulties. Like a bridge connecting two peaks, the riders had no choice but to face the challenge of the pass. They now led their horses up the steep

slope, climbing as upon steps its folded layers, ever rising towards the crest. The road remained firm; their footing sure despite the loose rocks that layered the mountainside. Greynol paused at its height where bitter winds blew across their noses a stray snowflake or two.

"Have something to eat while I take a moment to myself," he said to the shivering others, each reluctant to rest between the imposing peaks.

Kairn to the north, thick and brooding, swallowed the horizon within her massive arms, like a mother hen guarding her chicks; and opposite, Sorindon, tall and majestic, a snowstorm sweeping down its lofty heights. They could do nothing more than wait, surrounded by boulders where little grew save mountain fescue and thorny shrubs, wherever they could take hold. They munched dried provisions while their anxious mounts pulled precious grass from the cracks between the rocks.

Andro bit into a hard cracker, watching with wonder the actions of Greynol who seemed to change since Merthanir House. "He has taken no meat and eats sparingly – now look how he stands alone at the edge of the cliff. What is he looking for in the sky?" he asked.

"And his expression, so distant now," added Rogan, shivering in his mantle.

Greynol perched on the broken rim of a great gulf that dropped away to the lower levels of the pass. Facing west, a strong gust blew down from the heights; he seemed to revel in it. Suddenly he drew back his hood, and as if by command, and the sun broke through an ashen bank of cloud. He breathed again, stretching out his arms, the Timlet stone was in his hand.

The others watched in wonder: would he jump, or even fly away in some magical flight? Brenn saw enough and drew near, concerned that the old man might loose balance and tumble to his death. He reached for Greynol's cloak and found it strangely warm. He was at peace.

"Not to worry, friend. I only wished to great him when he passed by," said Greynol with a smile.

Brenn thought for a moment.

"Do you mean your Emiarra?"

Greynol raised a brow. "Yes, Emiarra – the Breath of Fawarra."

"Is this his home?"

"He is in all places, Brenn. Should I ride the far oceans, he is there. Walk the dread halls of Ghorammar, or the blessed forests of the Falliscade; his hand is on my shoulder."

"And this Mountain?"

"A special place of greeting. I always found it so."

The others abided their time until Greynol and Brenn returned. Drago was first to complain. "Well, is that all of it? When do we leave this hilltop? It is still early and this is no place to set camp."

"We may go now. Thank you for your patience – it will be warmer below," replied Greynol, pacified as one after a delightful meal beside a glowing hearth. The horses calmed as he walked between them, gathering Toryche's tether; but not all were put at ease.

The pass behind them, Armond felt eyes upon his back. Looking about revealed nothing, but he could not shake this new presence. Consequently, Rogan realized a familiar pain of his own: the discomfort he last felt upon the Arrither Road returned unexpectedly; it seized his arm and surged throughout his body. Holding fast to his wrist, he bit his lip and hoped it would soon depart. *After so long, how could it return?* He asked of the wind, but the wind gave no answer.

In file, they descended the deep vale of Sorindon's keeping: a slope full of rocks and broken pieces of wagon wheels and wreaked carriages – fellow travelers that lost control while attempting the dangerous pass. Conditions changed rapidly on the southern side. Once beneath the tree line, their view became cloaked in a white cloud that seemed to extend from the Mountain itself.

Rogan's pain increased and his breaths grew into labored

sighs; he tried in vain to control his panic. A fire nipped at his fingers, climbed up his arm, and into his shoulder. It was as if he never left Dagoraust. He grimaced and cursed aloud, this time catching Greynol's ear.

"Rogan, why do you speak in that manner?" he asked angrily.

"I am sorry. I do not know why it is so," gasped Rogan, holding his arm close, "but I will tell you more once this pain subsides."

"Pain? What sort of pain?"

By this time, Armond discovered an unhappy sight of his own. Turning away from the commotion, he surveyed a nearby rock wall across a field of broken white boulders. His mind was alerted to something in the heights. He tried to pierce the windswept cloud that obscured his vision, tracing the line of the wall, and there upon a rocky outcrop a dark figure stood. Armond froze for a moment, trying to grasp what lurched upon the stone – then its fire appeared in a strange violent blaze burst. Andro caught sight of it burning like a giant beacon through the mist.

"Armond look, it is much closer now. And why does Rogan hurt so with the flames near?" he asked.

Armond drew his sword. "We shall soon find out."

"What are you doing? You don't know what is out there," Andro panicked.

But Armond did not wait to argue and continued as a moth drawn to flame. Andro removed his bow from Ambarr's saddle scabbard and hurried to catch up.

Greynol examined Rogan's arm, but found no answers to his malady. Zerrin stuck his nose between the two.

"Maybe you got a wasp in your shirt, or a spider."

"There are no markings to show so much as a scratch," replied Greynol.

"I can't explain it here. Give it some time and it may go away, just as before," said Rogan, revealing more than he wished.

"This is not the first time? I want some answers…and soon."

Leonin felt remorse for keeping the secret of Rogan's affliction. "I said nothing at the time, but Rogan was acting strangely after Dagoraust. His arm pained as it does now, but it ended as soon as we left the Arrither road," he said.

"Rogan, why did you keep this from me?" asked Greynol.

"The pain departed so suddenly and stayed away. I thought it was gone for good," he replied. "But ever since the chamber room of Dagoraust, I have been troubled."

"What do you mean? Do not fear in telling me."

Rogan swallowed hard and recollected his thoughts. "I hid the truth from you, and I am sorry for it. In the chamber at Dagoraust, I touched the stone – the *Corih Thair*. A shock ran through my arm and into my body, like lightning, but the pain came later on. It since departed only to return this day, as if a searing iron burns my very flesh. What can it all mean?"

Greynol shook his head unknowing.

Suddenly their attentions where drawn to Armond and Andro whom had wandered away, scrambling along the rocks beneath the wall. Something lurked in the gray shadows above.

"What's the matter with those two?" asked Brenn.

"Armond's sword is drawn, and look, there seems an strange fire on the rim of the overhang. See how it moves back and forth upon the ledge, quite unnaturally," replied Leonin, unhappy that it eluded him until now.

Greynol came forward. "And if I know better, they are where they need not be."

Armond scaled a large stone trying in vain to close in on the source of the blaze, but his advance fell back at the sound of wings. The fire suddenly rose into the cloud supported by a large shadowy form. Then it fell forward with speed, lunging towards the others.

"A Drake!" cried Drago, ducking behind his shield.

The flame swooped down with a loud screeching cry. Before Leonin could loose an arrow, it rose high into the mists and back towards the mountain. They watched the skies awaiting its return, but it did not come.

"Drago, I am not certain of your guess. A Drake flies not so swiftly," said Greynol once things fell silent again.

"What else can it be? They burn with fire and they can fly. They are cousins to the dragons after all."

"Have you ever seen one? A drake will not approach man without good reason – such as mutton on the spit," replied the Acolyte, turning his attention to Rogan. "Speak to me, son, how do you feel now?"

"Better now that the fire is out of sight. But what would that thing have to do with my arm?" asked Rogan, rubbing his fingers.

Zerrin recalled Kuirian mountain lore. "Could it be a Fury?" he asked.

Greynol peered warily into the skies. "Let us hope it is nothing of the kind."

Armond and Andro returned to the others. Greynol's look demanded an answer to their foolishness.

"I know you are angry, but Andro and I have seen this thing before – first near Dagoraust, then here," replied Armond, shaking off his angst. "Does this have anything to do with your prayer at the pass?"

"No, Armond, my prayer may have kept that thing away."

"Then let your prayer protect us off this mountainside."

Hope came to pass as they descended the rift into a deep-forested valley. Odd sounds were heard in the skies above, both earthly and infernal. Andro was pleased the veil of cloud held its place. Once under the cover of forest the mists cleared and the feeling of unease lifted. They managed several leagues by nightfall and set watch beneath an aging spruce stand where the earth was deep and dark. Mount Sorindon remained in full view, seen from its southern face: its frozen peak bright orange from the setting sun. Strong winds pushed all trace of cloud eastward and the sky gave no clue of fire.

Despite the early clearing, rain greeted them the next morning. Their ride began chilly and wet, over rocky foothills beneath forests of cedar that soon gave way to a broad sweeping valley. The last stretch of Ainiald carried them across a wide green land of tilled fields, woodland, and a swift flowing river – the Binarra, which marked the border of Ainiald and Fanael.

Against the river's bank a town emerged: Finar, the lone hospitable place upon the Werithain Road. Muddied trails descended from every direction to converge at the supply post from settlements with names like Corthad, Rorish, and Kuirtol – a Kuirian village east of Sorindon. Finar's gates were open during respectable hours; a welcome to any whom wished to enter, including a tired party from the North. Here the skies cleared, and the men, like many a traveler, turned to the town for a respite, provisions, and a full mug in the city tavern.

They entered Finar with the mid-day sun warming their rain-soaked cloaks. Main Street was unswerving and neat, and a short distance away the south gate exposed a stone bridge where the Binarra River rushed within a deep gorge.

"Let us secure a room while there is time," said Greynol, dismounting in the middle of the lane. "Remember, the gates are shut from midnight until dawn. You won't get back in if left outside."

He recalled the town well, imperceptibly changed from past visits. "Mayor Ermal is a gracious man, typical Ainurian, and easy to find; kind too, is Callis, a fellow Acolyte and an old friend. His home lie on South Street, but I will not call on him right away. Finar House is our destination, kept in the tradition of a Larin hostel – hospitable and welcoming."

"In ages past many gatherings found their place in Finar – a holiday of sorts, full of conversation amid the beauty of its fields, river, and mountains. But traditions wear thin and so had many allegiances."

Finar House was nestled between several neatly ordered homes, which seemed the common theme of the village. The manor had a stately look, brightly painted, windows opened wide to catch the breeze. Greynol procured eight beds for two nights and a stable pen for the horses. A promise of comfort and a place to rest their heads had no one objecting. They left their baggage in an upper floor room and spent the remainder of the day in the rathskeller, a well-attended ale-hall capable of handling a hundred thirsty travelers in comfort. The inn held a steady crowd for a Wednesday.

In an inconspicuous spot along the back wall, they enjoyed the main course of the house – lamb, potatoes, broth with bacon, cheese, and pan bread served hot and steaming. They ate and drank vigorously, either beer, or in Andro and Leonin's case, an orrisroot mead. They delighted in each other's company. For many, talk during dinner is impolite, but encouraged at Finar House where discussions ran between the weather, idle complaints, and war. An old farmer and common face in town, Gord Greenhall, continued a nearby conversation:

"…I'm tellin' you, the war's starting to take its toll and ol' Turgulant ain't ready to stand down," he said in a loud voice, the only manner he was used to speaking. "Them Raugulon got a plan in mind, and it ain't gettin' easier for any of us. Everyday I see more of 'em pass my fields, wagons going south, now wagons headed north, and those ones ain't lookin' too healthy – full of wounded and dyin'."

"Forty years ago times was bad, and I remember it like yesse'. But this time drukon are sneakin' west. I always said the Long Road needed watchin'. All they 'ave to do is come along and sack everything – including old Finar."

The young men listened while Gord rambled on to anyone who within shouting distance. Greynol chuckled, whispering to the others, "Gord has never tasted a hot meal, at home or over there in his favorite chair. Funny how some things never change. Gord will talk even if by himself. But he's got a wit about him; most who live off the land do."

"You're a worrier, Greenhall," returned a well-kempt steel merchant seated nearby. "Fanael and the Kuirian are fit to fight Illutar alone."

Armond could not resist putting in a word of his own. "And if trouble brews, my people will have something more to say about it," he called, raising a mug.

"Your people? Well, young man, let us hope times grow not so dire," he replied. "Shall I venture a guess who you might be? You do have a northern look."

Greynol responded before Armond could open his mouth again. "A northern look, yes, for the passes grow cold at night," he said, deflecting attention. Gord Greenhall put a quick end to the diversion.

"I know that voice. You ain't been 'round here lately – you're Callis' friend, Aren…Arrowin. Folks been asking about you."

"Arowen, I am Greynol Arowen," he replied, shaking his head in futility.

"And clearly not Ainurian," added the merchant. "I would say, given a guess, your party is Nordic, or from Bardol, possibly both."

This time Armond held his tongue awaiting the Acolyte's response. Greynol gave in to the question for deception was not his skill.

"Four of us hail from Nordhiem, one Carrinth, the others from Northern Gandol."

Several patrons turned their attention to the company upon hearing his disclosure, revealing their conversation was not entirely their own. Greynol's desire for concealment never had a chance in such a place.

"Say, if you've come all this way to fight, there ain't enough of you!" called Gord, nearly shouting.

"We are the first of many – Nordhiem shall answer Fanael's call," replied Armond, who could not resist.

"That settles it: if Fanael asks for help, then there's trouble brewin' indeed. And you Arrowin are much too old to fight – if acolytes fight at all."

"Not with swords, Mister Greenhall."

Dusk brought a cool breeze that swept through the tavern,

clearing out the stale, smoke-filled air. A fearful thought came to Andro – the reality of sitting on the border of Fanael finally sank in. Gord did not make matters any better.

"I've got nephews fighin' down south. I'll wager they ain't comin' back anytime soon. Never been fighters, the two of them; but no matter, we've got troubles of our own right here. Something's been brewin' – bad magic. They used to say drake and dragons have no place north of the King City, but just today I saw flames in the sky above my fields."

"You saw a fire in the sky? Do you think it was a drake?" asked Brenn, recalling the events on the mountain pass.

"Beggin' your pardon, but what the 'ell else could it be? What else flies and breathes fire? It weren't big enough for a dragon," replied Gord. He stared longingly into his empty mug. "Strange times indeed – odd sights, odd faces, lots of questions being asked…"

Andro heard enough and his thoughts drifted away from Gord's rambling. He surveyed the crowded barroom in his usual perceptive manner. "Good plain-folk," he thought, "much like those at home."

But the mood soon changed as a grim figure stepped down into the tavern from the lane. Andro found him peculiar for that place, if not menacing. His habit was like Greynol's, but of a darker shade of gray, matching the forked beard upon his chin. The man searched the room with purpose – a terrible gaze of which Andro wanted no part.

He strode towards a table near the entrance to sit down, keeping a wary eye on the crowd, but froze in place when he noticed Greynol conversing in the shadows with Leonin and Brenn. Greynol did not immediately perceive the fellow. Andro found it odd: the stranger seemed to deliberate whether to stay or go, standing in place, then made up his mind to approach.

"Oh, look what has crawled up from the Bottoms," said Gord in a rueful voice, quick to leave his chair for the man. "Here *Watcher,* take my seat. Got better things to do than sit 'ere and listen to one of yer speeches. Don't they need you on the other side of the bridge tonight?"

The glare in the man's eyes was answer enough, but he remained composed, ignoring Gord who trudged his way back home through the fields. The man turned to Greynol whose sudden bewilderment gave way to surprise.

"Thairidain, is it you? Seeing you now is beyond all expectation! How long has it been?" asked Greynol, leaving his chair.

"Stay seated Arowen. Might I find your presence in Finar any less expected?" he replied coldly. Dark narrow-set eyes and a pointed nose gave his words even more bite. "Many supposed you dead, but here you sit. Looking once again into the past for answers? How long must a *vagabond* live before he realizes it is too late?"

"*This* vagabond is now eighty and not yet dead – so until that day, it is far from late. Many years have passed since my last visit to the Werithain, and find it fair still. But what has time taught *the Watcher*?" returned Greynol with a dash of sincerity. But Andro, for one, could feel the tension between the two.

"I abide my time, spending the days the way I choose, unbridled by formula and contrition. That should not surprise you," he answered. "First I am here, next there; only I decide. Just now I came in looking for a friend, but since he is not here I shall go."

"I see little has changed since our travels together with the old alliance," replied Greynol.

Thairidain's jaw jutted and a grievous smirk came across his lips, spewing his response. "There you are wrong, Greynol Arowen. You are a conformer; a worrier over matters beyond your control. Just like Callis, you assume to know many things – idle wisdom drips from your words. But your ways are tested and found tiring. My mind has progressed far from the simple path. And you dare judge me? Common men are foolish to deduce my ways," he exclaimed, laughing haughtily. His words struck Greynol to the heart, and he continued his charge:

"Where to now, Arowen? Off to recapture past glories? Perhaps make new disciples for the Exarch's folly? Or do you still search for the one you lost so long ago? Time to give up the quest, old man."

Thairidain broke a smile of satisfaction, leaving with the last word – a short and strange visit.

"How rude?" asked Brenn once Thairidain rushed out of the place. "What was that all about, anyway?"

Greynol's eyes turned downward – his spirit was broken. Doubt sounded in his voice and his hands began to tremble.

"Thairidain was an old acquaintance and travel companion, but never really a friend," he replied candidly. "Our relationship strained due to pride on both ends. He was part of a fellowship of nearly forty years ago when I led a party of men and consecrated south to try once again to find Aliane and the others lost when Tier was overrun. Those days remain dark for me; but I clung to the hope given me by Callis, Wetherton, and Greylady Feldspar. All were young in their professions back then, convicted in the ways of Fawarra. I soon joined them, relinquishing my sword."

"Thairidain was different, yet for a while he embraced the discipline of an acolyte. He spurned instruction to go his own way – wherever that direction lie. I aptly named him 'Watcher', and the title stuck, since his attention was drawn towards prying, always concerned of other's motives. He was secretive then, and it appears little has changed."

"From his dress, he looks some sort of acolyte," said Andro.

"He holds fast to a discipline that is all his own," replied Greynol. He was glad it was over.

The merchant listened nearby, taking in the conversation between sips of mead. As he raised a mug to his lips, the rings upon his sleeve jangled. "Aye, I know him too," he said. "Promise a look at my wares and I'll tell you more – I have the finest merchandise in all the Werithain."

He leaned in close, gaining their attention. Glancing this way and that, he continued in a low voice:

"This Thairidain frequents 'the Bottoms' across the river – a place that has fallen in with bandits and revelers. Even the Fawoeran border-keep is thought ill. The previous captain perished, unexpectedly; no one is certain how, but speculation speaks of murder. Thairidain is oft seen with their new captain, Ernild, and his foul crew."

"How can this be?" asked Brenn.

"War takes the strongest men, leaving Ernild and his brood to enter in. That is when the problems started. Now Ernild is Captain. The good folk of Finar do what they can to avoid the bridge crossing. As long as they keep from the bottoms, they'll be safe...for now."

"As for myself, I go now and again: a sale up in Lonarion, a buy down river; one must make a livin', you know. But those guards keep a close eye on things – my things."

"Dishonor among the Fanael guard, just like Gandol. How does this persist?" asked Andro.

"War claims too much. The focus is more than always upon the South – the northern border holds small concern," he answered, spinning the rings on his fat hand. "Perhaps there's something a fine looking crew like yourselves can do about it. Now if you'll excuse me, it's late and almost time to put my cart under lock and key – nothing left to trust these days."

The man stood up and gave a bow, which caused his entire jacket to chime like sleigh bells. "Now about that promise..."

Armond and Drago found his wagon just outside the inn, and when the merchant opened its doors, the unmistakable clang of cutlery rang in their ears. They found his wares fare-priced and fairer made. Armond discovered a short-sword that caught his fancy; slightly longer than a dirk, broad and ready to take on a sharp edge.

"A little something worth holding onto," he thought, tossing the man ten schillings.

The fellow flipped his cap and rolled homeward for the night. Armond and Drago went to their room for a well-deserved rest, where the others had already gathered.

Although lumpy and several too hard, their beds beat lying out on the open ground. Sleep came not without effort, for the manor served ale until just before midnight when the gate-bell tolled: a signal that the city was preparing to close. The sound of chatter and song dispersed with the crowd.

Despite the relative calm, Andro slept light that evening, his mind filled with anxious thoughts: Fanael lay at their doorstep, and talk of strange men, fires in the sky, and 'the Watcher' kept him turning beneath his covers. Once settled into a peaceful dream, the sound of a barking dog jolted him awake.

"This'll never do," he muttered in frustration, crawling out of bed. In the next cot Armond slept soundly, his first good night's rest since Larin and the attack; the smell of fresh balm thick upon his stitches.

Andro crept over to the window, quietly so not to wake the others, pushing aside the shutters to expose a sleeping village now bathed in moonlight. "What time is it?" he thought, poking out his head out to take in the air. The streets were empty. A glimpse south exposed the gate where guards stood unseen outside a smaller gate-door; and beyond the walls, the far end of a bridge with iron cressets blazing. To its left a shadowy keep, barely visible along the river channel – the Binarra exposed only by its churning waters.

Warily, Andro turned north, the words of Gord lingering in his mind of a fire in the sky. "Nothing," he sighed, relieved to find only stillness and dark. The silhouettes of Mount's Kairn and Sorindon, barely visible from the light of the moon, ruled the clear night. Just then, a strange noise caught his ears.

A whistling sound arose from out of the northern skies, closing in at great speed. As he leaned out the dormer, Andro saw it plain: towards Finar it came, a reddish glow just above the trees beyond the north-gate. A loud screech erupted as it passed; a sound Andro never heard in his young life. High above the rooftops it swooped, a monster with long black wings and fire at its mouth that bristled down its thick torso with sparks and sputters. Like a great night beast, it plunged over the manor. Andro fell away from the window so not to be seen. Another cry and it continued away.

"Is it gone?" he wondered, shaking from fright. He turned to find the others half-awake from the alarm – save Rogan, still in the throes of an uncomfortable dream, tugging at his arm in silent pain.

"I am sorry, friend," whispered Andro. "Why did we ever leave Logan?"

Chapter Thirteen – Revelation

The second day in Finar began as one of ease and preparation before entrance into Fanael. This was a good time to sharpen weapons, check bridling, and inspect the horses. Greynol and Brenn went off early to purchase supplies, some of the best quality in all Turra Arrither.

"Salt, candles, oil, and the finest rope I've ever seen. What strange place is Finar to have such choice items on hand," said Brenn, holding up a tightly braided leader.

"This is only a small town, but one of great importance along several well-traveled routes," answered Greynol who noticed a familiar face walking towards them.

Mayor Ermal approached, nearly as wide as he was tall, and greeted them as if they met only the week before. Greynol gave an ear, listening politely as the Mayor spoke on many subjects that had little to do with anything at all.

"Remember young Mister Linderfell, sometimes patience requires long listening," whispered Greynol once they broke away. "Lord-Mayor Ermal appreciates a receptive listener; he was once a dominant figure in the region and many valued his wisdom. I fear with age his words are met with ignorance."

"Will they vote him out?"

"He is a Lord-Mayor, a relative of King Emeraith's mother, and this is his place in the world. The only vote that counts here belongs to the King."

They walked a leisurely circle about the village, arriving at last upon South Street, passing Callis' modest house where the elder acolyte greeted them from his garden. He was quick to invite the entire party over for dinner. Afterwards, Greynol and Brenn gathered with the others in the stable behind Finar House.

Zerrin looked up with a brush in his hand, smoothing over his steed's fine coat as they returned. "Well, you're back, with supplies I see," he said. "Andro was just tellin' us about something he saw last night. Some screeching thing that passed over Finar in a rush."

"I didn't hear a thing. Takes more than some hoot-owl to rouse me from sleep," laughed Drago.

"It was a Fury, and no hoot-owl. Gord Greenhall was right; there are strange sights in the skies these days," replied Andro, unhappy the subject came up.

"In the Lanfersi we call them Fire-gyres, but it is a name given to creatures seen rarely since days of old," said Leonin. "Some say they are flesh and bone, others demons; servants of Turgulant sent to find the Jewels of Firdom."

"Whatever they are, they are feared indeed," said Drago, and his mood turned. "One of their kind haunts the Vanadium Mountains: since my childhood came stories of Grunthagamor, Prince of Furies."

"You speak of Nordic legend, right?" asked Rogan.

"No Rogan, the Vanadium's hold a lore all their own. The Lord of Huork lives day and night from that creature's curse – the sword made black and his flesh to rot by the touch of that foul beast," answered Armond, and even his courage was tested with the thought of such an encounter.

"The curse befalling Lord Turan-Set is an unfortunate tale, but bringing up old terrors does us no good here," replied Greynol, setting down a bag loaded with fresh vegetables.

"But what of this new creature?" asked Brenn. "Armond has seen these fires since Dagoraust. And what of the noises above the camp in the East-wilds?"

"I cannot answer everything."

"No matter, sir, we will stand firm even should Grunthagamor leap upon our trail," said Armond.

"Speak no more of such things. Rest up, for we have a dinner invitation at Callis' this evening. Make yourselves presentable."

An hour before dusk, Greynol and company, having spent a leisurely day about Finar, its shops, fields, and river, arrived at the parsonage of Acolyte Callis. A woman greeted them at the door, her neat yellow smock matching the kerchief upon her head.

"Welcome Master Arowen, welcome all," she said in a kind voice that hinted a Fawoeran accent. "I am Elsie. Been working at the master's house for years – Arowen will tell you. Let me take you to Acolyte Callis, he is waiting at table. I hope you young men are hungry – dinner comes shortly."

"Thank you, yes," they replied in unison, following her lead.

Callis awaited them in a front dining room where candles were lit and oil lamps burned. Dressed in a plain woolen shirt and gray breeches, he looked odd for an acolyte, but right at home with the folk of the Binarra Valley, which he favored himself.

"Thank you all for coming," he said, rising slowly to his feet. "I was anxious to meet Arowen's new fellowship. Or what is it they call you now? Greynol."

"Whichever you wish," replied Greynol bowing, "and thank you for your hospitality."

"Think nothing of it. There's a bounty of corn, squash, and tomatoes this year – more than enough. No use in letting them rot on the vine," said Callis, motioning to the men.

"Please take a seat, all of you. This reminds me of old times indeed. Arowen and I go back sixty years, although he joined the order much later – a story worth hearing when you have the time. We were both fighters in the old Fanael brigades back then, just footmen, for both of us had Fawoeran blood in our veins. But I knew early on a fighter's life eluded me. Arowen was a fine soldier and skilled with a horse; he went on to marry a beautiful Earlon girl. What was her name?"

"Aliane," replied Greynol somberly.

"Those were fairer times. Aliane was a good choice for you –

strong-willed despite losing her father at a young age. I joined your hands in marriage at the house in Tier; a modest but adequate place to start a family. Does it stand still? I wonder."

"It was razed with every other home in the village; but that was a long time for anyone to remember," replied Greynol, placing a hand upon Callis' to reassure him.

"Foolish me, of course," he said. "My mind has lost its edge. I recall those days now when I played more a physician than anything else, doctoring soldiers after the line broke. Now it comes again – war has returned to the South. The enemy seems to want one thing, to take every piece of Fanael it can."

"We heard yesterday that the tide goes well," responded Armond.

"It is true, the surge has been met and thwarted. But the enemy is cunning – they plan every move far in advance," replied Callis, moving aside to let Elsie place a cool pitcher of milk before them. Brenn broke a smile, stuffing a napkin in his shirt in anticipation of a home-cooked meal.

"With any luck, the battle will be over before we get there," said the Mihtrir, quite comfortable with the thought.

Callis did not understand the comment. "Arowen, I believed you did not intend to return to Earlon."

"Asengard is my destination, no other. I will not venture again into Earlon. But these fine men might have other plans; continue on and become battle mercenaries, or go home. The choice belongs to them alone," explained Greynol.

"Indeed, but they are so young and deserve better than to be treated like some hoard of brigands. I do not wish to intrude, but I would hate to see fighters of honor grow corrupt like those who live in that keep across river; men depraved because of a few bad seeds. Men of ill-fortune you might say."

"Thank you, Acolyte Callis, we appreciate all good advice," replied Andro; "and speaking for myself, I'd like to focus on helping Greynol first – not what comes next."

"Sounds like you have a wise one in this group," laughed Callis. Andro blushed and lowered his head, sipping his drink.

Andro tried to look past the compliment, and quickly changed the subject. "Greynol, have you mentioned the scroll to Callis? He might know something of its whereabouts."

"We spoke of many things earlier, including the scroll."

"...and I told Arowen that his message arrived here last fall, unopened," replied Callis.

"This is news indeed. So far we know it was opened prior to Roallin and after Finar," said Leonin, removing his cloak. Callis gave him a strange look, a look Leonin was quite accustomed to away from the Lanfersi, as if the Acolyte gazed upon a Farrian for the very first time.

"Well, that leaves Larin again as the best choice; although we discovered nothing about the scroll there," said Rogan.

"My guess is that the spy who attacked Armond did it," replied Brenn. "If he read it, then he is linked to it; and that would explain his evil deeds."

"Then the question remains: how would the spy manage to steal it from a messenger and return it unnoticed?" asked Leonin.

"Unless the messenger and the spy are in league with each other," countered Rogan.

Callis listened attentively, following the discussion with great interest. He drummed his fingers on the table waiting to interject.

"Messengers are loyal bunch," he said at once, "from all I have ever encountered. They earn a sacred trust to serve their masters, be that king, lord, or noble. The privilege of their office comes at a severe price if made corrupt; but times are different now and trust thrown easily to the winds. My hope is that all young men are not so easily profaned."

Andro couldn't help but laugh. He found irony at odd occasions.

"Youth may have their wiles, but we've seen some older sorts that have a sinister look about them."

"Andro, of whom are you speaking?" asked Greynol in a curious voice.

"Well, just last night, that 'so-called' friend of yours showed up

– Thairidain. Even now the thought of those prying eyes and tone of his voice makes my skin crawl."

"Thairidain? I am not surprised you ran into *him*. He's been handy of late, turning up now and again unexpected. I believe he stays with associates near the mill on the Fanael side, along 'the Bottoms' and up river," replied Callis.

"Andro is having a jest," explained Greynol. "I gave an account of the subject of Thairidain and our stormy past; any attempt to call him 'friend' would be false indeed."

Elsie returned from the kitchen bearing fresh rolls and butter, then a modest portion of ham and game-pie, her specialty; next came steaming bowls of fresh corn on the cob, diced potatoes with rosemary, and honeyed yam. Brenn offered to help, but she would hear nothing of it.

The young men savored the home-cooked meal, eating and drinking until sated. Callis enjoyed watching them, a reminder of earlier times, giving a wink to Greynol now and again in remembrance. The discourse jogged his memory; thoughts of Thairidain and the scroll came to mind:

"If I may interrupt your dinner," he started, placing his knife and fork down. "I was reminded of Thairidain since you mentioned him earlier in your concerns. Like I said before, he has been handy of late, appearing at my door on several occasions since last fall. An old acquaintance, I bring him in for a hot meal; he eagerly accepts, of course, for even a stubborn soul like Thairidain cannot resist Elsie's cooking. I am trying to recall a particular visit last year. Elsie, are you busy? I need to ask you a question."

She promptly returned bearing a fresh pitcher of raspberry cordials, another specialty. "Yes sir, you have a question? May it wait until after dinner? I am busy as you can tell; pies to slice – pear and apple, mind you," she replied, talking all the way back to the kitchen.

Callis leaned in whispering: "Need I tell you who is the true master of this house. Prelate Anicarr, whom resides here with me, could tell you as much. He is in Rintar until the end of the month."

"It is good to have a prelate residing in the valley again," replied Greynol.

"Yes, and he is a busy one at that, drawn thin with the demands of the people. Father Anicarr is called far and wide for blessings, healings, and council. The demands of the prelate far outweigh the subtleties of an acolyte. Now all of you clean your plates before it gets late. Elsie likes to be home before dark."

They readily obeyed and drew back their chairs, stuffed to the gills. Several pipes were lit, as deep shadows poured across the front yard of Callis' residence. Plates were cleared and the table wiped – this time Elsie accepted Brenn and Rogan's help, spent as she was after such a meal. She rarely cooked for more than a few.

With a shawl thrown over her shoulders, she poked her head in to take her leave. "It is twilight now and time for me to head home. What was it you wanted to ask me?" she asked.

"Yes Elsie, thank you. Just one question if you have a moment to spare," replied Callorn.

"Only a moment."

"Of course. Do you recall last fall, we had a messenger arrive here with a scroll addressed to Greynol Arowen? He left it in our safekeeping until it could be taken north. It was getting late in the year, you know, and the passes less traveled; and emissaries can be in such demand these days."

Greynol pulled the scroll out of its pouch and laid it upon the table to jog her memory. Elsie recognized it at once.

"I remember it well; I am not so old, you know. And there was a smaller note with it. We held both letters here until the rider from Larin came for his pickup at the Finar House, and I recall greatly that dreadful red seal. I am surprised that you do not, Master Callis – you are far too forgetful these days," she answered. "I recall Prelate Anicarr being too busy to worry about it, and you fussed over it for a time, but set the thing aside."

"Was it opened here? Perhaps Anicarr had a look," asked Armond.

"Oh, he would never open what was not his."

"Pardon the question, Elsie," replied Greynol in kind, "we are trying to determine who may have opened the message between Larin and here."

"Well, thinking back, none of us would have done such a thing. It was left for me to take to Finar House before the messenger arrived. It was unopened then, but wait..."

Elsie pondered the question – her thin lips tensed and she searched her thoughts. "Now that I think about it, I recall at that time Callis' odd friend, Thairidain, hanging about. That was the one occasion he actually volunteered to help anyone with anything."

"How did he help?" asked an attentive Brenn.

"Well, as Master Callis clearly knows, I detest that manor with every sort of idler and drunk hanging about. Thairidain was happy to take the scroll for me. A past acquaintance of Arowen, I saw no problem in allowing him to bear it. Since you have it with you, he must have done as he said he would. Any other questions you will have to take up with him."

"Yes Elsie, and thank you for your assistance. It has helped us greatly," replied Greynol with emotions mixed between relief and a new burden.

Elsie nodded, untroubled by the strange needs of a traveling Acolyte. Callis saw her to the door, watching from the porch as she made her way down South Street – a short walk to her house near the river wall. Turning back, he noticed a rustling in the hedgerow at the edge of his yard.

"Hey! Come out of there. What are you doing in my bushes?" he called suddenly.

The others ran to the window and door to see the reason for the commotion, and the source of feet running up the lane.

"What is it, friend?" asked Greynol, standing from his chair.

"A man was lurking behind the hedges. He backed away when Elsie passed. She did not see him, but I did. He was watching us. As soon as I called, he ran off."

"That sounds like our man," said Armond, heading outside for the street. The others were right behind him.

"Who, Thairidain? He would never steal behind my hedges. Would he?" asked Callis, raising his hands to his face as they passed.

"Not Thairidain, but another man. One set out to do us harm," answered Greynol, leading his friend to the lane.

They turned towards Main Street, a stone's throw away, and saw a shrouded man at the corner. He paused at the south gate, turning back with a glance. Just then, a taller gentleman joined him on the road.

"There is Thairidain now," gaped Callis, "and what is he doing with that man from my bushes?"

"That's what we are about to find out," answered Armond. He stomped off in their direction.

"You must go Greynol – your men will not wait. Go and find the answer to your questions. You can explain the rest to me later," said Callis, urging him forward.

Just as the others bore down upon Main Street, Thairidain and the cloaked man turned the corner for the bridge.

"Is one sword enough?" asked Andro, stumbling over his shoes to keep up with Armond's gait.

"Don't you worry, my one sword will undo that assassin's dirk – my skin's a little thicker this time," replied Armond with a sly grin, shaking the chain of mail beneath his shirt.

"Not so fast," said Drago as they met the gate. "Look, they are tryin' to sneak into Fanael."

"...and we'll be right behind them."

The bridge stood in the long shadows of dusk with two figures seen in a hurry on the opposite side. Upon the left a stone keep sat in darkness.

"They have crossed over, but the guards have them stopped," said Leonin.

"Then they can't get away," replied Armond with satisfaction, drawing his sword.

"Lower that weapon. Give the guards no reason for

provocation," commanded Greynol, as anxious to confront Thairidain as Armond his attacker; although the Acolyte's motives were less violent.

The dark waters of the Binarra slid beneath the broad wooden span, seen by an orange glow of fire upon its surface – a reflection of the beacons that framed its length. Thairidain and his companion conversed with a group of watchmen; and suddenly as Greynol and company came within earshot, the two were left to pass.

"Armond, I told you once, put that weapon away," whispered Greynol, taking the lead as they came to face an unsavory garrison.

One of the guards stepped forward to end their progress. A red feather on his metal cap showed him to be one of authority. "Halt! Who wishes to enter Fanael so late in the evening?" he called.

"Those two you let pass, they must be stopped. One of them is a spy...if not worse," said Armond, jumping in before Greynol could answer.

"And who are you?" asked the man with a smirk, arms crossed at his chest.

"We are allies and friends of Fanael."

"Allies? You Northerners?" he scoffed. "The fact is, I cannot let you pass, not without first paying the toll."

"Again? Is that all corruption brings, a thirst for bribery?" replied Greynol to the scheme. "I have crossed this bridge as long as you have lived: it was built by Fawoerian and Kuirian hands for the needs of all men, and it is free. But if you demand a price, name it and let us pass."

"...and hurry, those two are getting away," mumbled Rogan at his back.

"Well, let's see, who can count here? Not many smarts here at the bottoms," said the man with a foolish laugh that reeked of drink, playing a game he enjoyed all too well.

"I count eight, Ernild," said one fowl guard.

"Make it nine!" shouted another.

"Come now, I am no thief. There are eight before us; so that'll be eight pounds – sixteen silver marks, old man," scoffed Ernild. His eyes were serious now and the jest left his lips. Thairidain and the cloaked man were seen mounting steeds tied nearby, and started away into the night.

"What kind of foolish men are you? What am I to say when I meet with your lords in Rintar?" asked Greynol angrily.

"They have greater concerns to tend. How would you like to double that toll?"

Armond came between them, unhappy by the turn of events.

"You dog, those traitors paid you off!" he fired back. He grabbed Ernild by the arm and punched him square in the face.

A ruckus broke out and bodies clashed upon the bridge, save Greynol who stood his ground. The young party was outnumbered, but had the size advantage of Armond and Andro rattling bones up front. Ernild climbed to his feet, now enraged and shaken. He snatched Brenn by the throat, the nearest and smallest opponent he could manage; and with a flick of the wrist, pressed a dagger against his neck.

"Enough, or he dies!" cried Ernild, red-faced and nose bloodied. "I'll kill this wretch if I have to."

The scrum ended immediately. Fists were lowered, but the guards brought out spears against the Alliance, who carried only dirks and Armond's broadsword, which he drew upon seeing their weapons.

"Don't be fools!" called Greynol. "There is no reason for this violence."

"You should have paid!" snapped Ernild, a strong hand across Brenn's chest, pointing the edge of the blade just below his chin. "Now put your weapons away."

They each complied, save Armond who strode forward within a sword's stroke. "Let him go, or should I offer you a taste of Nordic steel to change your mind. What do you want him for anyway?"

Ernild gave a wink to one of his men.

"Maybe your right, Turrar. I will throw this one back for a bigger catch…"

Without warning, a stout-bodied guard came from behind and struck Armond across the back of his head with a club, felling him at once. Brenn was tossed aside as several guards tackled Armond to the ground. There was no time to react. Armond's sword fell, kicked aside during the struggle, landing at Ernild's feet – he picked it up and slid it under his belt. Andro, Drago and Zerrin rushed forward, but the spears held them back. Several more guards ran up from the keep with pikes and swords as the situation worsened.

Leonin held the edge of his knife, quite prepared to cast it, calling out in a surprisingly loud voice. "Do him no harm, Ernild, or I will fall you myself! Do you wish to test my skill?"

Ernild pulled the limp and bleeding Armond before him, several blades now pointed at the Turrar's chest. "Do you wish to take that chance – whatever you are?"

"Give him back to us, or things will go bad for you. Everything is even now. To push things further will prove ill indeed," replied Greynol. Ernild laughed it off.

"What can you do, Acolyte? He's my prisoner now. How dare this barbarian strike the captain of the guard," he said, dragging a sleeve across his bloodied nose. "Bind him. I am the lord of this bridge, and all who cross it are subject to my rule. I own it by right. Yes indeed, Thairidain's money looks rather pretty, but for the game at hand, I'd do it free. I'll give you a reprieve, acolyte, my original offer: eight pounds and you may pass – but your friend remains."

A ruffian guard tapped Ernild from behind. "Cap'n, we 'ave no shackles for 'is bones. They're too tight and some are rusted through."

"Don't you know how to do anything?"

"We've never 'rested anyone before."

"Brom, Tark, rope the prisoner and take him to the dungeon. I'll deal with this vermin later."

Andro pressed forward, his face flushed and trembling, hands gripping the hilt of a dagger. Leonin beside him held the throwing knife tight in his hand, eager to do something to free Armond.

"Greynol, we can't let this happen."

Greynol stood frozen and unsure; their prospects had grown sour. Outnumbered two-to-one and Armond now being carried away by four guards, he could only shake his head.

"We must return to the manor," he said before long. He turned to Ernild for one last warning. "If Armond is harmed, you excite the wrath already laid against you; one murder hangs over you in judgment, do not allow a second. Time has come for you to choose your fate."

"Go back to your weeping and prayer, Acolyte. Your friend will be fortunate to glimpse another day," replied the foul leader with great irreverence. He wiped the blood from his nose and led his troop away from the bridge and into the keep, leaving several armed guards at the bridgehead.

"Greynol, we cannot leave!" cried Zerrin, watching helplessly as Armond disappeared within.

"We are not leaving."

"But he is hurt among murderers," sobbed Brenn.

"They will not slay him this way – there is money on Ernild's mind, a ransom," returned Greynol. Reluctantly, the others followed him back to the inn where word of the commotion spread rapidly throughout the village.

Chapter Fourteen – Northern Fire

Finar House teemed with a larger than usual crowd that night. A throng gathered about Andro and company, including the Mayor Ermal, Gord Greenhall, and several gate-guards whom had retired for the evening – witnesses to the incident upon the bridge. Knights Leomund of Rintar and Corull of Larin were also present; they were cousins passing through town after duties upriver. The tavern fell silent, listening intently to Andro's re-telling of Armond's capture, but no one had a quick solution.

"I wish Greynol were here to tell us what to do next," said Brenn whose distress pushed him to the point of losing his appetite.

"He and Callis are doing their part – whatever part that is," replied a dejected Andro.

"Despair not young lads, I will do all I can to help," said Mayor Ermal seated nearby. He rubbed his chin repeatedly while listening to the tale, but his voice was reassuring. "I will be certain to alert my friends along the border. I have no charge across the river, but more than one associate from 'the Bottoms' owes me a favor. Aside from that, the city watch will assist you; they shall remain vigilant throughout the night should any news come out of that place of corruption. Ernild is a scoundrel and won't get away with his devilry this time."

"It's 'bout time somebody did somethin' to stop those rabblers. Ol' Patch has taken over just where we looked for 'im least; and he's got Ernild who loves one thing, 'is money. Ain't no honor across that bridge," bellowed Gord from the next table, smoking pipe in hand.

"Well, I for one don't like being helpless here," uttered Rogan, leaning upon his elbows as his temper simmered; "and on top of that, Thairidain and his spy are long gone."

Leomund sat nearby minding his own mug until he heard enough and approached the dejected party. The tall Fawoerian knight wore his common clothes and a linen jacket emblazoned with an eagle, and a great sword hung at his side within its gilded scabbard. Corull was similarly arrayed, but in Ainurian fashion, with a doublet of the four-square design upon his sleeves, which matched the shield hanging from his saddle outside the door.

"It sounds like this Ernild has come to the end of his rope. I cannot help you with the two escaped accomplices, but I hold authority over any Keep-warden in Fanael," said Leomund in a reassuring manner. His voice carried command, a trait common to the lords of Fanael. "Lord-Mayor Ermal, Corull and I are bound by oath to serve against injustice within our realms. With your permission we request to assume command of the Finar watch; that is, until a just resolution is met."

"Yes indeed, whatever you require," replied Ermal bowing against the girth of his supple belly.

"What will you do?" asked Brenn.

"Arrest Ernild and the guilty, and displace the others until a tribune is formed to rule on the issue. I will assume captaincy of the keep until then."

"This has altered our previous directives, but security of the bridge and border take priority, this time," added Corull. "Seems evil has crept into the quiet of Finar."

Andro jumped to his feet, a glint of hope in his eyes. "Then let us be at your service – at least until our friend is released. But if you may, could you hold off on any swift action until Greynol returns? He is wise and cares greatly for Armond's safety."

"Very well, then," answered Leomund. "You men shall join us should we need to breech the keep. We will wait for Greynol, but only until the midnight hour."

Andro nodded, gazing soberly into the eyes of his friends – they wondered the same two thoughts as he: "Where was Greynol? And what does he mean by, *breech the keep*?"

Greynol paced across the parlor floor, awaiting Callis who dressed within his room. He prepared to turn in for the night when Greynol came knocking upon his door. Callis returned wearing a traditional gray frock and sandals with a Timlet Stone in hand.

"Brother, do you think Armond will survive this trial? And what of Thairidain, how did he come to this bad end?" asked Callis, quite shaken over the news.

Greynol stopped pacing. "I never held a fair impression of our associate. In younger days he showed passing respect for the order, but siding with a man like Ernild is beyond my expectations. His kind I know all too well; he seeks a bounty at any cost. This time he may realize he has gone too far – there are witnesses to his crime. What Ernild might do to Armond I fear to guess? Much depends upon his rational mind."

"As for Thairidain, long have we known each other, and his thoughts were ever far from me. But you Callis remained in his favor; you are a humbler man than I am, and seldom one to criticize. I on the other hand told him straight away my feelings and what he lacked. I assure you, he remembers every word."

"He deserved your criticism, for it was fair advice. That is why you are a sound leader."

"A leader who is put to the test. Friend, I do not wish to burden you more than necessary, but I thought you should be alerted to the circumstances. I must go back to my men and decide a plan of action. A crowd had already gathered when I left the inn."

Callis smiled remorsefully. "You are not troubling me at all. I will go with you."

"Thank you, but first let us do what we can here to assist Armond," replied Greynol.

In the light of an oil-lamp they sat, each bearing a Timlet

Stone that glowed with warm light. Callis searched an aging First Volume of Tuirowe.

"Here are the verses," he said clearing his throat:

"*...No shackle shall bind, no door remain closed, blindness removed with the light of Fawarra. Hearken not to the darkness, for a great light has come to fill the empty halls and still the raging waters. The messenger calls from the sea to the shore, to still the heart and resist the sword...*"

Callis finished the reading and closed his eyes. Greynol listened intently, then proclaimed the prayer on his heart: "Spare your land the bloodshed of its own, and mercy to those whose care I claim..."

With that, a gust of wind swept through the house and the light of the stones seemed to lift away into the night, carry above the city wall, and drift across the river. Only a whisper remained behind, soft as a breeze, then it faded into silence.

Armond awoke to a sound and a soft light that roused him before drifting away. His eyes were caked with blood, barely opened to mere slits; the throbbing in his head a reminder of what happened upon the bridge. His wrists were tied at his back – his arms numb and stretched. The wound upon his shoulder burned with new pain, as several stitches were torn open in the melee. Blood wetted the front of his shirt.

The sound of men's voices echoed down from an upper chamber; the rush of water made it evident that he lay close to the river in a lower level of the keep. He managed to open his eyes a little: the room was black, save the poor light of a lantern that hung outside the door of his cell.

"I'm in a dungeon, that much is clear. Now were did that light go?" muttered Armond. He managed a deep breath, only to catch the reek of mold and decay, dung and stagnant water. He knew not the time, nor how long he had remained in that state. His skull ached from the blow of the club, struggling with the rope tied in a bulky knot about his wrists, placed by hands without the skill to manage such things.

"I can wriggle my way out of this with a bit of struggle, but I'll save my wrists some nasty cuts," he said, leaning away from the wall. He pulled his hands up beneath his mail shirt. "They made a mistake leaving me in my chain – I made it and I know every link by heart, and I also know there's a sharp edge or two I can use."

He found a belt underneath his coat sporting a jagged edge upon a small buckle. Rubbing the dry-rotted rope against its edge, he swiftly splayed a section of knot. A little more and the piece cut through, but the knot held.

"Just a bit further," he said, struggling as beads of sweat formed upon his brow.

"There!" as his hands came apart. He unwrapped the remaining rope. "These fools can't even tie a knot."

Next he loosed his legs, which were bound at the ankles: the length of rope could not make up for the lack of skill among an undisciplined troop more accustomed to drink and mischief. Armond was their second attempt at subduing a prisoner; the first no less an unkind act, overcoming their previous captain. He then spit into his hands and wiped the caked blood from his eyes – its sting gnawed his anger.

He struggled to his feet and walked warily over to the iron bars of his cell door. Peering into the dim torchlight revealed a long corridor in each direction lined with cells. The dungeon remained eerily silent save for the churn of the river outside and stray water droplets that fell in puddles along the rough stone floor. He caught a breath of fresh air that funneled down the passage – sweet and invigorating. Suddenly, a steel door opened from a stairwell to the left and a single set of footsteps was heard upon stairs.

"Only one...good," muttered Armond, backing away from the cell door. He acted quickly, retaking his position upon the floor. He wrapped a piece of rope about his feet and held the second in his hands behind his back. Closing his eyes, he lowered his head to his knees and waited.

"Brom do this, Brom do that. Put him in shackles, Brom – all fer Ernie's fun," muttered the fat henchman of Ernild's company as he shambled down the corridor. With a jingle of keys and a clank, he unlocked another cell. The guard and his lantern disappeared within, but Armond heard his grumblings.

"Rats, they're all rusted. Ah, 'ere's a good set – now we can shackle'm up sound. Then *I'll* have some fun," he said, clanking fetters in his hand.

A shuffle of feet approached Armond's cell door. Brom leaned against the gate with his lantern aglow against the bars. "There's the scum. You awake in there?" he bellowed, unlocking the door. Armond gave no answer, his face buried in his knees.

"I oughta put another lump on you. Gotta string you up first," he said, chortling. A heavy thud and Brom kicked the door open, hanging the lantern upon a peg within. He took a deep breath and leaned upon a gnarled club. "Hey sleepyhead, remember this stick, or should I give ya another smack?"

"You'll never get the chance," replied Armond, raising his head. Brom nearly leapt out of his skin.

"Why you grimy good-fer-nothing! All tied up and throwin' a challenge."

Brom rushed over with his club raised, but Armond cast aside the tattered ropes and threw a kick into the guard's knees, knocking him off-balance. Jumping to his feet, he punched Brom squarely in the jaw and drove a shoulder into his torso, pinning him against the cell wall. Brom let out a breathless groan as the club fell from his hand. He dropped to the floor, clutching at his belt, a dagger appeared in his hand.

"Not so fast," growled Armond, his eyes ablaze. He smacked away the Brom's hand and delivered a blow of his own with the fallen club – the same weapon he used on Armond upon the bridge. Brom dropped like a sack of flour.

"Now we're even."

Armond dragged the unconscious guard to the back of the cell, removed his keys and locked the door behind him. He tossed the crude club away with disdain.

"That is no weapon for a fighter to carry." He also left behind the knife that was covered with grime and felt greasy in his hands. "What filth?" he muttered.

Armond started down the right passage towards fresher air, passing rows of empty cells to the bottom of a stairwell with a windowless iron door.

"Up or down?" he wondered.

Armond leapt down a shorter flight to the lower door. Unbarring it, a rush of wind stilled his anxiety and stiffened his battered and bruised body. He was outside. Then he descended a row of stairs just above the darkness of the river; the wall of Finar seen in the shadows across the distance. At the bottom he found a landing: a secluded vantage point beneath the firelights of the bridge, and nary a soul to be seen.

He dropped to a knee splashing his face and hair with water, preparing himself for the fight yet to come. The blood washed from his eyes and face; another douse to the back of his head where Brom struck with the club. His senses awakened. Suddenly, the iron door of the keep creaked open.

Armond fell flat against the hillside as a guardsman stepped out into the night. The landing was a popular place to drop a line, sneak a nap, or enjoy a smoke when on duty, and the guard intended to enjoy a break in a commotion-filled night. Halfway down the stairs an invisible hand gripped his leg. Out of the darkness Armond lay in wait, and with one swift motion tossed the fellow head over heels into the river. With no more than a muffled groan the guard fell headlong with a splash.

"Serves you right you wet rat," called Armond as the man tumbled downstream against the current. His journey would be a long, cold ride before reaching dry ground.

"Damn, I should've grabbed his sword," he thought. Then he recalled losing his own in the fight. "I'll bet one of those dogs has it."

Nordic Steel is as precious as gold to a Turrar, and far too valuable to leave behind, at least in Armond's mind. He could hear Andro's admonition in his ears as he started back towards the keep:

"Your freedom isn't worth the price of a sword." But he did not listen. Armond leapt up the stairs and paused at the door; gazing back, he heard a horn blow and the sound of men gathering near the south gate of Finar. Without waiting, he turned and re-entered the darkness of the dungeon.

"This looks like war," said Callis as he and Greynol found an assembly forming outside Finar House. Knights Leomund and Corull formed a procession beginning with the Alliance, who explained all that had transpired; the city-watch, consisting of a dozen footmen; and lastly, a gathering of towns-folk who rarely found such excitement in all the chronicle's of Finar.

The Fawoerian knight now bore a full mail hauberk and breast-plated armor painted with the design of a golden eagle. Corull was similarly arrayed, but in Ainurian fashion, with green and blue plumes on the battle helm tucked under his arm.

"Consecrated brothers, judging everything that has happened here, we are bound to act upon our oaths to secure the land from dishonor. I am Corull, and my authority gives me lead over the watchmen of Ainiald," said the Larin knight, Corull, proud upon his gray steed.

"And I am Leomund, my authority lie in Fanael; the keep will remain under my authority once taken. Come with us and bless the service we must now perform," added the Knight from Rintar, displaying his respect for the holy men with a bow.

Callis hardly knew what to think; in fact, he knew little of warfare. "Greynol, you must go with them. I will walk in the rear with the townspeople – out of everybody's way," he said.

"I will go once I find out what is the plan," replied Greynol concerned by the look of things. "A siege seems a bit overdone."

"Indeed, father," replied Leomund, "but a show of force may be what is needed to eradicate this Ernild. Chains await the malefactor. Unfortunate that he was able to commit these crimes: first, to murder a captain of Fanael; and second, to extort our allies while aiding a spy. Your man's capture must be avenged."

"He did strike a captain of Fanael, be he just or unjust," replied Greynol, knowing in time all truths would be told concerning the matter.

"We will sort out everything once Ernild is disposed."

"The previous captain, Furim, was a good man. If Ernild had anything to do with his death, as most believe, he must be punished," called one of the crowd. The rally was complete and ready at their backs.

But looking over the situation, Greynol sought to keep order. "Lords, be wary for Armond is in my service; harm may come to him if Ernild is pressed. I pray that unnecessary bloodshed not come of this action. I understand your faithfulness to the kingdom, but be mindful, these are not Drukon you challenge in that stronghold — many of these men have been mislead."

"Father, your wisdom guides us. Recall the mantra of our calling: *the Knighthood and Fawarra are one*. Mercy rides before us and justice is our shield," replied Leomund in a sure voice, his gauntlet at rest upon the hilt of a gleaming brand.

Greynol regrouped with the others at the gate. The call was given that each should prepare his bow and that no one should fire unless fired upon.

"I don't like any of this," said Drago, setting a bolt in place upon his crossbow, "we should be inside freeing Armond by now. The seven of us can handle those dogs."

The others echoed his sentiments.

"We are no longer in Nordhiem, and the problem of Ernild involves all of Finar. We have little choice now but to follow Leomund and Corull," replied Greynol.

"These knights have no allegiance to Armond — they are not concerned with his safety," muttered Zerrin as a horn blew. The whole company came to order at the opening of the gate.

Leomund sat tall upon his white steed, raising his hands to

silence the crowd. "My cousin and I will ride ahead with the Acolyte's company close behind. The rest will come only after I give the signal, and do so with speed."

The knights healed forward, empty-handed with weapons sheathed, while the Alliance brought up the rear on foot. The night rolled in deep over the Binarra valley and a light mist fell about the bridge – a dankness that sank skin-deep. Four figures stood in the shadows on the opposite side: keep guards that held their ground upon nervous legs. Their perturbation mounted as the knights came into view.

"What tidings of home, brothers? Duty has borne me away for a time and I am pleased to find Fanael soil before me," called Leomund in a calm, yet sobering tone. Corull remained stoic and silent at his side, but no less imposing.

The watchmen were stymied until one managed to speak. "We...we heard a horn and expected trouble."

"Trouble? What are you saying?" asked Leomund, coming to a sudden halt just off the bridge where the four guards waited. "What sort of trouble do you expect from Ainiald, your ally? Here sits my cousin Corull, an Ainurian Knight. Are you telling me that Ainiald now wars with Fanael?"

"No sir. But those men behind you...are *they* with you?"

"These gentlemen? What is this concern of yours, brother? I have many friends."

The guards' distress heightened. They were each young and timid, merely hirelings from the bottoms drawn into Ernild's scheme. "Indeed lord, there are no concerns here. You are all free to pass, if you so wish."

"And so is any friend who travels the highroad," snorted Leomund, growing indignant. "Now brothers, do me one last favor – bring to me your captain so I may speak to him here."

All four men hurried back to the keep without concern for the bridge; none dare remain to endure Leomund's gaze. After a vociferous argument within, Ernild marched out of the keep with a dozen armed men in his wake, like a weasel extracted suddenly from its hole. His eyes raced back and forth expecting a trap.

"What is it you need – I have no time to greet every passerby," grumbled Ernild with a flippant gesture. He refused to come close, preferring to stand at a distance.

"Who do you think you are speaking, Keep-warden? I am Leomund, a knight of the realm, and no mere sojourner. You have been accused of transgressing our law."

"What law are you talking about? Do these fools have your ear?" sniped Ernild with a nervous laugh, pointing out Greynol's party. "*They* are the only lawbreakers here. One of their lot has been detained – a bleedin' Turrar who struck me without provocation."

Ernild stepped into the torchlight to display a fresh black eye. Leomund couldn't help but laugh. "We will get to the bottom of...*everything*," he replied. "Now tell me, why did you allow a murderer and a thief passage while refusing to let the Acolyte pass without demanding a toll?"

"I know nothing of what you say. There is no proof of his claim – just the word of foreigners."

"Very well, bring me the prisoner and await my next command," continued Leomund, as he and Corull dismounted.

"Is that all? No need to get unruly here. I will do as you ask; but first order these others from here. My responsibility is to protect the border, and I find them a threat. Let them get on with their business, far away from here," replied Ernild, already backing away.

He started at once the keep whispering to one of his henchmen. "Tark, time to shut the door. If there is any trouble, the Turrar dies and we ride out of here. We know the east hollows better than any of these fools – they will never find us."

Quickly, Armond passed the shadow of his cell where Brom still lay shackled and disoriented, groaning upon the floor. At the end of the corridor, he found the way open; stepping into a second stairwell without exit, save for a straight flight of stairs leading to the upper floor. He raced to the top in darkness, hesitating as he reached a half-opened door. A loud conversation continued in a nearby room.

Armond slipped through the opening into seemingly empty quarters; but around the corner sat an unsuspecting bearded man, lining arrows on the cot where he sat. After a strange moment of disbelief, the man gripped the weapon at his feet – a battle-axe. He drew a scowl and came forward; all the while, the commotion within the next room escalated.

"Ernild, look what I gots in 'ere!" called the bearded man, but no response came as the voices faded outdoors. "Get in here you louts, the prisoner..."

Armond did not hesitate. The only item within reach was a round sharpening stone. He picked it up and whipped it, striking the man squarely on the forehead before he could react. Stunned, two quick blows of a fist dropped him and the axe fell from his hand. Armond's instincts took over; he picked up the fallen weapon and turned quickly to find a second guard at the door.

"Where is that scoundrel, Ernild – and my blade?" growled Armond to a gaunt-looking ward with a poor-man's sword in hand. He answered with a charge.

Armond blocked a sudden slash – then countered with the blunt end of the axe, breaking several ribs. The man was sent to the floor writhing in pain. He gave up at once, laying his sword at the Turrar's feet.

"Please do not kill me. I am no fighter," he begged.

"I should end things for you now, but Nordhiem knows honor. You may be dogs, but I will not shed Fawoerian blood – unnecessarily," replied Armond, kicking the sword away. He shut the door to the outer room that appeared now empty, and barred it from within; about the time Ernild faced Leomund at the bridge,

"Your ribs may hurt," said Armond as he turned to the thin guard who sat upon his haunches, clutching his side, "but you've still a job to do."

Armond forced him to drag the semi-conscience bearded man down to the dungeon and locked them both in a cell with the keys he lifted from Brom. Then he returned to the quarters to search for his lost weapon, listening through the door to a new commotion opposite the other side.

Ernild entered the stronghold after his meeting with Leomund: the four young guards addressed by the knight earlier did not follow him into the keep, choosing no more part in the illicit company.

"Are you fools coming? We are shutting the way," hissed Ernild not much above a whisper, trying hard not to rouse suspicion from those upon the bridge. The young men did not listen.

"Have it your way!" he shouted, slamming the steel door at his back. "Be quick and bar the way – those bastards will not enter."

Ernild turned to find other problems inside.

"Chief, the door to the chamber is locked. Our weapons are in there," said another man, standing opposite the door where Armond, unknowingly, lay in wait. Ernild fumed, tugging at the handle.

"Well, don't just stand there, go around. And someone find Brom with those keys – now!"

"I fear Ernild has chosen to make a stand," said Leomund, turning to the four deserters, each younger than Rogan's eighteen. They gave up their weapons, laying several spears and dirks at the knight's feet.

"Your choice is wise. Tell us now, how many guards remain in the keep?"

"All are not guards, like we who began early last year when the call went out for replacements," replied one of the young men; "that was before Ernild came along. He brought in many of his own kind after our previous captain…disappeared. In all, sixteen remain."

Corull signaled the others in wait to advance, and so they came, city watch and townspeople alike in a long advance that stretched across the bridge.

"My apologies, Greynol, but a fight appears imminent. Ernild has chosen the difficult path," said Leomund.

"He still has power while inside the keep: iron bars and steel doors aid him for the moment, but there are things mightier than steel," replied the Acolyte, hoping his prayer had an answer.

"But Armond is in there," fretted Andro, feeling helpless where he waited.

In angst, Andro stepped away from the others, searching his thoughts. Desperately, his eyes tried to pierce the granite walls for an answer to ease his worry. That is when he caught a happy sight.

"Leomund, sir, we've waited long enough. My friends and I are going inside. Look, the bottom door is opened, if only a crack. I missed it until now."

The back door that Armond re-entered only a short while before was left ajar, only slightly, but plain to see away from the bridge beacons.

"I will go with you," declared Corull, handing the reins of his proud steed to one of the young guardsmen. "Prepare your weapons and follow my lead – we shall find your friend. But be wary of traps."

Corull led the Alliance around the underside of the bridge and down a grassy slope to the steel door. Greynol looked on anxiously from above with Leomund at his side.

"Do not fret," exclaimed the knight, "they are in good company with my cousin – he is courageous and forthright in every circumstance."

Greynol kept silent. He could only watch as they unknowingly retraced Armond steps and entered within.

Armond laughed, listening as Ernild and the others tried to pry open the door.

"Good firm oak – solid workmanship. They shall do nothing against her without these," he said jangling the keys in his hand.

The noise on the other side stopped. Armond remembered the dungeon door; it would take little for them to reach him from the back stairs. He ran to the bottom to secure the wooden postern just as Ernild and his men came into view at the far end of the dungeon corridor. He could hear their calls.

"Where is the barbarian? Brom, what are you doing in there?" bellowed Ernild at Armond's cell door.

"I dunno. He musta' jumped me and taken the keys," muttered the plump henchman seated clumsily upon the floor.

"The other set is in the quarters, I'll go get 'em," said the brawler Tark. Two other voices called from a second cell.

They found the frail guard still grasping his injured ribs, and the bearded man seated on the floor rubbing his forehead.

"We are locked in," said the guard. "The Turrar forced us in here. Now he is in our quarters."

Tark tried to enter the stairwell, but its door held tight. "No getting through here without a fight."

"He's a cunning one," grumbled Ernild. "That Turrar-dog expects to thwart my plans, but I am not finished yet. Go back the other way, all of you. Tark, stay here with me – use your axe."

Tark started upon the door, driving his weapon hard against the boards. Ernild assisted, hacking with a sword that was not his own; both men looked more like desperate escapees than the captain of the keep and his lieutenant.

The others returned the way they came into the stairwell, but were met at once by several angry bowmen. The henchmen set themselves to charge until Leonin sent an arrow purposefully past one's ear.

"You will fall before a sword is raised!" thundered Corull, brand in hand with the Alliance at his back. "Whom shall die first?"

Six guards, mostly young men from the bottoms, came forward throwing their weapons down; but the last five, delinquent friends of Ernild, hurried back the other way to chance the only means of escape. Corull escorted the prisoners out while Andro and the others remained behind to block the way.

"Why are you here? Where are the others?" shouted Ernild

when the remaining men returned.

"They chickened out," answered one. "There are men with bows on our tail."

"We shall see what kind of fool they think I am. You can all run off to your doom, but I will not take the blame for that fool's murder. No prison for me. If anyone is man enough, then follow my lead," called Ernild, bursting through the hacked door with a sudden thrust. Reaching the top of the stairs, he and others where surprised to find both doors leading into the chamber open.

"He is not here – the prisoner waited for us to go into the dungeons, and now he is gone," said one, peaking through the door leading into the main chamber. "And look, the front door is open wide."

"Cowards – all of you!" shouted Ernild who ran straight for the front door where Leomund stood outside with a dozen spearmen. Onlookers from Finar waited nearby, even folk from the bottoms whom lined up despite the late hour, curious to learn what trouble Ernild had gotten himself into.

"Do you still desire a fight? Shall I become a siege-lord this fine summer morning? This place has not the means for a long holdout," said Leomund, entering the building. The henchmen stood petrified at the sight of the knight and a number of Ainiald guardsmen entering the hall. Ernild desired nothing of the justice they sought, sliding against the rear wall to make his escape. Tark was already gone.

"Where is your prisoner, captain?" asked Leomund with eyes as sharp as the sword he bore.

"What are you asking? You of all should know he has escaped," returned Ernild.

"And so he has," returned a voice in the far corner of the room. Armond stood to show himself, flipping the table where he hid upon its side. "I hoped to get another shot at you before it was over."

Ernild cocked a crooked smile.

"If the knight is a sporting man, you may yet, Turrar," he replied, drawing a sword from his belt that rang clear and unmistakable in Armond's ear.

"There is a reason I remained in your filthy keep: the sword you hold is mine, given me by my father, forged within my grandsire's Vanyor furnace, and belongs not in the hand of a dog."

"Then the pleasure of slaying you with it will be all the more sweet," mocked Ernild, spitting upon the blade.

Armond strode forward with the borrowed axe in hand, flinging the ring of keys to a Finar guardsman. "You will need those to lock these mutts up – Ernild too, if spared," he replied, stopping between Ernild and the knight whom he eyed with curiosity.

"You are a knight of the realm?" asked Armond.

"I am."

"Then watch a Turrar whose blade was taken from him," he replied, crouching into a wide stance not two meters from the compromised captain. Leomund gave him a hard look then backed way.

"And know this, each of you!" called Armond in a loud voice; "Nordic steel will never betray its rightful owner."

Ernild did not fear the boast and leapt forward. Armond lunged in response, forcing the butt of the axe into Ernild's stomach; but he spun back, cleaving the axe-handle in two. Armond's eyes lit up in awe at the sight of his weapon, even when used against himself. Taking the advantage, the foul captain charged against his weaponless opponent, waving the sword like a madman. Armond backed away, contemplating every movement of the sword. Ernild took it as senseless audacity. *Does every Turrar fight as if possessed?* he wondered.

Armond reached for a chair to block the onslaught and caught the blade on its downward stroke, causing it to be lodged – a saving block destined to cleave the Turrar from neck to sternum. Ernild tried to pull it free, but Armond shoved him back with the legs of the chair, and pulled back with a sudden jerk – sword, chair, and all. He flipped the seat to its upright position, placed his boot on top, and with one single motion, pulled the blade straight out like a sword from a stone.

"Well now, the turn of the tide," said Armond, sporting a wicked smile that backed his opponent away.

"The fight is over. The guards will take it from here," replied Leomund, unsure of what to make of Armond. "Ernild shall be arrested and tried – we do not slay men outright like heathen."

"One more thing: my sword-belt and hilt. Give them to me now," demanded Armond, pointing the blade within inches of Ernild's chest. He complied and threw them to the floor.

A Finar city-guard entered from the stairwell with keys in hand. "We found three other prisoners and unlocked them from their cells," he said, escorting Brom and the two-wounded watchman from the dungeon. "They claimed to have no part with Ernild, but I recognize each of them as bridge-wardens and close to the captain, especially the fat one."

"You should have left them be for they are going back with their captain to await judgment," replied Leomund.

The Finar guard took hold of the four remaining henchmen who offered no fight. But Ernild turned into a trapped animal, leaping before they could grab him. He threw everything he could find at his back to block the way, bolting into the quarters for the rear stairwell, but Andro and company were making their way up. Ernild ran to the back of the room into what seemed a closet and a narrow door, slid a lock, and started up a twisted staircase.

Andro saw it plain, but was distracted at the sight of Armond entering the room. Brenn slipped past and got to him first.

"Armond, it is you! Are you alright?" he cried with a hug, elated to greet his friend.

"Never better, shorty. And now the rat is caught in a trap," he replied, turning to a guard. "Anyone know where this door leads?"

He did not wait long for an answer: disposing of proper manners, Armond proceeded to bash the door with his foot, causing a hole big enough for Brenn to reach a latch within. In file, they marched up the narrow stairs into what appeared a small bedroom. A candle lamp burned upon a cluttered table beside an unmade cot and opened window, but Ernild was not there.

"Quick, to the window," said Rogan, rushing over for a look.

Below stood an unkempt stable yard, fit only for swine; and there sat Tark upon a large horse, holding the reigns of another while Ernild climbed up.

Armond was first to step out the window onto the sloped roof of a small porch; the others followed behind as well as they could manage. Andro saw how the trap was set.

Leomund, Corull, and Greynol came into view with a band of guards and townspeople circling the front of the keep towards the stable – the commotion drawing everyone's attention. Ernild and Tark attempted a hasty exit, but the horses were nervous and uncooperative, neglected as they were.

"Move you damn beast!" shouted Tark as the animals stomped and circled about. He kicked his mount and gave it several hard lashes. Ernild managed his steed out into the yard where he spun away from the oncoming hoard.

"Time, Tark! or else the gallows await," he called, turning to face the mob. "You won't have Ernild this day."

But a disturbance erupted from the midst of the crowd. "You ain't gettin' away without me – not on my horse!" came a shout. It was Brom. He broke the hold of the guards and shoved his way out of the circle of pike-men. In a fit, he came running towards the two riders.

"You ain't leavin' without me!" he cried again, shouting and pounding them with balled fists.

"Get off me you oaf, there is no room for the two of us," said Tark with a kick, escaping Brom's clutches. He rode off without stopping or turning to look back, disappearing quickly along an eastern river trail.

But Brom made things worse for Ernild: the crowd surrounded them on all sides with the Alliance coming in from the stable yard, leaving only the river free.

"You can't leave me here to hang or burn. They'll nab us for murder for sure!" panicked the paunchy guard.

"You'll stay behind if I say so," answered Ernild, drawing a long dagger from his coat, "and I say – stay!"

Ernild slashed Brom across the throat and he fell back, but managed to cling to the horse with groping hands. Blood showered from his neck onto Ernild, the horse, and dust of the yard. That fateful moment Brom perished with a loud gasp. The horse went wild with fear, kicking as it bolted away from the others that hemmed it in – Ernild held on for his very life.

The ebony steed, set mad from the attack and smell and feel of blood upon its flesh, galloped hard to the edge of the river bluff. It leapt and reared back, toppling over onto Ernild whom tried to stay her. Both horse and rider tumbled over a ledge and down into the rapids.

The onlookers witnessed with horror sights that would remain long in the memory of Finar: Brom as he lay dead upon the ground in a pool of steaming blood, and the grim sight of Ernild face down in the Binarra drifting downstream. The horse, for those concerned, swam for a time and found footing down river to escape the swifter rapids. The mare returned several days later; but wild now, she would never let another ride her, nor dare anyone try.

The remaining third of murderous conspirators, Tark, was never seen again. Rumor spoke that he was lost in the wilderness and died alone that winter, but no one knew for certain. The remaining keep guards were eventually vindicated, victims of Ernild's insolence. None, save the three were found to have a part in the killing of the previous captain, and after a time were set free; but long after Greynol and company departed that place.

Surrounded by his friends, Finar elite, and the curious, Armond had grown accustomed to being the center of attention. Knight Corull, a veteran of many field dressings, re-stitched Armond's newly opened wound; at the same time, Leomund discussed the events of that night. The manor crowd pressed close to hear every word.

"Armond, son of Baldor, I have met several Nordic in my time, mostly fighters, and from what can be told, you sport a brave lot in your land of ice and snow," said the Fawoerian knight.

"Cold is our land, but hot runs our blood in the fight," replied Armond, grimacing as a needle passed through his skin, Corull pulling each stitch tight. "I would like to hone my skills, perhaps learn how you knights spar in play."

"Play is one thing – battle another," replied Leomund, watching as the last knot was tied.

"He is fortunate to be alive," grimaced Andro nearby, turned by the sight.

"Indeed, fate has smiled upon your friend."

Greynol shook his head. "Seems Armond has the nine lives of a cat – I wish he wouldn't use them all at once."

"How did you manage your way out of that dungeon cell, anyway?" asked Zerrin.

"I may never know how to explain it," replied Armond with an honest look. "Something roused me from a nasty knock to the head; then I loosened my bonds with just enough time to surprise that fat guard. Now he is dead. I should have escaped then, but my sword was lost and I returned for it."

Greynol laughed. "Should we be surprised? As Callis and I pray for your safe release, you go running back for your sword."

"Say what you will, but if I had not returned things may have gone differently: that murderer, Ernild, could be miles from here with my sword, searching for mischief," replied Armond, draining his first beer. A second replaced it just as soon as he put his mug down – a royal treatment insisted by Mayor Ermal. "But if your prayers opened my eyes, not my strength alone, then I owe your Fawarra a favor and one day I'll repay him – I'm good for it,"

Acolyte Callis nearly gasped. "Do all Turrar speak in such a manner?"

"Only the foolhardy," replied Greynol. "And now that

everything is settled, I am turning in for the night, although it is more likely morning by now."

He got up and started for bed, leaving one last bit of instruction:

"Enjoy the moment for tomorrow we depart Finar; but later than usual since we were *delayed*. Each of you should get his rest. I'll be sound asleep before you lads consider the thought."

After a while, the onlookers slowly dispersed. The midnight gate-rules dispensed for the night – for the first time in memory. Armond and the Mihtrir were last and remained deep into the morning hours. After so much excitement, they drifted off with their heads upon the bar surrounded by empty mugs, only to be roused at sun-up by the innkeeper's wife who chased the party to their beds.

But the time for revelry was soon to end; for deep in the southern range lingered one who never slept, ate, or drank. Wreathed in flame it watched and waited. The time approached to do its master's bidding.

Here ends the first part the Passage of the Acolyte.
Book two concludes Greynol's journey into Fanael and Asenrael to find Fauglir and face his master.

The End.

Copies of this book may be purchased at:
www.createspace.com/3501592

Part Two of Passage of the Acolyte:
www.createspace.com/3539685

Copies also available online at most popular booksellers, including Amazon and Kindle.

For more info try:
http://passageoftheacolyte.blogspot.com/

Made in the USA
Charleston, SC
23 February 2011